MAGIC AND MADNESS

"There were demons," said Ryle, frowning. "Great fanged ones with claws like green daggers—surely you saw them."

"I saw Wastelanders, boy," the captain said testily. "Though for the way they fight they could be demons."

Imrie turned on the magician and his boy. "What did you see? Townsfolk come with pitch and pig-slops to turn you out of town?"

"Nothing of the sort," the magician said, looking indignant. "It's not safe to stay here, my lord, we should move on."

"And you, lass?" Valon said.

"I saw a cavern with a big green rock in it, and as I got closer to the rock, the air became denser. I saw you hacking and shouting and prancing about and almost killing one another, and I told you that they were afraid of fire, and I led you out."

They fell silent. "Perhaps," the captain said after a while, "none of us saw the truth in there. There are places where men—where people see what they wish to see. Yet you saw nothing, lass."

Imrie put her hand in her pouch and curled her fingers around her amulet, finding some comfort in its worn shape.

(From "A Question of Magic," by Marta Randall)

Tor books by Andre Norton

Caroline (with Enid Cushing)
The Crystal Gryphon
Dare To Go A-Hunting
Flight in Yiktor
Forerunner
Forerunner: The Second Venture
Gryphon's Eyrie (with A. C. Crispin)
Here Abide Monsters
House of Shadows (with Phyllis Miller)
Imperial Lady (with Susan Shwartz)
The Jekyll Legacy (with Robert Bloch)
Moon Called
Moon Mirror
The Prince Commands
Ralestone Luck
Stand and Deliver
Wheel of Stars
Wizards' Worlds

THE WITCH WORLD (editor)

Tales of the Witch World 1
Tales of the Witch World 2
Four from the Witch World
Tales of the Witch World 3
Storms of Victory

MAGIC IN ITHKAR (editor, with Robert Adams)

Magic in Ithkar 1
Magic in Ithkar 2
Magic in Ithkar 3
Magic in Ithkar 4

Andre Norton

Tales of the Witch World

3

TOR
fantasy

A TOM DOHERTY ASSOCIATES BOOK
NEW YORK

TALES OF THE WITCH WORLD 3

Copyright © 1990 by Andre Norton, Ltd.
Maps copyright © 1990 by John M. Ford

A Tor Book
Published by Tom Doherty Associates, Inc.
49 West 24th Street
New York, N.Y. 10010

Cover art by Victoria Lisi
Maps by John M. Ford

ISBN: 0-812-51336-3

First edition: July 1990
First mass market printing: April 1991

Printed in the United States of America

0 9 8 7 6 5 4 3 2 1

CONTENTS

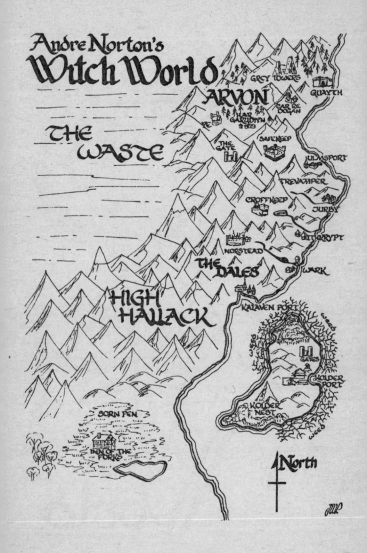

Introduction

As I have said elsewhere Witch World never was intended to be more than a one-volume book, a fragment of which had been originally jotted down for a historical novel that never came into being. However there seems to be that about Witch World itself that continues to draw both the writer and readers—the latter, judging by letters received, eager to know more and more.

First there was the eastern continent comprising Estcarp, and the traditional enemies Karsten and Alizon. Then, out of nowhere, there arrived the first adventure in High Hallack to the west: *Year of the Unicorn*. This was also the first to have a female protagonist, and though it was not warmly welcomed by male readers, women greeted it with enthusiasm.

However, more and more letters brought questions as well as suggestions for new adventures of favorite characters. The first sharing and building of such a tale was with Ann Crispin whose collaboration in *Gryphon's Eyrie* was, to my mind, a widening and enriching experience. Nor were either of us satisfied to allow our characters to remain mute at the end of that adventure. The idea of *Songsmith,* carrying on into a second generation, developed before the last word of the first was set on paper.

1

Unfortunately, other commitments faced both of us and we did not get much further than an introduction and a somewhat vague outline of the following events. Though we hope to have the book finished soon.

Though *Songsmith* might be delayed, fellow wordsmiths, whose work I admired and thought sympathetic to my own ideas of fantasy, contributed short stories for what was to be four volumes of *Tales*. A meeting with Robert Bloch was responsible for the first two stories in volume one. We discussed and decided upon doing two versions of the same plot, one to be seen through the eyes of accepted "good" and the other "evil." This experiment intrigued us both.

But, with the putting together of the volume that was slated to be number three in the series, a change was suggested by the editor. The manuscripts that had been selected numbered four, all of novelette length with fine character development and excellent plotting. Because of this factor the book was lifted from the original series and was published separately as *Four From the Witch World*.

There remains this third book of shorter stories.

I was and am so enthusiastic about these new dimensions and the enlarging of Witch World by these other writers that a greater belief in the existence of another level world into which others also can enter becomes firm. Now I am eager to learn more and more about that which may lie within the Dales, beyond the mountains, in strange seas where even the Sulcar have not yet ventured.

Thus five of us, Pauline Griffin, Mary Schaub, Patricia Mathews, Sasha Miller, and I have recently completed another project: *The Witch World Chronicles*. These are set in Lormt, that repository of knowledge (though, alas, there must have been already too much lost through parchments crumbled into dust and books left to rot for centuries). Lormt surely holds a treasury of adventures, each more exciting than the last.

The second turning of the mountains (which brought an end to the witch rule that had strangled Estcarp into decline) by exhausting the witch power and killing many of those using it, marked the end of an era. What had happened, is happening now, that customs are broken? What of the Dark perhaps free now to rise anew? What of menacing manifestations in the Dales and Arvon? Who will rule Karsten? What of Alizon, licking her wounds after her defeat in the Dales?

What of those Dales, exhausted of manpower, bled white by the long war? Does Alizon still threaten, and even more boldly, Estcarp? Will Karsten remain long in the chaos into which Pagan's death plunged that country?

There are separate groups such as the Falconers and the Sulcars. Their long-held sanctuaries are gone. How do they now fare?

This is a period of drastic change, of a need for new leaders to seek other goals and methods of reaching them. Witch World is no longer the same and the changes will bring pain and strife as some of these tales foretell.

But this volume is in a way introduction to the *Chronicles* in laying the groundwork for those changes. They do not cover vast areas of any nation nor numbers of people, but rather deal with the fates of small groups here and there, plucked out of their normal way of life and sent into actions they are not always prepared to accept.

So the *Tales* will become the *Chronicles* and those will lead to an ever wider knowledge of that other world and perhaps a new assessment of all.

To me is left the pleasure of knowing that my world is enriched and expanded through the efforts of others of whose embellishments I am often envious and for which I am delighted.

To those who have willingly, and with very real interest and concern, added to the portraying of characters, the expanding of maps, the advancement of new causes and ventures I am grateful. For me they have glorified a history that somewhere I am sure is real. They have truly shared.

—Andre Norton

VOICE OF MEMORY

by

M. E. Allen

"... And on this day, did Logrin, brother to Lady Alyss, die, having completed his fifty-third year, and some three months and also two days." Sibley tilted the quill upward so that the ink would not blot and tried to think of a way to end the entry. When Lady Alyss's elder brother died six years ago, Master Logrin had filled half a page of the commonplace book recording Geran's bravery on the battlefield. But what could she say about a scholar who even as a young man had never been a warrior. Sibley admired him for his learning, but there were few others in the keep who felt that Logrin's attempt to understand the nature of language had been more than a complicated game, a jest even, played at the expense of harried fighters.

Sibley lay the quill in its rest and began to leaf through the pages of the book. Every bushel of wheat, every pound of dry flesh brought into the keep, was recorded in Logrin's economical hand. Each birth, wedding, and death; all building and repair; every increase in the herd of sheep, was listed. Logrin had noted every raid by the Alizon, every shipwreck off the keep's coast. There were the records Logrin kept of the stubby dairy cattle he had tried to breed for his sister before deciding that if

Gunnora had wanted cattle to live by the sea edge, she would have made some grass other than a few wiry tufts grow on the cliffs.

Sibley paused at one entry written nearly eighteen years earlier: "For fostering, Sibley from Ithrypt. The girl is some two years of age and seems completely without hearing; she makes no cry. No one can tell if she was born thus or lost her hearing through some cause as she has been kept apart from the family and her nurse is now dead." Those few words told how she had come to the keep.

Sibley had gleaned a little more information from Lady Alyss. Her mother, the youngest daughter of the lord of Ithrypt, died bearing a bastard daughter. She never named the father of her infant. Lady Alyss chose to believe that Sibley's father had been a knight, but Sibley thought this unlikely. Sibley was given to a woodcutter's widow to nurse until she was old enough to be sent to the Dames and the family did their best to forget the scandal.

When Sibley was less than two, robbers killed her nurse, hacking off the woman's head. Sibley and her three-year-old milk brother were found under the bed. The killers had slashed the mattress and run pikes through the board: the little boy was dead of stab wounds, but Sibley was unharmed. Word of this event spread through the Dales, and Logrin, who had long been interested in trying to create a sophisticated silent language, offered a home for the child. Her grandparents, who were thankful for the chance to be rid of her, quickly accepted.

She took up the pen again and turned back the pages to end her own entry, "Always the first to plan for battle, the design of war machines was among his skills, also the use of herbs and much other learning." She left the book open, ready for the next day's entry. The book was nearly half used: neat columns, marching week after week, month after month across the large pages. It had taken Logrin a lifetime to fill that much. Sibley suddenly realized that she would spend her life filling the rest, transcribing the steward's tally sticks, recording the sergeant-at-arms's report. And she would fill her days as she had with Logrin, reading his books, borrowing and lending manuscripts between the other keeps and the Abbeys, silently sewing with

Lady Alyss's maidens, and then, when the lady died, with those of Blodnath, Lady Alyss's mealy-mouthed daughter-in-law. The maidens would become wives, and she, Sibley, would stay a maiden.

"You're not beautiful, but still you look well enough, more's the pity," Blodnath had said when Sibley was twelve. A year later Sibley had understood what she meant when a neighbor's young son had asked permission to court her. Lady Alyss had explained that any child Sibley bore might also be "afflicted." Sibley must reconcile herself to spinsterhood. "Perhaps we should send you to the Dames, you would be safe there . . ." But Sibley had no wish to leave the only home she knew, and so braided her yellow hair under her cap, kept her brown eyes lowered, wore simple clothes, and told herself what Logrin taught her was more important than babies.

"And I am reconciled," she told herself as she looked out the window, watching the surf break on the cliffs, "and I am content." Sibley thought of Jenneth, who had befriended her ten years ago, when she had stopped sleeping in the closet where Logrin kept his books and been moved into the maidens' room. Jenneth was twelve then, the youngest girl fostered with Lady Alyss, and the only person beside Logrin to master the finger speech Logrin had devised. At times it was a game among the maidens to learn Sibley's language, but no one, save Jenneth, had ever bothered to learn enough to let Sibley have a proper gossip with her.

But Jenneth had left three years ago to marry a widowed lord and Sibley would probably never see her again. Sibley touched the arm band Jenneth had sent her shortly after arriving at her husband's keep. It was made of green stone and large enough that Sibley could push it above her elbow and wear it hidden under her sleeve. Now she slid it off her arm. It was smooth, warm from her own warmth. Jenneth had seen it hanging outside a house, part of a wreath of dried Angelica-Vervain and Moly, put there to keep off the evil eye. The villager said that his uncle had dug it up years ago, and had been happy enough to sell it to his lord as a gift for his pretty young bride. Sibley remembered the letter Jenneth sent with it, telling her about the journey and her new life, how exciting everything was. But lately Jenneth's letters had been short. Between her husband's half-grown children and her own two babies, Jenneth seemed to have little time for herself. *Yes,* thought Sibley, *it's better this way.*

The chamber felt confining, and everywhere Sibley looked she saw reminders of Logrin. It was a chilly spring evening, but the evenings were long now. She had time to take a walk before the evening meal. The air would clear her head. She put on the heavy boots she had worn to go herb gathering with Logrin and went outside.

At the gate she signed, "Good evening," hand turned up at chest level, then raised above her head, fingers bent over palm. She pointed to the headland, and down, indicating that she would walk on the beach, and then pointed to the sun and lowered her fingers a few degrees to tell him that she would return when the sun had moved that much. It would still be a little before dark.

"All right, Sibley." She and the gatekeeper had worked out this crude method years ago. Now it rankled Sibley, why did she have to use gestures when she had words? She had only gone a few steps when she felt a hand on her shoulder. It was the gatekeeper. "Mind you're back for dinner, now."

Sibley nodded and tapped once on her shoulder. Of course she'd be back in time. Why did everyone treat her as a child?

The beach was only a narrow strip, high tide would crest very soon. Sibley wandered along, letting her mind drift. *It's natural that I should be sad now, all winter, even, with Logrin so ill, but the grief will pass. That's why I feel so unsettled now. Soon all will be well again.* The movement of a seagull caught her eye and she watched it as it dived.

By the time Sibley reached the cliff base at the foot of the headland the tide was at its fullest. Even so, there was enough beach uncovered that if she wanted to scramble across the rocks she could reach the next cove. For a moment she hesitated, she hadn't told the gatekeeper that she might go there: that would have involved drawing a map in the muddy earth. Then she drew an arrow in the sand and wrote her name next to it. If anyone came looking for her, the way she'd gone would be clear enough. But what if someone just glanced along the beach and did not see anyone? They might raise the alarm without even looking for the arrow. But why would anyone even come looking for her? There was time enough before the gatekeeper expected her back.

Sibley gathered up her skirts and started around the cliff base. The wind was strong here, tugging at the brown fabric. Her green cloak billowed behind her and she grabbed the loose end to tuck under one arm before it could trail into one of the tidal ponds. She had to keep her eyes down, looking for gaps in the slippery seaweed where she could step, but once on sand again she let loose her hold on her skirts and cloak and looked up.

Halfway down the beach men in helmets and leather jerkins were pushing a rowing boat into the sea. She did not recognize any of them. Raiders! Sibley turned to run, to raise the alarm. Halfway across the rocks she slipped into a pool and fell. She struggled on, soaking wet with the wind like ice across her face and her dripping clothing twisting around her legs. Had they seen her? She glanced back, she could no longer see the beach, but there was no one on the rock behind her. *Please, Neave, let the noise seem like the sea to them.*

Sibley clawed at the wet tapes of her cloak, trying to untie them and drop the sodden weight. She broke a nail on the knot and pulled it to her mouth to try her teeth on it. Her heart pounded and she could feel the blood rushing in her ears. Then something struck her on the back, knocking her to the ground. She twisted her head around and saw one of the strangers standing over her. He grabbed a wrist and pulled her to her feet, his mouth was moving but Sibley could not make out the words. She struggled to free herself and he cuffed her lightly, then backhanded her sharply when she did not stop fighting. Finally the man stuffed a corner of her wet and sandy cloak into her mouth. He held it there with one hand, put the other around her waist, and carried her across the rocks.

The others had already launched the boat. Sibley's captor dragged her behind him and dumped her into the boat. At once other hands replaced his over her mouth. The man heaved himself into the boat and crouched next to her. Shivering, Sibley inched away from him. Someone else pushed her aside. The oars were unshipped, and hugging the coast, the boat moved away from the keep.

Twice Sibley tried to raise her head above the gunwale; each time she was pushed back to the bottom of the boat. The man holding her was trying to tell her something, but she couldn't understand the words his lips made. So she lay there, shivering in the bilge. Obviously, these men hoped that no one from the keep would spot them. They had picked a good time to try it, ebbing tide and dusk. Many of the men were dark—were they from Alizon? But what were men of Alizon doing here? There had been no recent storms, so they were not wreck survivors. These were fighting men, although their equipment was shoddy. Perhaps a scouting party?

Eventually her captor loosened his grip. Sibley sat in the bottom of the boat, legs pulled up to her chin. Here, at least, she was out of the wind. No one objected when she spat out the corner of her cloak. One of the men draped it over her and she soon realized that even wet it helped cut the wind. She fell into a half sleep, aware that she was cold and bruised, but almost detached from the discomfort. And she blamed herself: *I should have never left the cove. But if Logrin hadn't died . . .*

Sibley had no idea how long the journey took, but it was still dark when they reached a ship. The men scrambled up a rope ladder, but Sibley's legs were painfully asleep and couldn't bear her weight. She was carried on board like a sack of meal and dumped on the deck. With stiff fingers she rubbed life back into her numb legs. There were no lights on the ship. In the darkness she could see the shapes of men moving about. It wasn't a large ship, but the crew seemed numerous. Like all the keep children, Sibley had been taken on the fishing boats along the estuary, but she had never been on a seafaring vessel. The motion was unsettling and when she finally managed to stand she nearly pitched to the deck again.

Someone took her arm and hurried her down the companionway into the cabin. It was small and close. A man sat at a table, and a younger man—not yet grown tall enough to have to stoop in the low cabin—stood next to him. Her escort pointed to a bench bolted to the bulkhead, and Sibley lurched over to sit there. The taller of the two men—Sibley assumed he was the captain as the others deferred to him—turned to her. When he spoke, she could not understand him. With her right hand she mimed holding a pen, making strokes on her left palm.

The captain spoke again, then turned to the other man. Sibley followed the captain's gaze. The young man said something, then, after his captain turned back to Sibley, he winked at her. She quickly looked away and he left the cabin.

The captain gave Sibley a bit of slate and a lead rule. Since the men did not use the tongue of the Dales, she doubted they could read it. Logrin had taught her to read the language of Alizon, but she had never tried to make herself understood in it. She carefully printed, "I do not hear you."

The captain at least could make out what she had written. He read it out to the others, pointing to each word. After some discussion the captain touched his lips with an exaggerated gesture.

"No, I cannot speak," Sibley wrote, trying for an even hand despite the ship's lurching. "Who are you? Why did you take me? What—"

The captain took the slate and rule, and smudged out her words. "I am Estban, captain. My ship." He printed clumsily. "Be good. Go with the boy."

Sibley reached for the slate, but Estban pushed her hand away. When the young man returned, the captain spoke to him. He pulled a blanket off the bed, pocketed the slate and rule, and held out a hand to Sibley.

Sibley stumbled after him. The captain's few remarks had not reassured her at all. She had no idea of what would happen to her. Was this man going to take her back on deck and pitch her overboard? She tried to calm herself. Why did he take the slate if he was just going to kill her? To trick her? Fighting fear, Sibley realized that panic would only make her more helpless.

The young man took her to the galley. He roused the cook from his bed, and the man shuffled off, scowling at Sibley. He had only one eye and was missing a hand. Sibley hoped he'd find somewhere else to sleep that night. She sat gingerly on the side of the dirty bunk while the man poured her a drink of water. It tasted stale, but Sibley's mouth was raw from the salt

and sand and the wool of her cloak, and she drank gratefully
before making the sign for thank you.

The man had taken out the slate and drawn on it a picture of
a stick figure with long braids, wrapped in a blanket lying on
the bunk. He plucked at her sleeve, pointed to the open doorway, then turned his back. Sibley stamped her foot, a good way
to get someone's attention. He turned around and looked her
straight in the eye.

Sibley noticed then that his eyes were green. That in itself
was not too unusual, but they were slitted like a cat's. He was
drawing again, a picture of someone plucking a chicken. He
pointed to the picture, then to Sibley.

Sibley understood: undress or be stripped. With poor grace
she nodded and pointed to the doorway. At least he could wait
outside. She removed her dress and stockings and, after much
fumbling, the woolen shirt she wore under her chemise. She
was going to keep the chemise to sleep in even though it was
damp. Then she tossed the wet clothes into the hall and
climbed into the bunk. As an afterthought she removed her
cap. It was half dry, and she was so tired that she pulled it off
over her face rather than trying to untie it. She wondered how
she would brush her hair, and fell asleep still wondering.

When she woke, she knew at once she was not in the keep.
She remembered everything from the night before. Unlike the
poor girl in *The Dalemaid's Litany* who awoke every morning in
the Abbey thinking she was still in her parents' home, Sibley
knew where she was. She could feel the footsteps of men on the
deck above her and smell some sort of strong spirit. Turning
her head she saw the fierce cook pouring a dark liquid into a
kettle. A sailor took it off the fire and carried it out of the
galley. The cook carefully banked down the fire, then rum-
maged through a sack on the floor. As Sibley watched horrified,
he crushed a brick of hard bread, picking out maggots, poured
hot water from another kettle over it, and added a little of the
spirit. He put the dish next to Sibley, made sure once again the
fire in the sandbox was banked, and left the galley. So this was
her breakfast.

Her clothes were hanging from the ceiling, dry, but stiff and
scratchy. During the night someone had tacked a bit of sail

cloth across the doorway. It didn't hang all the way to the floor. Sibley assumed it was too short to reach the sandbox: fire was an even greater risk at sea than on land. She put her shirt on over her chemise. Her cap was a crumpled rag. She broke off one of the tapes and used it to tie back her hair. After she dressed she choked down her breakfast, the spirit was bitter but warming. While she was still eating the cat-eyed man brought her a bucket and drew a picture of the girl with braids carrying the bucket onto the deck. Then he left her.

Sibley spent the morning on deck, huddled out of the wind. She dared not return to the galley and face the cook. The sailors ignored her. Once the captain came over and absently patted her shoulder. She supposed that was his way of saying that she was being good.

When the sun was high, the cat-eyed man brought her a cup of water and another dish of the watered bread. She took the dish from him and set it on the deck. As the ship rolled, the dish slid, and he stopped it with his foot. Sibley pointed to herself, then to several points on the horizon. Would he understand that she was asking where the keep was?

He smiled at her and pointed to her meal. As he handed her the cup he spoke: "'Poor little maid, waiting by the sea.'"

Sibley recognized the words, they were part of a children's rhyme. She put a figure to her lips, reached to touch his ear, then touched his lips and the corner of her own eye.

He looked straight at her, and his eyes narrowed. "So you can see my words, is that it, lass?"

His lips moved slowly, and he shaped his words oddly, but Sibley could make out his meaning. She pretended to write, and he gave her the slate and rule.

She sketched a picture of High Hallack's coast, then pointed to him and the ship.

"It makes no odds where we are."

Sibley shook her head and drew again. The stick figure with braids stood with both feet on High Hallack. Then on a boat shape with wavy lines underneath, and finally on the outline of a ship. Sibley pointed to him.

"How did I get here? Well, I was born about there near Kalaven Port—however did you learn to draw a chart?"

Sibley shrugged. It was an inelegant gesture, one which Lady Alyss forbade her, but it would be too complicated to explain about Logrin. The cat-eyed man spoke again, repeating words when she shook her head, and before long she had his story.

"My father was off a Sulcar ship, my mother a chandler's daughter. My father wintered with us each year, and when my mother died—I was eight—he took me to sea with him. He—died, he's dead now, and I'm working my passage home."

Sibley wondered what he wasn't telling her.

"But, little maid, you're not to let them know I'm of High Hallack. They think I'm Sulcar, and that suits me. I've no wish for them to send me spying out against my mother's people. You understand?"

Sibley nodded. He took the empty cup and dish. "I'll be back later, rest easy."

Sibley signed, "Good-bye." This man—she would have to learn his name—did not seem altogether trustworthy. But he seemed loyal to his mother's people, and he was kindly disposed toward her. Perhaps he would help her escape. She would have to talk with him more, try to understand him. She remembered Logrin talking about the art of siege warfare, "always have a friend within the gates."

When the sun started to set the cat-eyed man took her back to the galley, where the cook made her the same meal again. Then he cut chunks of dried meat into a bucket—for the crew's dinner, Sibley guessed. The meat smelled foul, and Sibley was thankful that she didn't have to eat it. She was thirsty, but when she held out her cup, hoping the cook would refill it, he shook his head. When he left the galley, the cat-eyed man explained that water was rationed.

He gave Sibley the slate, and she began to make her clumsy drawings again while the man tried to guess her meaning.

"By the Horned Man, lass, I would that you could write."

"And what makes you think I can't?" Sibley wrote.

"However did they teach you?"

"However did they teach you to read?"

"My grandfather Chandler taught me, though I'm out of practice."

"What is your name?"

"Herol. But they call me Woldor, a good Sulcar name, or Boy. What's yours?"

"Mistress Sibley." She didn't really have any right to the title, but Lady Alyss had encouraged people to use it, and Sibley was beginning to suspect Herol was younger than she was. It would do him good to show a little respect.

He looked at her stained, simple clothes, and nodded. "Mistress."

Sibley spelled out his name with her fingers. "Or I could call you this," she wrote. She held out her right hand, palm facing her, thumb holding back the little figure so that the other three pointed to her left, like whiskers. It was the sign for "cat."

He laughed, pointing to himself, then making the sign.

Sibley taught him the verb "to be" and a few pronouns. Cat learned quickly. She told him about Logrin and how she'd come to be captured, then showed him a few more signs, ones useful in emergencies, and told him that if he stamped his foot, she'd feel it. "Or thump on a table if I'm writing on it, anything that makes vibrations."

"Can you feel the waves against the ship?"

"Yes, and when the sailors run across the deck, just like you could if you felt for it," Sibley wrote, then scrubbed the slate clean. The rule was bent and she pinched it back into shape. Now that she and Cat were on friendly footing she'd trust him more. "I do miss home."

Cat grinned. "Can I help you escape, you mean?"

"What will happen to me? Will Estban try to get a ransom for me?"

Cat reached to touch her hand, then stopped.

Sibley understood that he wished to comfort her and smiled.

"Estban isn't going to risk something like that, even if he knew your rank. Suppose your family set a trap for him when he went to collect the gold. No, he'll sell you."

"But who'd want a deaf servant, even one who can read and write? I'd be too much trouble, and no one would trust me to keep accounts or anything like that."

"No, he'll sell you—to a place where your deafness won't matter." He fell silent, a hard look on his face. "I'll think of something."

"But no one's touched me." Sibley knew exactly what he was talking about.

"It wouldn't be good for the men's morale to let them . . . er."

Sibley tapped her shoulder, she understood. "When the ship gets into port, bribe the greediest sailor to let us off."

Cat laughed so much she couldn't understand him. When he could speak clearly he said, "There are enough holes there to sail a fleet through. There is always someone on guard, for a start, and what shall I bribe them with—my shirt?"

Sibley smiled and took Jenneth's arm band off.

Cat took it, turning it over and over. "Where did you get this?"

"A gift. I think it's valuable. Even Logrin had never seen stone like it."

"It was made by the Old Ones."

Sibley made the question sign.

"I can feel it, I've held their relics before. Can you read this writing?" Cat held the bracelet out to her.

"There isn't any writing."

"Here, but very faint, I can just see silver letters; they must have been painted on."

Sibley couldn't see any writing, but perhaps Cat's eyes were sharper. A real cat could see in the dark, after all.

"Can you read it?" she asked.

"No." He copied the writing onto the slate, but the language was foreign to Sibley. "Take it back, lass—mistress, I should be saying."

"Keep it, in case you get a chance."

"Have you thought what you'd do once you got away. You'd be in a strange place—"

Sibley tugged at his sleeve, and he read from the slate. "I would have you to speak for me."

"In Alizon, I'd be killed on sight if I left the ship. You, too, if you're with me."

"Why?"

"Less than a week ago, the horn was sounded thrice against the Old Race. I have the blood of the Old Ones in me." He pointed to his eyes. "These let me see in the dark, but in Alizon it would be taken as a mark of the Old Race." He paused. "I was in Alizon when it happened, drinking wine with my father and a merchant, a friend of his near the docks. Suddenly there was a hue and cry in the streets. Before I could make out the cause, my father had pushed me out the back door. He was— he died in the street trying to bar the front door. I could hear, I think the merchant did it. Then I ran.

"I hid all day in a warehouse, made my way to the ship at night and saw her watched by the Hounds. I was afraid that if I tried to board, they would attack and my shipmates would be killed trying to aid me. So I crept along the docks, keeping to the shadows. When I saw old Estban's tub I thought I was saved. He's a scoundrel and a slaver—we've had a couple of run-ins with him over the years, but I thought he'd let me buy passage with him. Half his crew is outside the law, I didn't think he'd turn on me. Well, he took every coin I had, and yesterday morning, before we were in sight of High Hallack, he had me tied below. I know what that means. He wants to keep me as a slave—forever. He knows I'm afraid to be seen in Alizon, and he won't let me get near enough to land anywhere else.

"But don't worry, I'm going to find a way off, and I'll take you with me." He took up the lantern and stepped across the tiny galley, then turned, "And, Sibley, I'm sleeping across the door, Estban's orders, though I'll be up and gone when you wake. Don't worry if it gets rough tonight."

Sibley took up her arm band. The air was damp and cold, but the stone felt unusually warm, and in the poor light, its green color seemed paler than it really was. She pulled off her boots and lay down fully dressed. She was awake for hours, trying to make plans, and fell asleep to dream of Cat and herself swimming away in the night. In the dream it didn't matter that she did not know how to swim.

The sea was much rougher the next morning. The cook did not light the fire, and sent up hard biscuits to the men, although he took the time to grind Sibley's into a paste with cold water and gave her a slice of dried apple. Sibley ate and took her slops bucket onto the deck. She had a hard time keeping her footing, but once she had huddled into the same space she had taken the day before, she decided to stay above deck. Here at least the air was fresh and the ship's movement bothered her less.

The weather did not improve, and Sibley had to eat biscuit paste again at noon. She wondered if the cook thought she had no teeth, but after she saw that the sailors had to suck their biscuit rather than chewing it, she was grateful he bothered. While she was still eating, the sails were reefed, and she was not surprised when Cat came and took her below.

"There is going to be a storm," he told her as soon as they were in the galley. "You'll have to stay here where you'll be safe."

"Will it be bad?" she signed.

Cat understood the question and roughly signed, "No bad."

The storm was very bad. It hit suddenly, and Sibley could feel the ship's timbers pulling apart under strain. She tried to lie in the bunk, but after rolling out of it a couple of times, she wedged herself between the bulkhead and the fire box. Warm ashes spilled over her. Before long she had been sick, and huddled miserably under the cloak. It was very dark. When waves broke over the deck, water rushed between the boards.

Sibley did not notice when morning came with a sick gray light. She was balanced between exhausted sleep and a fear that if she slept the ship might go down and carry her with it. Death might be preferable to seasickness, but drowning, trapped in a small room, was a horror she could not even bear to think about.

Cat passed into her sight, working the bung from the water barrel, and fresh water sloshed everywhere. Even Cat was having trouble keeping his balance. He crawled over to her and pressed a wet rag against her lips. She sucked, but the water made her stomach heave. He wiped her face instead. He said something that she couldn't understand.

"More clearly," she signed. It was an effort to move her hands.

"What?"

She managed to sign, "Go on."

"I'm going to take you on deck."

Cat half dragged, half carried her up the companionway and helped her lie down against the cabin. There was a cold gray light; the rain was hard and driving. Estban and the men crouched around the wheel. "The cable snapped," Cat explained, "and over there, hidden in the fog, are the Long Sisters. The wind is driving us onto them. There's no point in taking the boat, it would capsize in this sea. But we may get washed over The Hands, the low bit that joins the two big reefs. If so, we'll be driven onto the shore."

Sibley ached with cold and sickness and had not understood every word, but she thought she could manage to drown out here and not disgrace herself by panicking. She wouldn't be trapped. The fresh air cleared her head a little. With stiff fingers she worried her arm band from under her wet sleeve. "Take it, swim, buy passage home." She had never heard of the Long Sisters: they must be off the Alizon coast. Cat would be in danger there. "Close eyes," she added.

"I don't understand?" Cat said.

Sibley tried to explain once more, if only she'd taught him more signs. He kept pushing the bracelet away, but finally took it. He folded his hands about it, fingers threaded through the hole. Sibley closed her eyes. *It was all right now, if he swam, or even if he didn't. He'd wake up on the beach . . . cats had nine lives, after all.*

A short while later the wind dropped. Sibley felt a little warmer. There was a jolt, and she thought the ship had finally struck, but instead she turned to. Sibley opened her eyes.

Sailors were climbing the rigging, hoisting sails. Estban waved his arms. Cat sat beside her, bent over, his arms pulled to his chest. His face was white, eyes rolled back. Sibley stumbled to her feet, the sea was still rough, and as she tried to walk, a wave broke over the ship, and sea water rushed around her knees, knocking her to the deck. Cat now lay on the deck, legs drawn up, his head in water. Sibley pulled him more or less upright. She'd do better to stay with him than trying to get help.

Sibley held him while the wind dropped and the fog lifted. Soon the rain stopped, and the sun shone through a thin haze of clouds. Estban had a rudder jury-rigged, and a minimum of canvas raised.

Cat was still in her arms breathing rapidly. No one took any

notice of them. Suddenly he began to shake. For a moment
Sibley was even more frightened, then she realized that his
color was coming back and that his eyes were closed. He was
limp, like a sleeping child. She turned him on his back and his
legs flopped straight. The arm band was grasped loosely in his
hands. It was white, the color gone. As Sibley pulled it free she
noticed that the palms of his hands were red as if they had been
scorched, but the marks were already fading. She pushed the
bracelet onto her arm. Cat, it seemed, had worked some sort of
magic with it.

Someone was standing next to them; Sibley looked up at Estban. He knelt and began to feel Cat's head. Cat stirred, Estban
spoke, and Cat nodded. Estban pulled Cat to his feet. Cat
glanced at Sibley and encircled his wrist with the fingers of the
other hand. Sibley pointed to her own arm and nodded. Cat
winked and went to join the working men. Estban looked at
her. Sibley could not read his expression. Then he shook his
head and left her.

No one paid any attention to Sibley that day, and she kept
out of the way. She worried about Cat and her arm band.
When the men were given water, she expected some, but was
not brought any. She wondered if she were being punished. At
dusk the cook took her back to the galley. She thought she was
too worried and thirsty to sleep, but did so as soon as she
climbed into the bunk.

Cat was there in the morning, holding a cup of water, the
now-cracked slate, and a piece of crumbly chalk. He had a split
lip and a bruise on his left cheek.

"Sorry," Sibley signed. She meant, "Oh, poor Cat."

He grinned lopsidedly. "Sleeping on watch. Estban said he
wishes he could learn to drop off like that. Thank the Horned
One he thinks of me as a boy, otherwise I'd have been keel-
hauled."

Sibley hoped he was teasing her.

It was raining again, and Sibley stayed in the galley. She
watched the cook with fascination as he set the galley to rights
and boiled meat for the crew. When he noticed her interest, he
entertained her by mending a shirt. Sibley, who hated people
staring when she signed, felt embarrassed by her own interest.

She crushed her own biscuits for something to do, and borrowed the cook's needle and thread to mend a rent in her cloak. Even with the fire lit, it was cold in the galley, and her clothes were damp.

Cat came to see her in the evening, and the cook left. "Changing of the guard," Cat joked. His bruise was just starting to turn purple at the edges, and his lip was very swollen. Sibley had a hard time understanding him. He'd brought a new bit of lead to replace the almost finished chalk. "I have a plan: we were blown off course, almost as far south as Estcarp."

"Witches!" signed Sibley, then wrote it for Cat.

"Yes, but they won't hunt the Old Race, it would be like killing their own people. If we were wrecked there, then we, you and I, we could run inland. Both Estcarp and High Hallack stand against Kolder and Alizon. I'm sure I could find a Sulcar ship and arrange for you to go home."

"But we'd have to wait for a storm, and pray it blew us in the right direction," Sibley wrote, wishing that written words had the nuances signs did: she wanted to draw information out of Cat.

"Sibley, that arm band of yours, you know I wore it before the storm dropped."

She tapped her shoulder.

"Well, I was thinking about the storm, how the wind was blowing from the east, and a little south, and that if it veered to the south, we might pass over The Hands. And I felt the band grow warmer. Then I thought why couldn't the wind just rise higher, high enough to leave us calm, and blow the clouds away. The stone grew even warmer. And I knew it was magic, my thoughts were bringing it to life. It was a terrible knowledge. I was frightened, and I wondered what I'd done to deserve it.

"I thought about the storm, and suddenly it was as if I were above it, looking down. But I didn't really see it. Sibley, I say I can see in the dark, but I can't really. I just know where things are if I'm moving toward them. This was the same sort of thing. I was the wind. I pushed against the ship, it was a something there instead of nothing, and it moved. Then I drove away the clouds. When I stopped pushing, it was as though I was drifting away. I thought I was dying. Then I was on the deck with you by me and the standing captain over me. My hand burned all day, and my chest, where the stone had pressed against me, although there wasn't a mark on me or my clothes."

Sibley drew off the arm band. She had looked at it the few times the cook left the galley. Each time it was darker. Now it had almost returned to its usual dusky green, and for the first time she could remember it was cold to the touch. She told him how it had been nearly white when she had taken it from him.

"Perhaps I used up its power, or maybe it just goes white when it's being used. I just hope it will work again. We're going south and west now, I'll have to drive us east before a storm."

"How can you use it without anyone noticing."

"I'll have to get sick. I hope you don't mind sharing the galley with a sick man. I'll drink seawater and pretend I feel worse than I do."

Sibley went on deck the next morning. It was only the fifth morning she had woken on the ship, and she was sick of biscuit gruel and not enough water to drink. She felt dirtier than she ever had. Halfway through the morning Cat collapsed on deck, and after he had been pulled to his feet and fallen several times, he was carried into the galley. Sibley followed. Cat was given a drink of water and left alone with her.

"I drank seawater and brought it up four times last night. Everyone heard. Cook won't be here for a bit, and by then I'll be asleep—not really asleep you know."

"Doing magic," Sibley signed. "Slate?"

"Captain took it back. He does his talleys on it."

Sibley handed him the arm band. "Luck," she signed.

"Once I've really got the storm blowing, I'll try to wake up. If I don't, just walk along the coast until you find someone." He closed his eyes and tightened his grasp on the stone.

Sibley found his instructions rather inadequate. Since she couldn't swim, she wondered how she was supposed to get to shore. But she didn't want to disturb him to ask, for she suspected that if he didn't wake she wouldn't be able to manage without his help. There was no point in worrying him.

When the cook came down Cat lay curled up, facing the wall. The cook looked at him, but didn't touch him, and went about his work. Sibley spent the afternoon sitting by Cat, hoping to feel some difference in the weather. It seemed a little colder, but that might just be wishful thinking.

She spent the night sitting by the bunk. Sometimes she slept, her head resting against the boards. She was awake when Cat began to shiver again. She put her cloak over him and waited until he slept normally, then took the arm band back again. The cook came at first light and made biscuit gruel for both Sibley and Cat. Cat made faces at her while he ate his.

His hands were still red when Estban came to see him, but the captain seemed to believe he was well, because he sent Cat up on deck. Later Cat explained that Estban thought his hands were red with a rash from fever.

"Storm?" signed Sibley.

"I've made a wind; can't you feel it? By tonight it will be driving us back. I'll work a little more on it this evening."

Sibley thought he seemed very sure of himself.

"The captain will be furious," he continued. "He wants to put in somewhere safe for water: several casks were broached during the last storm. When you're outlawed in your own land, it's hard to find a safe bay, and I'll be driving him away from one he likes."

"When will we go?" Sibley asked, trying to use signs he knew.

"In a day or two, if we're driven fast enough."

Sibley wondered how many days of storm she could endure. "I do not swim."

"I'll tow you. Don't worry."

But Sibley did. Cat was no longer afraid of using the stone, in fact he had lost his awe of it. Sibley found it hard to believe he had mastered its magic so soon. However, as the day went on, the wind grew stronger until it was a gale. The ship was no longer able to tack, and, as Cat had predicted, ran before the wind. There was no rain, but the seas were high, and once the waves began to break over the deck, Sibley was sent below. Cat took the band with him into the passageway when he went to sleep that night.

Sibley awoke as the ship struck something, drew back, and struck again. This time the motion stopped, although she could feel the timbers strain as the ship was pounded by the waves. It was dark, and she barked her shins against the sandbox. She found the doorway by blundering into the sailcloth curtain. There was a little moonlight in the passage, and she saw Cat, legs and arms drawn up, body curled. She bent to look at his face: it was contorted. She tried to draw his hands away from his chest and saw scorch marks on his shirt: the stone had finally grown too hot. There was a skin of seawater kept over the fire box, and she hurried to get it. It cooled the skin around the stone, but she still could not pull it free.

There was water spilling around her feet. It drew back, and rushed again. The ship must have struck a rock! Sibley grabbed Cat by the legs and dragged. She was smaller than he was and slighter, and she thought she could never lift him. She got him up the ladder by working an arm under one of his and pulling him up rung by rung. Her arm felt as though it would tear loose from its socket. The deck was deserted, the boat gone. The men had left—even the cook—with no thought for them. Sibley felt anger and with it, strength. She dumped Cat on the deck and, no longer caring if she hurt him, forced his fingers from the stone. It burned her slightly, but it soon cooled, and she pushed it back on her arm. One did not discard something of its power easily.

Then she propped him against the hatch and went to the railings. As she walked around the ship she could see no sign of a rock. The ship seemed caught below the water line, and not in danger of sinking at once, but Sibley was sure the vessel was being broken apart. Twice she settled with a lurch. Sibley had to find something to keep her and Cat afloat. She searched his pocket for his clasp knife and cut several lengths of rope. Then she looked for something she could use. The hatch cover bound with iron was too heavy for her to lift, so she cut a spar free. As she worked, she felt the ship drop again.

The spar was twice her height in length, and thicker than her arm could span, but she could roll and push it along the deck. She found seamen's harnesses, hanging from the rigging where they had been abandoned, and manhandled Cat into one. He was less stiff now, but his eyes were still open and rolled back. She pushed the spar through the stern railings, then fastened a length of cable to the end nearest the sea, passed the cable over the railings, and tied the other end to Cat's harness, thanking Neave she had learned her knots as a child. Then she struggled into a harness and fastened herself to the spar as she had Cat.

It seemed to take forever to heave Cat over the railing. As soon as he dropped, she was pushing the spar into the water, trying not to tangle the rope, and climbing over the railing herself. For an awful moment she thought she was not going to make it, but would jam against the railing, held there by the weight of the dangling spar. Suddenly she felt herself falling, then the cold shock of the sea, colder than she had expected. She pulled herself hand over hand until she felt the spar, then fumbled for the rope attached to Cat. Twice she pulled on her own rope before she drew him up to her. She felt his warm breath on her hand and she knew he lived.

With them both at one end, the spar rode unevenly in the water, the far end poking above their heads, so Sibley dragged them toward the middle. She had planned to lash them firmly to the spar, but had the strength only to cling to the wood with one arm and keep Cat's head above water.

The tide did the rest. At least Cat had been right about that, although it was a morning ebb, not an evening one. Surely Gunnora was watching over them. The wind must have blown much more strongly than Cat had planned, and they could easily have come when the tide was flowing. Sibley just let wave after wave carry them onto the shore. After a long while her feet touched bottom. The beach was very long with a gentle slope. The waves crested and broke far from land. The force of the tide was strong. The tide turned when the water was still up to Sibley's waist, and rushed out quickly. She struggled to drag Cat and the spar behind her: there was no time to cut them free.

She collapsed in the surf and waited while the sea withdrew and the sun rose. Cat lay still in his trance. With an effort Sibley pushed herself to her knees and drew out the clasp knife. She had eaten nothing but biscuit and dried apple for five days and was thirsty as usual. She cut the ropes and harnesses; it was easier than trying to untie the knots. There was wet seaweed

heaped along the beach, and she bound Cat's blistered hands
with it. When she looked at the stone it was white and cracked.

There was a high sea wall behind them with stairs shaped into
it. There would be a village above them. Sooner or later someone would come onto the beach, and be they Alizon, witches,
or moss wives, Sibley would be glad to see them. The tide was
far out now. Sibley could barely see water across the sand. She
wondered how far she and Cat had drifted. Well, she'd rest a
little too and if no one had found them by the time they woke,
they'd have to find the village themselves.

The sun shining through her eyelids woke her. She put her
arm over her face to block it, then decided to get up and see
how Cat was. As she looked at the sea she blanched. The tide
had turned—the sea was rushing toward them. The same strong
rush that had carried them onto the beach would trap them.
Now she noticed high water marks on the sea wall, marks
higher than her head. They had to get off the beach.

Cat did not stir when she shook him. She slapped him and his
lips moved, but not clearly enough for her to understand. She
pulled at his arm, but she was at the end of her strength and
could not lift him. She could not even drag him.

They had to move, or they would die. Dimly, words formed
in her mind, "Don't move, don't make a sound!" She shook
her head to clear it and tugged at Cat again. Her head was
whirling with faintness. She collapsed over him.

*There was sunlight spilling through the cottage door. Sibbie sat
on the floor, watching Islak pile up four wooden blocks for her
to knock over. She put out a hand and the blocks flew everywhere. "More, more, Issie put up now," she demanded, laughing as she scattered the stack.*

*Nana sitting on the doorstep knitting said, "Say 'please,' Sib-
bie."*

*"P'ease more, Issie?" she said, and Islak made the tower
again. Suddenly Nana pushed her under the bed. Outraged, for
she'd done nothing wrong, Sibbie yelled.*

*"Hold her, Islak, don't let her cry," Nana commanded. It was
dark under the bed; the dangling quilt blocked most of the light.
She heard the door slam. "Don't cry." Islak held her tightly, his
hand over her mouth.*

Sibley felt Cat's body jerk under her, convulsed. She moved her hands, making his name sign.

There was thudding against the door. Sibbie heard a groan as it was forced open. A scream from Nana. Islak's hands were over ears now, but she could still hear. Peeking under the quilt, Sibbie saw Nana fall, saw a stick driven into her. Islak screamed.

There were terrible vibrations in Cat's chest.

There was a thud as the mattress landed over Nana. Islak let go of Sibbie, and she drew back against the wall, covering her ears with her own hands. A stick, like the one that had hurt Nana, came through the bed, then another. One stuck Islak, and his screams grew shriller. Sibbie bit her lip to keep from crying for Nana. She was not to make a sound or the stick would get her.

Islak stopped screaming. Sibbie couldn't hear anything.

Sibley looked at Cat's face. He was moving his lips again. She glanced at the sea, it was advancing faster than a man could run.

Islak squirmed and kicked.

Cat kicked; his arms flailed.

Nana lay half covered by the mattress. "Don't cry, don't listen."

Cat lay still.

Sibbie was silent, not hearing.

Sibley screamed, "Cat, Cat." She chafed his hand.

He moaned.

"Cat, what is it, what do you need?" The words sounded strange to her own ears.

"So far, go so far," Cat murmured.

"Come back, come here, to me. Cat."

"Above the clouds . . . the wind."

"It's over, Cat, come back, you don't have the band, you aren't doing magic."

He lay still while Sibley repeated his name, calling him back. His color improved. Then his eyes opened, and he whispered, "Water."

"Stand!" cried Sibley. "Look at the sea!"

Cat looked and scrambled up. A wave broke a hand's width from his feet, drew back to break again, soaking him to his knees. Clutching each other they stumbled up the stairs, pulling themselves by their hands when they slipped.

They sat on the top step with the sea whirling below them. Sibley rested her head on Cat's shoulder. Suddenly he twisted his head to look directly at her. "You can speak!"

"And hear. As soon as you can walk again we'll go along that path and find someone to help us. But while we rest let me tell you . . ."

Afterword

My brothers and I all found a great deal of pleasure in Miss Norton's work. I remember many days spent playing at Star Man's Son. *Unfortunately, I didn't manage to interest the boys in the Witch World books—magic just wasn't their thing. The fact that the eldest boy was only eight when I discovered the Witch World may have had something to do with it.*

Years later, when I was all grown up (or so I thought) my friend Susan Shwartz told me there was finally a way I could play Witch World. I could write a story for the Witch World anthology—at that point the first volume hadn't yet been published. I jumped at the chance and settled down to reread the Witch World novels and Sandra Miesel's excellent introduction to the Gregg Press hardcover edition of the first Witch World book, which saved me the trouble of making my own time line and gave me a number of insights into the universe of the Witch World.

I sent "Voice of Memory" to Miss Norton just after the first volume was closed, but she was kind enough to buy the story for this volume. In the time between the sale of the story and the publication of this anthology, my novel was published, but I'm still very proud of the fact that my first fiction sale was to Andre Norton.

—M. E. Allen

PLUMDUFF POTATO-EYE

by

Jayge Carr

Know your enemy was one of the necessities of winning any struggle, thought the young challenger as he peered through the underbrush at the giant. But—he chewed on a full pink lower lip—

He wished he hadn't.

Known.

The giant was so very—very—

Gigantic!

The giant lay down his axe, picked up the split logs, and walked over to add them to the neat pile under the rush covering—and the ground shook with each stride.

Seven and a half feet, maybe eight, and built broad for his height. A boulder moving. Thick and tough and—

The young man shuddered. Even in his carefully preserved quilted-leather armor, with his sword, would he be able to—

His shoulders stiffened, and that young, vulnerable lip pulled tight.

He would.

He had to.

*   *   *

Plumduff was aware of the intruder almost as soon as he established himself under the crisp-smelling mint bush.

Not that he heard him, the crisp *ka-chunk, ka-thwack* of the axe splitting dried wood would have covered louder sounds than dry leaves rustling.

Not sight, because the figure was well hidden in the dimness of the underbrush and late afternoon.

But this was Plumduff's woods, he had lived there long enough to be a part of it, his heartbeat pulsing somehow with the life around him, his senses so finely attuned that any disturbance out of the normal tugged at him.

He sighed, and lifted the axe extra high for the next stroke.

Another one.

He sighed again, brought the axe down, and the log split with a reluctant *chuffff* into two neat sections.

(The watcher in the shadows saw and winced. One blow. The giant hadn't used a wedge and hammer, just the axe to split a log as thick as his own massive body.)

Plumduff carefully propped the axe against the stump he was using as a platform, and picked up the two sections, all senses alert.

Now?

Or later?

He straightened, knowing it was later. If it was now, he would have been attacked when he was most vulnerable, weaponless, bending over.

Small favors.

But was he condemned for the rest of his life to be a rite of passage, the demon each fledgling must conquer—or at least face?

What if one of them, lucky or skilled or whatever, succeeded.

With a world-weary shrug, he piled the two sections neatly in with the rest.

Enough splitting for a while. He looked over the branches he had brought in, selected the straightest one. Yes—he sniffed the spicy pine, discarded a couple of them, picked through— elm. His new chair would definitely be elm.

He held the branch up, measured it against his own brawny

forearm. Too small. He sorted through the pile of branches, chopped off, saved for kindling, patching, whatever.

That one. Yes—good size. And that one.

In a few minutes, he had four nicely straight pieces picked out, and was seated comfortably on his stump, working the bark off, carving them smooth and straight. The new legs. For his new chair.

The challenger slithered back through the underbrush. He would get his weapons, prepare himself, and—

Hit the giant at sundown, when he would be weary and slower?

But so would his opponent.

Tomorrow sunrise, when he would be sleepy and unaware?

Should he challenge first, and give up the advantage of surprise, or attack without warning, try to make the first blow the telling one.

Plumduff was wondering the same thing.

Would the lad challenge first, or attack without warning?

The young challenger was far enough away that he had risen to his feet and was about to return to his hidden gear when Plumduff spoke up, loudly, to his apparently empty clearing. "I'm getting rather tired of this, you know."

The youth in the woods froze. The giant was well away from him, but his voice was as large as the rest of him, and his conversational tones penetrated easily through the underbrush.

"What do you people think I am, anyway, a punching bag?"

The youth gasped. *The giant knew he was here!*

"Have you ever thought about it from my point of view?"

Was he going to attack?

"Here I am minding my own business, working away in my wood pile, and you're planning to rush up and attack me."

The youth in the wood debated running.

"Is that fair? What have I ever done to you, anyway?"

"You're a giant!" the interloper squeaked.

"No." Plumduff lined his four to-be chair legs up and lopped a fingerspan off one of them. "You're too short."

"I am not!" Without realizing what he was doing, the young man had drawn closer.

Plumduff took off another bit of wood. "Of course you are," he said calmly. "If we stood front to front, I doubt you'd come past my belt buckle. Obviously, you're far too short."

"I'd come well past your belt buckle, you—you giant," the young man asserted, glaring out of the bushes on the edge of Plumduff's clearing. "Giant," he repeated bitterly. "And"—getting his first good look at Plumduff's features—"you're ugly, too!"

Plumduff sighed. He'd looked at his own reflection often enough to know that, by normal human standards, he would never come in better than last in a male beauty contest.

"Yaaa." The attacker was working himself up. "Your mother was a demon, and your father a spavined horse!"

"Pffffaaa," Plumduff sputtered. "Do I really look like a horse, villager."

"Yes, you do, you—" the heckler started—and stopped. Plumduff's question had been asked in such a whimsical, mildly curious tone that it was hard to keep his own anger going.

"Look at me, do I really look like a horse," Plumduff repeated, still in that light (for such a deep voice) almost-teasing note.

The intruder looked.

"A *horse*?"

The youngster snickered. "No." Then, a rush of honesty: "Like a frog."

Plumduff frowned.

"Sort of. You have such a big jaw, the rest of your head looks too small, and those little black eyes, and—"

For the second time in as many minutes, Plumduff gazed at his four branches dubiously, and as he frowned in concentration, his tongue protruded to tuck into the groove between cheek and wispy-bearded chin.

"Your tongue comes out just like a frog," the young man finished triumphantly.

Plumduff, who would have sworn he had no shred of male vanity left, hastily pulled the offending organ back within the confines of his (it was rather large) mouth.

And too hastily shortened one of his to-be chair legs.

The youngster again, on a rude note: "If you're making chips for your fire, you're doing it right."

Plumduff frowned. Without his realizing it, the tongue crept out again. "It's going to be a chair," he informed. And lopped at the other three to match the too-short one.

Curious, Plumduff's would-be challenger wandered a little closer. "At the rate you're going at it," he observed, forgetting that he was talking quite amiably to the dreaded giant, "it's going to be about high enough for a two-year-old."

Plumduff's frown at that was ferocious—but somehow not frightening. The youngster smothered another snicker and said, "It's a job for two." His girlfriend was the village carpenter's daughter, and he had picked up plenty, though he himself was apprenticed to the smith. "Look, lay them flat on the ground, I'll line them up with another branch, and you can straighten them easily. And get them all the same length."

"All right." Hesitantly: "Thank you."

With both of them kneeling, staring at their work on the ground, Plumduff didn't look quite so large and menacing.

"My name's Gregoriat," the newcomer said suddenly as they were lining the pieces up.

"Plumduff," he replied automatically.

"Plum—" Gregoriat rocked back on his haunches and stared at the kneeling giant. He had a bald spot in the thicket of graying black on his head, and it somehow made him look both less formidable and—and more human. "—*duff*?" He burst out laughing. "I never heard a name like that before," he managed to get out between spasms.

Plumduff sat back himself, rubbing absentmindedly at one eye, where a bit of grit or sawdust had gotten in and was irritating him. "My mother"—a smile—"who was not a demon, but a very, very wise woman, said that was the name of her favorite dessert, where she came from." He rubbed at the eye, again, squinting. "Far from here," he added.

"Must have been." Gregoriat's own eyes were watering— from laughter.

"She said that Plumduff was warm and rich and infinitely satisfying." He smiled, reminiscently. "And so was I. But she was the one who was—" He sighed. "I miss her," he said, mouth drooping, "even now. And it's been many years."

Gregoriat's own mouth drooped. "I miss my mother, too," he admitted.

Both men were silent for a bit, grieving.

Until Gregoriat noticed Plumduff rubbing at his eye again. "Why do you keep grinding your eye?" he asked with all the directness of his youth.

"Was I?" Plumduff frowned. "Acch, there must be something in it."

"Well, don't rub at it like that, you'll just make it worse," Gregoriat scolded. "Here, turn so what's left of the light is on it—" He tugged at the man kneeling across the sticks, and Plumduff obediently rotated his large self.

"Now—" Gregoriat squinted, and his own tongue crept out from between his teeth. "Let's see—" He rolled down the lower lid of a huge but definitely human eye. "I don't see—yes I do! Wait a minute—" He tugged the tail of his not-too-clean shirt out and began gently probing.

"Hold still now—I think—yes—" He leaned back triumphantly, still holding the tail of his shirt.

"No, you don't, it still hurts. But thanks for trying."

"I did get it." He looked again, carefully. "I don't see anything else. Maybe it just scratched the lid a little and that's what hurts now. Do you have some water to clean it out with."

"Pond's just a few steps." Plumduff rose, and Gregoriat, still kneeling, realized once again just how very, very large the giant was. "I'll be right back—or would you like a drink, too?" He reached out his large, grimy hand.

Gregoriat stared at the hand for a second, as large as the rest of the giant, and took in its unwavering offer of help, as well as its size. "Yes, I think I would—" He put his own hand in the large one—gingerly—and allowed himself to be drawn upward.

Big as he was, Plumduff wasn't clumsy. Gregoriat found himself neatly on his feet, and his hand wasn't even bruised.

"All the comforts." Plumduff laughed a few minutes later, drying his face on the tail of his own shirt. (Which had begun life as a bright red plaid blanket, on another world.)

"Fish." Gregoriat watched as a large shadow glided near the

surface and snapped up a fat dragonfly that had been trying for
its own meal, and instead became one. "Water, and—" He
couldn't help grinning. "Frogs?"

Plumduff grinned amiably back. "Fat ones."

"You're not fat," Gregoriat hastened to assure him.

Plumduff grinned wider. "Doubt I'd make as good eating as
a frog." His face wrinkled ferociously. "But I'm sure hungry.
How 'bout you?"

Gregoriat stiffened. Everybody knew about giants— "Bad
time of day to catch frogs," he mumbled.

"Haven't been fishing either." Plumduff sighed. "Have to be
'taties again."

"'Taties?" Gregoriat wasn't sure what a 'taties was; he just
hoped it wasn't any part of a Gregoriat!

"Um. Got plenty. Last year's, in my root cellar. Take a while
to bake, though. Want to roast some pine nuts?"

Gregoriat was hungry. "Sounds good."

"To me, too. Cabin's there—" He pointed, though the small
thatched-roof log building was pretty hard to miss. "Bank up
the fire, I'll get the 'taties out of the cellar, get 'em started, then
go out and gather some pine nuts while it's light enough to
see—"

Gregoriat had been well brought up. "I'll help. Two gather
faster'n one."

"Sure thing." Plumduff was already heading down some
wood-planked steps. "Be right back with the 'taties."

Gregoriat leaned back against a rough wall in Plumduff's single room, comfortably overstuffed. The 'taties turned out to be
lumpy, brown-skinned root vegetables that tasted mouth-watering eaten with chopped wild shallots and something Plumduff
called tomatoes. The tomatoes had also gone into a wild greens
salad, whose crispness had topped off the meal admirably.
Along with some wild-honey mead, as smooth as anything the
village could produce.

Gregoriat belched contentedly. That last round of mead had
really been too much. But it had been so good. Like the 'taties.

He said so.

"Taste better with a little melted cheese," Plumduff said with a sly glint in his eye the tired youngster missed entirely. "Or butter. Now there's a feast for the gods themselves, 'taties slathered with butter and cheese, chopped onion, and maybe a little crumbled bacon—'course, can't keep a cow, m'self. But when I was younger 'n' smaller, 'n' folk didn't fear me so much, mother used to trade 'taties for cheese and butter— Never told 'em 'bout the 'tatie eyes, though—"

"'Tatie eyes," Gregoriat said on a contented yawn.

"Ummm." Plumduff had gotten out a carved pipe and filled it with dried leaves. "'Tatie's a root vegetable," he informed, carefully tamping. "Don't grow from seed, grows from pieces of the root—that is, the 'tatie itself. Eye's the part"—he chose a long slender twig, and thrust it into the glowing coals—"part of the 'tatie you need to plant to have the crop next year—" He drew in, and tossed the twig onto the coals.

"Eyes are like nuts," Gregoriat said on another yawn.

"Ah-um." Plumduff drew in contentedly. "Take a whole 'tatie, cut it in pieces, each piece grows a new plant next harvest. Lots of 'taties on each plant."

"Good crop." Gregoriat was almost asleep. But he was curious, too. There were times when the village went hungry.

"Real good crop." Plumduff was watching the half-sleeping young man through a plume of blue smoke.

"How you tell"—Gregoriat slumped a little more, his eyelids half closed—"where the eye is."

"Oh, you can see them." Plumduff's deep voice was infinitely soothing. "And if you're not sure, you just leave your 'taties in a warm humid room for a bit, 'stead of a root cellar. The eyes sprout, can't miss them then."

"Ummmm." Gregoriat snuggled down farther, his eyes closing all the way.

Plumduff gazed at him sadly. The problem was only postponed. Liking or not, come morning, the man would still feel impelled to challenge him. And he was getting older. Once he had been pretty sure of his abilities, could disable an opponent without doing too much permanent damage. But size or not, skill or not, he was getting older and his opponents younger.

Sooner or later it would be kill or be killed.

But not young Gregoriat.
Please, not young Gregoriat.

Gregoriat woke up slowly, started to stretch—
And finished waking up *very* fast.

Because he couldn't stretch. He was tied, hand and foot. He pulled, but the vines were strong ones.

He was tied! Helpless! In the giant's lair!

"Let me loose!" he yelled furiously, knowing it was futile. "You—you traitorous giant, you—you—vile betrayer, you—let me LOOSE!"

Nobody answered. Nobody came.

"Let me *LOOSE*!"

By the time Plumduff opened the hide door, some ten or so minutes later, Gregoriat was so hoarse, he was almost unintelligible, and his curses had degenerated to a monotonous sameness.

Plumduff waited until his captive had to stop to draw breath, and then he inserted calmly, "No. I'm sorry."

Loud enough that the hide door quivered: *"LET ME LOOSE!"*

"No." Plumduff walked over and squatted by the bound and furious Gregoriat. "I can't, son. But don't worry. You'll come out of this fine, just fine and dandy."

"Whatever that means, and whatever your word's worth," Gregoriat muttered hoarsely, his eyes shining with tears of pure fury.

Plumduff sighed. "Mam always used it, fine and dandy," he informed. "Means just what it sounds like, better than just plain good."

"Oh, sure." Gregoriat managed a creditable sneer. "Here I am, bound and helpless, and I'm going to be better than good? Oh, yes. Definitely. I do believe you."

Plumduff grinned. "What you mean is, go tell it to the Marines." Gregoriat just looked puzzled. "Never mind, lad. Those vines I tied you with stretch when they're wet. Once I'm gone, all you have to do is wriggle yourself out to the pond, it's not so far, and soak your wrists and ankles. Tied your wrists in front so you could do it without the risk of falling in and drowning. Take a while, I'll have a good head start, but you'll be free and safe enough."

"Only—" Gregoriat bit his lip.

"Only you were supposed to come here and challenge the mean, nasty old giant—" Even bound, Gregoriat snickered. "Don't you see, lad, you've succeeded. You challenged me, and I'll be gone. Never come back. You won, lad."

Gregoriat surprised Plumduff. "Why are you doing this for me?"

"Besides that I like you, lad?"

"That's not enough reason." Gregoriat sounded very grown up, all of a sudden.

"Well, son, want the truth?"

Gregoriat nodded.

"Doing it for me. You think it's fun, think it's pleasure, being the big, mean giant every would-be anything has to come and try his strength on? One challenger after another, and not taking no for an answer, neither? And sooner or later one of 'em wins and I'm dead, for what? For nothing? Because I'm tall and ugly? Because everybody who looks at me runs screaming, 'Giant'?

"What's in it for me, I ask you? Besides staying alive, which wouldn't be no problem at all, if people would just stop treating me like some sort of monster, and leave me to it?"

He glared down at the silent Gregoriat. "How would you like to live like that?"

Gregoriat's gaze dropped.

"You wouldn't, would you?"

It was unanswerable. But Gregoriat tried. "If you explained—"

Plumduff snorted. "You think people stop and wait and listen. Unh-unh. It's get out the weapons and attack, 'fore I can open my mouth. You're the first one I've talked to in years, and you was just waiting till morn, wasn't you?" Gregoriat dropped his gaze again. "Well, wasn't you?"

Sullenly. "Yes."

"Even though I think you liked me, a little. 'Cause, young'n, I liked you."

"I have to." Gregoriat tried not to make it a whine; he didn't succeed.

"See." Plumduff spread his hands. "Case closed."

"But it isn't fair," Gregoriat burst out.

"Young'n"—Plumduff's deep voice was as close to a growl as it could get—"you're alive and you could be dead."

"I meant you."

Plumduff's jaw dropped.

"You. It's not fair. Living alone, being driven along, never having a chance for—for—" He swallowed.

"Well," Plumduff snorted, "how you gonna change it?"

Very small voice: "I can't."

Plumduff shrugged. "Neither can I. Way it is, way it gotta be." He stood up and groaned, and stretched to work the kinks out. "Ain't as young as I used to be, neither. Which is why—" He gestured to the vines, binding Gregoriat's wrists and feet. "This way, we both live. Your way, one of us gets hurt bad, maybe killed. So we do it my way. Used to be, big as I am, could take on most anybody, rough 'em up a bit, dump 'em somewhere, they'd be sore as Hades, but they'd live, be fine eventually. But I'm getting old and stiff, someday I can't be sure of winning, maybe I have to hurt someone real bad to get free. Don't want to do that. You asked what I get out of it. Easy answer. I get out with my conscience clear, didn't hurt no one bad when I could avoid it, didn't risk having someone's crippling or worse on my conscience."

Gregoriat didn't say anything, but his eyes, blue in the morning light, were clear and bleak.

"You thinking, I'm worried about losing. Yeah, that too, but not for a while, not a good long while. Less someone like you sneaks up from behind and bashes my skull in." He grinned. "Not as easy to do as you'd think." He hesitated, spread out his hands. "Son, I just don't want to have to hurt you. Don't you see?"

Gregoriat refused to meet his gaze.

"Damn all, boy, you won. You're safe. Once you get out of here, tell any tale you please. I won't be around to contradict it."

"It's not fair," Gregoriat muttered.

"You the winner," Plumduff said heavily. "Why you keep complaining."

"Because—" The blue eyes glistened with unshed tears, but their gaze was as straight as a sword. "It isn't fair, not to either of us."

"Don't worry about it." He cuffed the boy on the shoulder. "You the winner, all that counts." He turned toward the door.

"But it isn't." Gregoriat's soft young voice froze him as he was reaching for his pack. "It doesn't. I haven't won anything that counts, it's just one big fraud."

Plumduff slung on his backpack, threw over his shoulder: "Nobody'll know."

"I'll know," Gregoriat retorted.

Plumduff whirled to face him again, the light from outside turning him into a huge black silhouette of menace. "Well, what do you want, boy? A fight? The chance to be hurt or maybe killed?" Voice dropping, with, for the first time, an under-note of menace: "You think you can take me."

"Oh, no!" It was said with such a note of wistful sincerity that Plumduff snorted, and the menace was suddenly gone, though he was no smaller, and his voice still a deep bear growl. "Then what do you want?" he asked on a sigh.

"I—I want—" Gregoriat's bound hands stretched out in a pleading gesture. "I don't know—I *need*—"

Plumduff let out his breath on a long sigh. Then: "How old are you?"

"Twenty."

"Any man in your village you can't lick?"

Gregoriat shook his head.

"No other challenges but me?"

Another head shake. Then: "There's a war, but it's far, far away. We hope it never comes here, but—"

"There's always a war somewhere, humans being humans, and sooner or later they all come 'here.' And you want to be sure that when it does, you'll be able to handle it." He shook his shaggy head. "Son, never works that way. Never can tell how you'll do in an emergency till it comes." Softer: "There must be some other way for you to prove yourself to yourself."

Gregoriat only shook his bowed head.

With finality: "Then I'm sorry, son. Ain't gonna be me."

Gregoriat knew when he had come smack up against an uncrossable crevasse. He swallowed. "Good luck, then, Plumduff. Good luck."

A grin that made his giant frog face somehow immensely likable. "You, too, youngster. Worry 'bout each day and each problem as it comes, say I." He shrugged on his heavy pack. "Gonna be far, far from here by nightfall." He looked around his little cabin and sighed. "Snug."

"Gunnora watch over you, Plumduff," Gregoriat said softly.

"And you, lad," Plumduff replied. "I'm off."

He went out through the hide door.

He meant to use his long legs to put distance between him and Gregoriat, his village, and the homey little cabin.

He had forgotten one item.

Gregoriat's wasn't the only village around.

And even if he had had time to realize the wrongness of his little patch of woods, he would have put it down to Gregoriat's presence.

It wasn't.

The second would-be giant killer, hidden in the underbrush, had never planned to issue an honest, open challenge. The giant was a danger. The giant was a menace. The giant should be taken care of.

The hidden archer had no intention of taking any risks at all. He drew back his bow carefully—

What saved Plumduff, once again, was his size.

The archer expected a giant and aimed very high. Plumduff stepped out, humming, and the archer lowered his aim—but not enough. The bowstring cracked, the arrow sped—and buried itself, not in Plumduff's heart, but in his massive shoulder.

Inside, Gregoriat could not hear the twig *snap* of the bow launching, or even the butcher-shop cleaver-split-meat *splat* of the arrow hitting solid bone and meat. But Plumduff's howl of agony and rage would have penetrated solid stone, much less a flap of leather.

Gregoriat stopped feeling sorry for himself and rolled over to hooch himself frantically on knees and hands toward the doorway. He knew he would probably be too late—and what could he do in his helpless position—but he *tried*—

Outside, the archer had automatically put a second arrow on the string; then he made his second mistake: he looked up to find his target.

Plumduff, his rabbit-fur cape bouncing around him to make him look even bigger, his convulsed-with-pain-and-fury frog face topped by a helmet of shaggy hair, bounding across the small clearing toward his attacker, was a sight to freeze the coolest blooded of men.

The archer gasped, and rose slightly, revealing himself, as Armageddon rumbled toward him.

"YaaaHHHHHHHHH—" Plumduff roared, all but ignoring the blood blooming on his shoulder, and the arrow sticking halfway through it.

The archer hurriedly let fly again. This time he miscalculated the other way, and the arrow went through fur and cloth and skin and muscle and—midriff. Low midriff.

He didn't have time for a third arrow.

Plumduff slammed up to him, and one clenched fist, the size and hardness of a sledgehammer, landed square to the point of his blond-bearded chin.

The archer went up with the force of the blow, his head snapped back—and in the back of its arc hit the tree behind him with a crack almost as loud as Plumduff splitting a log.

He was unconscious even before his limp body slithered down to fall in a heap at Plumduff's feet.

"YOU—" Plumduff roared again, before realizing that he didn't have an opponent anymore.

He shook his head dazedly, looked down, saw his opponent, drew back his foot for an angry kick that would probably have stove in the unfortunate archer's rib cage—and hesitated—

Wavered—

Fell slowly, with a crash louder than Jack's beanstalk giant landing.

Luckily for the archer, he landed next to him, not on him.

Gregoriat, hearing the shout, the crash, redoubled his efforts.

But it was still an agony of time later that he could push himself out the hide and look around.

To see two still, unmoving figures, lying at the edge of the clearing.

The archer regained consciousness first.

With a little help.

Shaking his head reflexively, spraying the water that had just been tossed on it, he heard a voice ask grimly, "Do you know as much about getting arrows out as putting them in?"

"Wha wha wha—"

"I said"—Gregoriat's voice was grim—"*do* you know as much about getting arrows out as putting them in?"

The newcomer blinked.

He was still in the clearing, the giant was lying almost at his feet, his head *ached,* and—

Somebody had tied his hands and feet with his own bowstring. He growled, an angry lion's threat. Somebody was going to pay and pay *dear*—

Gregoriat asked for the third time, "Do you know anything about getting arrows out?"

The archer blinked and looked down. "The giant. I got him," he said with amazed triumph. "He's dead."

"Not if I can do anything about it, you worm," Gregoriat snapped. "Are you gonna help or not?"

"Help a giant? You crazy!"

"Then I'll do it myself." He had only the faintest idea of what one did. But he had memories of the midwife boiling water, so he had built the fire up inside and been looking for a container to boil water in. Plumduff had no pots, but he himself had brought a small metal shield, with enough curvature to hold some water. It was on the fire now, water in it bubbling.

"You crazy," the archer repeated.

Gregoriat looked at him. Saw a strange face. "You're not from my village," he stated the obvious.

"You're not from mine," the archer shot back.

"What did Plumduff ever do to you, huh?" Gregoriat began tugging at the bright red plaid shirt, to try to see how bad the damage was.

"Plum-what?"

"Plumduff. Him. The giant."

"Plum—" The archer thought the name as funny as Gregoriat had when he first heard it.

"What did he ever do to you?" Gregoriat had the shirt out of the waistband and began tugging it from around the lower shaft sticking out.

"What—he's a giant." As though that explained everything.

"He is not!" Gregoriat exclaimed fiercely. He was using the knife he had taken from the belt-sheath of the other man, cutting through the heavy, now stained red, plaid blanketing material, to expose the two shafts sticking out from the huge mound of black-pelted muscle that was Plumduff.

"Shorter than either of us, is he," the archer snickered.

Gregoriat glared, than turned back to his task. "He's not *that kind* of giant," he bit out.

"He's worse." The other man started pulling on his bonds, gasping in pain as the bowstring cut in.

"He's *nice*." Gregoriat chewed on his lip—hard. Both arrows were buried past the heads.

"You're crazy." A sneer. "Goldmantler. Only a crazy Golder would try to help a giant."

Gregoriat was looking from the knife to the two arrows standing up from Plumduff's hairy hide. There was only one way to get them out, and he knew it. "Only a cowardly Redmantler would ambush without warning," he sneered back. He stood up. Vague memories. The knife would need to be cleaned. In the boiling water, he guessed, and hoped he was guessing right.

"Nyaaaaa." The archer couldn't believe somebody would actually help a fearsome giant. This odd fellow was, which meant— Bet you're a giant too, you just ain't grown up yet. Nyaaaa— Bet you're—"

Gregoriat went into the cabin, put the knife in the boiling water, and, thinking about it, came back out and walked over to the archer, who was getting unimaginative in his cursing.

But he started anew when he realized what Gregoriat was doing. "That's my shirt!"

"I need bandages. You wounded him, don't see why I should shiver," Gregoriat said, finishing cutting the homespun shirt off the archer's back.

"You—" He was already shivering.

Gregoriat began cutting the shirt into strips.

Then he went back in and dropped some of the strips into the boiling water. Clean the wound with them, yeah.

The archer was still cursing, despite that his teeth were chattering.

"Shut your mouth," Gregoriat said, "and I might pull you into the sunlight. Be warmer there."

The archer thought it over, shut his mouth.

Sighing, Gregoriat dragged him down below Plumduff's huge body and into the bright sunshine.

The archer hunkered himself into a sitting position. "You really gonna try to do something?"

Gregoriat gave a tentative tug on the arrow in Plumduff's midriff. It didn't move.

He tried the one in his shoulder. It moved—a little. It was the simpler problem, buried in a massive muscle. He wriggled it again. Not the bone, he was pretty sure. Maybe— He pursed his lips. Maybe it would be easier to push it through, break off the fletching, and just draw it out.

The other one—

He chewed his lip hard.

"Ain't nothing you can do," the archer informed. "He a deader. Just going to take a while."

Gregoriat didn't bother to answer. He was feeling under the shoulder. Yes, he could almost feel the sharpness of the point. There. If he just—

He used the knife to clumsily hack off the fletching, raised the massive shoulder as high as he could with one hand, jammed down with the other.

Triumph!

The bloody point protruded. Just a finger-span.

He shoved again.

A little more point, plus oozing blood, dark and angry-looking.

He rolled Plumduff onto his side, knelt, legs on either side, supporting the hugeness with his own thighs, braced the knife under the back of the barb—and *pulled*.

The shaft emerged slowly, reluctantly, with a sucking sound. Then abruptly, he almost fell when the last length of it popped out.

"That's one," Gregoriat sighed, looking at the two bleeding holes.

"Can't do that with the other one," the archer observed.

"Shaddup, or I'll drag you into the pond," Gregoriat said in a calm voice that was somehow more threatening than a shout.

Somehow he managed to clean the wounds, with cloths soaked in the boiling water, and wrung-out-as-dry-as-he-could ones to bind it. The blood seemed to be stopping but—

The arrow in Plumduff's midsection seemed to be mocking him. He swiped at his sweating forehead, adding, though he didn't know it, blood and grime to the sweat.

How was he to get the bloody thing out?

He knew.

He just didn't want to do it.

The archer knew too. "Cut it out, only way," he offered.

Gregoriat shuddered. He went and cleaned the knife again.

"Vertical." The archer had gotten intrigued by the problem. "Shaft went in vertical. Cut along it, until you can pull it back out."

"I know." Almost a moan: "What if he dies?"

The archer didn't say what he thought was obvious. No matter what Gregoriat did, the giant was going to die.

Gregoriat wriggled the shaft again, and, before he could lose his courage altogether, cut in as hard as he could, vertically, along the shaft.

Plumduff's huge body convulsed, and he emitted a gigantic roar of sheer pain.

Gregoriat threw himself atop the massive, heaving form. "Oh, Plumduff, I'm sorry, please be still, you're hurting yourself—"

Plumduff had lost a lot of blood. His own weakness made him subside. He blinked unfocused eyes. "Wha—wha happ'n?"

"You got shot." A sneer: "A cowardly Redmantler. In the trees."

"Oh." Plumduff blinked, but he couldn't seem to really see anything.

"There's an arrow in you, Plumduff." His words almost trampled one another in his hurry. "I'm sorry. But it's gotta come out."

"Oh. Ye'." A hesitation. "Who—"

"Me. Gregoriat." A wail: "If there's a better way, tell me, Plumduff!"

Plumduff blinked again. He was lying out in his own clearing, with something—it was his pack—propping his head up. He could see down.

Yes. An arrow. Sticking out of himself. "Gre—Gregoriat?"

A child on the edge of a precipice: "It *won't* come *out*!"

Plumduff reached up, patted the shaking shoulders he could only see fuzzily. "'S OK, lad. Not your fault."

Muffled sobbing, only intelligible phrase: "—hurt you!"

Plumduff was weak and groggy, but one fact was clear: The arrow would have to come out, and he couldn't do it himself. Which left—

"You doin' fine 'n' dand', Gre"—a breath—"gor'at. Just gotta fin'sh job."

"I—I can't!"

Softly: "What you sayin' 'fore, 'bout provin' you'se' to"—another gasp—"you'se'f?"

Gregoriat straightened up. "It's going to hurt."

"Gotta be"—gasp—"done. Do it. Now." There were beads of sweat on his forehead, matting down the shaggy brindled hair. Lines of pain around the frog mouth. Knowledge in the brown eyes.

Gregoriat nodded. He tugged on the arrow. Plumduff stiffened, gasped, but swallowed his howl of agony.

"I'm gonna have to cut more," Gregoriat apologized.

"Yeah. Do what you must." A weary ghost of his normal broad grin. "Ain't blamin' you."

Gregoriat sent a look to the archer. *He* knew who to blame!

Plumduff knew he had only moments of consciousness left. "Gre—" he rumbled.

"Yes—" He leaned down.

"In pack. Herbs. Stop wounds—festerin'. Get 'em . . ." His voice trailed off.

"All right." Gregoriat crawled over, reached into the leather pack, began pulling out its contents, trying to leave enough to still support the massive head.

"Know—herbs?" The words were slurred, almost unintelligible. Gregoriat saw that the heavy lids were almost down.

"No. Tell me quick."

"Look for the yarrow, for healin'; seal, help the bleeding. Boil water, dump in whole packet, soak clean cloths . . ." His voice trailed off.

"Which ones are they?" Gregoriat asked desperately. There

were dozens of the small packets, little leather pouches full of crisp dried herbs—

"Red . . . sewn wi' red . . . ones cross . . . three . . ." Again the voice was slurred.

"Liquor," contributed the archer suddenly.

"What?" Gregoriat has almost forgotten him.

"Liquor. Help him. Lessen the pain. Lessen the—whatever it is, kills a man when you cut at him."

Gregoriat shuddered.

"Do it now," the archer said. He didn't have to add, *Or else.*

"Gonna get you some honey mead," Gregoriat told the grim gray-under-brown shut-eyed face. "Make it easier—" But he didn't think Plumduff was conscious to hear.

But Plumduff surprised him. "Gre—" It was so weak, he leaned down to hear. "Yours—what I left. All." A shuddering breath. "'Taties in the cellar—'member—eyes—"

"They're not going to be any left," Gregoriat asserted fiercely, almost leaping to his feet. "'Cause you're going to be eating them, while you get better!" He ran into the cabin.

But when he tried to get Plumduff to drink the last skin of honey mead, it only dribbled out of his mouth to soak his scraggly dark beard.

"Why bother," the archer asked, a shrug in his voice.

"I'm gonna," Gregoriat asserted fiercely. "And—" A challenge to every god living and dead: "He's gonna live!"

The archer looked around. A clearing, wind gently rustling through leaves, himself, Gregoriat—and the wounded giant, lying limp, eyes shut, each breath making the great chest shudder like an oldster dying of lung sickness.

The archer settled himself as comfortably as he could, given that his wrists and ankles were bound. All he had to worry about was that the crazy Golder—he didn't think he was a giant, was full grown, and no taller than any normal man—wouldn't kill him in a rage when the giant died, if not under his inexpert knife, then the aftereffects of the wound and the removal of the arrow.

Gregoriat settled Plumduff as best he could, picked up the knife—

Again Plumduff's howl split the clearing, and tiny rustles in

the underbrush said that it scared any small creatures whose
curiosity or luck had drawn them to the vicinity.

Gregoriat was as pale as his patient.

The next howl was the loudest of all.

There was no howl after that.

The archer gave his parole almost as soon as Gregoriat had
finished his crude operation and sewn up the gaping wound
with needles and sinew thread found in the invaluable pack.

After all, it was all over with but the claiming of glory, and
he was pretty sure the other wouldn't take any of his credit.

He'd stick around to the end, but afterward—

Anyway, he was hungry, even if the crazy Golder wasn't.

Gregoriat accepted, on condition that the archer—his name
was Andor, he informed—help with the chores and Plumduff.

Andor agreed. His stomach was rumbling. And his wrists and
ankles had gone beyond pain to numbness.

They got Plumduff into his cabin and on the pile of furs he
used as a bed, by making a primitive sled out of the hide door
and two long branches from the wood pile. He was too heavy
for them to carry, even after Andor's feet and hands woke up.

But once they had him settled under shelter, there was nothing to do but wait.

Andor went fishing, using what was left of his bowstring and
a crooked twig, and Gregoriat fussed around the cabin, making
medicine in his shield, and feeling Plumduff's forehead for
fever every minute or two.

A day passed, two, and Plumduff didn't die—but he didn't
recover consciousness, either.

But his size and vitality conquered wound and clumsy nurs-
ing. On the third day he opened puzzled eyes, and it was downhill from there.

Andor slowly cleaned his catch of fish, listening to Plumduff
and Gregoriat arguing over the game called checkers that
Plumduff had taught his young friend.

It was the same argument they had been having ever since
Plumduff had regained enough strength to talk in more than
short, gasped phrases.

"But I'll tell my village, and Andor'll tell his, and you'll be safe, truly, Plumduff—" Gregoriat had said some variation of this a hundred times.

Plumduff sighed. He had answered it a hundred times. "More like they'll just think I've ensorceled you somehow. You think it's better for three to run than one?"

Andor, who agreed, sighed as he neatly gutted a fish so small he had debated tossing it back to grow. But Plumduff's bulk needed a lot of food, and the local animals had gotten wary of his traps, and the root cellar was almost empty.

Andor sighed again. He had learned to appreciate Plumduff, who was a much more patient patient than his own father had been, that time he had fallen off Widow Emmiet's roof and broken his leg. Andor grinned in memory, he knew how the Widow had intended to "pay" for the fixing of her roof. Probably it was the waiting as well as the pain that had made his father so irritable.

But Plumduff, who must have been in far more pain, had an immense store of patience, and a sweet disposition that surprised Andor, who thought that hermits must invariably be of sour mien, to say nothing of Plumduff's being a fearsome giant.

"King me," said the dreaded giant smugly, and Gregoriat sighed.

"You'll get better, just takes practice," Plumduff encouraged.

"Will I get any, without you," Gregoriat asked.

Plumduff looked down at his matted chest, still swathed in bandages after ten days. He was propped up on his bed of furs, because he still hadn't the strength to sit up long on his own. "Reckon so for a bit, lad."

Gregoriat ground his teeth.

Andor, who now understood why Gregoriat liked the giant, shook his head. People were people.

"It's not fair," Gregoriat muttered for the *n*th time.

"No," said Plumduff gently, "it's not. But that's the way it *be,* lad, and I've accepted, and you must too."

Gregoriat's fists were clenched, and he was staring at the board carved into crude squares without seeing it. "There must be a way," he gritted out. "I'll find one. There must be."

Plumduff sighed, caught Andor's gaze, and shook his shaggy head wryly.

Andor found himself wishing there was a way, too. Giant or not, Plumduff was fun to be around, for his stories if nothing else.

Trouble was, *everybody* knew about giants.

Plumduff was well enough to sit quietly on the bank of the pond with a fishing line when Gregoriat flung himself down beside him, his sullen expression easier to see through than the clear waters of the pond.

"I like wandering, you know," Plumduff said gently. "I wouldn't stay in one place all the time if'n I had the choice." His gaze flicked over to the cabin, a ribbon of smoke pluming out the hole in the roof. "But 'twas nice," he said, unconsciously wistful, "to have a snug home to come back to."

"Friends are nice, too." Gregoriat had discovered that even Redders could be pleasant to have around.

"Aye." Plumduff drew in on his pipe. "Reckon so."

"It's not fair!"

Plumduff answered obliquely. "You done a good job on me. I'll be ready to move on, soon."

Gregoriat sighed.

"You lads gonna try to stop me."

"You think two of us could?"

"Well—" He grinned. "Mighty glad you cut Andor's bowstring, that first day."

"I want you to have a snug home to come back to. I want you to have friends."

Plumduff cuffed him lightly on the shoulder. "Friends ain't any less friends, for distance atween 'em."

"But I want—it's not fair."

"Mam used to say, If wishes were horses, beggars would ride."

"There's gotta—"

"Any luck." Andor, a single unwary squirrel at his belt, flopped down next to them.

"More 'taties than anything else in the stew tonight," Gregoriat informed.

Andor shrugged. "I like 'taties."

"There's gotta be a way," Gregoriat repeated. A sigh. "Have you ever seen or heard of a giant that was—was accepted," he asked, more to himself than his companions.

"Yes." Andor had pulled off one of his boots and was poking around for the bit of whatever that had been digging in.

"Of course no—*what did you say*!"

"'Course he wasn't a real giant," Andor said casually, more interested in his boot's interior than his words. "Just looked like it."

"Looked like a giant but wasn't—like Plumduff!"

"No." He had shaken out the offending bit of bark and was putting the boot back on. "Not like Plumduff. He was just a man. But he looked like a giant. At a fair. You know. He was one of the entertainers."

"At a fair," Gregoriat repeated slowly. "A fair."

"Mam took me to a fair, when I was a little tad," Plumduff said, dreamily remembering. "Even traveled with one, for a while. She told fortunes." He sighed. "Told 'em too accurate. We had to leave."

"Pity," said Gregoriat, wheels turning behind his blue eyes.

"Yeah. Friends, and travelin', and snug for the winter, usually. I liked the fair."

"People expect to see giants and demons and magic beings at a fair. But—"

"Not real ones," Andor pointed out. "And nothing you say will make Plumduff any shorter. He is a giant."

"I've only been to a fair once. But I remember it. Remember all about it," Gregoriat's words tumbled out. "Listen. I saw a man I thought was a giant, too. Only he was just a man on stilts. I remember how tall I thought he looked, I knew he was on stilts, but he still looked so tall—"

"So." Andor shrugged. "When he got down, he wasn't a giant, was he."

"No, but he looked truly tall on the stilts. Even when I could see the stilts. Now, suppose—suppose Plumduff were up on stilts. People would see him, and think, Oh, he looks like a giant, but that's just because he's on stilts—"

Plumduff shook his head. "I've never been on stilts in my

life. And if I learned, do you think I could be on them all the day and night, too."

Gregoriat was literally bouncing on the pond bank. "That's it, that's it. Suppose they thought he was on stilts, but he wasn't."

Andor snickered.

"Jesters!" Gregoriat went on. "They do all sorts of things to make themselves look odd. Pad their clothes, stand on stilts, wear funny costumes, paint their faces—"

"A jester—"

"And you could make a great big club out of cloth, and go around with it on your shoulder, saying, Ho ho ho, I'm a giant, and whack people with it—"

Andor was leaning back on the bank and laughing, but Plumduff was watching Gregoriat with a hopeful expression.

"And wear funny clothes, and hike your belt high so you look like you're on stilts and paint your nose red and make big floppy ears out of cloth and tell your tales and travel wherever you pleased and come back here in the winter—"

"Here?" It was a hopeful question.

"Sure. Andor and I will tell our folk that you aren't a real giant at all—"

Andor sat up. "I don't tell lies."

"*Is* he a *real* giant?" Slyly: "Everybody knows what real giants are like?"

"No." Andor didn't have to think about it. "He's not a real giant. He—he's only big."

"But you are a jester. And you got hurt, so we stuck around to help until you got better—"

"But I'm not a jester."

Even more slyly: "A jester with friends in the village could trade for butter and cheese to put on his 'taties." Suddenly solemn: "Are 'taties as good a crop as you said."

"Better. Maybe too good. My mam warned me about never depending on them. They are liable to bugs, and wilt. And if the crop goes, it all goes, lucky to salvage enough for seed. Happen now and again. But mostly—good crop. Easy." He sighed. "But I'm not a jester."

Andor spoke thoughtfully. "You tell mighty good tales,

Plumduff. Tales I've never heard. Plenty of jesters pay their way with tales."

"You could travel and make friends, and have friends to come back to, too," Gregoriat added.

"Trade 'taties, too," Andor added. "Good crop. I like 'taties."

"Friends . . ." Plumduff murmured.

Thus began the saga of Plumduff Potato-Eye, the traveling tale-teller, he of the enormous height and padded club, the flapping breeches and bright red nose—and the marvelous tales and potatoes he traded, so that potatoes became a new crop, a new staple—

In later years, after he had made his rounds many times, it became an open secret that Plumduff really was quite tall, but of course, all those in his enthralled audiences, from the smallest sweet-sucking child to the oldest grand dame, knew that he was not a giant.

Everybody knew about giants.

And Plumduff.

Afterword

I've always been fascinated by the Wereriders of Witch World. One of my most favorite stories—like Will Rogers, I never met a Witch World story that didn't become a favorite instantly—is "The Jargoon Pard." So when I set out to write a Witch World story myself, I thought of Arvon, the forest where Kethan learned what he truly was. I even planned to have Herrel, Gillan, Aylinn, and Kethan in one scene.

I reread several Witch World novels. I worked the plot all out in my head, a despairing young man treated as Were, hurt and twisted.

I sat down to write that story. I intended to write that story. I was going to write that story.

But as my fingers poised, I had a sudden vision of a tall, very tall, ugly man—a giant. What do people think of giants in a world of magic? And I was hooked, as helpless as any fish on Plumduff's line.

"Plumduff Potato-Eye" wrote itself in one glorious splurge of creativity. I loved him immediately. Long may he tell his tales!

So, for those readers who are completists, Plumduff's tale unfolds in an Arvon forest like the one surrounding the star tower, but far away in a no-man's-land between clan territories. The sort of off-the-beaten-trail, nobody-wants-it, half-forgotten place where so many Witch World adventures take place.

I like to think that sometime in his childhood, Kethan saw the happy clown Plumduff at a fair and heard his tales. Or perhaps the young, pre-Exile Herrel. Or any of the others whose stories I have enjoyed so much. I hope so. Because then I will have given something to Witch World, which has given so much to me.

—Jayge Carr

THE SCENT OF MAGIC

by

Juanita Coulson

Joa gulped as she peered over the rocky ledge. The Vupsall encampment lay far below. Tentholds, hounds, sleds, the people and their ownings were but tiny marks in the Escore valley. The sight dizzied the girl. Her clan was well sheltered from the early spring wind's teeth. Here, on the mountain's knees, there was no haven. The air was a knife of ice, slashing at Joa's dark skin, whipping her red-gold braids.

Not for the first time, she regretted undertaking this search. It surely was not the houndmaster's wish that she venture her very life to find the lost whelp. Were Desst beside her, Joa knew he would bid her turn back, before she was lost, too.

Strength grew strength, and in a season of much ill luck the death of even one small girl-child would diminish the tribe. It would especially grieve her sister Omithi. Their kindred and Omithi's husband had been among those who had perished this past winter. Many grave pits were dug. With misfortune upon misfortune, now ran rumors of mysterious slave raiders, roaming the game trails and preying on weakened Vupsall bands. The tale much affrighted the clan. They had used their ancient rituals to fend off such evil, but were afflicted in that. Omithi

58

was the most skillful at the women's charm-making dance. However, she was great with child and no longer able to move in the necessary patterns. Some of the people fretted and whispered that the tribe must be cursed. They wondered which of them had so angered the gods.

Naschellu, first wife of Joa's tenthold, would have cast the lots toward her fellow widow, Omithi, if she had dared, for the elder was strong unfriend to the younger, and to Omithi's sister. Omithi's pregnancy and position protected them, and Naschellu was forced to swallow her spiteful resentment of the second wife sharing her cup and tent. She often vented her frustrations on Joa. Indeed, that shrew would rejoice, if the girl died on the mountain.

Joa leaned into the buffeting wind and resolved not to give the first wife that satisfaction. As she turned to retrace her path, a keening cry made her look toward the peaks, where a vrang hovered. "Hai! Cloud ruler! Tell me, where is the lost one?"

Vupsalls had never tamed these feathered allies of the People of the Green Silence. Yet Joa felt confident in seeking the great bird's aid. Did not the smith-priests assure the clans that the vrangs were creatures of the Light and therefore to be trusted? Joa tilted her head back, like an animal on the track of its quarry, sniffing. She stretched out her thoughts to the sky lord.

She would not have revealed this skill in the encampment. It was a secret she hid from all save Omithi. Unfriends such as Naschellu might name it evil and call for the girl's casting out, should they learn of it.

This mind-scenting talent had come upon Joa scant moons ago. It bound her to those of earth, water, and air. Of late, as she approached her entry to women's rituals, the ability grew. This power was very disturbing, but it was too useful to be put aside willingly.

The vrang's senses were hers. For a heartbeat, Joa was suspended over nothingness as the bird soared out above the valley. A seemingly fathomless gorge opened beneath them. As the vrang circled back, Joa carefully separated her will from his, reminding herself that she stood on solid ground. The feathered one was a voice she felt rather than heard: *"You are not of the crags, Vupsall youngling. What do you here?"*

"Farseeing One, I have come upon a duty to serve my people," Joa replied in the same speech without words. It was truth and not truth. The lost whelp *was* the most promising of his litter. Expertly trained, he would make a fine hunter. But she would not have undertaken this search had not Desst requested it. When Kynor, the clan's hound trainer, had died this winter, his young kinsman had assumed his tasks. Vupsall custom bound him to be shield and spear to his brother's widows as well, particularly since Omithi was pregnant. To the first wife Naschellu, Desst offered nothing beyond the law. To Omithi, he was heart-touched, and his kindness extended to his beloved's younger sister. To repay him, Joa had eagerly given herself to find the stray pup.

Despite the cold and peril, this searching had been far better suited to her spirit than what she must do in camp. Joa had little desire for women's work. Her fingers were clumsy at weaving and hide scraping and the other expected occupations. And Vupsall girls were never permitted to accompany the boys when they tracked and killed small game for the cook pots. A final insult had come this daybreak, as Naschellu ordered Joa to gather wood. That was a chore for an infant, not one approaching moonblood beginnings!

Before Desst left camp with the hunters, he had spoken of the strayed houndling to the girl, and Joa had seized her opportunity. Did Desst suspect she possessed some skill beyond the normal in such things? Perhaps not. However, he had seen her sure touch with the pack and trusted her. If she could, she would find the houndling, for Desst, and for her whom Desst loved, Omithi.

Majestically, wheeling, the vrang advised, *"Look to the copse yonder, Vupsall child."*

An excited "yip" confirmed his sighting. Joa trotted across a patch of snow-raddled stones, heading toward the thicket. "To me, Clever Little One," she called, "you have played this chase overlong."

As she neared the tangle of trees and brush, the pup's mind-scent grew as strong as a well-braided cord. She determinedly traced it through the brambles. Joa's leather breeches turned aside the thorns. But her loosely belted coat billowed in the wind, baring her unbudded breasts to sharp limbs and the wind. She forced herself to go on to the very end of the copse, hard against the mountain's side. Her hands closed there on the pup's creamy mane. Laughing, she knelt beside him, and he greeted her as he would a little mate, his rough tongue laving her scratches.

The vrang and Joa touched the pup's curiosity as he turned to investigating once more what he had sought ere he was discovered. He thrust his pointed muzzle deeper into the brush, uttering happy noises. Her wonder aroused, Joa asked, "What is it, Clever Little One?" and followed him.

Suddenly she and the animal were falling.

Joa did not have time to cry out in fear, for they did not tumble far—no more than twice her length. The pair landed on soft earth. For several moments, they lay stunned, the breath jolted from them. Then the pup stirred and Joa pushed herself upright, staring about.

The copse had hidden a cave's entrance. She and the pup had plunged over its lip. Pale, dappled sunlight penetrated the leafless branches, casting rays into this rocky womb. The interior, the size of a Vupsall tent, was empty but for a dusting of snow and scattering of pebbles. Joa wrinkled her nose. A musty odor was proof of long disuse. Her footprints and the whelp's were the first the earthen floor had known for uncounted seasons. Seeing that, her apprehension eased, and she stopped clutching her knife.

Then the girl discovered a series of carven steps rising to the sunlit opening. Above that entrance, a blue stone had been set into the lintel. Runes adorned both narrow stairs and door cap.

Joa's wariness rekindled. Runes! These, she had been told, were things of sorcery. Had she blundered into the lair of a seeress? And if so, did ill magic, the Power of the Shadow, lie here?

The houndling had no fear. Tail up, his slitted amber eyes bright, his small ears aprick, he snuffled along the steps and around the chamber's edges. Plainly he was not on guard against an enemy—and Joa herself had witnessed how the

clan's pack reacted with terror whenever the people's travels
took them too near the ancient sources of dark wizardry.

There was no obvious touch of the Shadow. Yet Joa sensed a
presence. Puzzled, she walked slowly away from the steps, into
the cave's recesses. As her eyes adjusted to the dimness, she
detected an eerie blue-green glow emanating from the rear
wall. Was this light akin to the circles of stone sought out by
Vupsalls? Such menhirs were desired camps, protected from
evil and especially prized by tribes like Joa's that were not lucky
enough to have a wise woman's guidance. It was said that those
clans counseled by seeresses of the Old Race were ever safe
from danger, not at risk with each day's trek they took.

Luck! How little of that had Joa's people known of late!

Her father and uncles dead. Kynor dead. Hunters, women,
children, babes . . . so *many* dead. Game scarce. Journey food
turned foul. Clashes with rival clans, costing them in wounded
and stolen hounds from their already half-starved packs. Little
wonder ill-seekers such as Naschellu muttered of curses.

Ah! But that might change, for all of them, if Joa had discovered a place of Power.

Tentatively she stroked the wall. A peculiar warmth snaked
up her arm, healing her scratches instantly. She did not know
whether to react with delight or alarm. Surely this craft was a
good one. However, what created the magic and the blue glow?
Was it something a Vupsall child should not touch?

Kynor, the dead houndmaster, seemed to thunder in her
memory: "Do not ask so many questions, girl! The world *is*!
The way of it!"

Yet she *did* question. It was a wanting, as unbidden as the
mind-scenting, and as much a part of her. Now Joa questioned
if this heal craft could be taken to the camp. What a gift it
would be for Omithi, to ease her time of birthing.

Without warning, that presence she had felt earlier invaded
her. The houndling and the vrang felt the questing touch also,
without concern. Joa would have fled, but she was held
moveless by unseen cords.

Vivid images flowed from the wall into her thoughts, bearing
Joa into the past. She saw two sorceresses, guarding an ancient
palace and creating magic to forestall magic. One woman was

of the Old Race, her hair raven black, her skin snowy, her
robes long and full. The other was a Vupsall. Her dark flesh
and her elaborately coiled gem-pinned red hair were much like
that seen among the tribeswomen of Joa's clan. And like them,
she painted her breasts, though not with flower designs common among the nomads; her adornments were arcane symbols.
As Raven Hair watched, the Vupsall witch wove a charm
dance, as Joa's sister had often done. About the pair swarmed
their allies in sorcery—birds and beasts of breeds Joa had heard
of only in legends.

The girl was reassured to see that the palace was constructed
of blue stones. Then surely these wise women were of the
Light. For did not the clans' elders proclaim that Darkness
dared not enter such sanctuaries?

As scenes unfolded, Joa realized the blue stones were *not*
always proof against the Shadow. She witnessed segments of a
terrible war waged eons before her race had arrived in Escore.
In that remote time, the wizards' struggle had maimed and
blasted Escore. Indeed, the land was still much scarred as a
result.

Abruptly, Joa was thrust forward into another time that was
generations later, yet still long ere her own. Practitioners destruction wielded an awesome power, as Escore was maimed
and blasted by forces whose marks still lay ugly upon the land.
The sorceresses fought with runes, crystals, and bone wands,
abetted by their peculiar creatures. An ominous reverberation
rang through the palace. Joa started, knowing the sound for a
spirit gong. *How* had she known? And how could she be part of
these things that had happened generations before she had
been conceived? This was not possible! Yet . . . she was one
with the wise women, sharing their cup, and their fate.

Sacrifice had been necessary in that war. To gain space for
other witches and warlocks elsewhere, Raven Hair and the
Vupsall deliberately challenged the Dark, calling it down. And
it smote with a terrible vengeance, rending the very stones of
their palace to ashes.

As it struck, its victims vanished. They could not escape such
dreadful power whole. On magic's wings, they had transferred
their presences, and that of their beastly companions, to this

haven that they had prepared ere the holocaust. Here they were entombed while the eons passed. Neither living nor dead, they awaited the touch of one who would wake them to the world anew.

The tale had been told. Joa indeed had partaken of the wise women's cup, and feared greatly. She licked her lips and found no taste of bone breaker or blood seeker. Then the witches did not desire her death, or she would have sensed it. What *did* they want?

Raven Hair spoke in the flowing images and also within Joa's skull. Her words were foreign gibberish, that tongue of the Old Race. Seeing that she was not understood, she gave way to the Vupsall. The flame-haired witch's words were clear, though certain phrases seemed those of Vupsall ancestors long since dead. *"I am Aisli, girl, and this is Kotyan. We know from your thoughts that you are Joa, as we read your life and your people's. Ah! So you call your Gifting 'a mind-scent.' We will teach you far straighter terms for the sorcerous arts."*

Raven Hair, her accent heavy, adopted the other woman's tongue, saying, *"Do not fear us, Joa. We are in your debt, as you shall be in ours. You are already of our kind, you and the beasts whose spirits you can touch—or you would never have opened this sanctuary."*

"I but dream," Joa murmured, trying to make herself believe. *"I but dream."*

The Vupsall ignored her. *"All her clan's tales are in her thoughts,"* Aisli exclaimed. *"Thus we see what occurred after we two were rift from the battle, Kotyan. How Escore was hurt! But the Shadow was not victorious! Ah! What is this? My people have fallen back into barbarism. That is ill fortune to my house!"*

"They were victims," Raven Hair said. *"As were many, including you and I. Gaze upon the farseeing, sister, at what must be done. Vupsall will climb. Necessary. Lest the Dark overcome . . ."*

"The clans ever distrusted sorcery," Aisli muttered. *"But they took the weapon I offered them. They shall again, through this girl. The senseless feuding among the tribes must cease . . ."*

"Hsst!" Kotyan radiated intensity. *"The enemy!"*

The seeresses seemed to listen. Fascinated, Joa listened too, and caught some of their apprehension. About her there was a soft growling and clacking of beaks, an approving chorus from those alien creatures entombed in the stone. They also tracked prey. Evil, entering the valley. Joa smelled a stench she knew at once for Dark Powers and through that saw a man of the Old Race, followed by an ugly group of Vupsall hunters. No, *not* hunters. Slave takers! Their master, the berobed, sharp-faced warlock, wove spells, working some grim mischief aimed at Joa's encampment. At her feet, the houndling whined, then made a puppyish attempt to sound a warning bark and alert the people.

"They do not hear you, Little Clever One," she murmured. "No matter. It is magic, only dream-weaving . . ."

"Think you so, daughter?" Aisli demanded curtly. *"Your mind-scenting Gift is impressive. Yet you are a babe, unskilled in its use. You deny your destiny—which is to join us."*

"No!" To Joa's relief, she could move a trifle now, and she pressed cold fingers against her head, trying to drive out the visions and voices. "Leave me! I am no witch!"

"You shall be," Kotyan said. *"You will have no choice. You were born to it, as were we."*

"In time, you will yield," Aisli agreed. *"The enemy, fed with slaves, will have leisure to grow, and the Shadow will reign anew. Wish you that for the Vupsalls, for all races?"* Blue light danced on the wall, mesmerizing the girl. Aisli nodded, satisfied. *"She will come to it, with courage,"* she said fondly, as though she saw something of herself, long ago, in the youngling standing before her.

"Dreaming, only dreaming," Joa breathed. "None of it is so."

"She will follow the way we trod," Raven Hair said solemnly. *"We cannot outrun that which is written for us. Go now, girl, until your will concedes that you are sealed to the Power."*

The invisible cords dropped away, releasing Joa. She was free! Seizing the pup's collar, she dragged him toward the rune-carved steps. Ghostly, tingling laughter rushed through her veins as Joa fled. The houndling longed to stay with the beasts locked within the wall, but she picked him up, carrying him to the top of the stairs and forcing him out into the copse beyond.

This time, as she tore her way through the thicket, the thorns did not harm her. They seemed to turn aside, allowing her to win bloodlessly to the icy mountain trail. Joa, still carrying the whelp, skidded on rocks and ran downward, nearly falling in her panic.

For a while the vrang accompanied her. He flew a tree length above the girl, his puzzlement a thing she could reach out and touch. When she did not respond to his unspoken questions, his wonder became disinterest. As he returned to his crags, Joa hastily wished him her thanks for his help in finding the pup. But she did not pause in her reckless descent.

Slowly, the images and voices and talk of inescapable destiny faded from her mind. Joa knew she dared not tell anyone of this, not even Omithi, lest the clan deem her headsick and shun her. No. It had, after all, been as dreaming. She and the pup had wakened spirits, and spirits did not like to be disturbed. Joa made the ritual two-fingered gesture to ward off ill luck hurled by the dead. *That* would keep the sorceresses' ghosts at bay!

She did not slacken her pace overmuch until she had reached the tree line, not far from camp. By then, the sun was falling behind the mountains. Twilight was fast settling on the game path Joa had used to make her way into the mountain and back again. She felt safe, now, in setting the houndling on his feet, though she held tightly to his collar. For a bit he strained to get loose and run up the trail. Joa chided him and untied her belt, fastening the leash to the pup's little jeweled necklet. As they continued down the path, he gradually lost interest in what he had smelled in the cave.

New leaves clung to the branches overhead, shutting out what little of day remained, shadowing the animal run Joa was tracing. She had to depend on the pup's nose and his hunger for his dam's teat to lead them the rest of the road. On every side, they heard twitterings and peepings that marked the hiding places of spring-awakened birds and forest beasts. There was no sound of predator or enemy, however, and more and more Joa felt secure. Soon she would be home.

What would be her welcome there? Hard, curious eyes? Some in the clan thought Omithi's sister a strangeling, lazy girl.

As she reached the edge of the encampment, Joa was grateful that Desst kept his hounds aside; she would not need to walk the length of the tentholds, enduring scowls, in order to return the pup to the pack. She stole past the back of the horn worker's tent and the gem fashioner's and the smith's, now and then peeping beyond the woven hide structures to the camp's center. Hunting spears were stacked. Fresh game was dressed, hanging from low limbs. The younger women were dancing the charm-making ritual, slowly, gracefully, though none did so well as Joa's sister Omithi—or as the Vupsall witch in those visions. The men were gathering at the smith's tent to reminisce about the day's hunt. No doubt they would also discuss the morrow and when it was best to strike camp and move.

Desst was still tending to his animals when Joa crept into the glow of his fire. The hounds, recognizing her, set up no din, but greeted the girl and the errant pup with soft growls. Desst glanced sternly at Joa while she fumbled with the makeshift leash, untying her captive. The whelp lunged forward eagerly. He and his litter mates tumbled together in a fierce welcome of bared fangs and lolling tongues. These were the rituals of the pack, as firm as the women's charm-making dance and the men's gatherings under the smith's guidance.

Joa refastened the belt, cinching her much-patched tunic. A big hand tugged at her braids. Beneath Desst's scolding expression there was a glimmer of amusement. He shrugged off his hunter's cloak and pushed back his green-fringed hood, eyeing the girl narrowly. She knew that she must endure a scolding, but hoped it would not be too severe. "See? I found him," she said, pointing to the houndling.

"Girl, did I command you to become yourself a stray?" Desst tried to sound angry, with small success. Responsibilities had weighed hard upon him and sometimes made him look older than his twenty winters. Now, however, there was an easiness in his manner belying the sharp words. Joa realized with guilt that Desst had been sincerely worried for her. He hid that, saying, "Omithi was concerned. Ill favored of you to cause her pain. Why did you search so long?"

"I—I am sorry. I wanted to fetch back Little Clever One. I *did*. Are you not pleased?"

He tugged at her braids again, more gently, then thrust his thumbs into his wide, gem-set belt. "Happy I am to have the pup to my hand again, it is true. Yet he was not worth a full sun's search." Desst shook his head. "Naschellu will be rough with you, girl, and rightly. The first wife had to do everything this day. Omithi could give her no help. The midwife says the birth waters will come soon . . ."

"Has it begun?" Joa cried.

The houndmaster grinned. "No, Kynor's babe does not join the clan, girl, so far. But he binds Omithi to her bed. You are not to trouble her. Heed me! She should not be given hurt for your sake. You are all she has."

Painful memory held them both silent for a pace. They saw their kin—Joa's father and uncles and Desst's brother Kynor—crashing through the river ice to their deaths. "I am not all, no," Joa said softly. "Omithi is heart-touched by Kynor's near blood, him that will have her to wife . . ."

Desst laid a callused, scarred hand over her mouth. "Talk not of that. When custom decrees I may bring Omithi bride gift and wipe the paint from her breasts and claim her, I shall. Not sooner." Chastened, Joa nodded. The houndmaster sighed and asked, "Where did you find the pup?"

"On the mountain. There was a . . ." She stopped herself and finished lamely, "He—he had chased a vrang up to the crags."

"This is the season for *all* the clan's younglings to neglect duty," Desst grumbled. He shook a finger at the unrepentant whelp, then at Joa, telling her, "Go now. Comfort Omithi."

She moved away reluctantly. She was eager to see her sister, but their tenthold was dominated by the first wife, and Naschellu, unlike Desst, would not be happy with the girl's return. Staying to the shadows as much as possible, Joa walked through the cluster of woven-hide dwellings. Tethered hounds outside each tent sniffed at her, identified her as part of the clan, and lain back down once more. Small children played in the circles around each owning's fires, set, as was the pattern, before the tent flaps. Women joined in the charm-making dance or gossiped, as did the Vupsall men, in their way. Some of the girls, Joa's age mates, glanced at her, knowing her dread.

Those she called fellow smiled and spoke sympathy. Unfriends, wishing her ill, taunted her with promises of the punishment she should receive from her holding's first wife.

That wife, Naschellu, had shunned the usual gatherings tonight. The dour-faced widow poked viciously at her fire and glared at Joa. "So! Honored I am that you chose to come home! What would you, girl? Are you the daughter of some great leader, that I dance attendance on you?"

"I—I am sorry I did not gather the wood, but Desst . . ."

"You serve this tent, not Desst," Naschellu snapped.

Others were watching and listening. A few smirked, amused to see a disobedient child lessoned. Firelight shone on the women's naked, painted breasts, their jeweled collars, the gems in their elaborately coiled and pinned hair. Men looked toward Kynor's tent and shrugged, dismissing the scene there as mere female squabbling.

Naschellu got to her feet and rested her hands on her skinny hips. The chief wife's ever-bitter nature was a stink, one so strong Joa had no need of a secret art to detect it. A snake striking, Naschellu pinched the girl's neck fast in a painful grip. "Hear me! You obey *my* commands, not Desst's!"

Squirming vainly, Joa protested, "He is the hunter for this . . . ow! . . . kinfast. Desst put on Kynor's cloak, and he trains Kynor's hounds. And he barters them for the things we need. And he shares his hunt-kills with us, as Kynor did . . . ow!"

Naschellu shook her, like a hound a bone. "I *told* you to oil the traveling boxes, lest the leather crack. You did not! Nor did you sew garments or dig roots. You mended no light nets, collected no glow insects to inhabit the gauzes and bring day to the tent when darkness comes . . ."

The chief wife punctuated her words with cuffs. Onlookers did not interfere. Such rough discipline was common among the Vupsall clans. All in the tribes had suffered it, as younglings. Now Joa must pay her debt for ill-serving her tent.

But she did her best to dodge Naschellu's blows. That, too, was a common trick, and she hoped to waken on the morrow with no more than bruises from this chastisement.

"Tracking a lost whelp! Unfit task for women-children!" the first wife bellowed. And around her, oddly, the tribe's hounds were setting up a din. They had been near many a similar punishing, and rarely reacted so. Now their angry barking added to Joa's confusion. Naschellu pummeled her mercilessly, the slaps hardening, beginning to break the skin. And a new and terrifying glint came to her eyes.

Some neighbors called objections. This went far past the laws!

Naschellu did not hear them. Spittle flecked her thick lips, and her expression was wild. "Bewitcher! You and your sister and your mother before you! All of you cursed me, sealed my womb, made me barren! It was *your* doing!"

She struck again and again, until Joa reeled, her vision blurring. Even when Naschellu released her hold on the girl's neck—the better to use both hands in assaulting her victim—Joa could not flee; she was too dazed to take advantage of the opportunity. Brutal fists knocked her to and fro.

An unseen force was ruling Naschellu, maddening her. And two other invisible presences witnessed the clash through Joa. Dimly, amid pain, she felt Raven Hair, Aisli, and their companion creatures enter her mind. She knew they were angry for her sake.

They were not alone. Omithi, big-bellied, struggled from her fur-covered bed and lurched to the tent entrance. There she knelt on the threshold, flinging her arms protectively about her sister. "Leave by, Naschellu!" Omithi shouted. "You may not punish her to death. She is free born! Stop!"

By now, the uproar from the hounds was deafening. It seemed to worsen Naschellu's rage. Her heavy hands fell upon Omithi as well as Joa, making neighbors gasp in horror.

"Stay her, daughter," Aisli commanded. The silent voice rattled in Joa's skull. *"You have the power, schooled by us. It is the* enemy *who abuses you. Naschellu is but his tool."*

"Ai!" Kotyan agreed. *"She, the hounds, and even your death will be diversions for his purpose. Observe!"*

For a twinkling moment, Joa was outside her body, a spirit flying into the surrounding forest to a nearby glade. The veil of night parted for her, though not for those lurking in that hiding place. A net of glow insects might have hung over their heads, showing Joa the enemy warlock. Like Kotyan, he was of the

Old Race; but where she was of the Light, he was Shadow-sworn, suffused with evil. His stench assaulted the girl, turning her stomach. At the warlock's back stood two hands' count of Vupsall warriors, dull-eyed, cruel men, shorn of all honor to the patterns. They marched to the wizard's bidding, and en-slaved or killed as he ordered.

In an instant, Joa returned to herself. No time had seemed to pass while she viewed those dread lurkers. As before, the first wife pummeled her and Omithi. Naschellu was shrieking in-coherently. Tortured by the will of the hidden warlock, she was his captive, catching up a brand from the fire and raising it to smash over the cowering sisters.

At last the clan's women ran to restrain her. They had not moved to save an impertinent child. Now, however, Naschellu threatened a pregnant widow. A crime most foul! It must be prevented!

The rescuers could not reach her in time to stop the blow. *"Act, daughter! Strike!"* A dual mind-scent overwhelmed Joa, and she sensed this was her only course. Power washed away the pain Naschellu had dealt. Joa was strength, extending from her thoughts, though she was crouched and whimpering beside Omithi.

Bonds froze Naschellu. She was helpless, her fiery club held high, descending no farther.

Joa was one with Aisli and Kotyan. As she lifted her head and stared at Naschellu, the girl knelt amid an encampment of woven-hide tents—and she stood in a blue-stoned palace that was destroyed numberless seasons ago. Through her, that pal-ace's mistresses and their beastly allies conquered time and death. Joa realized, with both despair and exultation, that she had accepted the cup fate had poured for her. She, too, was a witch!

Tribeswomen swarmed about Naschellu, prying the brand from her fingers, enfolding her in their arms. She thrashed wildly, and they were forced to pull her off her feet, pinning her as they prayed to the gods to restore her sanity.

They did not know their gods had no part in Naschellu's af-fliction. That Shadow-sworn warlock was her tormentor, and the hounds'.

The hounds! Would their clamor never cease?

Not so long as it served the enemy.

Hunters, shaken out of their unconcern by these events, began to resort to boots and whips, attempting to quiet the crazed pack. To no avail.

"In a breath or two, the slave takers will attack," Kotyan murmured deep within Joa's being. *"Their master has not yet detected your Gifts, daughter. He would scorn you, for he believes himself unmatched in sorcery."*

Without sound, in the same mental touching the witches employed, the girl asked, *"What does he here? Why does he enslave the Vupsalls?"*

Aisli answered her. *"Our people are to be his army, and the Shadow's. The terrible conflict will resume. Escore again will be rift, uncounted tribes slain, to establish the Dark forces supreme. He crushes the wills of the Vupsalls his minions take in slavery, for our people have no wizardry to oppose him. With our blood, he will construct his foundations, then thrust murderously throughout the land, from the eastern sea to the Green Valley to all the rivers and hills and woodlands. When he is done, Escore is lost forever to the Shadow . . ."*

The hounds! Howling, snapping at those who fed them, in a witless fury despite the worst the hunters could do to punish them.

It was a tactic, Joa saw, sent by the enemy. Distracted thus, off guard, the hunters would have no spears to hand as the slave takers swept upon them.

Escore—and her people—forever lost!

Joa gently pushed away from Omithi and rose to her feet. Heal craft, a gift of Kotyan and Aisli, flowed along the girl's veins, soothing hurts, clearing her brain.

She stood at a spot where many trails divided. Which must she travel? They were roads of destiny. Some led to enslavement. Others to a kind of living death, where her mind-scenting skill would be smothered and serve no use, nor would she. And one led to sorcery. On that path there was power, the victory of saving her clan from destruction and Escore from the Shadow. But there was also loneliness and a painful separation from those she loved.

"Necessary, child," Kotyan told her, with tenderness. *"We knew what you shall know. A worker of magic is apart. Those who do not possess the arts do not understand, and they will always fear us. It is the way of it."*

Aisli added, *"Courage is required, girl. It is not easy. Choose. And quickly. Or Vupsall dies. Which path will you take?"*

"I am but a child," Joa murmured, half aloud. "I cannot . . ."

"He is one. You are three and many," and with the sorceresses spoke those alien hordes of creatures. Like the witches, the beasts owned Power, and offered it to this battle, and to future ones, upon the path Joa was invited to walk.

Naschellu was howling, a human hound, and driven, as they, to madness.

At that moment, the enemy again shifted his focus, creating yet another diversion to occupy the attention of his victims. Omithi clutched her swollen belly. Her eyes widened with fear. "The—the babe! Aaa! It—it is not yet time. . . !"

A midwife ran to help the young widow. The tribe muttered in surprise at this latest event. Were they indeed cursed, as had seemed all this winter?

Joa wondered. Had the warlock spread his evil spells far ahead, to pave his conquest? Was he responsible for the ill luck bedeviling her clan, and for the deaths of her kin and Omithi's husband? Anger was a heady odor, stimulating her and prodding her into decision.

Desst, his expression twisted with worry, hurried toward his brother's tent as the women carried Omithi inside. Joa shared his anxiety, but knew a far greater matter now demanded their power. She took hold of the houndmaster's arm. Startled by the strength in her touch, he halted and peered down at her.

"Open your mind-scent to him, and to us," the unseen sorceresses pleaded. *"He will be our weapon."*

Was Desst, then, to be the first necessary sacrifice on the path Joa was about to trod? No! She would strive to insure his life, and the lives of Omithi and the rest in the encampment.

Trusting her allies, Joa did as they bade. A peculiar look came into Desst's dark eyes. He was his own man, yet he bent to the will of a child and those who strengthened her.

"You must release the hounds," Joa instructed calmly.

She gave this much—that Desst was shown the enemy and something of what the warlock's presence meant. Rage twisted the houndmaster's face. "So that is what he thinks? Vupsall will not submit so tamely!"

Man and girl-child confronted each other for a heartbeat. And Desst stepped onto the path *he* must follow. But had he chosen in time to save the people?

He ran from tent to tent, slipping the tethers from straining hounds' collars. Fellow hunters gaped at him, fearing that he like Naschellu was mad. Was this to be the last curse to befall the clan? That they all lost their wits?

"Slave takers!" Desst roared, pointing to the forest. "The beasts smell them. Come. Take spear!"

And within the wood surrounding the lurkers' glade, the furred and feathered denizens of the valley set up a horrendous racket. The noisy assault was as a blow to the spellcasting enemy leader. It was something he had never expected. Frantically, he cast sorcerous nets, seeking his foe, and would crush that witch, should he find her.

Joa was taught and guided, moving in her first effort in such arts. Alone, she would have been as nothing, her untrained abilities a melting snowflake before the burning blast of an adept. But she was not alone. And in the distant time Kotyan and Aisli had lived, they had been among the Light's most skillful servants. They poured their Power into Joa, becoming part of her, showing her the way to manipulate Desst, the hounds, and the forest creatures. In that last, the witches' entombed animal allies had no peer; like called to like, across the ages, in this rough-made young army of the Light.

The clan's hunters were pelting into the trees, and Joa of Many Forces was able to press aside barricades of branches and shrubs to hasten their counterattack. She was a night wind, hammering the warlock and his slave takers mercilessly, as he had forced Naschellu to hammer Joa.

Little Clever One and his dam led the hunters and the pack. The cacophony was deafening. Those women who were not with Omithi in the birthing tent stared in terror in the direction of such noise. Children wept and babes clung desperately to their mothers' painted breasts.

Joa was not with them, save in body. She was with Desst, following the hounds, seeing beyond, to the creature-harassed enemies.

The wind was at her back, aiding her. Forest vrang and bat and ground hopper and tree serpent fell upon the warlock's men, clinging, biting, raking with talons.

It was thus when the men of the clan burst into the glade and Desst hurled his spear at the slave takers' master.

The sorcerer was incredulous. Joa read his thought: Did the barbarian seriously hope to harm one who commanded great magic? Negligently, the warlock wove a spell to shunt aside that spear lancing toward his heart.

And his spell was met with countering magic, wielded by women sacrificed in an earlier war between good and evil, and focused through a gifted Vupsall girl.

Again, it was a thing he had never expected. So arrogant was he that he had not called upon any farseeing to warn him of this. He deemed himself invincible.

Wrongly.

There was no space for him to retighten his glamour and build another spell.

Desst's spear penetrated the sorcerous veil and the enemy leader's breast. Coruscating energies filled the glade for a moment. It was a starburst of colors none of the clan had seen, save Joa; she had learned their hues in a cave, the living burial place of her invisible allies.

Bereft of the wizard's shield and guidance, the slave takers were trapped. Once, no doubt, they had been strong men, knowledgeable in use of point and blade. Now, they had been too-long puppets. Their courage, like their spirit, was vanished. Joa's people cut them down, aware that had they failed, these Vupsall foes would have done the same to any of the tribe who resisted them.

Joa felt Kotyan's shudder of revulsion. *"Patience, sister,"* Aisli comforted the woman of the Old Race. *"It is not your way, but at present it is the Vupsalls'. There will come an age, with Joa's labor, when Vupsall will no more need to survive through their spears. That path, however, is not yet beneath their feet. For tonight, it is good that they* are *barbarians, and friend to blade and blood."*

Kotyan sighed. *"Ai! You see it, too, do you not, daughter? Much is required to raise your clans to the civilization they used to own."*

Doubt assailed the girl. This small battle had been won. The battles ahead? Had she the strength to endure them?

She was tired as she had never been. Her wounds were almost mended, and the weakness did not come from that source. Sorcery had taxed her severely. Joa had not understood the demands her mind-scenting Gift would place upon her. As she leaned against the tent pole, listening to Omithi's birthing grunts inside the dwelling, Joa sniffed the air—and the unseen trails of magic.

The stench of the enemy warlock was gone. She smelled blood and the ugly and strong reek of murderous satisfaction, as was so for successful warriors. The hunters, flaunting booty, were returning to the camp. Desst, in the lead, waved the dead wizard's mantle above his head and shouted the triumph song. Women, realizing they were safe, cheered and greeted their men. Children laughed. Naschellu was abandoned, for her thrashing and screaming had ceased and her madness had vanished when the warlock died. Left alone, she sat up, groaning, and gazed about her at the happy scene, perplexed. Joa scented the woman's deep shame and anguish.

Hounds ran untethered through the tentholds. They exulted, as did their masters. One galloped past Joa, and she saw that the beast held a severed forearm in its teeth. The arm's flesh was pale. The wizard's! Desst and the hunters had not been content to pierce his evil heart. They had hacked him to pieces and given him as carrion to the pack. Ill fate, well deserved!

Joa trembled, sickened. Confused, she examined her reaction. What feeling was this, for a Vupsall child? She should be used to blood and violent death, for the nomadic clans had encountered these things all her young life. Yet she trembled. Had she absorbed some of Kotyan's squeamishness? Was this to be part of that civilized behavior she must learn, along with witch's arts?

Much would change. For her. For the tribe. All of them were setting forth on a different path from that which they trod before.

Behind the tent flap, the midwife encouraged the young widow in her birthing struggle. Then Joa heard Omithi cry out in victory, and there was a smaller, petulant squeal.

"The boy will live," Kotyan assured Joa. *"That we foresee."*

"He will become a clan leader of influence. Desst will stand at his side," Aisli said. *"Both will consult you, girl, to the clan's good luck."*

Without words, Joa asked, *"And does your farseeing tell you how much they will fear me? And how much I must be separated from them, from Omithi, from those I would embrace?"*

There was a silence of sympathy.

Naschellu was weeping, hiding her face. Joa reached to touch and her mind-scent told her of the first wife's pain. A twinge of pity argued with Joa's resentment of that woman. She knew Naschellu's emptiness that had soured her soul and spirit. The cry of Omithi's newborn son had been as a knife in Naschellu's heart. Kynor's second widow bore his seed, and Naschellu was barren. A sad trail stretched ahead, upon which no man of the tribe would put hand to hand with her nor take the paint from her breasts. Empty, she would go alone. It was that emptiness that had made her a ready vessel for an enemy's usage. In part the fault was hers, for her spiteful nature. But great was Naschellu's punishment, and her sorrow.

"There are sacrifices," Aisli spoke soundlessly, echoing the thought Joa held. *"We are sacrificed, too, girl, that the Light prevail."*

Little Clever One padded up to Joa. He put his paws on her knee, begging to be petted. Smiling, she did so, seeing that he, at least, would prove a faithful companion. Beast and bird would be her friends henceforth and ever, not fearing her powers as would humans. In *that,* she would not walk the path unpartnered.

A bit of the triumph had eased for Desst. He approached his dead brother's tent, staring at the closed flap. Joa turned her wistful smile from Little Clever One to the houndmaster and said, "It is well. Omithi is all right, and her son is healthy."

The words were scarce out of her mouth when the midwife unpinned the flap and stepped into the camp light. She held aloft the swaddled, bawling newborn and loudly proclaimed,

"A man-child! Ai! He will be a mighty hunter. Kynor's seed is yet with us! Rejoice!"

People set up fresh cheers and called for the brew pots to be opened and the music festers to make merry. This was a night of celebration indeed!

As women paraded to Omithi's tent, to honor her and praise her babe, Desst stared wonderingly at Joa. How much of her mind-scent touch did he remember? And what did he feel of it? Plainly, he longed to enter the hold and be with his beloved. But that was not permitted him till Omithi was purified and once more sealed to the clan's gods. Uncertain, unaccustomedly shy, he moved from one foot to another, eyeing Joa warily.

Then, of a sudden, he pulled off the warlock's cloak, which he was wearing, and offered it to the girl. "This is by rights yours, youngl . . ." He broke off, looking afraid. His manner was that of a man who had shown dangerous disrespect to a powerful chieftain.

So! She had taken but the first steps onto her chosen path. And already the separations began! Joa took a deep, weary breath. "No, Desst. Keep the cloak. It is your prize, honestly won."

Gratitude brightened his face. He wrapped the blade-rent garment about his broad shoulders proudly. "Ai! I did!" Then he glanced scornfully at Naschellu, who still sobbed in the dirt. "That one will not trouble you again. I'll see to it. I am your guard, and Omithi's."

Joa's smile widened. "Indeed! We will be as one, kinfast."

Whistling, swirling his cape, Desst went to rejoin his comrades. *"Well worked, daughter,"* the sorceresses said in Joa's mind. *"He is henceforth your ally. You will acquire many others. For we see you have skills beyond your mind-scenting. The wise witch moves gently with the souls of those who do not share her Gifts, and makes them hers by their own wish."*

Little Clever One again pawed at the girl's knee. Laughing, she sat beside him, ruffling his fur. "Friend! *You* do not fear me, do you, houndling? Together we will walk the way and serve the Light and our people."

No, she would not be alone. No doubt in the time to come

there would be pain. And no doubt some days she must deal hurt to those who would follow her, in order to accomplish good. But for now, she was Joa, and the scent she touched eased her. Allies, human and not, living and not, looked and approved as a girl played, and readied for her long future amid the weavings of Power.

Afterword

Andre Norton's work has entranced me for years. Long before I began my writing career, I became annoyed with critics who didn't fully appreciate her books. Trying to correct that injustice, I wrote a laudatory analysis of her series, printing it in Yandro, *a fanzine my husband and I published. As a "thank you," Andre graciously invited us to join her and her guests at a special brunch during the 1966 World Science Fiction Convention. It was a stunning experience, leaving an aspiring young author walking on air and even more devoted to the lady than previously.*

And then she gave us Witch World, opening still more horizons to challenge our imaginations. Her characters, concepts, and alien cultures not only delighted but inspired me while I was struggling to create my own fantasy novels. Of all the ideas that Andre introduced, I found the Vupsalls, described in Sorceress of the Witch World, *particularly intriguing. How did those colorful people fit into the larger scheme of that magical universe? What was their true history, shrouded in a mysterious past? What were the further details of their barbaric customs? I itched to explore such questions, never dreaming I'd have the opportunity to do so.*

I had forgotten how generous Andre is. She extended a new invitation: asking if I'd like to contribute to the mythos. Of course! Like my story's heroine, I, too, am an apprentice, learning from an exceedingly skillful mentor, the creative mistress of the Witch World. Now I have satisfied my urge to answer those queries about the Vupsalls, and it's my turn to say "thank you" to the lady who made it all possible and who has given us so much pleasure.

—Juanita Coulson

HEARTSPELL

by

A. C. Crispin

Rain splashed noisily into the puddles in the soot-streaked alley lying between the Silver Spur tavern and the Wayfarer's Rest Inn. Shivering, Branwyn Stormgerd turned her mount off the main street and halted him at the opening of the alley, peering into the dimness from beneath the dripping hood of her cloak. "Well, Cinder, here we are. I suppose I'd better get to it."

The massive black ox she bestrode whuffled inquiringly, as though asking whether she *really* wanted him to enter such a dark, noisome place. In answer, Branwyn tapped her mount's shoulder with the rowan switch that served her as a cattle goad. "Hup, Cinder. There's a shed at the end where you can wait, out of the rain."

Reluctantly the ox splashed forward, grunting a complaint, but obedient to Branwyn's command. When they reached the rickety lean-to, the young woman slid off, then guided the gigantic beast within. "Stay, Cinder," she told him, resting a hand between his eyes in a gesture that was part caress, part signal. "I won't be long. I hope."

Drawing the sodden folds of her cloak about her, Branwyn made her way back up the alley, skirting puddles as well as she

81

might in the dimness. A sullen rumble of thunder made her start. *Stop it,* she ordered herself sternly. *This is no time to lose your nerve.*

As she approached the tavern door, it burst open and two men, laughing raucously, reeled out. The taller slipped in the mud and fell full-length, but his mishap only made his companion roar louder. After hoisting his soaked comrade to his feet, the two staggered away, arm in arm.

Branwyn, who had stepped into the shadow of the massive rain barrel for concealment, watched them go, her resolve failing again. *What if they're all like that in there? I couldn't bear it! Rum-soaked breath, sweaty hands . . . perhaps I should go back. Maybe becoming one of the witches of Estcarp wouldn't be so terrible . . .*

But that would mean leaving behind all that she'd struggled to keep and build for the past eight years, ever since her mother had died and she had been left, a child of ten, to fend for herself.

Branwyn had hired herself out to Squire Barkas as dairymaid, so she could pay the lord-tithe and the taxes on her little farm until she had saved enough to hire someone to help her work it again. Leaving Ravensmere would mean abandoning the sleek cattle she had raised from orphan calves and that the squire, in gratitude, had given her over the years. Cinder, and Callie, Goldhorn, Primrose, and little Ebony Star—all of them like her children, with their patient brown eyes. Her animals loved her, and she could not—*would not*—abandon them!

Squaring her sturdy shoulders beneath the sopping cloak, Branwyn opened the door and entered the taproom. She paused for a moment in the shadows, unseen, to peel off her mantle, her eyes wandering over the men sitting sprawled at the tables, drinking. Most of them were strangers, in town for the spring horse-fair. Tavernmaids circulated among the patrons with slopping mugs on trays. Branwyn's eyes widened at the expanse of bosom the girls' slack bodice lacings revealed. *Is that what attracts these men? I could never, never, in a thousand years . . .*

But after a moment of indecision, she unbuttoned the first few inches of her embroidered blouse, then tugged at her own laces, until a hint of cleavage showed. *That will have to do. Now, which one shall I choose?* Head high, Branwyn moved out into the lights, trying without much success to assume the hip-swaying walk the other girls used.

Conversation in the Silver Spur died to a mutter as most of those present swung to look at her. The young woman felt her face flame, but she held her chin high, and her eyes were busy, studying each male face as the patrons gradually lost interest in her and resumed their drinking. *That one? No, too drunk . . . that one? No, look at those rotten teeth—ugh! How about the black-bearded one in the green jersey, he's—no, no, I once saw a bull with eyes like that, and the poor creature was as mad as a pack of rasti . . .*

Slowly she picked her way across the greasy floor, treacherous with wine sloppings, until she had scanned each of the faces. *There's no man here I'd sell a freemartin heifer to, much less . . .* She sighed, as she sat down at an empty table. *Blessed Gunnora, what shall I do?*

One of the blowsy tavernmaids tapped her on the shoulder, making her jump. "What'll it be, dearie?"

Branwyn shrugged, trying to look casual, as though she frequented taverns all the time. "Oh, wine I guess."

"Red, white, or mulled?"

"Mulled?" Branwyn repeated doubtfully—she'd never had spirits in her life.

"That's hot wine with spices, dearie." The tavernmaid gave her a reassuring smile. "Goes down good on a night like this, I can tell you."

"Mulled, then," Branwyn said gratefully. *I'll drink my wine, and give them all one more glance. Then I suppose I'll have to try the taproom at the Wayfarer's Rest . . .*

"Here you be, dearie." The tavernmaid set a steamy mug down before the young woman.

"Thank you." Branwyn laid a silver coin on the table. "Keep the rest for your trouble." She sipped the hot wine, feeling its warmth rush through her body, making even her toes tingle. *Must be careful, or I'll end up falling over in the street like that fellow outside.*

"May I buy you another of those, mistress?" inquired a light voice from behind her.

Branwyn turned with a start to see a man standing at her elbow. He had not been in the taproom when she'd originally entered, for his face was not one she could have overlooked. His well-cut features were typical of the Old Race—long, oval countenance, black hair and dark gray eyes, but the dour expression shared by most of her countrymen was missing. This young man—it was impossible to tell his age, but Branwyn thought he could not be much over thirty—wore an impish grin, revealing excellent white teeth.

Branwyn gaped at him, forgetting his question. "Where did you come from?"

One black eyebrow lifted sardonically. "Where do all men come from, mistress? I claim no more extraordinary origin than they, I assure you." He made a mocking half bow.

"I mean—I meant—" Branwyn sputtered. "I didn't see you before," she finished lamely.

"That is because I wasn't here." He swung a leg over the bench and settled down beside her. "I was in the back room, educating some of the local farmers in the finer points of dicing."

Branwyn glared at him, irritated. *She* was a farmer. "You mean cheating, most likely."

His faintly derisive smile never wavered. "I assure you, no. I reserve my cheating skills for worthier opponents."

"Then you're a gambler, by trade." *He might be the one,* she was thinking. *True, he's as full of conceit as an egg is meat, but he looks clean, and he has all his teeth. And a gambler will be gone tomorrow, never to bother me again.*

"No, actually I'm a horse trader. My name is Lorin. And you, mistress?"

"Branwyn," she told him absently.

"Are you from Ravensmere, Mistress Branwyn?"

"Yes." *He's not drunk, and that's something unusual in this crowd. I'll probably do no better at the inn . . .*

"Really? With that dark red hair, I'd have taken you for a Sulcar lass. On my travels I've seen sailors with that shade of hair."

She smiled. "My father, Rannulf Stormgerd, *was* Sulcar. He met my mother at Eslee Port, when she came up to the fair there."

"And they married and he gave up the sea." His smile broadened. "He settled down to live happily forever, farming."

Branwyn met his gaze squarely. "For two years, he did. Then he went back to sea, and his ship was lost. There are worse things than farming."

Lorin nodded sober agreement, but his eyes still held that spark of mockery. "To be sure, Mistress Branwyn. May I buy you another drink?"

"No, thank you," she said, feeling her heart pound. She'd made her decision; best get on with it. "I should be heading home. Would you like to join me?"

He looked a bit startled, then laughed. "Of course. But perhaps we'd better settle the business end of the deal first." He touched the purse hanging at his belt and she heard the jingle of coin. "How much?"

Branwyn gaped at him, shocked. *He thinks I'm a trull! A whore!* Part of her mind argued that the assumption made sense on his part, but that small, reasoning voice was quenched in a flood of indignation. "How *dare* you!" she gasped, jumping up from the table. "I'm not—I've *never*—" She swung at him, furious, but he caught her wrist, stopping her blow in midair. "Let go of me!" she raged, breaking his grip.

Without looking at him again, Branwyn whirled and fled for the door, snatching her wet cloak off its peg and around her shoulders.

When she reached the street, she paused for a second, trying to gather her wits. The outrage that had pulsed so hotly through her veins died, leaving her shivering with the cold and wet. *I can't go through with this,* she realized, looking over at the Wayfarer's Rest. *I just can't. The witches will just have to take me—or perhaps I can run away, hide myself . . .* But she knew that was a very forlorn hope. The witches were pitiless and determined, with men-at-arms to do their bidding. It was highly unlikely that one auburn-haired dairymaid would be able to—

"Good even' to you, mistress!" A steaming blast of rum-

soaked breath nearly knocked Branwyn down, but a brawny
arm swept out to encircle her, keeping her on her feet. "I heard
what ye said t' the young cockerel in there, an' how he insulted
ye. But don't cry, missy, ol' Tomlin here'll be glad t' go home
with ye!"

A black-whiskered face tried to nuzzle her own, and Branwyn pulled back with a choked cry, recognizing the man from
the tavern. In the faint light from the tavern window, his eyes
gleamed small, vicious—and madder than ever. "No!" Branwyn pulled away with all the strength of her wiry muscles.
"Stop it!"

"Now come on, sweeting!" Give ol' Tomlin a kiss!"

Realizing she would gain nothing by struggling, Branwyn let
him pull her toward him. At the last possible second before his
mouth captured her own, her knee shot upward with all her
might.

The blow was hampered by her heavy, wet skirts and did not
land true. But it staggered her would-be escort enough so that
Branwyn was able to send her small, hard fist crashing against
the side of Tomlin's jaw. He wavered, then sat down hard in a
puddle. Snatching up her skirts, Branwyn ran.

Even as she approached the shed where Cinder waited, she
could hear the oaf following her, bellowing with rage and pain.
"Cinder!" she cried desperately, dragging the great beast out of
his shelter by tugging at his ear.

Branwyn usually mounted by ordering the ox to kneel, but
there was no time for that now. She flung herself at Cinder's
back, higher than her own head, her legs thrashing wildly as she
forced her body upward, sobbing for breath.

As she clawed, teetering for purchase, a brutal hand seized
her ankle. Branwyn shrieked, kicking frantically at Tomlin, as
she was pulled down off the ox. She landed in a filthy puddle
with a yell, then struggled to get up. Tomlin moved toward her,
chuckling.

Beside Branwyn, Cinder bawled as he swung his great head
around, catching the man between his horns. His huge shoulders rippled as he flung his head—and Tomlin—to the side.
The black-bearded brute sailed into the air, flying clean across
the alley. He struck the wall and slid down it, to lie there, unmoving.

Branwyn darted over to feel the man's pulse, reassured to find that he still lived. "Let me up, Cinder," she commanded the ox, tapping his knee with her cattle goad. Ponderously, the big creature knelt, and the girl scrambled up.

Then, grunting in concern, Cinder sniffed the fallen man anxiously. After a second, the ox began licking the black-whiskered face.

"By the Sword Arm of Karthen the Fair," said a voice. "I rushed out here to see if you needed help, but I guess you don't. Not with *that* monster fighting for you, mistress. I swear, I never saw anything like it!"

Lorin the horse trader stepped out of the shadows.

Branwyn leaned over to pat the ox. "Good Cinder. Thank you, baby. You'd better stop licking him, or he'll not have a face left on the morrow when he wakes up." She glanced over at Lorin. "Their tongues are as rough as any cat's," she explained, and saw the white flash of his teeth as he grinned.

"I know," he replied. "That ruffian deserves worse than a flayed face if he hurt you. Did he?"

"No, I'm all right." Branwyn gathered her cloak around her, remembering suddenly the scene in the tavern. "I'm sorry I tried to hit you . . . and my thanks for trying to help. I'd better be getting on home."

Lorin walked over to gaze up at her in the rain. "I want to beg pardon for what I said in there. I should have known just to look at you that you weren't . . ." He cleared his throat delicately. "But I don't understand why you . . . I mean . . ."

"It's a long story," Branwyn told him, feeling her face grow hot despite the cold rain.

"Are you in some kind of trouble? Perhaps I can help."

Branwyn gazed down at him for a long moment as the rain spattered onto his upturned face. Finally she nodded, then held out her hand. "Very well. Come on up."

They did not speak during the ride; Branwyn concentrated on guiding Cinder through the wet streets, then down the muddy back road, and Lorin sat behind her, head huddled into a fold of her cloak. She wondered if the man regretted his impulse to help her, but the idea of talking to anyone—even a cheating horse trader—about her dilemma brought such relief that she did not turn and invite him to climb down. No one in all Ravensmere had dared offer her even sympathy in her plight . . . the witches were still too feared.

Cinder finally stopped before a dark, slate-roofed stone cottage. The little house nestled behind a clump of trees, making it invisible from the main road, even in daylight. A flash of lightning revealed fenced meadows stretching behind the house and outbuildings. "Get off here, Trader," Branwyn directed. "I'll take my ox on to the stable. The door's open, and there's a lamp ready for lighting on the table to your right as you go in. Have you a striker?"

"Yes."

When Branwyn returned from the barn minutes later, she found the lamp lit, and Lorin crouched on his heels before a snapping fire that was rapidly spreading in the huge fireplace. "That was fast work," she said, hanging up her cloak. She went into her small bedroom to change her dress, then came out to stand beside him, warming herself before the hearth.

Branwyn frowned when she saw the puddle of water growing beneath him from his soaked clothes. "You're wet through! You should have at least taken your cloak before you bolted out to go a-rescuing!"

He climbed to his feet, regarding his dripping jerkin and breeches ruefully. "You have the right of it, Mistress Branwyn, but when I saw that black-bearded brute follow you, I forgot the rain, in truth."

"Well, let's see." Branwyn went into the bigger bedroom, the one that had been her parents'. "Here you go," she called, handing him a shirt and a pair of trousers. "I sold everything else, but I couldn't bear to part with Dad's work clothes. Put these on until your own things dry."

Minutes later Lorin emerged from the bedroom, looking much abashed, holding up the waistband of the pants with both hands. "I forgot you said your father was Sulcar," he said, shaking his head. "They're a tall, brawny lot, aren't they?"

Branwyn giggled as she spread her long hair over her shoulders to dry. "You probably needn't have bothered with the breeches," she said. "The shirt would no doubt cover you decently enough!"

His rueful laughter mingled with hers. "Do you have a rope to serve as belt?"

Minutes later, a hemp cord holding the sagging trousers around his slender waist, Lorin sat before the fire, sipping a mug of tea and looking about him at the whitewashed walls with their smoke-darkened beams, the raised stone hearth with the black cat curled up asleep, the caned chairs, and the colorful quilt padding the seat of the hand-carved oak chest. Herbs hung in bunches from the beams in the small kitchen, their sharp, spicy scents warring with the smell of wet homespun and earth. "I like your cottage, Mistress Branwyn. Reminds me of the place I grew up in."

"A farm?"

"Oh, yes. I was the eldest of six, and I learned to feed the stock and scythe the wheat before I could recognize gold from brass."

"Why did you leave?" Branwyn sat down on the hearth-stones, trying to draw him out. Now that he was actually here, she found herself with a strange desire to postpone telling him about her dilemma . . . she wanted to know him better, before she confided in him. After all, what if he laughed at her? She didn't think he would, but still . . .

Lorin hesitated for a moment before replying, and Branwyn knew that he was not the sort of man to speak easily about things close to his heart. "Two reasons," he told her finally, a strange mixture of wistful longing and contempt shadowing his handsome features for a moment. "I wanted to see the world, and I wanted to control my own destiny.

"For my folks, the world consisted of their few acres and naught else, and they were forever at the mercy of the weather, or the weevils, or the whims of those in power. I had no mind to live my life grubbing in the fields all day with my head cocked over my shoulder, just waiting for someone with authority to appear and take whatever of mine they pleased."

He leaned over to nudge his tall leather riding boots away from the fire so they would dry without cracking. "I'd always had some skill at riding and tending horses, so I joined a traveling horse trader who came through one spring, and I never went back."

"How old were you then?"

"Fifteen." He looked down, picking at a loose thread in the hem of the old shirt. "I've wondered often how they all fared, but"—he shrugged—"somehow my wanderings have never taken me back to the village of Torview."

"Are you afraid to go back again?"

He gave her a hard, quick glance, startled out of his studied indifference. "Afraid? Of course not! Why do you say that?"

"Farming gets into one's blood," she said quietly, pouring more tea. "Mayhap you miss it, but won't admit that to yourself. If you went back, you might find yourself wanting to stay."

Lorin shook his head in a quick, dismissive manner, then had to push his damp black hair out of his eyes. "Not me. I like roving."

"But don't you get tired of never having a place to call your own? It seems to me that even traveling might lose its lure, given enough of it. Haven't you ever wanted to build something, make some kind of dream come true?" Branwyn gazed intently into his gray eyes.

He smiled at her, a crooked smile that held genuine warmth, no mockery. "A dream? Well, yes . . . but I've never spoken of it to anyone."

Branwyn said nothing, only waited, listening.

"I'd like to breed a new kind of horse, one combining the beauty of the small southern stock, the size and strength of the tall northern breed, and the speed and endurance of the horses from the fens of Tor. I have some southern mares, and a northern stallion, but horses of the Torgian breed are rare, and expensive. There was a man with a fine Torgian stud at the horse fair today, but he wanted twice what I could offer. But someday, perhaps . . ." He shrugged, then shook his head wonderingly. "You are amazingly easy to talk to, mistress."

"I enjoy listening to people talk about dreams. I have"—*had,* a jeering inner voice reminded her—"a few of my own."

"But enough of me. I came here to help you." He patted the seat beside him and she sat down. "You inherited this place from your parents?"

Branwyn nodded, then quickly explained how she had hired out to earn enough to keep the farm, how she had nearly saved enough money to work it again, and how Squire Barkas had generously given her the orphaned calves she'd raised throughout the years, so that now she had the beginnings of a small herd of her own. "And folk don't know how I do it," she concluded proudly, "but they say the milk, cream, and cheese from my cows is the sweetest and best they've ever tasted. If I could just stay on here, I know I could do well and be happy!" Her fists clenched against the faded homespun of the old housegown she'd put on in place of her wet dress.

"I assume that brings us to why you were out at the Silver Spur tonight. What did you hope to gain there?"

Branwyn shrugged. "I thought I made that perfectly clear. I came to find a man to bed tonight, and I picked you."

Lorin choked on his tea. "You picked—why *me*?" he sputtered, his face reddening, whether from embarrassment or from the tea that had gone down the wrong pipe Branwyn wasn't sure.

"Because you were the best of the lot in there," she said calmly. "I'm only too aware of the results of poor breeding, and if I had to take the chance of bearing a child from the night's bedding, I wanted it to have the best sire possible. No cast-eye or lackwit for me! Your eyes were clear, you appear to be in good health, and it was obvious to me that, however shaky your honor when it came to dicing, your wits are sharp enough."

He gazed at her with unconcealed dismay, then chuckled halfheartedly. "Well, I suppose I should feel flattered, but I don't. Especially after that slur on my honor. You mean you wanted a man to bed just for a night, and not after? Why?"

Branwyn sighed. "Because of the witches of Estcarp."

She saw Lorin's unwilling start and the look of horror he wasn't quick enough to hide. "Oh, yes, whatever you've heard, I can tell you that the real thing is worse. Just to stand near one of them made me tremble—I could feel the Power emanating from her! It gave me chills. She came through Ravensmere with her escort three days ago, on one of their Searches. I'm nearly eighteen, and have never been tested, because I take after my father in my looks."

Branwyn loosened a tangle in her hair, then began brushing out the heavy mass as she continued: "I suppose they never before guessed I might have the Talent, because I don't look at all like the Old Race. My hair is auburn, my eyes are green, my face is round—nothing could be further from the way they look. From the way *you* look," she said, studying his features in the firelight. She wondered why they seemed faintly familiar, when she was certain she had never seen him before . . . "One would expect the Talent more from you, if you weren't male," she added.

Lorin's eyes were hooded, his expression bland. "Yes, of course. But everyone knows men can't have the Power. Go on with your tale, pray."

"Well, since the Turning—you've heard of the Turning, haven't you?" she asked.

"You mean when the witches combined their Power to shake the border mountains to keep Duke Pagar from invading? Of course, that's an old story by now. It happened when I was a babe in my cradle."

"Well, you've been traveling in far lands, so you may not know that the witches still haven't regained their former strength. Many of them died or lost their Power that night, and in recent years, they've been combing the country for girl children with any spark of the Talent. So it was that, when the witch came through with her mounted guards this past time, I was one of those summoned to lay finger upon her Jewel of Power."

Lorin was listening intently, his face still void of any expression, but Branwyn sensed that her story, while it had shocked him, came as no surprise. "The moment I touched the stone, it began to glow softly, changing from a plain gray rock to a thing of shining beauty. The witch took down my name, telling me that I have a touch of the Talent, and that I had three days to settle my affairs here in Ravensmere, before I must travel with her back to Es City."

"And you don't want to go," Lorin finished for her.

"I hate the idea!" Branwyn burst out. "I've worked so hard here to make a place for myself, and to see it all plucked away—well, it's just cruel! I don't want to be a witch! I've always thought that someday I'd like to wed, have children. And there are my cows—I've raised them all from the moment they were born, and they depend on me!"

"So what does all this have to do with finding me in the Silver Spur?"

Branwyn pulled her hair over her shoulder and began braiding it into a loose rope, not meeting his eyes. "Everyone knows that if a witch lies with a man, she loses her Power. Then the witches wouldn't want me anymore."

Lorin leaned back in his chair, the firelight throwing the angles of his face into sharp-chiseled relief. His eyes were still half-closed, their expression unreadable. "What about the Lady Jaelithe? She wed Lord Simon Tregarth, their union was fruitful, and yet she still retains her Power."

"That's what folk say, but don't forget that they also say Lord Simon is an outlander with his own brand of Power, from some distant land—some even say from another world altogether! Mayhap the Lady Jaelithe's feat is a result of that." Branwyn shrugged, rising to her feet to pace up and down the well-swept stone floor. "Maybe it wasn't such a clever notion, but it was the only thing I could think of."

"And now?" he looked up at her. "What will you do now?"

"Go with the witch tomorrow afternoon," she said miserably, then raised her eyes to his. "Unless you would consider, uh . . ." Her voice died away as her gaze dropped. She stood smoothing her skirt with shaky fingers, blushing hotly.

Lorin thumped his mug down on the hearth with a muffled curse. "No, I won't. I'm not sure I even . . . could . . . knowing I'd been chosen with no more warmth than I'd select a stallion for one of my mares. And there's something else you should know, my dear Branwyn. All those old grandsire tales about the Power are naught more than the same stuff you rake out of Cinder's stall each morning! It's likely true enough that a woman who is taken by force is so shocked and brutalized that her Power departs, but when a man and woman lie down together with love, or at least liking, such is not the case! I *know*."

Her green eyes were puzzled as they met his. "How could you possibly know that?"

"Because *I* have a touch of the Talent myself!" he burst out. "It runs in my family. My two younger sisters had it, too. The three of us lived in well-justified fear that we'd be discovered.

Before the witches took Betha and Jennis, my sisters warned
me never to reveal that I had it, lest I be persecuted by those
thrice-cursed bitches who rule in Es City! I've never admitted
this to a living soul, either, and I'm damned if I know why I'm
telling you now, but it's true!''

Lorin stood up abruptly, then had to hitch awkwardly at his
sagging trousers to keep them from skidding down around his
shanks, but somehow Branwyn felt no desire to laugh. The
horse trader's eyes blazed with a strange intensity, and something uncanny thickened and curdled the air around him. The
girl had a sudden, sharp memory of the witch who had tested
her . . . the woman had carried the same aura of dangerous,
waiting Power. She shivered.

Lorin's voice softened as he noticed her fear. "I've always
been able to whisper wild horses tame, diagnose lameness just
by looking into an afflicted animal's eyes, control mounts with
neither rein nor spur—inspire even the shoddiest animal to
show to its best advantage while I'm astride it.'' He grinned
wryly. "I can also tell you what the weather will be like on any
morrow, and start fires without a striker . . . as I did tonight.''
He gestured at her hearth. "But most of my Talent, such as it
is, is linked to horses, which should be nothing new to you. It's
my guess you've been doing similar things with your cattle without realizing it for years.''

"A *man* with the Power?" Branwyn whispered, dazed. Her
mind was rocked by this admission, so opposite to what she'd
grown up believing.

"Yes, and there are enough women who could testify to that
to let me know that you won't lose your Power by bedding
someone any more than I did.''

Branwyn sank down onto a bench. "Oh . . . and to think that
I almost—" She began to tremble, remembering.

He came over to kneel before her, take her hands in his. "It's
all right. Nothing happened. Here, I'll get you some tea.''

She was nearly sobbing with anger and frustration. "I don't
want any tea. When I think what I nearly did, in desperation, it
makes me hate the witches all the more! That horrible Tomlin!
I feel st-stupid," she finished, her teeth beginning to chatter.

"You're just worn out with worry, and feeling the reaction

from tonight's danger," he said, urging her up out of her seat.
"Come on, lie down, and you'll feel better."

"You'd better stay here tonight," Branwyn said as she
stretched out on her parents' bed and he pulled the quilt over
her. "You can sleep in the little bedroom."

"It *is* late," he admitted, "and my clothes and boots are still
wet. Not to mention that I couldn't find my way back to town in
the dark."

Branwyn grinned wryly as she settled her head against the
pillow. "*I* can't get lost. I suppose that's part of my Talent."

"I suppose," he said soothingly, brushing her hair away from
her face as though she were one of his mares who had been
frightened.

"Lorin," she said suddenly, urgently, "do something for me.
There's a loose stone on the right side of the hearth. Pry it up
and bring what's beneath it to me."

He gave her a wondering glance, but obediently left the
room. He was back in a moment with a small, heavy bag. "Silver," he said, peering inside.

"My savings," she told him. "I want you to have it. I won't
need it where I am going tomorrow. Buy that Torgian stallion
you saw. I want you to have your dream. At least that way one
of us will."

"I couldn't!" he protested, shoving the bag beneath her pillow. "No, Branwyn. Rest now. Get some sleep."

"Please," she whispered, sitting up to press the bag into his
hand. "I want you to have it, Lorin. Otherwise the witch will
probably take it, for the treasuries in Es City."

"They would, wouldn't they," he murmured bitterly. "Well,
all right. Thank you. Now lie down again, and good night." He
stood up to blow out the candle, and then the room was lit only
by the faint glow from the fireplace.

"Will you be here tomorrow?" Branwyn whispered as he
turned to leave.

He sat back down beside her, shaking his head. "Tomorrow
will be a fine sunny day, and I'll be gone before dawn, so this is
good-bye, Branwyn."

"I know," she whispered, searching out his features in the
dimness. She could barely make out the planes of his face,

edged by the fireglow. The dark lock of hair had fallen down over his brow again, and she reached up to push it back, her fingers trailing blindly down his cheek. "You're a kind man, Lorin, even if you don't let yourself realize it."

He cleared his throat. "I'd better leave. If you need me, call."

But before he could stand up, her hand came out to close on his forearm. "No," she whispered, and, when he turned back to her, repeated it. "No, don't go. Stay with me, even if just for tonight. For no other reason than that I want you to stay, Lorin. After tonight, I'll be alone for the rest of my life. I want to be able to remember you, when I'm alone."

He hesitated for many heartbeats. "But, Branwyn . . ."

"Stay."

Her arms came up to encircle him, draw him down. Their mouths met in a long kiss that was the antithesis of the chill, wet loneliness outside, and after that, Lorin argued no more, but stayed.

Branwyn awoke before dawn, as she did every day. She lay facing the window, seeing darkness still outside. The rain had stopped, as Lorin had promised. *Lorin . . .*

She lay there, thinking of him, of their hours together, loathe to roll over and start the day. For as soon as she turned over, she knew she would find the other side of the bed empty, naught but a dent in the pillow where his dark head had rested; but until she did that, she could pretend that he was still there, beside her, and that everything would be all right.

If only it could be so, she mused, remembering the warmth of his lean, muscled body, his gentle, knowing hands. *But such things don't happen, only in love ballads sung by songsmiths,* her rational mind argued, mocking her fantasies. *But it happened to my parents!* Branwyn thought defiantly. *They loved each other, they did!*

Tears threatened her eyes, and she fiercely blinked them away. *You have too much to do today to lie here abed, dreaming of things that can never be. Get up!* Resolutely, she turned over and sat up, forcing herself to touch the other pillow.

The opposite side of the bed was empty, of course.

Branwyn went out to milk her cows, talking to each of them as she did so, soft words of farewell, of well-wishing. When she was finished storing the pails of milk in the cold cellar, the sun had risen, so she turned each animal out to pasture with a last pat. After cleaning the stalls, she swept the aisle, making sure the whole byre was neat and clean. Squire Barkas would be coming by later to take charge of her place, and Branwyn wanted to leave everything in order.

She let the chickens out of the henhouse, scattering feed for them. Then she went into the cottage and made the bed, fed Jet, the cat, then swept and dusted the house. She had no appetite for breakfast, but forced herself to eat, remembering she would be traveling all day.

Finally, chores done, she stripped and washed, putting on her best dress, which had dried overnight. After putting a change of clothing into one of her father's old sea bags, she was ready. She packed nothing of a personal nature—the witch had warned her that ties to her old life were not permitted.

When everything was done, Branwyn sat on the edge of her swept and tidy hearth, trying vainly to think of other chores she could do to fill the hours until the witch arrived. While she'd been busy, she had been able to focus her mind on the task at hand, pushing away the grief. Now, with nothing left to do, it threatened to overwhelm her. Her throat tightened and her eyes filled.

Outside, in the back pasture, Cinder lowed mournfully. Branwyn wiped away her tears. *What ails him? Could he be hurt?*

Catching up the cattle goad she used to signal and guide her beasts, Branwyn went out. She stood for a moment on the front step, shading her eyes against the morning sun, looking down the lane that led through the trees to the road. There was no sign of the witch, but she was not due until after noon.

Cinder bawled again, and Branwyn hurried around the house, past the neat rows of her vegetable garden, back to the cow pasture. The ox was standing against the rails of the gate, as close to the cottage as possible. When he saw Branwyn coming, he bawled again, butting his enormous head against the fence. "Poor Cinder," she whispered, "you know something's wrong, don't you?"

She patted his head, then scrambled up onto the top rail to administer his favorite caress, using the pointed goad to gently scratch the big hump of muscle behind his neck. Soon Cinder stood, eyes half-closed in ecstasy, sighing with pleasure.

Perhaps I can take this with me, Branwyn thought, looking down at the cattle goad. *It holds so many memories for me, but to anyone else, it would seem naught but a length of rowan wood with a pointed end. Perhaps the witch won't—*

Her thoughts broke off as she stared down at the goad, suddenly remembering a piece of old, half-heard lore. *Rowan . . . what did they always say about rowan? That it is a bane against all magic, light or dark!*

A kernel of an idea began nibbling at the fringes of Branwyn's mind. She was still staring at the cattle goad, bemused, when she heard a hail from the front of the cottage. Her heart seemed to halt its beating. *She's come early! Blessed Gunnora, help me!*

Grasping the goad firmly, the girl ran back up the short lane from the pasture and around the house to find the witch just dismounting from her horse. Three men-at-arms sat at attention back near the end of the lane. One of them held a placid-looking gelding on a leading rein.

Branwyn curtsied. "Good morning, lady."

"Are you ready?" The witch was a woman in her mid-twenties, slightly above middle height, slender, with well-cut features and beautiful dark gray eyes. Branwyn had forgotten she was so young—perhaps because there was no youth left in those eyes. She wore a divided gray riding robe and traveling cloak, with the Jewel of her Order on a silver chain around her neck.

Branwyn curtsied again, her hand holding the rowan stick down amidst the folds of her dress. "I am ready, lady, but mayhap you no longer want me," she said, her voice pitched for the ears of the witch alone.

"What do you mean?" The woman's eyes flashed, and Branwyn could feel the Power coiled within her, waiting.

The girl took a deep breath, trying not to blush. "Lady, I have lain with a man since last we met. Everyone knows that a woman who does so loses her Power."

Anger raced across the witch's features, then was replaced by such coldness that Branwyn shivered, despite the bright sunlight. "Indeed," said the witch. "And why would you do such a thing?"

Before last night, Branwyn might have dared to answer, "because I did not want to go with you," but now she found herself responding, with equal truth, "Because I loved him, and I knew there would be no other chance."

The witch's lips thinned contemptuously, but she did not speak. "So you see, lady," Branwyn continued breathlessly, "I am no longer fit to become one of you. I might even be with child," she added as the thought struck her for the first time.

"Think you we are fools?" the witch spat. "Do you imagine, girl, that you are the only one to try such desperate measures to thwart us? The Jewel will tell me if you still hold Power within you. Touch it!"

Branwyn hesitated, eyeing the stone.

The witch thrust her Jewel of Power at the girl. "Now!"

The fingernails of her right hand digging into the wood of the rowan stick, Branwyn put out the forefinger of her left hand, laying it upon the dead, gray stone.

No Power. Quench the fire, don't spark! the girl thought desperately, feeling sweat bead her forehead. *No Power, none! Good rowan, help me!*

Beneath her touch the stone glimmered, glowed faintly, then, as Branwyn and the witch watched, the inner fire died out, leaving the Jewel gray and cold as yesterday's ash.

Branwyn pulled her hand away. *I did it! I kept the Jewel from glowing!* The effort of will she had expended had drained her— she had to use the last of her strength not to stagger with exhaustion. "See, my lady?"

"I see," the witch said, her voice colder than any winter's blast. "I see that you have more Power than I thought, girl. It is no small accomplishment to extinguish the fire in a Jewel of Power." Her hand came up to catch the girl's chin, hold it past any effort Branwyn could make to break free. "I also see that you are not lying about bedding a man, but that makes no difference. If the Power still resides in you, we care naught for your maidenhood. And if you should be with child, we will deal with *that*, too. Now fetch your things."

A small cry of dismay came from Branwyn's lips, but she forced herself to walk calmly as she went to obey. As she picked up her bag, she took a last look around her home, then, squaring her shoulders, went back outside, latching the door behind her.

The witch beckoned her toward the man-at-arms holding the palfrey. But even as Branwyn raised her foot to the stirrup, she paused, hearing trotting hoofbeats—many hoofbeats!

The girl lowered her foot back to the ground, staring, puzzled, at the lane leading to the road. Two mounted figures came into sight, each leading three riderless horses.

Branwyn shielded her eyes with her palm, squinting in the bright sunlight. *Who can that be?* Her dazzled eyes made out a youth with shaggy brown hair, perched atop a tall, heavy-boned, snorting stallion. The other was riding a dun-colored stallion, and he had black hair and a crooked grin—

"Lorin!" Branwyn gasped. She rubbed her eyes, wondering if the witch had put her under some kind of spell—was this an hallucination of some kind?

"Branwyn!" shouted her supposed illusion, then swore lamentably as his stallion nipped at one of the led mares.

"Lorin!" Branwyn cried, her immobility broken. She raced toward him, laughing and weeping at the same moment, completely forgetting the witch and her men-at-arms. "You came back!"

"Of course I did," he said testily. "I swear, you give me no credit at all. Where can we put the mares?"

"In here," Branwyn said, dropping the rails on the eastern pasture gate. The small, delicate-boned horses trotted inside and began cropping the grass within hungrily.

"Gareth"—Lorin swung off the dun-colored stallion and handed the reins to the lad—"put the stallions up in the barn for now."

Branwyn looked at Lorin's horse closely for the first time, then grinned excitedly. "The Torgian! You bought him!"

He grabbed her hands and exultantly swung her around, then stopped, his hands on her shoulders. "Thanks to you, my lady. Are you willing to make a partnership of it? My horses and your cows? We work the farm together?"

"A partnership?" Branwyn wasn't quite sure what he meant. And for the first time, she remembered the witch. "But I have to leave. The witch is already here."

"You're not going anywhere," he said.

"You came back to help me," she murmured, still barely able to believe it. "Why?"

"That should be obvious," he told her, his dark eyes dancing with all the mockery she remembered. "Or do you value yourself so lightly, my lady? Your Power isn't confined to cows, Branwyn. You've managed to ensorcel my heart completely."

Bending down, he brushed her mouth with a kiss that, brief as it was, made her lean against him. Then he slipped an arm around her, and together they turned to face the witch, who had walked down the lane to confront them. "This woman and I are handfasted," he declared. "We will be wed as soon as we can have the local squire witness our troth. She stays with—"

Lorin broke off, stiffening as he gazed fully at the witch, who was also staring at him, her eyes wide with shock.

"Betha!" he whispered. "It's you!"

Even as he spoke, the witch drew herself up, the coldness sweeping back down over her features, leaving them as stony as her Jewel. "This woman has been selected," she told him. "She must come with me. Now."

Lorin shook his head dazedly. "I never thought to see you again. That day that they carried you and Jennis away, I thought they had taken my heart with them. I left home myself less than a month later. I couldn't bear to stay there without you. How is Jennis? Is she well?"

"Jennis is dead," the witch told him, expressionlessly. "The training is difficult, and often dangerous. She did not survive the novitiate."

"Jennis . . . dead . . ." His features crumpled. "No . . ."

"Come, girl," the witch told Branwyn. "Get on the horse."

"But—" Lorin recovered himself with an effort. "Didn't you hear me, Betha? Branwyn is my betrothed. I love her. We will be wed—"

The witch ignored him. "Get on the horse, girl, or I'll have you carried."

"*No!*" Lorin pushed between them. "What's happened to

you, Betha? Don't you remember what it was like, that day they took you and Jennis? Would you do the same thing to me, now, as they did to you? Sister"—he reached out to touch her arm, imploringly—"listen to me! Are you dead, too? Don't do this!"

Something flickered behind the witch's eyes. "I have no family anymore. I am sworn. I have a duty to bring the girl with me."

"Betha . . ." Lorin's voice was still soft, but his expression was now as unyielding as the witch's. "I won't let you take her. I'll fight until your men slay me, if it needs must be that way. Don't do this, I beg you."

The witch stood staring at him, for a time measured only by the frightened thumps of Branwyn's heart. Finally the woman stirred. "My Jewel *did* die," she murmured, as if to herself. "Mayhap her Power *has* left her . . . 'twould not be the first time . . ."

"Oh, please!" Branwyn begged softly. "My Power is only with cattle—it would do you little good. Please, lady!"

The witch turned to her, and for the first time a real person gazed out of those beautiful eyes, so like Lorin's. "Very well," she said, finally. "But there will be a price."

Branwyn turned to Lorin, saw fear in his expression that echoed her own. She clutched his arm, almost ready to tell him no, it could not be worth it, but he was already saying, "Whatever it is, we agree, Betha. Name it."

That spark of humanity in the witch's eyes increased, until Branwyn almost thought she saw tears there. "Lorin, I charge you to go home, see to our parents' welfare. I am permitted no contact with them, though they receive money each year from the Council."

"I swear," Lorin said, relief filling his voice. "Torview is only a few days' journey, and I was planning to see them soon. I swear they will never want for aught."

The witch nodded. "Then farewell, Lorin. We will never meet again."

"Fare *you* well, dearest sister," Lorin said, his arm tightening about Branwyn's waist. "I will thank you all my days."

The witch turned and walked away without a backward

glance, mounted, beckoned to her men-at-arms, then they clattered out of sight.

They watched her go, then when the lane was empty, turned to each other. "You came back for me," Branwyn whispered, and then added irrelevantly, "you have the most beautiful eyes."

He chuckled, drawing her close. "Shall we travel to see my parents as soon as we've visited the squire?" he asked. "I must keep my promise to Betha."

"Who will watch the stock?"

"My stable lad, Gareth. He grew up on a farm, too."

Branwyn's heart felt so light she fancied giddily that it might rise straight up, pulling her into the air. "Very well," she agreed. "We'll leave the day after tomorrow, then."

"I can hardly wait to see my people again. It's been more than ten years. And they'll be twice as surprised to see me come home with a bride!" His eyes began to twinkle with the old mocking glint. "Wait till I tell them how we met . . . that you picked me up in a tavern. What a story that will make! Wait till our children are old enough to hear it!"

Branwyn's mouth dropped open in mock horror. "You wouldn't *dare*!"

Lorin winked over at the youth, who had come from stabling the stallions to join them. "Wouldn't I? Gareth, this is your new mistress, my lady Branwyn. Would you like to hear the story of how we met? It was a dark and stormy night . . ."

Afterword

Witch World is a rather grim place—not surprising, since it is a world where both continents have undergone destructive wars and their bitter aftermaths. Most stories placed in that world have been of a serious turn. Andre Norton's own "One-Spell Wizard" is a lightsome exception to this rule, and several of the Tales of the Witch World *stories (the one that comes readily to mind is "Cat and the Other") have also injected some humor. Still, lighthearted tales have been decidedly in the minority.*

So when Andre first mentioned that she was doing this project, and would like a story from me, I determined that I would write a humorous piece. So what did I do? I produced "Bloodspell" for Volume 1, probably the grimmest, most violent tale in the entire book!

Chagrined, I begged Andre for another chance, and she, gracious chatelaine of her world that she is, granted my request. The inspiration for my second try was the testing by the witches of the young maidens in Estcarp. Not everyone selected, I reasoned, would be eager to go and leave behind all that she had known. Since the witches of Estcarp scorn union with men and jealously guard their chastity, holding it as the key to their Power, it seemed to me that a girl who wished to avoid becoming one of their number might determine to intentionally divest herself of her virginity, so as to render herself unfit to become a witch. And if the man she chose for that purpose proved to be a lovable rogue, with a touch of the Power himself . . .

Thus "Heartspell" was born.

—A. C. Crispin

THE WEAVERS

by

Esther M. Friesner

The Moss Wife tracked the runaway's progress for some time before the girl was even marginally aware that she was being watched. In the gray-green quiet of the forest, the child's ragged, panting breath was a slash on the air, a harsh tearing of the veil so long, so dearly woven. With a sideways, shambling gait the Moss Wife moved from shadow to shadow, tree to tree, her wrinkled face wincing with each gasp that escaped the girl's lips. The young one sounded as if she were in pain. There were no wounds that the Moss Wife could see, but Fyuru knew to her cost how deep some wounds can run and leave no mark, never a surface mark.

She is healthy, the Moss Wife thought, absently running her fingers through the long, silky tendrils of her hair. *She will pass through here quickly. She will go away. She must go away. Her smell is too strong, too much like his, too much of a chain to bind me. The branches tear it from her as she passes, the curtains of moss hold it, weave the seeming of the face I once knew. I want her gone. For the sake of the silence, I want her gone.*

But the girl did not go. She ran more as one who seeks than as one who flies. She was driven, yes. She looked behind her

every several steps, paused in the forest's quiet to harken for
any sign of a pursuer. Her small, slender limbs trembled, her
hair came free of its braiding and floated about her until she
was another moss-draped sapling in the twilit world. Fear clung
to her, and the certainty of pursuit, and the wavering of a will
once strong, strong enough to have urged her into this mad
flight.

For all her fear, she did not use the endless minutes to add
distance between herself and whoever followed. She hesitated,
she paused, she lingered.

I want you gone. The thought pounded against the edges of
the girl's mind, but did not enter. *Go! Go! Why do you tarry?
What do you bring to my world? Let the leaves fall, and the past
lie beneath them, undisturbed. Child, child, I want you gone.*

It was no good. The girl lurched away, deeper into the forest.
Fyuru felt the very air bear the scarrings of her flight, and she
shuddered. If the girl had fled, he would follow. He was not
one to let a thing go, once his own.

Which would bring more pain? To bide and watch for his
coming or to follow the girl and see where her blood would lead
her? But that would be a path that would draw him too, eventually, inevitably. The silence shivered around her, a living entity that senses approaching pain and can anticipate its own
suffering.

Fyuru drifted back into the half light. She would go after the
girl. She was bought and bound to do so, a debt that now had
come due. She had learned of prices while she walked beyond
the forest, but she had never truly understood that all things
carry payment. Bitterness was in her bones. So many lessons,
all learned as one, too late.

She found the girl stretched full-length upon the softly yield-
ing moss of the forest floor, exhausted. Her cheek was cradled
roughly on her fist, her other arm flung up to cover her face.
Her ribs heaved hard, her legs were drawn up close to her
body. There was not a sign of a traveler's pack, or any supplies
for a journey. In the count of seasons, Fyuru knew that she was
scarcely fifteen. This knowledge surprised the Moss Wife, for
she had thought it all forgotten when she had returned to the
forest. The reckoning should be his, along with all the rest.

Strange, how much of memory will weave itself out of strands of the now and the present. As Fyuru gazed at the girl, another body rose from the forest floor, a weaving as seemingly tenuous, yet as strong as any moss-made tapestry of Fyuru's conjuring. The vision's hair was a darker, bolder gold than the girl's—itself colored like the ghost of a star—thicker, shorter, not half so fine. The body was larger, more powerful, a man's form, yet the strength of it drained away under the eyes of a younger Fyuru, that body's power seeping into the forest floor from a dozen bleeding cuts of the sword.

Memory's weave-work took her, gently parting the translucent layers of days and years that lay between *then* and *this*, forcing her to see. She was that younger Fyuru once more. She trembled, shaking with the remembrance of finding him in a silence that was no longer whole. The stillness screamed. His every groan of pain wrenched the woods around her until she thought she would die. To heal the silence, she must heal the man. Her whole being twisted inside in terror at the thought of touching him, and yet a coolness deep within her spirit calmed her, made her see the good reasons why she must help him, steadied her heart and her hands so that when he awoke in the vine-woven confines of her house, his wounds were already cleansed and bound.

And because she could not bear any further disturbance she had likewise woven and bound to herself an illusion of human appearance. Even she, the solitary, had learned from her sisters that humankind often found them hideous, frightening. Fear had done enough harm in the forest. Her belly was still sour with sharing this man's fear of betrayal and abandonment and death. She could stand no more. To his eye, she was a young woman of his own breed—no beauty, but fair and pleasing to see, with a wealth of hair that moved with its own unspoken poetry.

So she healed him, and when he was healed, he told her that his heart was still wounded. He would not let her go. He would not believe her when she said that she was happy as she was, where she was. The pain of his disappointment marred the peace. In peace was all her wholeness, and so to purchase it

again, she allowed him to love her. In this way, he was happy
for a time, and she was content.

But he grew beyond the point where her love, placidly given,
could satisfy him. He told her of the enemies who had driven
him into the forest in the first place, driven him there to die.
They held his lands, but he would have them again. He would
win back all that was his, and no one would ever take it from
him. She could feel the grasp of an invisible fist tightening as he
spoke. She tried not to fall into a thousand shaking strands
when the shrieking rasp of a sword drawn from its sheath filled
her little home.

They had gone from the forest together. Another choice
would have meant argument, and she was too weary for strife.
It was easier to give in, to float on every passing breeze like the
drapings of tree-limb moss, to give beneath the weight of a con-
queror's foot and spring back again when he had passed, like
the spongy carpet of the forest floor.

He was as good as his word. Ambition made him stronger,
bolder, more ruthless than his enemies, though he told her it
was love. He took back all that was his and laid it at the feet of
his fair wife. He stood beside her bed and smiled down at the
daughter she bore him, swearing that he would make the child
a great lady. He wove grand dreams with his words, and all she
gave him in return was a timid, peaceful smile. She thought it
was enough.

Not for him. He was ambitious, the young man who once had
told her that all he asked of life was to hold her love. Ambition
glinted with the edges of a hundred swords. She felt the bartered calm of her home among humankind begin to fray as her
man's ambitions made their myriad slashes. When he gazed at
their child he saw a coin, a puppet, a trading counter. When he
looked at her . . .

She ran away. In her own form, to her old home she ran. She
wrapped the silence more tightly around her than the silken
cascade of her own hair, closed her eyes into the perfect darkness, and rocked herself back and forth, back and forth until
she was again one with the slow, ageless serenity of growing
things, the endless peace of the forest.

Now this.

The ground shook. Fyuru felt his coming from the soles of her feet to her belly. He burst into the small open space where the girl lay, his eyes blood-blazing in the half light.

"So this is how you repay me!"

The girl gave a little cry and rolled into a ball of ice. Fyuru's teeth chattered with shared cold. Her arm shot through with the pain of his grip on the girl's arm, hauling her to her feet.

"Now you'll come home with me, and we'll hear no more of your foolishness. It's a good match. He's an honest man, and he'll do well by you. Not every father would find such a husband for his daughter—nor be able to, having a daughter like you! Your reputation . . ."

The girl grew bones, stood straight suddenly. Her chin came up, and her eyes thrilled with the green fire of sunlit woodland. "I have no cause to be ashamed of myself, and you have none to be ashamed of me."

"Don't I? With all your outspoken whinings of going off and earning your own way as a wanderer? Not content to stay at home like a wise woman, grateful for a solid roof over your head, but on the roads in all weathers. How will you find bread on the road, I'd like to know?"

The girl tossed her head. "You know how."

Her father spat. Fyuru passed her hand over her cheek, feeling an old stain. She had tried to speak to him once, to beg him to return with her to the forest. That had been his answer then, too.

"Singing nurse tales to the local brats was never any calling for a young woman of our house. If they praised you for your words and tunelets, do you think it was true?" His laughter raked the boles of the trees. "Flatter the daughter to curry favor with the father! That for your precious tales, my innocent! Take sweet words for your bread and you'll starve soon enough, if I'd let you."

Fyuru saw the girl's head droop under a weight of hair nearly as heavy as her own. Still, there was steel beneath that melodious, piping voice, tender with many dreams. "The first night out, I came to a house beyond your lands. No one knew me there. I was no one's daughter. I sang for my bread, and they gave it to me. That wasn't flattery." Her head rose sharply, and she met her father's eyes. "It wasn't pity, either! Not in a house so poor."

The man made a disgusted sound in his throat. "Here I'd hoped that these few nights with no roof over your head would have given you some sense. Will you sell dreams, and live on them yourself besides? A fine road you've taken into this wild-wood if you're seeking a new life!"

The girl's head dipped again. "I am seeking the old."

Now there was worse than scorn in her father's eyes. "You believe every lie you hear, don't you? That's what's puffed your head full of air. Your mother's dead, I told you. She took a chill and died the year after you were born. If you're looking for phantoms to put in your songs, we've more than enough closer to home, and home's where you're going." His hand closed around her wrist. His feet dug deep gouges in the mossy ground as he hauled her away.

The Moss Wife stepped from the shadows.

"Let my daughter go."

Her voice was unchanged. She saw him stiffen and stand still. The girl gave a joyous cry and twisted from his grasp. Blindly she ran toward the sound, toward the voice that was only an infant's memory.

Then she saw the Moss Wife's face, and she fell to her knees. The strangled sound she made caused the man to wheel about suddenly, sword ready to slay whatever nightmare had so af-frighted his child.

Fyuru threw up her hands automatically, pulling Power from the forest floor. Vines plunged from the overhanging branches, whipping around the man's sword arm, wrenching away the blade. He cursed her viciously, and with his free hand groped for his dagger, but more vines snaked out to bind his ankles, roping their way up his legs to lash him secure.

What have I done? Fyuru's head burned with the rending of the silence. She clapped her hands to her ears, but could not shut out the man's unholy ravings.

"Let him go!" the girl cried. There was much of the man's rage in her voice. "Let my father go, monster!"

"Monster?" Fyuru shook her head slowly. Disbelief was a numbing balm. She raised her hands to the crown of her head and began to weave the filaments of illusion. Her body shimmered in a gray mist, grew taller, more slender, sweeter to the human eye. When the weaving was done, she stepped forward so that man and girl together might see and not mistake.

He called her by the name she had used then, in the long ago time of bartered peace. It was at once welcome and invocation and thanks for answered prayers. "You've come back." His bonds still held, but they were forgotten. "I dreamed you would come back. Look, girl! Your mother's come to us again! Now all will be—"

"No," said the girl, shaking her head. "That's not my mother. Father, you didn't see her—not as she is. This is— nothing human."

"Curse your stubbornness, can't you *see*?" The man strained against his bonds. "She is your mother! If I ever told you she was dead, it was only to cover my own shame for losing her. Tell her! Tell her who you are!"

Fyuru knelt beside the girl. She made no attempt to touch her, though her fingertips burned with remembrance of an infant's velvet cheek. Before her eyes she saw small, sleep-heavy lips where a blue-white drop of milk still clung, and the vision stayed until her own tears blurred it.

"Your father is right," said the Moss Wife. She saw mixed horror and denial in the girl's eyes. "And so are you. Your mother, and nothing . . . human. You came here seeking me. You must take what you find."

The man was shouting again: "Don't believe her, girl! Living here in these forsaken woods, she hasn't any notion what she's saying. Come home with us now! Come, and this time I will be the healer."

The Moss Wife raised her eyes. "Of what will you heal me? Of being what I am? It is incurable, and the same illness is already deep in our daughter's heart. Will you heal her too, with your threats and your shouts?"

She turned from him and gave the girl her hand. "Come. You have yet to find all that you seek." She led the awestruck child away, deeper into the forest.

When she came back, she was alone. "Where is she?" the

man demanded, struggling against the vines again. "What have you done with our daughter?"

"Shown her the path." Still in human guise, the Moss Wife sat opposite him, arms embracing updrawn knees.

"What path?"

"The path through the forest. The safest, swiftest path for one who wishes to go so far." He would have spoken then—hot, angry words—but her pale palm flashed in the half-light. "If you pursue her, I will set my snares in your way. If you persist, I will follow, and I will stand between you and her even as you have tried to stand between her and her dream all these lost years."

His voice was a muffled growl. "Lost years . . . a lost life, loving you."

"Then I will heal you of that." She cast away the human seeming.

For a time, the woods were silent. Then he cried out: "Liar! Cheat! The tales they tell of your people don't tell half enough. Shy and meek, they claim, when you're as ready to feed on a man's heart as any wolf."

"And on what do you feed, man of swords?"

"Our child was right," he growled. "You are nothing human."

She stood up slowly. "She said she was sorry for saying that, before we parted. She said that maybe that was why she was so sure of becoming a singer, because of the half-blood. Nothing human. She weaves vision to melody even as I weave vine to vine and you weave land to land. She is truly the daughter of two bloods, but not like me and not like you. Let her go."

"I can't let her go as easily as you once did! Do you expect me to tear her memory from my heart? You don't know anything of human feeling."

The Moss Wife did not seem to answer the accusation. All she said was, "She will not be gone forever."

A canny look came into the man's eye. "You can't keep me bound here forever. You know how long my memory can be, when I'm determined on a thing. Here's a bargain: Come home with me again—put on your human shape—and let us be as we were before. Your love for her freedom. I will swear by any oath you name not to harry her if you consent."

Fyuru bowed her head. One by one the vines binding the man dropped away. One hand floated up to brush back the fall of her hair. The man flinched. She saw his distaste as a flicker of movement in the shadows of the trees.

"No bargain," she said. "Follow her, if you must, but first you must fight past me here. I have learned that some things are not to be bought with compromise."

The man stared at the Moss Wife, then at his fallen sword. His hand darted out to seize the blade before another vine could spring its snare. Nothing in the forest moved. His eyes danced from tree to tree, daring her magic to take him unaware. All was stillness.

"You must fight me," the Moss Wife said. "I will not fight you with anything but my death. This time it is I who set the price."

"Then let it be paid!" He raised his blade. It hovered for several heartbeats in the misty air, then came gradually down to his side. Fyuru drank the sound of its sheathing as if it were purest springwater.

"I loved you." The man's words were bitter. "But what did your folk ever know of love?"

She lowered her eyes, and her voice was a murmuring wind in the branches. "What we know, we know in silence, and we prove in time."

When she looked up, she was alone.

In the years that fall with the falling leaves, they say that a great singer emerged from nowhere and wove tales that caught the hearts and twined the souls of men in a web of living dreams. In all the years and places of her wandering, she would never speak her lineage except to say, "I am the child of forest and sword, I am the wage of fighter and free." When they implored her to stay, she would smile wistfully and reply that moss sets down no roots. Her songs were her only hearth and home.

But when the last years came to her, they found her with harp in hand on the grave where a minor lord lies buried, and over mound and maiden was woven an evergreen coverlet of moss starred with the fairest flowers. No man's hand or blade shall ever part that weaving.

Afterword

Because I started reading Lord of the Rings with the middle book, then worked my way out to either side, I'm used to not doing things in what others might call the natural order. I had done a story for Andre Norton and Robert Adams's Magic in Ithkar series, and so felt singularly honored when Andre asked me to contribute to Tales of the Witch World. Honored, yes, and a little nervous. I was not a born SF reader; indeed, in keeping with my not doing things in proper-order style, I only started reading it heavily after I started writing it. I had never read any of the Witch World books; I knew nothing about it. Thereat followed some quick makeup reading, with the helpful guidance of friends. And guess what? I learned I'd been missing something special. I found the rich variety of the Witch World's peoples fascinating; the moss wives most of all. Those who know me may think this is odd, but the shy, retiring nature of these forest dwellers spoke to something in me. I began to wonder what circumstance would be enough to compel one of them to come forward and take a stand. Thus the genesis of "The Weavers." So thank you, Andre, not only for inviting me to write "The Weavers," but also for bringing me (albeit tardily) into a wondrous new world of magic.

—Esther M. Friesner

THE ROOT OF ALL EVIL

by

Sharon Green

The Renthan brought us into the area of pillars, their gait rapid but short of a gallop of alarm. They, as we, knew there were sniffers at our heels out there in the night, but none were immediate pursuers of evil intent. Had they been able to follow us into that place of Power, the evil of their intent would likely have grown, but this the shining blue radiance of the place disallowed. We would be safe for the darkness, and perhaps by dawn the skulkers would be found to have gone elsewhere.

"Have any of you ever sheltered here before?" Derand asked the other men as he dismounted, the stroke of his hand thanking his Renthan for having carried him. "For all the riding I have done over Escore, never have I been in this place."

The others looked at one another as they, too, dismounted, but none spoke up as being familiar with the place we had taken shelter in. Even the Renthan were silent upon the point of familiarity, and this soured Derand to an even greater extent than the long day had done.

"So first we must ride into the unknown by day, and now we must trust ourselves to it for the darkness," he said to me, coming closer to assist me from the back of the Renthan who bore

me. "For all this we have you to thank, Merilan, and for what
pursuit we pick up as well. I sincerely hope you continue to find
yourself pleased with your actions."

"I do continue to find myself pleased with my actions," I returned as I accepted his assistance, determined not to show how
the sting of his words had upset me. "It was not I who set you
and these others to follow after me, nor was it I who refused to
return alone once I had been found. And this is a place of
Power. Surely we will be safe here if anywhere."

"What safety we find remains to be seen," he answered,
scowling down at me where I stood. "The blue of this place
feels a trifle odd, but in what manner I cannot say. And had it
not been for the pleading of your lady mother, we would not
have come in pursuit of you. Your own oddness has been a
thorn in our sides for too long, Merilan, and I, for one, have
tired of it. You will speak to me now of your purpose in leaving
our settlement alone, on foot, with none to guide or protect
you. What silly, female notion set you to such a thing?"

"My reasons are for my own thoughts, Derand," I replied,
feeling the heat rise to my cheeks as I sought a dignity I found
difficult to attain under his stare. "You have the need to pursue
warrior arts, and I pursue needs of my own."

"Once we have returned, you will pursue no other thing than
preparing to be wed to my brother," he said, heavy annoyance
clear in him despite the dusk we stood in. "Had he not been
otherwise occupied it would have been he who rode after you,
and his questioning would not have had the gentleness of mine.
As soon as you have been restored to your lady mother I will
speak with my brother, and then we will see whose thoughts
your reasons are for."

He turned then and stalked away to join the others who had
already begun building a fire and unpacking provisions, leaving
me with the heaviness of spirit I had come to expect at the
mention of Tullin, brother to Derand and the man chosen to be
my husband. Our manless, landless household had been honored when Tullin had spoken of his desire to take me to wife,
and my mother had accepted the honor with great relief. I,
knowing her happiness, had been unable to speak my own feelings upon the matter, which had left me bound into a situation I

found well-nigh repellent. Tullin was much like Derand, only more so, and had there perhaps been another about who was filled more with the true spirit of so many of Escore men, my mother might have seen him in his true light . . . If, perhaps, there had been another, only there had not been.

I turned away from the knot of men and their fire, finding the quickly gathering dark a good deal more appealing than their company. Among those pillars the darkness of night seemed softer than usual, untinged with the apprehensions usually to be found, a refuge and haven rather than a menacing threat. Even the cool of the night air urged one to stroll rather than to retreat to the warmth of a fire, therefore did I succumb to the urge and begin to move about the area.

Even without the light of day as an aid, I soon discovered that the pillars about us had runes upon them, and not the runes we were used to seeing here and there about Escore. The blue-glowing carvings seemed to be as odd as Derand had suggested, and in some way that very oddness put me at ease. It was, perhaps, an oddness to match my own, one I had never spoken of to anyone, but one that had sent me out into hostile lands alone, seeking what no other had ever sought.

I sighed as I thought of that errand again, dreading the time Tullin would demand an explanation of my actions. What woman of sense would go off on her own, he would shout, exposing herself to the evil that lived and lurked all about in our land? How was I to say that I disbelieved in evil, that I had found it necessary to seek it out where it dwelt in order to learn what it truly was? Even if he were to believe my words, which he would not, he would surely never understand what lay behind them. In Escore one grew up in the shadow of evil and Dark Powers, knowing their reality, only one who was bereft finding it possible to deny them . . .

And yet I found it necessary to do no other thing than deny them. I could not, of myself, *accept* the concept of evil, in a way I found difficult to put into words. Certainly there was evil, the results of the use of Dark Powers, and certainly both existed. But what *was* evil, at the very root of its reality and existence? What was it composed of, and why did everyone fear it rather than ignore it? I, myself, felt no fear of it, only an impatience with the very thought of it, and no attraction to it whatsoever. Why was it at the center and core of everyone's thinking? I had often wondered, but of late the wondering had grown to a burning demand within me . . .

Which had sent me out a-searching on my own, with supplies sufficient to keep me alive until I was able to return. A day and a half I had traveled alone, finding nothing, and then I had begun feeling that I neared what I sought. I continued on, taking encouragement from the very air around me, losing track of the days, suddenly discovering that my supplies were not as sufficient as I had thought, and then Derand and the others had found me—before I found what had called to me so.

A broken branch on the ground caught at the hem of my dress, distracting me from the distress of my thoughts but scarcely banishing that distress. I had little choice about returning home, but how was I to go back without finding what I so needed to find? And how was I to explain that need to those who would ask? Had I been able to speak to one of the Green Silences I might perhaps have made myself clear, but women of our settlement were forbidden to associate with those allies of Power. Our men fought in their cause because it was also our own, but they had no wish to see their women "tainted" with the doings of magic. They had had so difficult a time with the wise women of Estcarp . . .

Which meant none of our women were even permitted an examination to see if they possessed the capacity for Power of their own. Our men refused to consider the presence of witches in their midst, refused to allow even the thought of it, and those of us who had grown from childhood with an emptiness and yearning deep inside had early been taught never to speak of it. Or to question it. The yearning would cease when we married, we had been told, and that would be an end to it.

"But what am I to do until then?" I whispered to the soft, deepening dark, feeling as though it stretched an arm about me in an attempt at comfort. "And what if I have no desire for such an end? And what if, even after my marriage, the end fails to come? What will I do?"

For an instant it seemed as though the runes decorating the pillars shone a more intensified blue in answer, but when I

looked directly at them they were just as they had been. My
need for understanding and support was so intense, then, that I
was beginning to imagine things, I thought. Even the close
presence of odd, lifeless runes was preferable in my mind to
standing alone and friendless . . .

"Merilan, come here to the fire," Derand called, the command in his voice allowing no room for argument. "You have
indulged in enough wandering these past days, and I mean to
have no more of it."

I turned about to see that he stood by the fire, his eyes directly on me, at that distance no more than a dark outline of a
man. A dark shadow, I thought, vehemently on the side of
Light, but nevertheless of the Dark when viewed in a certain
way. Was that part of what I sought, a true understanding of
the difference between Light and Dark? To say that one was
good and the other bad was in reality saying very little, at least
to *my* mind. What was bad for one was a blessing for another,
no evil to be found in it at all. How could such a thing be, when
good and evil were supposedly entirely at odds with each other,
no points at all in common? One was expected to *know* the
difference between the two, and so most did. But did they
judge the matter weighing the two points separately, or was it
personal taste and bias that brought about decision . . .

"Merilan, bring yourself over here *now!*" Derand insisted,
his annoyance growing almost visibly. "Would you have me tell
Tullin you refused to obey me?"

I knew he would likely tell Tullin exactly that, but the
thought that he might not was enough to start me walking
quickly toward him. It would be difficult enough for me when I
returned, and I could scarcely bear the thought of additional
difficulty. I was in a turmoil of questioning and doubt, my mind
aching . . .

And then the sight of Derand was gone, along with the solidity of the ground under my feet! I cried out once as I began to
fall, my heart thumping wildly, but it was not a bottomless pit I
had been plunged into. I fell no more than a very short distance
before my booted feet hit something of slick metal, and then I
was seated and sliding, down, down, into the ground. At first,
shock kept me motionless and silent, but then a sense of the

absurd came to replace that. To be taken by the unknown was
cause for fear and trembling, but how frightening was sliding
expected to be?

My ride to the bottom was not long enough to answer the
question. A faint blue radiance had been visible from the very
first, and when I reached the bottom of the slide I was able to
see rather well by it. What I slid on was indeed of metal, and it
straightened at its bottom so that I came to a stop on it rather
than abruptly finding myself off it and into physical harm. The
distance was not all that much below ground, and rather than
being in the dark of a cavern I looked about to see the stately
walls of a large, neat room. The blue radiance seemed to spread
to all the corners of it, illuminating it gently for ease of viewing.

Swinging my legs off the metal slide brought me to my feet,
and I stood there brushing at the skirt of my dress, looking
about at the place I had unexpectedly come to. There were
runes and figures carved into the walls and others implanted in
the smooth marble of the floor, and as I stood there a faint
humming came to me, as though something in the room lived. I
moved some steps away from the slide, in some way knowing I
had nothing to fear there, and heard next the tinkling of a foun-
tain. Behind the happy tinkling was the faint, far-distant sound
of the joyous laughter of children, as though that, too, were
contained in the room. Looking about again showed me nothing but the room, a quiet door hidden beneath the metal slide,
but the sounds continued to follow me as though the very air
contained them.

I circled the room filled full with curiosity and enjoyment,
wondering how I knew I was welcome in that place, wondering
at the eager, vital life force to be found in so quiet and ordered
a chamber. The room was old, I knew, older than a mere lifetime or two, but the dust of ages had not come to smother the
lovely blue of its glow. I felt then that the room itself, rather
than something in it, lived and hummed, and rather than being
frightened the thought pleased me.

My circling at last returned me to the place beside the slide,
and when I glanced again into the center of the chamber I saw
something I had somehow missed the first time. In its very heart
stood two slim, shimmering silver pillars, and between them, as

though contained by their very presence, a cloud of soft, flowing blue. Calm was that cloud, and beautifully warm despite its
color, and filled with a peace that one had only to touch in
order to share. My need for that peace was so intense that I
found myself moving toward the pillars without thought, desire
alone enough to send me forward. I meant to touch it and gain
what my desperation cried out inside me for, but I was still four
or five steps from it when I was unexpectedly halted.

"Merilan, what are you doing in this accursed place?" Derand's voice came, harsh with fear and suspicion. "Why did you
fail to answer when I called to you?"

I turned to see that Derand and two of the others had already
come down the slide, a third arriving even as I watched. They
stood with swords bared and eyes narrowed, too far drawn in
upon themselves to feel what the chamber offered them. They
were intruders in a place never meant for their kind, but even
so the room continued to attempt to welcome them.

"I heard nothing of anyone calling," I answered, feeling
again that inner shrinking at the accusation. "Had I heard you I
would have responded. Surely you believe that."

"I believe only what my eyes and ears tell me," he replied,
still with that terrible harshness. "Or what my sword bites into
and draws blood from. Come over here to us now, and quickly,
for I mean to see us out of this place as rapidly as possible."

"I will join you in a moment," I said, glancing over my shoulder at the calm blue that awaited my approach and touch.
"There is something I must do before I leave here, and it will
take no more than a . . ."

"You will join us *now*," he growled, the glare from his dark
eyes refusing even to allow me to finish the words I spoke. "I
said I mean to see us quickly out of here, and your female foolishness will not be tolerated. To linger in a place like this is
madness, and we, at least, are not mad."

His gaze attempted to hold mine and draw me to him by its
strength and power, and almost I succumbed to the command.
If I refused to obey him he would surely tell Tullin, and naught
save ill would come from such a telling. I *had* to obey him, and
yet . . .

The peace of the blue cloud awaited me, making no demands, holding no sense of accusation in case of failure, compelling nothing but offering all. The choice was mine, and I found that I had no choice but to do as my own nature directed.

As I had deliberately turned my back upon the settlement, so did I then do the same with Derand and his insistences, moving again toward the waiting cloud of blue. The silver pillars seemed to shine even more brightly with the shouts of anger and outrage that arose from behind me, but those who stood by the slide were too far away to halt me. In four steps I was only a pace away from the beckoning cloud, and even as I took the final step my hand was rising and reaching forward to touch what I had so great a need of.

All sound in the chamber ceased as my hand reached and entered that blue softness. Not a cloud, I saw at once, but what a cloud would be with no moisture or mist in it, a palpable softness and warmth that nevertheless allowed penetration with ease. It gave me what I had had as a child, when my father, before bloody battle had claimed his life, would take my hand in his. I had never, before or since, experienced such strength and warmth and uncritical support, and I stood whole again as I had stood in those long-dead days, knowing the peace I had known then.

Until, that is, I heard the gasps and moans from those who stood by the slide. I opened eyes that had closed in satisfied accomplishment, to see that the thick blue cloud was no longer as thick as it had been. It had already thinned to show the shadow of a form within, and even as I watched it thinned further and yet further. I found that I had withdrawn my hand and had taken a step backward, but that failed to halt what had been begun. The shadow cleared more and more, taking on firm shape and color and detail, and then the cloud was completely gone, leaving only what it had hidden.

A man with dark hair and clothing the likes of which I had never before seen. A man who wore bright colors and a sword, but no mail. A man who stood framed between the silver pillars as though they guarded his safety.

A man who opened dark eyes to look out at those in the chamber, and one who undoubtedly lived!

*   *   *

"Merilan, what have you done?" Derand hissed in agony from where he stood, clearly having come no closer. "Now you have doomed us all with your madness! Magic such as that is *evil,* and you have loosed it upon us!"

"What fool is it who calls magic evil?" the figure who had appeared asked in a scorn-heavy voice, stepping out from between the silver pillars. "Have you never been taught the difference between good and evil?"

"Who are you?" Derand demanded in a quivering voice as I backed from the advancing figure, not so much frightened as wary. Here was someone who seemed to know well the concepts of good and evil, and the compulsion within me refused to take notice of the fearful manner of his sudden appearance.

"I am Baelialt, lord of those lands you now stand as guest upon," the man replied, calm rebuke in his words for the harshness of the demand put to him. "Or perhaps I should say I was once their lord. How long have I slept?"

"How could we know?" Derand asked in turn, confusion and a cautious diffidence now coloring his tone. "Never have I heard of one called Baelialt, nor have our allies spoken of a time within their memory that these lands were claimed. You slept, you say?"

"In a manner of speaking," Baelialt agreed with something of a smile, as though he shared a jest with himself. "It will be easier, I think, if I put my query in another way: How long is it now that Light and Dark have ceased to do battle?"

"How long—?" Derand echoed, and I saw that the others looked to one another and murmured in upset, adding to Derand's distress. "You ask how long the battle has ceased? Your second query is more meaningless than the first, for battle between good and evil continues to rage as ever it did. What gave you to believe it would be otherwise?"

"My spell demanded that it would be otherwise," Baelialt returned with a frown, fists to hips as he sought within for a meaning to what had occurred. "I was not to be awakened until— Not even to be approached unless— How could such a thing be?"

"Your spell," Derand said, his face pale in the blue radiance, those behind him equally as shaken. "You—you are an adept, then—? Not ensorceled by the will of another, but by—"

"By my own desire and ability?" Baelialt finished when Derand did not, the scorn having returned to his voice and eyes. "Yes, I am an adept, and all you say is true. You fear the fact that I am not a victim?"

"A man fears what is, not what is not," Derand answered with the harshness returned to him, his fist closed more tightly about the weapon he had not as yet resheathed, and then his gaze moved deliberately to where I stood. "Do you see now what you have done, female of foolishness? You have returned one of *them* to our midst, and it is we who shall pay the penalty for your folly."

"You need not concern yourself over the composition of those in you precious midst," Baelialt said, the dryness and words for Derand alone, not even a glance for she who stood well to his right. "Although my desire is great to revel in your unparalleled proximity, circumstances force me to deny myself the pleasure. I shall return to the sleep from which I came, and hopefully will next awaken when there are those about who have no 'midst.' Remain or depart as you please, it will all be the same to me."

He turned back toward the silver pillars then, his intentions clear, and the relief to be seen on the faces of Derand and his men was well-nigh painful. Their need to be free of the presence of one of Power was understood by me, but I, too, had a need that would not allow denial.

"Wait!" I called as I took a step forward, forcing myself to speak where my words were so clearly unwanted. "I must know what you thought to find when your sleep was ended."

Baelialt hesitated on the very threshold of the silver pillars, one pace away from returning between them. For a moment I was certain he would ignore my question, and then he turned his head to regard me over his shoulder.

"I had thought to find that men had at last discovered the root of all evil, and had managed to exterminate it," he replied, the words more courteous than those addressed to Derand. "My spell was to awaken me at such a time, for there is much to be done and I am eager to begin. Are you able to tell me how near I am to such a time, Witch?"

"I am Merilan, not a witch, and do not believe that such a time will ever be," I said, the words coming from me as though another spoke them. "Should you return to your sleep, you will slumber on even after all memory of this world has ceased to be so much as a shadow. Had you voiced your spell differently, you would not have slept at all."

"For one who denies witchhood, you speak with the assurance of knowledge beyond that of others," he said, turning from the pillars to face me squarely. "Even now, after having reviewed it, my spell seems to me entirely adequate. What flaw do *you* find in it?"

"I . . . have not the ability to find flaws in a spell," I stumbled, suddenly more than diffident but unable to keep silent. "I know only that men will never find the root of evil, for there is no such thing as evil. Should that be the manner in which you voiced your commands, you will—"

"Do not heed her maunderings of madness!" Derand called from where he and the others continued to stand, a frothing madness of his own clear in the fury of his voice and eyes. "She will only delay your intentions, lord, and for no reason related to sanity. Once you have returned to that which awaits you, we will take her from here with utmost speed, so that you will not again be disturbed."

"So that I will not again be disturbed," he repeated, looking to Derand thoughtfully before returning his gaze to me. "My mind must truly be addled from having passed the ages by, for it had not occurred to me to seek more deeply into the true reason for my having been awakened at a time when I should not have been. What was done here, and which of you performed the doing?"

"It was she, lord," Derand pounced in triumph, allowing me no opportunity to speak in my own defense. "She it was who intruded upon your sleep, and awoke you before the time you had commanded. I ask that you spare her for so intrusive an action, for she is promised to my brother, yet should your anger be too great to contain, my brother will grieve but surely understand."

I looked to Derand with the shock I felt, but he showed no more than grim satisfaction over having abandoned me to whatever fate his accusation would bring. From the others there were looks of unease and discomfort, yet not one of them stepped forward to speak an objection. That I was supposedly one of them had no bearing, nor the fact that they were there through no insistence of mine. I had been offered up to assure their own safety, for my loss was more acceptable than theirs.

"I would expect your brother's grief to be as full as your own," Baelialt responded, and I saw that he stared at Derand with what appeared to be anger before returning his gaze to me. "Does he speak the truth, girl? Was it you who awakened me?"

"Such a thing was not my intention," I admitted heavily, needing to voice the truth despite trembling reluctance. "I saw the cloud floating between the pillars and felt what was within it, and the driving need would not allow me to depart without touching hand to it. I would offer my apologies for having disturbed you, and must add that those others had no part in what I felt it necessary to do . . ."

"Of that I have no doubt whatsoever," he interrupted the flood of my confession, the dryness of tone having returned to him as he glanced to the knot of nervously waiting men. "My spell would not have chosen ones such as they to bring to my rescue. You, however, are another matter entirely, and I offer my thanks for having allowed yourself to be drawn here to my assistance. If you had not allowed it, I would still be unaware of my error. I thank you for that as well, and would offer you a boon before I take my leave."

"Leave?" I asked, too stunned to reply to what he had said concerning a boon. "You mean to return to your slumber after all?"

"No, not to my slumber," he answered with a smile, paying no mind to the stirring and muttering coming from the men of my settlement. "I am now able to see that the hopes I had for the progress of men were in vain, and must therefore do as I was previously reluctant to do. I shall find a place all of my own, and there will labor in an atmosphere that this world will never know."

"An atmosphere where good no longer battles evil," I said, in some manner certain of what I said. "Or where evil no

longer battles good. For what reason do you believe this world
will never know such a thing?"

"You should find it possible to answer that question more
fully than I," he replied, and then his hand was raised before
him, tracing a shape of some sort in the air. Naught save his
fingers moved, and yet where they passed the shape was drawn
in sparkling blue in midair, to hover between us before fading.
"You are a witch who has not been permitted to be a witch, and
for no reason other than that men have not found the root of
evil. I would say, should all men nowadays be as these who
accompany you, that never will they find the root and conquer
it. May I ask that you speak now of the boon you would have?"

"You believe that Dark will find victory over Light?" Derand
demanded, his outrage causing him to intrude in the conversation he had earlier kept from. "I, for one, refuse to accept that,
nor will I accept unjust accusation against my people! That the
woman has not been allowed witchhood is good rather than
evil, for great suffering has ever been the lot of those who permitted witches among them. We have not taken the lives of
those who would have been witches, merely have we refused
them the Power that would have brought misery to us all. We
acted for the greater good, and there can be no evil in doing
such as that!"

"Ah, you believe so, do you?" Baelialt asked, turning his full
attention to the man who had addressed him in such an outspoken manner, more of a purr to the words than an edge.
"Since you have taken no lives outright, you consider yourselves as having done good? It may, perhaps, be possible to
alter that view. Your accoutrements suggest that you are a warrior; is this so?"

"Yes, I am a warrior," Derand allowed cautiously, no longer
as forward as he had been a moment earlier. It was clear he
mistrusted the adept's lack of anger, and likely already regretted having spoken his mind.

"I, too, was given the training of a warrior," Baelialt confided with a warm smile, touching left palm to hilt in confirmation of what he said. "In my youth I had need of such
training, as you and those with you have need of it, but I no
longer find it the same. Should the girl ask it of me as the boon

I offered, I will speak a spell that will no longer permit you and the others to retain what warrior skills you have thus far attained, nor relearn what you will have lost once it is gone. You will never again find it possible to name yourselves warriors."

"You could not do such a thing!" Derand gasped in shock, backing a step as the others did the same. "We would be forever bereft, half our lives taken from us! You could not commit such an evil act upon us!"

"Evil?" Baelialt asked with one brow raised, still held by calm amusement. "Are not warriors those who cause death and destruction when they ride to battle, leaving widows and orphans in the wake of the steel they swing? Surely *those* are the actions of evil, the ruining of innocent lives? I shall merely exempt you from the guilt of such terrible doings, saving you from yourselves and the accusations of others. Will that not, in reality, be an example of good?"

"But—but—what of *us*?" Derand stuttered, beside himself with fear and horror. "We do battle only against those who are enemy to us, never against the innocent! We have done nothing to deserve being denied what others are allowed, to be made to live with the knowledge of what we shall never be permitted to be! It would be a waking nightmare, doing nothing to halt battle, only to disallow our participation!"

"And yet you and those of your ilk chose to keep this child from a complete knowledge of her Power," Baelialt returned, and now his voice and stare were cold as steel in ice. "She could not help but know and suffer from the lack within her, but those of you who had no such suffering to endure found the denial given her no more than a comfort! Others brought about ill with the use of Power, therefore was it clearly her lot to be made to pay for the misdeeds of those others. For what reason should you not be made to do the same? For the reason of your innocence? In what manner might she not be considered equally as innocent?"

The men of my settlement stared wildly about themselves, searching for a reply that refused to come within reach of their desperately groping minds. To me it was clear they knew there was a great difference between what had been done to me and what was proposed to be done to them, only they were unable, at that moment, to put the difference in words. Because of this inability, rage took them over, and almost as one, swords raised high, they launched themselves at the adept who had threatened more than their lives.

I gasped in renewed shock as they started forward, certain a calamity was about to occur, unprepared for what did in fact happen. To hear of the doings of adepts is not as seeing the reality of the thing, and when Baelialt raised his right hand, I thought his movement no more than reflex, a feeble attempt to ward off the attack of those who came at him. A moment passed before I realized that they should then be reaching him, and were not; I looked over to them in confusion, saw them frozen in place—indeed in midstride!—and gasped a second time.

"When I release them, they will emerge unharmed," the adept said, and I saw that he spoke gently to me. "Do you still believe there is no such thing as evil?"

"They would be poor examples of evil under any circumstances," I replied, surprised to find that he had heard and recalled what I had said. "They are no more than men filled with fear, for themselves and their loved ones, and therefore not to be blamed for their actions. You, I see, have not blamed them either, for you have said they will be unharmed. How could you expect the root of evil to be found and eliminated, if there is no such thing as evil?"

"Ah, but there is such a thing as evil," he said, his previous amusement returned to him. "You, I take it, have been searching for it, but have not yet found it. The reason for that is that you have searched in the wrong places."

"But those in Escore claim that evil is all about," I protested, then suddenly found myself too weary to remain standing. I folded to the marble under my booted feet, and looked up with the confusion weighing me down. "I searched even in areas that withered life as I know it, but found only what was wrong for me, nothing that was evil. Am I as mad, then, as Derand insisted, to pass evil by and not know it for what it is?"

"To know what evil is *not* is not to be mad," he said with firmness as he moved toward me, then took a place on the floor opposite to where I sat. "When the battling began between those of Power, I thought, like others, that that was true evil, but then I was granted deeper insight. The Dark, they say, is true evil, but what is dark but the absence of light? Without light ones misses most of what there is to see, clinging only to the known that makes the dark more bearable to exist in. Such dark is far too limiting, therefore is light the preferable mode of existence. Those who insist upon dwelling in the dark—or the Dark—consider themselves courageous and powerful, never realizing how pitifully they have constricted their every effort."

"I . . . cannot follow your reasoning," I said, nearly pleading for the understanding I had such a need of. This man before me *knew,* of that I was certain, and I, too, had to know.

"Let us return to the very beginning, then," he replied with a gaiety to him, as though he greatly enjoyed converse such as we were engaged in. "When one discusses a point, one must define one's terms. Is the taking of a human life a matter of good or evil?"

"Such a thing is considered an evil," I ventured, supplying the response I felt he sought. "Should the question have been put to Derand, he would likely have answered so."

"As would most, if not all, others addressed so," he agreed with a nod. "And yet, is a human life not taken when a man is executed for some heinous crime? And are lives not lost in large numbers when battle is engaged in? And what of the wild beast? Is it evil when it slays a human being to keep from starvation? In each of these instances lives are lost, and yet the taint of evil is seldom, if ever, attached to them. They are termed 'necessary evils,' and as such are accepted."

"You believe these things should not be?" I asked, much concerned with what his reply would consist of.

"I feel you already know the proper answer to that," he said with a gentle smile. "These things are not evil, necessary or otherwise, merely are they necessary. We, even those of us named adepts, are no other thing than men; for what reason do we so long insist to ourselves that we are as the gods?"

"To be what you are is no shame," I agreed, feeling a warmth within my breast. "To seek to be the best of what you are is a worthy act, to seek to be other than what you are is naught save foolishness."

"Alas for the lure of foolishness," he replied with a sigh, then immediately brightened. "And yet, not all of us need be foolish. Those who claim to be of the Dark are foolish, for they know not what they do. Is fire a good thing or an evil?"

"Why—how can fire be evil?" I asked, startled by the abruptness of the query. "It warms us, cooks our food, permits the hardening of iron into steel— How might it be considered an evil?"

"Would you ask that of a family who has just lost its home to a fire run wild?" he returned, the look in his dark eyes sharp. "They could scarcely be expected to consider fire a boon and an aid, and yet we have most of us learned that destruction is not caused by *fire,* but by carelessness in dealing with fire. To allow a child access to fire, as though it were a toy, would be inviting disaster in as an honored guest. Might the *child* then be considered evil for having caused a disaster with fire?"

This time I did no more than shake my head, at last beginning to see the trail he led me upon. Soon it would be clear before my eyes, of that I had no doubt.

"No more, then, might those of the Dark be considered evil," he said, a quiet statement accompanied by a quiet smile. "They are as children experimenting with that which they have no full understanding of, and the disasters they cause have ignorance at their roots, not what men call evil. Not all life forms are able to exist in peace and harmony with ours, and to bring these forms into our world, in order to attain what is considered great power, is more idiocy than evil. They have not as yet learned what truly great power might be theirs, were they to bring light into the dark in which they grope."

He sighed then, and lay back upon the marble of the floor to gaze up toward the ceiling of the chamber, lost in might-have-beens.

"All seem to be aware of the fact that there is a balance in nature and in life, and certainly in magic," he said, a murmur directed upward but to me as well. "Those of the Dark use foul balances, ones to turn the stomach of all who learn of them, and in their use lose part of themselves to complete the balance. Had they the intelligence of more than children, they would have brought light into their dark, to see that there are more balances to be found, ones that are not half measures and therefore more effective. And a good deal less damaging to themselves and those about them.

"When one wishes to use fire, one takes certain precautions to be certain that they will not be charred during their use of that fire. Light, brought into the dark as a guard and a guide, will allow the safe use of what is essentially fire, and so the fire may be used to benefit everyone. The look of fire is so lovely that an innocent child will reach out to it barehanded, in order to capture its beauty, but an adult knows better than to do the same. I, as an adult, wished to bring to my fellow men what there was of benefit to be found in what all consider the Dark, but could not do so in a world that contained the root of evil. I therefore set a spell of sleep upon myself, commanding that I be awakened when evil was gone, and had I not added protection to the spell I would have slept on till eternity was past and gone. I am now forced to admit that my work cannot be done here, therefore must I seek elsewhere, for the labors must be performed. I could scarcely call myself a man, were I to shirk a duty such as that."

"You mean to turn the Powers of the Dark into that which may be used by the Light," I said, shuddering within me at thought of such an undertaking. "I had considered myself fully grown, and yet—I know not whether I would have the courage for such a doing. But there is still a thing I fail to understand. We have eliminated so many things from the calling of evil, that surely there is nothing left? My conviction that there is no such entity as evil must be correct, and yet you say our world contains the root of evil. How could this be?"

"Your confusion is understandable," he said, rising to sit again and to smile at me. "For you, there *is* no such thing as evil, for there is none of it within you. This is the reason my spell called you here, to awaken me, for no other might have accomplished it. And as I said earlier, you have failed to find evil for the reason that you sought it in the wrong places. The root of all evil is fear."

"Fear?" I echoed, lost again in confusion. "How might fear be the root of evil? And should it be so, then I am scarcely one without evil. There are many things I fear."

"To have fear within one is not, in itself, evil," he said, his gentle understanding soothing me even as he spoke. "Fear is necessary in that it keeps one from overly reckless ventures that might well end one's life. Fear becomes true evil when it rules the one it resides in, making that one view happenings and others only in its light. In you, fear is no more than a sensible caution, what it was meant to be. In others, however, it becomes something else entirely.

"For what reason would a man turn to the Dark in order to accomplish his aims? For fear, and only that. Fear that he will not accomplish it otherwise, fear that he will die before his life wishes are completed. For what reason does he seek power? For fear that another will gain greater power, and therefore be a danger to him. Fear of death, fear of poverty, fear of hunger—these are all things one would consider natural to fear, and yet most are willing to do anything to avoid them, rather than simply take on the determination to see that they do not occur. It was fear that kept you from your birthright, fear of what Power you would learn to wield. Trust and fellowship go by the boards in the presence of fear, as does common sense. Had fire been feared in such a way, its benefits would not now be ours. But fear breeds fear, and so the root will grow rather than wither and die. I cannot remain here and see such a thing, therefore shall I seek other lands, other places where the root has not yet taken hold."

"So you, too, have fears," I said, but gently, so that he would know I meant no criticism nor wished to give pain. "To seek the avoidance of evil is understandable, and I wish you great success and happiness in your pursuits. You have shown me what I sought so long in vain for, and now the demand inside me is stilled. There *is* no such thing as evil, no more than those poor souls tormented by the twisting within them. Some may need to be removed from the society of men in order to protect the innocent from them, but the others— It may yet be possible to save them."

"As I said, there is no evil within you," he repeated with a smile, reaching out with a hand that halted before it touched me. "I have many long, lonely years ahead of me, and now I would ask a boon of *you*. Become my wife and accompany me where I go, and we may each learn from the other. There are so many things I would teach you—and so many I would learn from you."

"I . . . am honored to be asked such a thing," I answered, disconcerted and flustered and suddenly realizing that I wished it might truly be. "To learn and share would be a delight—but to abandon those of my world I might be able to aid would be to bring true meaning to the word evil. I . . . cannot leave them alone with their fears, for fears are always greater when one is alone."

"Yes, fears are always greater when one is alone," he agreed, his dark eyes now sad as they rested on me, and then he shook his head and sighed. "I should have known better than to become enmeshed with one lacking evil—or, if you prefer, one lacking fear. The disease is apparently contagious, for I have now myself contracted it. As you mean to remain, so shall I do the same, and together we will dig out the root and watch it die."

"Together," I agreed with great happiness, putting my hand in the one he extended to help me to stand. I would need to be extremely gentle with Tullin, but knowing that it was fear that moved him would allow me to be understanding of what he was. Understanding, I thought as we turned toward those who needed freeing from the positions they had been frozen in. Could that be the opposite of what I had been seeking?

If fear was true evil, could understanding be true good?

Afterword

While I was growing up, I somehow missed all of Andre Norton's work. Before you start feeling sorry for me, though, please remember that that means I had the pleasure of finding them after I was grown. They were instrumental in making me see how much pain some people go through, and very often for the wrong reason or no real reason at all. Everyone in charge of others, everyone in a position of authority, seems to think he or she knows just exactly what evil is. What they apparently have no trouble missing is that what you consider evil may be holy to the next guy, or fun, or perfectly acceptable in everyday life. The one basis of measurement—is someone being hurt by that practice—is considered as rarely today as when Heinlein first mentioned it. It doesn't mean "Are your feelings being hurt or your opinions offended?" It means "Is someone actually, directly, being hurt because this or that is being done?" Andre's work let me link up some of the ideas I hadn't put together before now, and that's only one of the things to thank her for.

—Sharon Green

KNOWLEDGE

by

P.M. Griffin

Aden moved swiftly along the familiar corridor, one of the nearly countless strands in the web uniting the chambers and rooms forming the heart of Lormt, the repository of the knowledge her very ancient people had accumulated through their long history.

The greater part of what was stored here was forgotten now, the records of it set down in languages or variations of languages no longer comprehensible to the most learned of her race, yet still that knowledge waited, ready to quicken the eager mind of one who could somehow learn once more the meaning of the words in which it was inscribed.

Such a sage was unlikely to come now, with the Old Race and, seemingly, every other of honor or worth beleaguered by foes and able to think of little beyond the waging of war to preserve themselves and the stark needs of survival. Under such conditions, small attention could or would be given to parchments and scrolls moldering away amidst the dust of time on the shelves of a repository that seemed to many more a shadow of a lifeway and a world long since faded and dead than a real part or any part of their own turbulent age.

The very residents of the place gave credit to such belief. It was not a living community in the usual sense. The greatest number of those dwelling and working here were men, very old men, who sat through long, quiet days at square tables or round tables in dimly lit chambers, reading or copying from disintegrating scrolls or merely dozing with the ancient manuscripts spread out unnoticed before them. Rare visitors to the silent rooms usually came forth again with the feeling that those they had seen, like the materials they purported to study, were but memories of what once had been.

The woman knew better. She, too, was part of Lormt, and she saw what outsiders did not. Truly, there were some here who drowsed gently through their days, but many only used sleep as a mask, a shield against the pain strangers roused in them. Their bodies might be frail, but the minds of most were fine. They disliked and resented pity and even more strongly detested the ignorance and indifference of the outer world. They mourned that so much of what was their trust and their love would almost certainly be lost because so few came to take up their work when their course in this life was at last run.

In one sense, Aden did not entirely regret that. She was not so long or so completely withdrawn from the violence and hardship of existence beyond these thick, gray walls that time had softened her memory of its ways. Perhaps it was better that the knowledge stored here should fade and die. Too much of it dealt with Power in one aspect or another, and she had little liking for the idea that something learned within this place should be used to bring still further misery on people already far too familiar with it. Certainly, she had not found much to comfort her in the handful who had come to Lormt on one quest or another during the period of her service here. A few of the seekers had patently been fine, high-souled beings right enough, but she put small trust in the rest of them.

All the same, despite her fears, a pang of grief shot through her, as it always did when she thought of the decay around her. Lormt held the history and heritage of her people, her world. The loss of what lay here would be the loss of their very birthright, an irreparable tragedy more wrenching than any wasting of goods or gold, although few outside these walls appreciated that danger, and fewer still were willing to trouble themselves at all to avert it. Even she and Jerro did not really do as much as they might . . .

The woman's eyes closed momentarily as fear knotted her stomach.

She tried to grip herself. There was no need for such concern, she told herself sharply. It was a common failing she had observed in her companions here, one she did not want to see develop in herself, this overresponse to any deviation from the norm in their peaceful existence, as if such were a major disaster.

The argument was logical, but Aden could not convince herself that it applied here. Jerro could be thoughtless enough at times, and he often came late when he promised to meet with her during his visits to Lormt. Occasionally, if he found some trail that really captured his interest, he missed an appointment entirely simply because he forgot it, but her brother was not completely insensitive. He would not vanish for two full days without sending some word as to his whereabouts and the nature of whatever held him. Indeed, he usually issued a call for her help in his digging if the project were in any way involved. Nay, she had to put enough trust in him in that respect to seek for him now.

She knew where to begin, at least. Like herself, Jerro had his favorite chambers, those that were rich in material on the topics he most loved to delve. There was no reason to panic until she had sought for him thoroughly in all of them.

The woman sighed, thinking of the task ahead of her. It seemed inconceivable on the surface that anyone could come into danger in Lormt, but with her brother, she simply could not be sure. When the mood struck him, he was as avid a seeker after knowledge as she, and when some hunt gripped him powerfully, there was little that could turn him from it. Unfortunately, whereas she was content to read and to know a thing in her mind, he had a tendency to try what he learned for himself, sometimes before he had gathered all the facts to him.

She stepped under an archway and passed through a door left carelessly ajar. It opened into one of the larger chambers, where a single, aged man sat, bent over a large tome bound in

KNOWLEDGE

leather that had once been brightly dyed but was now faded to
a muddy gray shade. There was no sleep on him. Ouen's expression was as quick and sharp as the wind of spring's first
month. It was welcoming, and she made him a good approx-
imation of a courtly bow although she did not otherwise pause.
He made no effort to stay her but only smiled and waved her
on.

Her own expression softened. This man was her teacher as
well as the one who had ordered her to her work, and he had
never held her back from any search she wanted to make, believing that to be more important than any shifting of dust. But
then, she had given him reason to trust her, always fulfilling her
duties even if she had to work far into the night to do it.

Aden left the chamber through a smaller door breaking the
wall opposite the entrance. She hesitated outside it. Ouen
would help her if he knew the weight on her . . .

Nay. It would be wrong to disturb him yet. If she failed to
find Jerro herself, aye, then she would call on him, on them all,
but for the moment, she must do her looking herself.

She would not be delayed long in the areas immediately
ahead of her. Her brother rarely tarried long here.

This was her territory, and even in her worry, her fingers
reached out almost of their own accord to caress a shelf on her
right as she passed close to it.

The ways of animals and plants fascinated Aden, as did the
sea and the workings of the land itself, all that made the world
what it was. The healing arts, she studied avidly, and she gave
freely of the knowledge she gained, to the good of a number of
people both in Lormt and in the village just beyond its walls
where she had been born.

Power did not interest her, possibly because she had no store
of it and was denied the wonders those possessing it and trained
in its use could wrought. Her motives for her lack of enthusiasm in this area did not worry her. No one could like or absorb
everything, and she had more than enough to do in the broad
fields that did captivate her.

If she did not care for witchery itself, the people who worked
with it were another matter. The woman sought out everything
she could discover about them, both records and tales of more

recent history, the better part of which she had learned before making her life in Lormt, and legends of mighty adepts who had lived and wielded Power and will in the dim past. Above all the rest, she strove to learn all she might about those Great Ones whom most considered to be gods, though some held them to have been men and women who had risen so far in their Power that they had advanced beyond humanity into another state entirely, a category that also held a larger number of other beings who had never been accorded the attributes of divinity.

They all drew the interest and efforts of her mind, but only Gunnora aroused any real feeling in her. That one was The Lady of life in all its fruitfulness and in its darker aspects as well, the patroness of women and their children. Although no man raised a sanctuary in her name or addressed petitions to her, Aden believed that to be the work of humankind and not the Goddess, if such she be, herself. Gunnora seemed too great a part and mistress of the balance apparent throughout all the rest of the world's realms to be the author of so unnatural a distinction.

For her own part, Aden did not worship Gunnora, for she was not certain in her heart that she was indeed a being to whom that honor should rightly be rendered, but her studies had, in truth, made her love that Great One and all she represented.

A wave of nervousness swept through her, stopping the ranging of her thoughts. Soon she would be leaving these familiar, well-browsed chambers for those less frequently visited, the ones in which Jerro was wont to roam during his increasingly frequent visits. Her search had been a cursory one to this point, but it must be carried in earnest from here on in, she hoped to a successful and pleasant conclusion. She had determined before starting out that he was not in any of Lormt's more public places or in the chamber assigned for his personal use. If she failed to discover him in the halls ahead, then she would know for a fact that there was probably very sound reason for the worry tearing her ever more sharply since yesterday evening.

*   *   *

Three long, weary hours went by without a break or brightening in the woman's search. She had by then passed through all her brother's normal haunts and came to rooms and corridors rarely if ever visited, perhaps not once in the year or in five years, places never coming under her care or any other's within the memory of Lormt's oldest citizen.

That very neglect helped to keep her moving, kept the hope alive in her heart although it seemed to her that she must have traveled the entire length of the huge building, as a measuring of the convoluted ways she walked would have proved to be the case several times over. The dust lay thickly here, on floor as well as on shelf, and it had been so disturbed as to indicate that some other had come this way not too very long in the past. The tracks seemed to be going in but one direction, and she thought, though she had not the skill to read them with any certainty, that they had been made by a man, or at least by someone with feet much larger than her own.

Aden continued on for another half hour. She was too tired by then and too concerned to wonder even fleetingly about the contents of these seemingly eternal rows of shelves although she probed every recess and space between them.

When would she come to the end of this infernal trail? What would she find there?

She battled down the panic threatening to overwhelm her. Very well, she thought. That mental outburst was a warning to her. She must stop, rest for a while and eat, or her body would betray her. The last thing she needed at this point was to lose control of herself.

The woman looked around the next chamber she entered and spotted a stone bench set beneath one of the tall, narrow windows. It looked inviting despite the inevitable layer of dust, and she went over to it. Her clothes were already so begrimed after her day's efforts that a few more stains would scarcely be noticeable.

She slid her light pack from her shoulders and took out the supplies she had brought with her, bread of her own baking and a small traveler's bottle of water.

As Aden ate, her thoughts drifted back through the years.

She could not recall a time when she and Jerro were not comrades. They had been born within a year of each other, and because fate had decreed that there were no others of quite that age in their village, they had grown up closer than was normally the case with siblings of different genders.

Life had been good to them. The offspring of the tanner in a little community that had been spared the horrors and most of the hardships vested on so many others, they had been raised in a good measure of what their kind termed comfort and in a reasonable degree of freedom.

Her brother had nearly always been the leader in exercising that last. Although the younger of the pair, all the courage and daring seemed to be his, and many had been the time she had followed him only because she, then considerably larger and stronger, felt bound to protect and care for him when they were away from their mother's watchful eye.

It was through him that they had first come to Lormt. When Aden was in her eighth year, Jerro had idolized his older cousins and followed them everywhere. To rid themselves of their small shadow, they had told him that he must scout Lormt's halls and report back to them if he wished to be part of their company, feeling certain that would cow him. The strange old building was a source of awe and dread to all the younger children and perhaps still had been a little daunting even to them.

They had underestimated her brother's determination, and that very afternoon he had set out with her as his very unwilling accomplice.

They had been caught almost at once, of course, as soon as they passed into the first courtyard. Terror had held them in place, or they should readily have been able to outrun their captor, but they were soon put at ease. The man who had taken them introduced himself as Ouen and told them of the work being done in the ancient place, then he had brought them around some of the rooms so that they could see the old books and scrolls for themselves.

The two children had returned again and again. Her eyes brightened, glowing almost like coals in a dark room as that memory rose up in her. They learned to read those scrolls and discovered how words changed and grew in meaning as years rolled by until their old significance could be and frequently was completely forgotten. They both became expert, even as were their teachers, at ferreting out those meanings and pushing back with them to discover those more ancient still. As they grew older, their duties at home inexorably increased, but they still had found the time or made the time or, on occasion, stole the time to keep coming back.

Eventually, Jerro was apprenticed to his father, and she had taken service in Lormt, a move her kin much favored, for her skill in heal craft had already aided them, both themselves and their beasts, and they saw it to their benefit that she acquire still more of that learning.

Since that time, she had maintained herself by preparing her teachers' food and caring for their few garments and their chambers, both those where they slept and the larger places they frequented most in their labors. It was light work compared with what she had done in her father's house or would have faced had she been wed with one of the village lads, and through it all, she was given good time and good training in her explorations until in the end she had won an equal's place among the others. Indeed, the need to perform the labor to which she had originally bound herself had been lifted from her nearly two years previously, when Jerro had become his own master, and she continued with it chiefly to honor and comfort these ones who had become as dear to her as any blood kin.

Her existence in Lormt was good. She did miss the company of others like herself now and then, and she regretted that there was so little of laughter and nothing of song here, but Jerro came often—even through the long years of his apprenticeship, he had come—and his visits always cheered and brightened her, even as did those she herself made to her own people.

She bit down hard on her lip. He had arrived three days before, and on that first evening, he had all but flown into the small hall in an excitement he had refused to share, saying this was a trail he wanted to follow to its conclusion first. She had not seen him since then.

Aden buried her face in her hands. If only she had pressed him while she had had the chance!

Her fingers sought the tight little pocket she had sewn in her tunic and closed over the object it held. She drew it forth and clasped it tightly, drawing comfort from it, as she always did when some trouble was on her.

She opened her hand after a moment and looked at it. Gunnora's amulet, but like no other of its kind that she had ever seen. It was fashioned of bronze but was exquisite in the perfection and detail of its workmanship, so that stalk and vine seemed minute versions of reality in all save color and material. Tiny, brilliant white stones formed the grains crowning the stalk, and dull, round ones, equally small, represented the fruit of the vine encircling it. She had found it at the very back of a shelf, buried under an unsalvageably decayed manuscript, during her first week of service in Lormt. Although she had loved it, she had dutifully offered it to Ouen, but the old man had refused it, telling her it was like to a gift from the Goddess herself and that it was not a thing to which any man had a right. He had charged her to care for it well, an unnecessary caution in her case, and to treasure it.

Aden did not return it to her pocket now although she felt immeasurably calmer. She continued to hold it as she sat back, her eyes closed, trying to think.

The woman had not come this way before, but all of Lormt was mapped, and she made herself recall the sketches she had seen of its buildings and the winding ways within them, seemingly winding, for this was in actuality no maze but only a complex of rooms laid out to fill a purpose no longer really familiar to the descendants of those who had planned it. Her people had fallen back, in that respect, at least.

She thought she knew where she was. If she were right, this should be nearly the end, with only one long hall and a final room to be examined. If she found nothing in either, her hope would be exhausted.

Aden passed out of the chamber where she had taken her rest and started down the hall beyond it. This was indeed long, and she found it oppressive although she could not at first say why she thought it so. No less light reached it than any of the others through which she had come. No greater volume of dust lay upon it, yet it seemed almost unbearably dismal to her.

Her step faltered. Nay. It was more than that. She felt threatened here, and the sensation of danger grew ever stronger the nearer she drew to the door at its farther end.

Nerves! Night shadows! she screamed at herself, but she clutched the amulet more tightly as she pressed determinedly onward. The tracks still led on before her, and where that walker had gone, she could right well follow.

The door, one like all the many others in the ancient repository, was closed, but it gave easily under the pressure of her hand, revealing a small, close room. No other exit that she could see led from it.

No one seemed to be inside. Her heart sank, but she stepped forward. The tracks were there, but they were now much confused, as if some seeker had ranged from one packed shelf to another in the joy and drive of his searching.

She, too, wandered up and down those aisles, looking for any sign of her missing kinsman, or of the author of the tracks she had followed should he be another.

The woman had examined more than half of them when she came suddenly to a halt, held by surprise. There on the wall before her, so set that it caught and reflected the full light of the window opposite it, was a glass, taller and broader than herself, such as a great lady might yearn to own. It was truly a wonderful thing, not only large but remarkably clear and free of distortion.

She peered into it. Her image looked back at her with scarcely a waver to mar it . . .

Aden screamed. The body was hers, but the face—the face was Jerro's!

She looked again. Nay. It was only herself.

She took a deep breath to steady herself. She knew what she had seen. Aden fought down her fear and the numbing lash of shock. This was a thing, a work, of Power, and it was essential that she be calm and in full control of herself when she dealt with it, or tried to deal with it.

How she wished now that she had availed herself of the wealth of information that had been laid out for her taking all these years! Even that which could still be read would have vastly fortified her for this challenge. At the very least, she might have learned with what she was contending and how best to move against it.

Regret, too, she put from her. It was too late for that. She must go forward with what she had.

The woman gazed into the mirror once more. Aye, her brother's face was there in place of her own. His eyes were starting in terror, and his lips were moving. Her heart twisted in anguish. He did not appear to be aware of her, but he was calling her. Over and over again, he was calling her name.

Emotion must not take her now! Think! Utilize what she had learned. It might have come to her indirectly while she had studied other matters, but she still had gathered in a great deal of information upon which she could and must now draw in her need.

Of all the things this accursed glass might be, the woman realized it was probably one of three. It could be a Gate into some other realm that Jerro had tried to enter and failed, or else failed to effect the return. It could be a device set long ages past to trap men or maybe any living creature blundering into it. Lastly, it could be a creature that fed upon the life substance of those it ensnared or a device to aid in such feeding.

The first, she discounted. People were sealed on one side or the other of a Gate, not, to her knowledge, actually within one. The third was almost too terrible to contemplate, a thing of the true and deep Dark. Such did exist, but always, they emitted that which struck horror and sickness into the very souls of even those like herself possessing no shadow of Power, warning, if sometimes too late, what they were. She was uneasy, but she did not feel that. Logic said the second possibility was the soundest, that this was a trap, but nothing very much more.

Very well, she would accept that, at least as a working premise. It was quite enough. How was she to move against it, free Jerro from its infernal hold?

She pressed herself against it, but all she could feel was the cool smoothness of the glass. Her fingers ran over it, carefully sliding across the whole of its surface and then along its unframed sides and bottom. A large tome dragged from the shelf beside it gave her the height necessary to perform the same search of its top.

To no avail. There was no break or seam, nothing to give entrance or release.

Tears sprang to her eyes. What was she to do? She knew enough not to try smashing the foul thing. That would only serve to slay her brother outright or, worse, to lose him, bind him forever in whatever state of existence or nonexistence he was presently held.

She had to move soon. That, too, was clear. His face, his lips, had an ugly blue cast to them. He had already been trapped for some two days, and the air that had been sucked in with him must be well-nigh exhausted. If she could not free him almost at once, then she had come to this place merely to watch him die.

Her hands balled convulsively. This was wrong, so very wrong, a violation of all justice! Some men, a very few, might merit such an end, but not Jerro. He was kind, open, loving, with nothing at all of villainy or guile in him . . .

A sharp pain in her right hand restored her to her senses. She willed her fingers to open and saw that she had clasped the amulet so tightly that the sharp little stalk had pierced her flesh, drawing blood.

"Oh, Gunnora," she whispered in desperation, "I know males are not supposed to be in your province, but he would be well worthy of your care, and I love him."

Aden stopped. Her hysteria vanished in the thought that had come suddenly to her.

Stones were used for polishing and cutting things, glass among them, and those tipping this symbol were very sharp. Perhaps they would be sharp enough and hard enough to serve her purpose.

It might avail her nothing even if she did cut the glass, or maybe she would only precipitate the same disaster that would come of breaking the mirror outright, but this was Gunnora's symbol, Gunnora who could not but be revolted by such foulness. If Jerro was a man, well, she was a woman, and it was she who strove, she who feared and grieved, she who loved.

Fighting to still the trembling of her hand, Aden moved nearer the glass. Slowly, carefully, she began to trace as closely as she could the outline of her body as it was reflected there, pressing as hard and steadily as she could with the sparkling head of the stalk.

Her eyes flickered up to follow its progress, and her breath caught. Aye! It was working! A thin, seemingly very deep line now scored the once-smooth surface.

At first nothing happened besides that physical marring, but no sooner had she completed outlining the head of her image and Jerro's than a noise began, a hissing rush followed fast by a rumbling that seemed to her overwrought senses to be the dying of a world.

She hastened as much as she dared and tried not to look at her brother's face. It was slack now, the eyes closed. Were her efforts for nothing after all?

There was a cracking sound, the splintering of glass, and a great weight fell forward upon her.

She went down under it but quickly rolled the body off her so that it lay on its back.

Jerro, and his lungs no longer drew in air.

Aden's fingers pressed into the side of his neck and were met by the thrice-welcome throb that told her his heart still beat.

Steady, she commanded herself fiercely. Not one but many scrolls had told her what she must do.

The woman placed her mouth over her brother's, forcing air into him until his chest expanded with it. She let it remain thus a moment, then pressed down so that his lungs emptied once more.

Again and again, she repeated the process until her body screamed with such weariness that it threatened to collapse under the effort she was demanding of it.

Somewhere within herself, she found the will to continue. Jerro's heart still beat, and while it did, life remained his. If she stopped, she would be his slayer.

The light streaming in through the window paled and became gray. Aden drew in yet another lungful of air to give him when suddenly she heard a low moan. She looked down, hope and disbelief warring in her heart. His chest rose, fell, and rose again.

Minutes later, his eyes opened. They were slow to focus, but when they did, she saw with relief that they knew her.

"Aden . . . The Gate . . . A fair garden, then nothing . . ."
She pressed her fingers to his lips.

"Say nothing for a while. Gather your strength."

The woman looked up at the mirror for the first time since
she had freed her brother from it. The whole upper portion was
shattered, but some of the lower third remained. She glanced
about her, spotted the book she had used to aid her examination of the trap, and sent it hurtling through the glass, shattering it utterly. Never again would it snare the innocent and
unwary.

She picked up Gunnora's symbol from amongst the shards
and carefully returned it to its pocket, then turned back to
Jerro. He was sitting up, still weak but rapidly recovering his
strength. After a few days' rest, he should be fully himself once
more, although she fervently hoped that he would have acquired some measure of caution from his experience.

Wearily, she got to her feet and retrieved the torch she had
prudently put into her pack before starting out on her hunt.
They would need it before they had made their way half the
distance back to the living quarters.

Tomorrow, she would return here to sweep up the fragments
of the deadly mirror, after first consulting with Ouen as how to
best dispose of them, but she felt at ease in her heart about
leaving them for this night. No danger remained. The quiet
calm that was Lormt's mark filled the chamber in place of the
glowering threat that had struck at her earlier. Nothing was left
for her or anyone else to fear.

She smiled. Lormt was cleansed, Jerro was safe, and if she
would not forget the events of this day, the memory would be
one upon which she would be able to build to the enrichment of
her life and her mind. Perhaps by recording it, she might one
day help work a similar victory for others who stood the Light's
cause in the ancient and yet ever-new war with the Shadow and
the Dark.

Her head raised suddenly. That was the purpose of Lormt
itself, the reason, the paramount reason, why it had been
founded in the distant past, and in recognizing that, in subscrib-
ing herself, instinctively, to that purpose, she had vindicated
Lormt's continued existence and the worth of the life's work
she had chosen to make her own.

Afterword

Andre Norton's Witch World has always been a fascinating universe for me. It seems to hold a story for everyone, not only the nobly born lord or lady, the powerful witch, the valiant fighter. The battle of Light against the Dark involves everyone, those of humble origins, human abilities, and quiet lifeways as well as the great.

Of the many places mentioned in Andre's books, I find Lormt, that "repository of ancient knowledge," among the most intriguing. I have often thought about the place and the people living and laboring there—who those folk might be, the work they do, the purpose they serve in the great conflict. Thus was born in my own mind the tale of my part research librarian, part charwoman and her search through Lormt's halls that Andre's invitation allowed me to bring to life. It was a great pleasure to write the story, and I hope it will bring great pleasure to those who read it.

—P. M. Griffin

THE CIRCLE OF SLEEP

by

Caralyn Inks

Felde looked down at the ruddy puddle in the snow, admiring the pattern the frozen red crystals made. Appalled at finding beauty in Tamar's iced blood, when she lay dead not ten feet away, Felde began to walk. Tamar was the tenth person in her border patrol to die. By the Old One, they were only an hour from home. Would any of them make it back to Sharoon Keep alive, short one horse and with death stalking them?

She glanced at the unconscious prisoner, visually checking his bonds. His feet were securely tied to the saddle stirrups. With his body slumped, face buried in the horse's mane, it was hard to see his bound hands. Felde wondered if her father would consider him worth the price. Lord Alesanfar wanted a live Alizon to question. Felde was not sure what she was bringing him.

Who was this man that his Alizon companions fought to the death to protect? Obviously not their prisoner for he had fought alongside them, using Power against her border patrol.

Until now no one Alizonian had been known to possess the Gift of Power. Only a lucky blow had knocked him unconscious. Toward the end of the skirmish the Alizon leader had tried to kill him, rather than let him fall into their hands.

Though the Alizonian wore the outer guise of humanity,
their essence was completely alien to mankind. All humans
experienced total revulsion in their presence. Then why did
she not feel that when near the prisoner? What was he? A
half-breed? What woman could lie with one of the hated non-
humans and not die before giving birth to that unnatural melding?

Questions. They danced in her head, nearly driving her mad.
She did not have answers. At the moment all Felde wanted was
to get her hands on this four-footed fellow warrior.

That hell-spawned bitch had tracked them for the past six
days, trying to free its master. Eleven horses and ten men the
hound had killed. It seemed deathless, like one of the undead
wrapped in tattered shades of Power. The border patrol had
named it Ghost, and not until Felde saw the wounds that they
dealt to the great white dog appear on their prisoner did she
understand. The Alizonian wizard was not unconscious, but in
a trance that allowed him to take on the wounds of the hound
and then heal them both.

She set her feet down hard as if she could pound anger and
grief out through the heels of her boots. Rage and grief were
doors through which the Dark Ones could find entrance.
Within her, her Gift for the Power roiled and strained to be
unleashed. Felde was deeply troubled. Her distress grew when
as she walked past the prisoner, again the talisman she wore
beneath her clothing changed size and grew warm. It was the
sudden awakening of the talisman that had drawn her and the
border patrol to him and the hidden Alizonian war band.

Several years ago she had found the talisman in the ruins of a
place of the Old Ones. Though she had tried many times to use
it, the force within it slept. All these years she had sought the
key that would awaken it. Now the thing would not be still, but
constantly shifted, phasing into different sizes and weights as if
stretching itself after a long sleep. She wanted to deny the
truth, to shout, *NO, the wizard cannot be the key,* but could not
lie to herself. He was. Also he was the enemy. So Felde tamped
down the Power within, afraid of what would happen if she
used it.

"Mount up," she called out. The snow was beginning to fall

in fat, wet flakes. Good cover for Ghost. "Harn, double up with Lanis. Ierdon, you take the prisoner's reins. We all ride."

Behind her she heard the sound of claws scrabbling for purchase on stone. She wheeled about to peer through the falling snow. She saw nothing.

The gates of Sharoon Keep opened. Her father, Lord Alesanfar, and a small company of men rode out to meet them.

"By the Power of Min's Nine Words, Felde," shouted Alesanfar, "what happened to the patrol?"

"Watch and ward. I'll explain once we have the prisoner inside," she said.

Her father nodded, called out to his men, "Surround them, swords out! Prepare for attack."

Felde glanced nervously about. Until they were behind the walls of the keep, she would not feel secure. Tension crawled along her spine and her Gift lapped inside her as if storm-tossed. She knew Ghost was near.

The forefront of their group passed under gate-lintel. Felde glanced up at the face of Min her father had mounted above the gate. Felde herself had carved the likeness out of a blue stone she had found while wandering through the ruins of an Old One's place of Power. The stone still held traces of that Power, a ward against forces of the Dark.

There was a shout. She whirled. The prisoner was awake, standing upright in his stirrups. Behind the half-breed Alizonian, his guard's horses reared. Someone screamed, a mournful wail of anguish. Felde reined her mount around, kicking it in the side. She recognized that outcry. She had heard it several times during the harrowing trek here. Only the dying made that certain sound. She scanned the wildly bucking horses and was not surprised to see a gray-white streak weaving between and under the horses. Ghost!

"Ierdon, the hound!" she yelled. He did not hear her over the noise. She was relieved to see he still had a firm grip on the prisoner's mount.

The Alizonian! What *was* he doing? He stood in his stirrups, his mount unnaturally still in the midst of the melee. Though his wrists were bound, the half-breed held his arms stretched

upward to their limit, hands clenched into white-knuckled fists
as if they were indeed weapons. Felde looked at his face. His
concentration was focused on the image of Min. He was speaking words—words of Power. Bits and pieces of information she
had suddenly fell together.

Felde shouted in warning, "He's a Power shaper! Stay back."
She fought to reach his side. She gained an inch, then a few
more. Again Felde called, "Iredon!"

He glanced toward her. In that instant of distraction Ghost
appeared. The hound leaped upon Iredon's horse, paws scrabbling on the leathers. With a movement almost too rapid for
Felde to see, the hound slashed Iredon's throat and whirled to
face its next opponent.

Felde freed her feet from the stirrups and leaped from the
saddle, drawing her dagger. She crouched, readying herself to
leap onto Iredon's horse when the hound's eyes met hers. They
were a hot, blazing blue. In the instant their gazes locked,
Felde felt a buried, atavistic response rise inside her, a corre-
sponding wildness that matched the Ghost's feral intelligence.
She fell back, as if sword-struck, grabbing her mount's mane to
keep balanced. Felde stretched forth a hand to the blood-spat-
tered dog. Ghost whined, shook its head, and fell back to the
ground to crouch beneath its master's horse. The hound's
movement jerked her back into awareness of her surroundings.
Felde yanked her hand back.

Iredon's body slid to the ground. She had changed from her
horse to his, shoving aside all thoughts of the strange confrontation with Ghost. She whispered a word of Power into the
horse's ear, lending it the ability to stand still among the carnage and confusion.

The Power the Alizonian manipulated densified the air. She
labored to breathe. Felde raised her inner defenses to shield
against his Power. Her responses were turning sluggish, as if
wrapped in a heavy shroud. Felde forced herself to grab at the
reins of the Alizonian's mount. She missed. Tried again. The
moment she touched the mane of his horse, the half-breed
shouted words of release. The smothering Power surrounding
them shifted and the talisman on Felde's breast leaped in response, straining against the clothes that concealed it. Felde

looked from the wizard's extended fingers to the stone face of Min. The spell exploded on the Old One's image. Silver-gray sparks showered like shooting stars. The wood surrounding the blue stone burst into flame.

What was he doing? Felde strained to see through the smoke and dust. When the air cleared she saw a gouge in Min's cheek. It could not be! The wound was bleeding!

"By the Nine Words," she whispered, "the Alizonian can use the inanimate to make contact with the live Power it represented."

The half-breed wizard shouted in triumph and kneed his horse. Her hold on its mane broke. She lost her balance, fell to the ground, and froze. Above her loomed Ghost. The hound placed a paw on her arm and growled.

Felde gripped her knife. Its point rested between the hound's large, foremost pair of teats. Once again she met Ghost's eyes. The empathy that had been there before leaped between them again, stronger.

"Why can't I kill you?" Felde whispered. She felt bewildered by the strength of her response to this female beast. This was her enemy. Ghost had killed many of her men.

The huge dog leaned forward, pushed its nose through her hair, and sniffed her ear. Ghost whined. Then with a lunge it leaped over her, to nip at the heels of its master's horse, herding it away from Felde. The falling snow quickly hid them from view, and the men who gave chase.

"Felde!" Her father grabbed her by the shoulders and shook her. "Are you all right?" He sounded angry but she knew he was really frightened.

"I'm fine." She let him help her up. "Have someone sound the homing call. The men who followed the Alizonian will only be killed." She allowed herself to lean against him.

"No! I must have him. How else will we discover why the Alizonian are constantly attacking our valley? We cannot hold out much longer! Your mind must be fatigue-mazed to suggest such a thing."

She moved back and bowed formally. "Lord Alesanfar, call your men back. I know why we have been attacked and where the Alizonian is heading."

"Why and where."

"He is a Power shaper. He has the ability to find an Old One through their outer semblance. I fear he may then discover their inner name and take their Power to himself. That's why the Alizonians have been at our borders for so long—to allow their wizard-warrior access to Min of the Nine Words. That's where he's headed. Min is not dead like so many of the Old Ones, nor has she withdrawn from our world." She pointed at the stone face. "He reached her through the carving. Look! It bleeds. If the Alizonian has the Power of a living Old One at their command, not just the keep will fall, but the Dales as well."

White-faced, Lord Alesanfar gave the order for the homing call to sound. Alesanfar drew her close, "At ease. It is done. How soon do we leave?"

"Father, you cannot come with me." She gripped his arm. "Let me speak. It takes one with the Gift to track a Power shaper and hope to survive."

"I don't like it," Alesanfar said. He led her over to his own horse and tossed her into the saddle. "About the hound. When you fell to the ground there was a moment when you could have killed it. You did not. Why?"

Felde looked away. How to explain so that this man, her father and her lord, would understand? How to explain even to herself? She sighed and met his gaze. "Ghost fought to free its master just as I once sought to free you from Radnor the Dark One. The dog did everything it could to save the half-breed. I did the same for you. We are alike, that beast and I." Silence grew between them as Lord Alesanfar moved to adjust the stirrups to her shorter legs, each lost in the memories of the past. At last he spoke.

"It did not kill you when it had the chance either."

She nodded, and as she spoke unbidden tears came to her eyes. "I will not stay my hand a second time."

Felde pulled a glove off with her teeth and opened the bag of provisions her father had given her. Inside was a small stone bottle. Eagerly she opened it and took a single sip. The fermented brew was a welcome streak of warmth. Though she wanted more, she put the bottle back and pulled out a strip of jerked salmon. She needed the long-term energy it would provide.

Late afternoon the sky cleared, except for a few fast-moving clouds. Sunlight reflected off the snow in a sparkle of mirror-bright colors giving the muffled land a sensuous look that burned the eyes. She cupped a hand over her brow and scanned the area. She was at the westernmost tip of the valley that was Min's Hold. No one human lived there. The land was barren, riddled with boulders and funneled into a boxlike canyon surrounded by granite walls. She reined the horse into the canyon. Wind pushed at her back, whipped the horse's tail against her thigh. Constant gusts and cross-currents blew snow across the hard ground until it danced on the surface like white sand.

Felde slid to the ground and led the horse to a pair of boulders that formed a V-shaped windbreak. In the bag of supplies was some grain. She poured some onto a flat stone. The horse lipped at it and she knotted the reins, then let them fall free. The well-trained horse would stay here while she traveled the rest of the way on foot. The rugged land presented dangerous footing for a horse.

Her inner tension grew as she came closer to the Old One, Min of the Nine Words. The blood coursing through the pathways of her body thrummed with an anticipatory beat. Over her heart the talisman quivered.

Despite the cold, beads of sweat formed on her upper lip. Felde pulled the scarf up over her nose to prevent it from freezing. She couldn't afford frostbite now.

It wasn't just the confrontation with the Ghost and the Alizonian that disturbed her, but coming face-to-face with the embodiment of pure Power—Min. She was not Min's handmaiden, though the one who taught her how to use the Power was—Mag'ra the wise woman, channel for the Power of the Nine Words.

Felde had grieved, angry that she was not chosen to become the next wise woman. The Old One had given to Zaya, one with a lesser Gift than she, the use of Min's Nine Words. Mag'ra had comforted her, saying her destiny lay elsewhere.

Since then, Felde had sought that destiny in places where remnants of Power still clung, gathering knowledge to develop and nurture her talents.

Driven by curiosity she had come to this part of the valley several times. But she had never gone any farther. A gentle barrier arose each time and she had not tried to breach it. Now she felt a sense of urgency. Rounding a group of high-standing slabs of rock, Felde saw the Alizonian's mount. Disbelief flooded her. She had been certain she would arrive before the wizard for she knew the land as he did not. A cold knot formed in her chest. The contact he had forged through the stone image must have led him here. She touched the half-breed's horse. The skin was hot, minute flecks of sweat lay under its mane. Ghost and the Alizonian were not far ahead.

Though Felde could feel the emanation of Power from the Old One nearby, she did not know where Min's shrine actually lay. Among the rocks she saw a small stone pointed at one end. She picked it up and placed it on her palm and summoned a thread of Power. She breathed upon it. The rock-arrow quivered, lifted to point upward.

The sheer walls seemed to embrace the sky. Felde began to climb and soon found she needed both hands. She leaned against the cliff face and checked her guide. It still pointed upward. She placed it in her mouth. It was so cold it burned. The stone spun on her tongue until the point rested upward, supported against the back of her front teeth.

Felde reached for the next handhold and pulled. The small ledge crumbled. Unprepared, she slid downward. Wildly she searched with hands and feet until they found security. Legs trembling, she leaned against the snow-dusted rock until her heartbeat slowed. The fatigue that fought her driving will had made her careless. With more caution she began to move, testing each knob of rock before moving on.

It seemed a long time until the stone in her mouth shifted. Now, it lay flat on her tongue, its point turned a few degrees to the left. Felde turned her head and saw—a pawprint in the snow. Ghost! At that place the rock face curved. She inched her way around it and beyond the bend; on a ledge at eye level, she saw the beginnings of a narrow pathway leading to a crevice in the cliff face.

The arrow in her mouth shoved against her teeth. Felde spat it out and it skimmed into the dark gap, leaving a small narrow furrow in the snow. She followed. Enclosed by stone walls on either side, the path continued, relieved from total darkness by a crack in the granite above that allowed dim light to seep through. Felde did not think it happenstance the narrow band of light only fell on the footpath; it was the Old One's hand-iwork.

Felde strode through the opening ahead and found herself on a knoll, overlooking a small valley enclosed on all sides by sheer cliffs. At the far end was a desolate and long-abandoned keep. Bare-limbed trees and a swiftly moving stream were a framework for the Old One's place of Power.

Below was a large circular wall formed of glowing, translu-cent bricks. At the center of the circle, on a bier formed of the same metal that shaped Felde's talisman, lay Min of the Nine Words. The Old One was curled up on her side, hands under her head, asleep. On the exposed cheek Felde saw an injury outlined in dried blood. The half-breed's Power was as great as she feared.

Within the circle of Power others also slept: dark-haired men and women wearing crownlets of red metal. A horned, furred man (who had the look of the legend-told bear-kin) lay nearest to Min.

A touch of crimson drew Felde's attention. She saw a woman clothed in snow, with quiffs of scarlet feathers for hair—Arch-erydon! The Old One of Feathers and Fire. Next to her lay a slender winged form with foxfire scales for skin. Many of the hibernating dreamers were so covered in snow that Felde could not make out their true shapes. *Legends lived and breathed in that circle!*

Snow, icicles, and sheets of frozen rain draped the brick cir-cle, lending to its glow an eerie quality. Each row of bricks forming the wall was a different color, one shading into the next: rich, earthy brown, bright greens, yellow, blues, the scarlet and golds of autumn—the last, white. It gave her the

feeling she was looking at the true essence of each of the four
seasons.

With heightened senses she glimpsed, for a fleeting instant,
the essence of Min of the Nine Words. The Old One had immersed this valley in her Power until she became an integral
part of the earth's natural forces, changing with the seasons until she was now vulnerably tied to the earth-sleep of winter.

At the northern curve of the circle was the wizard and Ghost.
The half-breed moved slowly, hands extended flat as if against
an invisible wall. He was testing Min's shielding Power.

Felde ran down the hill toward them, drawing on her Gift
and all the knowledge she held. Whether he could influence her
Gift, she did not know. She must chance it or Min, the Dales,
and these wondrous dreamers would surely fall to the Alizonians.

Beneath her clothes something weighed against her breast,
growing heavier the closer she came to the circle. The talisman!
Maybe its Power could augment hers. Felde fumbled at the fas-
tenings of her jacket, fingers searching for the chain about her
neck. She pulled it forth, then dug in her heels and came to a
halt. The hearts of the flowers vining about the horseshoe-
shaped talisman glowed like small burning coals of fire. The
flowers' threads of light were braiding into a radiant spear. In a
hot streak of Power the weapon of light leaped from the talisman on Felde's palm to the circle. There came an answering
flash . . . not from the Old One or the half-breed wizard but
from the stone circle itself.

She heard a shout. Looking up, Felde saw the Alizonian
jump to the top of the brick wall. Her talisman had destroyed
the ward the Old One had placed around the circle!

Her heart pounded faster than her feet could run as she raced
to meet him. With that shattering Min had not awakened. Was
the Old One so united with the sleeping earth that she was
trapped?

Desperate thoughts lent her speed. Had she unknowingly
brought death here? She glanced at the object in her hand. The
flowers shone like night stars. With a jerk of repudiation she
tried to pull the chain over her head and toss that which betrayed her aside and met—resistance. She could not remove it.

In revulsion and fear she let go, and the talisman drifted down to lie on her breast.

When she was only a few feet away, she saw Ghost leap to the top of the multihued bricks. With a burst of speed Felde followed to land on the surface of the circle. Her feet slid on ice and she sat down hard. Opposite her, Ghost whimpered. The great dog faltered, then slowly folded, sliding down into a limp, ungainly heap among the sleepers. With tremendous effort the hound began to crawl slowly along.

Felde looked for the Alizonian. No longer were his movements sure and powerful. Now, he staggered among the sleepers toward Min. For a moment she was confused, then she, too, began to feel what he and the hound were experiencing—drowsiness. Whatever force kept the dreamers dreaming affected all who entered here.

Felde pushed off the wall. If the Alizonian managed to reach Min, he would gain the Power contained in all who lay here. Nothing could stop him then. Fear urged her onward but the Power in the circle forced her eyelids down. Her legs wobbled. Sleepy. So sleepy. A melting coldness, oozing down between the gap in the clothing about her neck, half roused her. Now she was facedown in the snow.

There was a burning sensation at her breast. Irritated, she turned on her side and brushed at the annoying heat. As her fingers touched fine chain, the talisman all but leaped into her palm. From its flowers came a bittersweet odor that banished the fog binding her thoughts.

She leaped to her feet. Keeping the talisman close to her nose, she stepped on or over those prone on the ground. The light from the center of the flowers increased, taking on the colors of the circle, matching and augmenting them! She took heart, maybe she had not brought betrayal here. Assurance welled up within her—the Power residing in the talisman had a purpose all its own!

The weight of the talisman continued to increase until she was barely able to carry it. Felde staggered to the bier. Across from her were the Alizonian and his hound. He pointed at her, then shouted at Ghost, "Attack!" For an instant the beast hesitated. Then Ghost leaped.

At that moment the talisman tripled in size. Felde was yanked forward, her forehead cracked against the metal edge of the bier. She felt the wind of Ghost's passage over her back. She tried to move, but could not. The weight of the talisman pinned her down. The chain it hung on rolled over her head, tearing out some of her hair. With an audible clang the talisman fell onto the bier, next to the Old One. It rose into the air, multiplying in size until it arched over Min's body. The U-shaped legs of the talisman extended down, fused to the bier with a hiss that echoed back and forth between its legs.

Min opened her eyes.

"No!" yelled the half-breed. "I will *not* be cheated." He began to chant. The Power behind those words slammed into Felde. She would have fallen but for her one-handed grasp on the talisman.

Behind her, Ghost growled and leaped onto the bier. Felde ducked, but the bitch ignored her, lowered its head, and advanced on the Old One. Before Felde could act Min pointed a finger at the dog. Ghost's muscles locked. No matter how the bitch strained, she could not move.

The Old One now wrought against the Alizonian in the same manner. With him immobilized, the forces he had been building sprang free to hover above them. Felde knew that if the forces were not contained they would implode, but her concern was wasted. In awe, she watched the Old One open one hand beneath that mass of Power. Slowly Min closed her hand. The force diminished, then was gone. Though the Old One did not use wands, elaborate gestures or words to call Power to her, even so it answered. Min shimmered with Power, like hot sunlight causes air to visibly ripple.

Felde gathered her courage and braced herself. Min of the Nine Words turned, rose up on her knees, and rested her long-fingered hand over Felde's. For the first time Min spoke.

"We have waited an eon of seasons for your coming and that which you carried over your heart. Welcome."

Felde swallowed fear and asked, "If you have waited so long, why did you put the barrier in the outer valley?"

"Child, I felt your presence on the edge of my dreams but the talisman you carried still slept. I could not call you here until it woke." Min pointed at the half-breed. "Did it not awaken when in his presence?"

"It did," said Felde, "but you cannot use him, he is of the Dark!"

"He is not. He walks a narrower road, that of Shadow. Light always casts shadow so we need him even more."

Rage swept away all the fear Felde felt toward the Old One. "Need him! He and his hound killed ten of my border patrol. He is of Alizon."

"Not completely," said Min. "The talisman is a Gate—one we have waited for all this time. You found our only means of attaining freedom and a new world. This world is only a shadow cast by our hopes. For it to become reality we need the Alizonian to call forth its true Shadow. Where there is an image the real is within grasp."

Gate? Felde was stunned. She had heard of such, whispered by those who followed the Light. All believed the Gates had long vanished.

Felde looked at Min, then shook her head. "Use him, then, but you'll have no part of me."

"Felde," said Min, using Power to underscore the word until Felde felt her name stirring the marrow of her bones. "Would you loose upon the land that which make the Alizonians appear as children?" The Old One pointed at the dreamers. "Look, they stir. It is the talisman that disturbs their slumber. Soon they will awake. Once again they will walk the earth that was their home. With their hopes in ashes they will loose their Power on the land that now rejects them. And woe to those who seek sustenance from this world for they will receive that which is worse than death."

As Min spoke Felde experienced each word Min of the Nine Words uttered; the grief of each of the awakened dreamers and their final descent into rage. She saw the destruction of her world. Felde heard someone sobbing and realized it was herself. She looked at the Old One. "What must I do?"

"Accept the unacceptable. Little sister, rise above personal grief and desire for revenge so greater good may be achieved. Set aside all hatred for the Alizonian. Remember Iredon? You called his name and he died. Power called the Alizonian's name and others died. He is no more guilty than you are. Think on this."

Min turned. "Shadowborn, will you lend yourself to the opening of the Gate."

"My people?" he asked.

The Old One looked deeply into his eyes, "Are they in truth your people? I don't believe so. They wanted you to walk the path of Darkness. You could not have the Light, would not choose the Dark, and so took the hard way, Shadow. You are more your mother's child. The Alizonian lord who forced your begetting upon a witch woman of Estcarp had no idea what he forged.

"This I can give in return. I will let down all the barriers to this valley and the circle. The Gate will remain open from moonrise to dawn. The Alizonians are world-walkers, trapped on this world. Those within hearing distance of the summoning will come, and once anyone responds to the song of the Gate they can't break away. Will you do what I ask, cast Shadow for the Light?"

He looked from Min to Felde. Felde gasped at what was in his eyes, a glimmer of a smile. To her surprise she found herself nodding at him in encouragement.

"Old One, I will do it." His chest rose and fell with the depth of his sigh.

"Then stand here," she said, positioning him so he faced away from the sleepers. "Call on your Gift and cast the true Shadow of the Gate, not upon the ground itself, but level with the Gateway. Lend support to the Light. Do not falter, for if you do the Gate will explode, destroying the valley and all within it. When you are called, grasp the Gate and begin." At his nod she left him and came to Felde.

"Have you considered what I asked of you? Without your consent and aid, the Gate cannot be used and we will be trapped here on this world. Now, little sister, will you stand for the Light?"

As Felde made to answer, the Old One held up her hand, "Wait. I am Min of the Nine Words. Words are the base of the Power I wield. You do not understand, yet, the definition that lies behind my words. Nor are you aware that when you picked up the Gate and chose it for your talisman, you became its soul Guardian.

"Long have I guarded this place alone, resting only during winter while my brothers, sisters, and mate dreamed. In ages past we began to fade." She pointed to those on the ground. "No longer was there balance between the Powers, and our time on this world drew to a close. We wished to find a world that would welcome us, so we forged the Gate. Before we could use it war erupted between Dark and Light. The talisman was lost. We built this place, a sanctuary against time and sent out the call that would eventually bring the talisman to us. So all were bound in sleep, except myself. I guarded the sleepers through the eons. I wish to leave, but how can I." She gestured with a wide-sweeping movement to the valley. "This land has sheltered us, absorbed a portion of our Power. Without someone to protect it and wield the circle wisely, there will come a time when one of Dark Power will make it their own. That must not happen!

"You grieved because I did not choose you to be my handmaiden; how could I? You are my heir."

Transfixed by Min's words, Felde said, "Heir? I am not an Old One."

"Not yet. Since finding the talisman you have been in the state of gestation. Today is your birth. Do not fear for there will come to you teachers to guide you. Now, answer. Guardian of the Gate, will you stand for the Light?"

Felde thought deeply. Concerned that she might never see her father again she asked, "Will I be bound to this valley as you were?"

"No. Not until those of Power come to you—those who must dream in the circle until the Gate opens again. This I can tell you, that time will not come again for many, many years."

Felde could hardly grasp what Min offered her—the fulfillment of a long-sought destiny. She stepped up onto the bier. As the Old One gave way, Felde took her place.

"Open the Gate, Guardian!"

Felde looked at the altered talisman and for a moment wondered how. She watched the energy flowing through the metal vine, flowers, and leaves that adorned the talisman Gate.

A glitter of gold caught her attention: the chain she had worn about her neck. At the apex of the arch it lay entangled about a leaf. She stepped forward to remove it, then halted. It felt right to leave it there. The longer she watched, the clearer came the pattern of Power governing the Gate. No longer hesitant, Felde touched first one flower, then another, brushed fingertips over vine and leaf. They took on life! Flowers came to bud and bloomed, leaves rustled to a melody Felde heard in mind and body. Now, as she could not before, she sensed why the half-breed Alizonian was needed. The song of the Gate was not complete.

"Shadow Wizard, take your place," Felde said.

Felde strained to hear the change that must come over the Gate when the Alizonian joined with her. It came so gradually she was never afterward sure if she could pinpoint the exact time of merging. His song was gentle and inexorable as twilight swallowing daylight. Between the sides of the Gate she could see a shadow of the talisman that was not there before. Just above that insubstantial, gray-silver arch there came a shimmer, a melding of Light and Shadow that formed a path—the Gateway!

Behind her she heard soft cries of hope-tinged greetings. Felde faced the awakened Old Ones. Felde was not surprised to see, standing beside Min, an arm lightly clasping her shoulders, the furred man who had lain close to the bier. His eyes were red, filled with a glow of unsurpassed joy.

Felde grasped a portion of the vine. At her touch a flare of brightness came from the flowers and leaves. It spread across those waiting, caught on the gems and silver weapons they wore and flowed outward to fill the walled circle. The pool of light lapped the top row of bricks, but not beyond their edges. Outside the circle all lay in the white darkness of falling snow.

"Well done, little sister," said Min, and pointed to the sky. Above, the exact circumference of the circle, was an invisible tunnel. It walled out the snow and reached far above them to a clear night sky.

"My brethren, the long wait is over. The moon is full and in the heart of the sky! Come, our new world awaits. The door is open."

Awe filled Felde as she watched the Old Ones line up to walk through the Gate. They were the stuff of fireside tales come to life. A part of her yearned to keep them in the valley so she could know them, learn from them. Then she remembered Min had promised her other teachers.

For now the avian woman stood before her. Somehow it didn't surprise Felde that Archerydon would be first.

"May I enter?"

Felde nodded. Archerydon started through and a clamoring of notes smote Felde's ear. "Hold!" she screamed. The man behind the bird woman dragged her back.

Min shoved her way to Felde, "What is wrong?"

"The Gate. It is not finished." Felde pointed at the red-feathered woman. "If Archerydon had gone through, she would have died."

Grim-faced, Min touched Felde's forehead. "May I listen through you?" At her nod Min shut her eyes. A fine line appeared between the Old One's eyebrows. "The Gate is no longer mine. I cannot tell what is wrong. You must listen instead."

Felde opened herself to the Gate. She felt its notes vibrating through the metal framework. The tune was as before. There! A small gap in the melody. She extended her awareness to include all in the circle. The one she needed lay behind and to the right of her. She turned. Ghost! The hound was still bound by Min's will. Felde had forgotten about the dog.

"Min! Release the hound." As the Old One gestured, Ghost gave a strangled whine and leaped off the bier. Felde leaned out, but could only see the Alizonian's hand that grasped the vine and part of his shoulder. She looked at Min.

"The dog that is more than beast is with its master pressed as close to him as flesh will allow," said Min.

Felde nodded, then listened again. The gap in the melody filled. Ghost's notes expressed deep abiding love. Felde let it fill her and knew the Gate complete.

"It is finished. The way is now truly open."

The Power in the Gate coursed through the Shadow wizard and Ghost, with Felde its focus. It expanded her awareness until she could sense those Gate Summoned walking the path in the cliff. Not all were Alizonian, though many of those did pass through. It took all of Felde's determination not to let go of the vine. Power surged through her, vaster than any she imagined. It stripped her of the Gift, then filled her again with more, until she felt she would burst asunder. Her skin glowed, took on the pearlized colors of circle and talisman.

At last, only Min and her mate remained. The Old One bent and kissed her forehead. With that kiss came blessings and a new gift, understanding of the circle. Beyond Min, Felde caught a glimpse of the furred man, his horned head bent as he talked with the Shadow wizard. Then, as he joined hands with Min and stepped from this world, the sun crested the horizon.

The Power in the Gate ceased. The way closed. Talisman was once again talisman. Felde staggered as she bent to pick it up and fell to her knees. The last she remembered, before falling asleep, was clutching it in her fist.

Beneath her was a fur robe and at her back warmth from a living body pressed against hers. She could hear the comforting snap and pop of burning wood. Between her lashes Felde looked about. Across the barrier of a small fire was the Alizonian, drinking a liquid that clouded his face with steam.

Though he had not harmed her while she slept and had lent his aid with the Gate—he was the enemy. Felde stiffened. Behind her the body that warmed her growled. Ghost!

"So, you're awake. We were beginning to think you'd sleep through another day. Didn't we, girl," he said, patting Ghost as the beast came to lie beside him. "My name is Janydon. Would you like some tea?" When she did not respond he added, "If we had intended harm, you'd already be dead."

He was right and hunger twisted in her. Felde sat and took the tea he offered.

Janydon leaned toward her. "The Alizonian who answered the call were part of the clan who bound us. Now that they are gone, we are free."

"We? Oh. You mean Ghost."

Janydon chuckled. "She is indeed ghostlike. Her name is Neve, my companion and birth sister. She was whelped at the same moment my mother birthed me. The clanlord felt that held great portent so we were raised together. She is more than beast!"

"I agree. Now, why all this?" Felde pointed at the fire. "Why didn't you leave?"

For the first time he looked her directly in the eyes and sustained it. She was startled to see that his eyes were the same intense blue as Ghost's—Neve's. She saw truth in them and listened intently.

"The Old One said teachers would come to you. I would like to be taught, if they will accept me as pupil, too."

He fell silent. The trembling of his fingers, pulling at Neve's ears, betrayed how much her answer meant. She thought about the changes she would undergo as she became an Old One. The years stretched before her, seeming empty of companionship. No one among her acquaintances, including her father, would understand the coming changes, or live to see them completed. Only this man and his companion knew. But she did not fully trust him.

Iredon's death flashed through her mind. Guilt welled up inside her, an inner wound more vicious than any injury of the flesh. She bit her lip, forcing herself to stifle a moan.

What had Min said to ease her? Yes, she remembered . . . "The Alizonian's name was called and others died. He is no more guilty than you are." Why that had comforted her and now did again, she did not know.

Felde looked at Janydon. Min had trusted him and her mate had spoken to him too. She could accept the Old One's faith in him and build on that for now.

They were warriors for Light and Shadow. Felde laughed, and answered the look of inquiry she saw in Janydon's eyes.

"Some Power has had its hand in bringing us together. Who am I to part us now?"

Janydon leaped to his feet and shouted in relief. Neve barked and nipped at his ankles in excitement.

Felde stood and looked about the valley. In the distance she could see the old keep. Exploring it would be a good way to start an adventure. And she would have two companions. Hadn't she, from the first hot blue-eyed glance, been drawn to Neve? She looked at the dog, then up at the bitch's master and met his blue eyes. For some reason she felt blood rushing to her cheeks and did not turn away as Janydon reached out to hug her. The hound braced its front paws against them, pushed its cold nose under her chin. Their bodies felt good. Felde did not question, just accepted, that for a time, she was not to be alone. This—was Min's and her horned mate's final gift.

Afterword

*"The Circle of Sleep" is a sequel to "Nine Words in Winter,"
a story I wrote for Volume 1 of* Tales *of the Witch World.
When I wrote that earlier story I thought I had said all there
was to say about this situation. But the people and places of
Witch World wouldn't leave me alone and the story you just
finished was obviously destined to come out, whether I
wanted it to or not. That a story can force its way into being is
an example of the magic of fiction and the powerful influence
of a vividly imagined world such as Andre's Witch World.
Now that the story is done, I'm glad it came out, though I'm
still not sure exactly how it happened. Writing is like that
sometimes.*

—Caralyn Inks

FALCON'S CHICK

by

Patricia Shaw Mathews

They call me the Wise Weaver on the Mountain, although I am a killer. Now I must kill again, or risk the murder of all the village, and Gunnora help me, I can do neither. Oh, give me the wisdom to see what must be done and do it!

Falcon Crag looms over our village like a giant's shadow. Once a year the Falconers come down to the huts at the trailhead we keep for their visits, and start our daughters growing in us. Children, the elders, and those with some ailment or difference are kept safely away from the Falconers, for they are all mad.

I remember curling on my mother Eina's lap once, when I was small, and asking, "What is 'mad'?"

She stroked my hair. "Jommy," she said softly, "you have seen babies who have not yet learned how to behave. When they are tired, or cannot make their wishes known, they have a tantrum."

"Like Aunt Lorin's grandbaby," I said knowingly. Aunt Lorin was my mother's sister-friend, but she had daughters with daughters, and my mother had only me.

"When a big person acts like that baby," my mother agreed, "we say she is mad, and stay out of her way until the fit passes. Sometimes it never passes and we cannot live with her, but must send her away as we did Mad Bethia in my great-grandmother's day, who killed three women she said were plotting against her." She made a falcon-away sign and cuddled me to her breast. "But that was long ago, Jommy, very long ago."

On the other side of the hearth, my foster-sister Jorra, Aunt Lorin's youngest daughter, was watching with wide, fascinated eyes. Now she left our watchdog Guardian's side to pull at Mother's sleeve and stare at me. "Lennis Meireith's-daughter says Jommy will be like that," she whispered, "because Jommy is a you-know-what."

"Lennis is mistaken," Mother said fiercely. "Look at Guardian! Her foremothers were wolves, but we brought them up properly, and now she and her pups are part of the family. I am bringing Jommy up properly and he is nothing like a Falconer."

That, to me, was that, and I was more interested in having another honey cake before being sent to bed. But that night I wondered what she meant by "you-know-what." For I had already learned I was not like the others, but which way did she mean?

One of my feet had grown twisted, and hurt when I tried to run. Elthea the weaver was lame like me, from falling into a pit while herding sheep. It was three days before they found her and brought her to the healer, and her bones had set all wrong. I was to be her apprentice and learn her trade when I was older. That was one difference.

The other I learned from watching the tiniest babies in the village. Some made their water gently, as they should. Others made theirs in a spouting stream, and had a little thing like mine they did it with. (Though Mother and Aunt Lorin and my foster-sisters had taught me to do it properly and not wet my robes.) Babies like this were called *boys*, and all were tiny but me, and their mothers all seemed very sad. None of them had names but me, either. "Why is this?" I asked Aunt Lorin once.

"They are not ours to keep, Jommy," she said soberly. "They belong to the Falconers, who will take them away and make Falconers of them if they like them." Then she swallowed hard. "Eina does not want you told, but there is no greater unkindness than a kindly lie. Jommy, if the Falconers do not like a boy, they kill him. They do not like twisted legs. So your mother hid you from them to rear as her own daughter, for she had none. For this reason you must never let a Falconer see you, ever, but do not think any more of it than that."

When I understood this, I began to have bad dreams in which women with falcon wings (for I had never seen a Falconer) swooped down and carried off bad babies. Mother comforted me, then stormed off to quarrel with Aunt Lorin, who moved out of our house and back in with her blood-kin. I thought it was my fault and cried for a week, until Mother relented and apologized, and we were all happy again.

Sometime after that, the Falconers came.

The sheep herders in the high hills that dot the plains across the river cried out, a falcon's cry, then hid themselves and the sheep. Half of our young women and older maidens scrambled into ugly, shapeless robes and veils, gave their knives and wolf-spears to their kin for safekeeping, and slowly walked to the trailhead huts, heads down.

The rest of us quenched our fires, packed our valuables, and ran to the caves in the base of the mountain, driving our animals before us. It was dark and cold in there, though we had food and water, and a nasty pile by the door where we could relieve our needs. A long time we sat there, while the old women taught us the warning cries and told Falconer tales. We build our houses in the forest, one said, because the Falconers would burn down any house a villager built for herself. As if they expected us to live in the trailhead huts, so rundown and ill-omened! How the Falconers kill any woman they catch with spear or knife. Of boys taken and boys killed; of women murdered for no fault. Truly they are mad!

"Why do we endure it?" Jorra cried out after the seventh such tale.

"How else can we get our daughters started within us?" an old woman answered helplessly.

"Jonkara, Avenger of Women, sees all these deeds," came a bitter whisper from the deep darkness, "and lets no evil go unpunished."

"Oh, hush!" my mother cried out frantically. "Remember the b-o-y."

"Maybe we need not endure the Falconers much longer," Aunt Lorin said thoughtfully.

When the all-clear sounded, the children were kept from the trailhead, but the healers and the priestess went. They brought back the body of Meireith, Lennis's mother.

"They do not like women too old to bear," my mother said with wet eyes at her burial, "and she was my age, but went anyway. But why did they try to start another daughter within her, and then kill her?" she demanded. "Why?"

"Why do we endure it?" Aunt Lorin asked again, and looked at me as if I had the answer, which I did not. I began to cry, from helplessness. Nobody answered either of us except to comfort us, which without an answer was no comfort at all.

The older girls take care of any children who can walk past their mothers' doorsteps, and Lennis Meireith's-daughter was one of them. I soon grew to hate and fear her above anybody in the village, even the blacksmith with her bulging arms and grimy face. I would raise my voice, or scuffle with another child, and Lennis's face would grow pinched and hard. "Falconer blood," she'd say, as if I were a mad wolf; or "what did you expect, seeing what he is?"

Then one day when I was struggling to keep up with the others, my lame foot twisted, I went down, and I used a word the sheep herders used. Lennis quickly herded the little girls away from me, with a loud whisper of "Watch out for him! He'll go mad next."

I struggled to my feet, angry that she made no move to help, and hobbled toward her. She sent the younger girls running, and stood before me in the path, taunting, "Come on, Falcon Boy, touch me, I dare you. Hit me, be like all the others." Her robe was stained and torn, and not too lately washed, which was strange, and the finger she jabbed underneath my nose was dirty, with its nail bitten to the quick. Her brown braids swung back and forth as she shook her head from side to side chanting, "Falcon Boy, killer, touch me, I dare you."

Rage rose in me; then, fear that she was right. I wanted to go mad and hit her; then I'd be sent from the village like a wolf

and never see my mother or Aunt Lorin or Jorra again. "Let
me by," I begged, and burst into tears; then I sat on the grass
and bawled like any infant.

Suddenly she was silent. I looked up and there was Noriel the
Blacksmith, her skirts hitched up and grime on her face. Gently
she helped me up and hugged me, then said, "I hope nobody
has been unkind to Jommy. It is very hard to be different from
the others, without letting unkind people make fun of his differences. You're a big girl, Lennis; you wouldn't let that happen. Would you? Because big girls protect little children, don't
they?"

I saw Lennis blush and look at the ground. The blacksmith
took me by the hand and walked me home. Once away from
Lennis, she said softly, "She mourns her mother, whom the
Falconers killed. It's a hard thing to have a mother die for a
mad wolf's whim."

"I am not a wolf," I said a little too loudly. "I am not!"

"You are a watchdog pup," the blacksmith agreed, "and you
would never be unkind to Lennis for saying things in her grief
that she does not mean."

But the next day my mother dressed me in my best robe,
braided my hair, and sent me to Elthea's to begin my apprenticeship.

It was a good exchange. I loved to watch the patterns in the
wool grow under Elthea's hands, and soon learned all the colors and shapes of the wool in her baskets. When she set me to
working a pattern of my own at a tiny upright loom, I treasured
it even beyond a new puppy or a kitten. I wove ribbons for my
mother and Aunt Lorin, and a very special one for Jorra, who
blushed and grinned as if someone had given her a friendship
token. Later, she brought me a tiny wooden box she had made
at the carpenter shop. I have it still.

So the years went, with the round of festivals, the Falconer
visits, the births and naming of babies, the councils and village
meetings, storms and fair weather. Once a year the lookouts
would hoot like doves and the women, dressed in their finest
robes, would bundle their best pots and weavings together and
ride out a trail through the forest that could not be seen from
the crag. There they would meet with women who said they

served the Good goddess Gunnora in her abbey. We would trade goods, and sometimes people; the priestess who taught us children had been abbey-trained. We would all grow big-eyed on the strangers' tales for another year, and would go home rich in metal, salt, and spices.

And the children of my age were growing tall. Unable as I was to join some play, because of my leg, I could still join their talk and quiet games, a little apart as always. I knew who was whose best friend; saw the handholding and the tokens exchanged; heard the chants of "Lennis and Marra, sitting in a tree, K-I-S-S-I-N-G!" I knew that sister-friends lived together like Mother and Aunt Lorin, and reared their children together as foster-sisters; and as I grew older, I started to think about Jorra in that way. I thought of her even at the loom, and at meals, and soon the chants were "Jommy and Jorra, sitting in a tree . . ." I blushed as hot as anyone, but was secretly pleased.

Lennis left her childhood behind and joined the maidens, and in two years her lot was drawn to visit the Falconers. She came back with her face drawn up as if she'd eaten something nasty. I thought of Jorra undergoing this ordeal when her time came, and was sick inside. But when Lennis grew big with child, and it proved a daughter she could keep, I thought of Jorra holding a baby and felt better. The priestess and the healers had explained to me that I would never be able to bear a child, which hurt, but I swore then to foster all Jorra's babies as if they had been my own, if she would let me.

Then one day Jorra woke up early and went to her mother, then to the healers', and stayed there while the moon waxed and waned. I started to weave her a fine stole of four colors for her Maiden Day gift and worked day and night on it, while her mother and mine sewed her the long gown of a grown-up. Her sisters wove her a pretty crown of flowers on the day she came out. Our mothers held a party for her that everybody came to, even Lennis, who disliked our whole family. We ate of everybody's cooking and grew tipsy on Cousin Annis's fruit wine, and giggled like children.

Jorra opened my gift, blushed, and said, "No maiden has ever had a finer Maiden Day gift, Jommy," and kissed me.

"Jorra, I love you," I said, greatly daring.

She looked at me then, not as a sister, but as a lover, and we sat with our arms around each other, talking all night.

If we had not lived in the same house, we would have spent night after night at each other's houses often. As it was, her room was mine and mine was hers. I wove her a fine bedcover, and she made me a hope chest, though I would never have a baby to make things and save them for. We dressed each others' hair and she told me how Lennis's sister used to taunt her "Firehead! Firehead!" for her red hair.

"They're just an unkind family," I said.

"That's an unkind word, but you're right," Jorra answered, and we giggled and cuddled together. Then she said, "It isn't fair, for a sourpuss like Lennis to have babies when you can't."

"I don't have any place to grow one," I explained, my eyes hot, "but I'd like to play with yours." She lay curled up against me, soft and fair for all her hard work, her hair like fire in my hand. I loved her and she loved me, for all my difference and strangeness.

Then suddenly I jumped up, shocked and ashamed, as the part of me I'd thought tamed in babyhood made a sticky wetness all over the bedclothes. I blushed and stammered, "I—I'm sorry."

Jorra's mind worked faster than mine, and she said, "Maybe it's what boys have instead of moonblood. Let's ask the healer." She went downstairs while I tried to clean up, and came back with both our mothers, talking excitedly as if she'd discovered something great and new, and I think she had.

"This is what Falconers do to start the babies growing in us," Aunt Lorin said while Mother nodded. We went to the healer, then to the priestess, who told me in detail what happened during a Falconer visit. "You can never bear a baby, Jommy," she said with sober joy, "but perhaps you can start one growing in someone."

I thought back on this and that. "I may—I may have already," I blurted out. "In Jorra."

I have never seen such rejoicing on any face, or one so carefully guarded. "Maybe we can do without the Falconers now," she said.

* * *

So it was that I spent a month in seclusion, learning the secrets of Falconer visits and childbirth. I came out and was given a long white robe and a lovely crown of flowers; my mother and Jorra gave a great party to which everyone came, even those who had disapproved of my mother keeping me. We ate and drank and danced, and only Lennis, who had a newborn boy in her arms, looked angry and sad.

For two Falconer visits after that, Jorra stayed out of the lot-drawing, and nobody said a word. Then came the day she showed the signs of a child growing within her, and Lennis led a fierce and bitter outcry. "It is not fair that she should have a child and be spared the Falconers," she raged; and she raged until a village meeting was called. I sat in the back, for my youth and barrenness, and was silent, for many people had never wanted me there at all. But when Lennis raised her cry again, I shook with anger.

Noriel the Blacksmith spoke then. "Many of us go to the trailhead every year, like my sister, and never have a child. Is that fair? Some of us are blind or deaf or lame or simple, while others are whole. Is that fair? Lennis wants the lucky punished to console the unlucky. Is that fair?"

There were shouts from Lennis's side, and more shouting from our side, on into the night, until finally Jorra stood up and cried out, "I will not cause quarreling in this village! I will put my lot in with the rest and go to the trailhead if it is drawn." Then she sat down, crying.

I will never know if the lots were fairly drawn, but she was chosen, and went, veiled and downcast like all the others. I waited in the caves, sick at heart. I knew there was a grim ordeal in store for her, but surely nothing else. She was whole in every part, unblemished, and lovely; laughing and clever and loving. She had friends and family to help soothe her heart when she came back.

She did not come back.

When the all-clear sounded, the first few women coming in turned their faces from our family, and my stomach grew very cold and still in me. Then came two strong women carrying a body shrouded in the ugly trailhead-visit robes, but flame-red hair spilled out from under the hood. I struggled to my feet. Lennis stood before Jorra's mother, crying.

"I'm sorry!" she wailed. "I didn't know!"

Aunt Lorin held both Lennis's arms and looked in her eyes. Lennis tried to shrink down; Aunt Lorin stayed on a level with her. "What happened?" she demanded.

It was simple, and totally senseless. The Falconer who was trying to start a daughter in Jorra knew by her breasts and belly that one was already growing, and grew angry. Not because he wasn't needed, but because she had been with another man. All the Falconers then put their knives to the women's throats, and many thought they would all die; but Jorra did not betray the village.

"She retold the Tale of Kallile," Lennis whimpered, "that a man had come to her in the fields and did what Falconers do, and because he had a knife, she let him. The other Falconers wanted to question her under torture, but this one said it would spend their time needlessly, and cut her throat."

"What did he look like?" I asked her, forcing my way up front.

There was a babble of voices. He was short; he was tall; Falconers are taller than we are. He was breastless and arm-heavy as they are, with hair on his face. Fair hair like Elthea's; gray eyes like mine. Lennis looked at me exactly as a small child who has secretly gotten even with another, and I shoved myself between her and Aunt Lorin. "You know how to tell him if you see him again," I said, my head beginning to cloud with a distant redness. "Tell me!"

Defiantly she said, "It's not my fault! I told her we shouldn't have let her start babies by herself."

Unthinking, I lashed out and slapped her face, hard. My mother and Aunt Lorin took me by the arms and led me away. It's well they did, or I would have run mad like a Falconer and choked the truth from her smug, defensive face. Jorra always had a word that calmed my rage and made me laugh. Jorra was no longer here. Jorra would have babies and we would rear them together. There would be no babies and there was no Jorra. Mother tried to get me to eat, but I would not; Aunt Lorin expected me to cry, but I could not. Nor did I sleep.

Before the dawn I hobbled down to the kitchen and took a bowl of soup from the great ceramic pot that always sat in the coals. My mother was there, sitting next to Aunt Lorin, who had cried herself to sleep. Both were in heavy night-robes, now all wrinkled; their hair, all gray, fell uncombed and unbraided around their shoulders. They had lost a daughter and I could not comfort them, only go berserk.

"Mother, I must leave, before I run mad and kill Lennis," I said.

I have never seen her face so old. "Take the back trail to the forest shrine of Gunnora and pray her help, Jommy," she said, "and forget Lennis. You were in grief, and she's had that slap coming since she was old enough to speak."

I could not speak for a few minutes. "I have a Falconer's madness, Mother," I forced out of a tight throat. "Please."

At last, as a feeble gray light began to show around the edge of the shutters, she went upstairs and brought down everything I owned, including all that Jorra had given me. She came back with a fine mule, its saddlebags full of food; a rare and expensive long-knife; and the short robe and trousers of a field worker. I shaved my head in grief and laid the long, dark braids across the bedcover I had woven for us, and took only the ring she had carved for my fifteenth birthday.

I would never see my sixteenth, for I was going to kill a mad, trained killer. I kissed her, and kissed Aunt Lorin who still slept, and patted Guardian's-daughter, and rode off before the sun rose above the mountains. I thought I would never see my home again.

Gunnora's shrine stood in a clearing, with offerings all about it, but I called on another goddess. "Jonkara, Avenger of Women, help me avenge Jorra's death and the baby's. Jonkara, who slays men who harm women, help me now, even though I am a boy."

I heard a falcon's cry and saw before me a falcon-headed woman of the sort that had haunted my childhood nightmares. "Are you sure?" she asked with a mocking, Lennis-like laugh.

"You would not harm my village or my family," I said boldly. "And if you want my life, I am ready to die."

Jonkara screeched like a falcon again. "Avenge a wrong your kinswomen have all consented to?" she demanded.

I stood my ground. "You know why. Let them get daughters without enduring the whims of madmen every year, or every day." I added that last because of a legend that the Falconers had once lived among us, until we could endure their conduct no more and drove them out.

Her eyes filled with hate as Lennis's were, the goddess cried, "You have your wish," and flew off to Falcon Crag with a victory call that haunted me all the way down the trail.

The trail opened onto a wide, smooth road. Every once in a while I saw gardens or buildings, terribly exposed; and from time to time people passed on foot or horseback. I knew none of them and could not speak to them, but at night when I stopped and lit a fire, a woman spoke. "What do you do on this road alone, lad?" she asked me in a strange accent.

"Darthis," her companion warned, exactly as a big girl speaks to a wandering little one. The one who spoke had the breastless, flat, arm-heavy look of a Falconer, but his hair was brown-gray and he did not look mad. All the same, I stood ready to flee.

"It's only a boy, and a shy one," she argued, much like a little girl debating an elder. "And, Corin, I don't imagine he's ever been out of native village in all his life."

"I have not," I agreed, looking between them. "My name is Jommy Eina's-son, and I am looking for a Falconer. He has fair hair and gray eyes."

"It's bad business, seeking out Falconers," Elder Corin said soberly. "But there's a market in the city where they are sometimes seen. We're going partway there; after that you're on your own."

I thanked them, and helped Darthis with food and fire, as was proper. Then I saw my mother had packed my smallest ribbon-loom and some wool in my saddlebags, so after supper I set it up and began to weave. "If we are together long," I told them, "I'll make you a ribbon each, for your kindness." Darthis smiled, but Corin looked at me strangely.

However strange, they were a kindly pair, and I missed them when they left. The road grew more and more crowded as I drew closer to the town, and I was often frightened.

Most of those on the road were men, with hair on their faces, and manners rougher than I have ever seen, even to fighting among themselves like beasts, for pleasure; yet many seemed kind. Some mocked my bad leg and timid manners; others offered to share fire and food.

Of one such I will not speak, except to say that now I know what the women in my village must endure during a Falconer visit, and marvel that any of them ever let their lot be drawn. Oh, I did right to call upon Jonkara the Avenger to help us!

All this while I kept Falcon Crag in view, and watched for the bird-masks everybody said the Falconers wore among men. I ate very sparingly of the food my mother had packed for me, and wove ribbons, and sold them along the road for food and wool to make more, and endlessly searched. I dreamed of home and often woke up crying; I dreamed of Jorra living, and awakening was the nightmare; I dreamed of her dead and cried for vengeance once again. But now I had learned to call it "justice."

At last the Goddess favored me and I saw the falcon helmet of a man who was, as the women said, short for a man. He carried a curved sword—another word I had learned among men—and the hair on the back of his hands was fair. I followed him as quietly as I could, but like a bird, he had eyes in the back of his head. In a deserted place along the road we were on, he turned and snapped, "Well, boy? What do you want?"

"I want to see if you have gray eyes," I said, my hand finding the wolf-spear I had bought along the way. "I seek a Falconer with fair hair and gray eyes."

He stared at me, then laughed and took off his helmet. He was the one. I stared, shocked, then threw the spear. It went into his guts and he came raging at me. "Why, you treacherous little rat?"

Even lame I could sidestep him. "You killed Jorra and the baby," I shouted. How could he not know?

He was losing strength rapidly as his blood ran from him, but his anger remained. "I killed no woman," he snarled. "We never touch women, you little fool. Bad enough to be around them in the world of men!"

I drew the knife my mother had given me and stared him

down in sick rage. "She had red hair and was going to have a child. That angered you and you killed her. Deny it if you can, madman."

He was down on his knees now, doubled up, but he raised his head and snarled, "What do we care what one of your witches does and with whom? The only woman with red hair I know of was one of ours, who had defiled herself with some outlaw. My brother Haakon killed her before she could infect the rest of the stupid herd with her notions. And"—he was snarling in agony now—"if your father had cared enough to beat better manners into you the way mine did me, you wouldn't be butting your nose into things that don't concern you!"

I started to cut his throat, but he fought me with his hands until I found the end of the spear and twisted it. He grunted and fell down. I pulled it out and half his gut came with it. Then I cut his throat, mounted my mule, and rode off as if Jonkara and all the Falconer tribe were after me. His cries and grunts, like those of a pig being butchered, rang in my ears. His odd and hateful words—"one of ours"; "stupid herd"; "*beat* better manners into you"—was *that* how Falconers made boys into Falconers?—followed me. But they could not drown out the only words with any meaning: *"my brother Haakon."* I had killed the wrong man.

It was good that I fled, for when I reached the marketplace, the streets were abuzz with grim-faced men in bird-masks. They had not seen me yet. I must warn the village of what I had done and learned, and we had friends in the abbey. I stopped and put on the robe my mother had given me for this, made some attempt to comb my shorn hair, and threw away the spearpoint in the nearest midden, keeping the shaft for a walking stick. I rode as far as the abbey gates, dismounted, and slowly started up the steps.

"Here, Mother," a man's voice said suddenly, and he stepped in front of me. "Where would you be going today?"

Did he mean me? "To the abbey, with a message," I croaked, my voice raw from a dry throat.

"Well, be careful," he said gently. "Some mad dog took out a Falconer last night, and he's still loose on the streets. If he can do that—and is mad enough to try—he's dangerous!"

"Thank you," I choked, and hobbled up to the abbey door. Thank Gunnora for my bad leg; it had saved my life twice! Once from the Falconers; and now, by making the man think I was old. I rang the bell and stood panting by the gate. An abbey servant came; I wheezed, "I am Jommy Eina's-daughter and I must see the abbess."

She gave me a stern look and let me in, but led me to an outbuilding and bid me remain there. I sat down and tried to breathe, but my heart was bursting in my chest and my throat was pounding. Soon a woman in a long, plain gray robe stood before me and said, "This is a refuge for women, and you have lied before the Goddess. Well, sir?"

I looked straight at her, a slender, proud old woman who could have been the Goddess's own self. "I gave the name I am called at home. I have stirred up the Falconers, and they must not be allowed to harm my village for what I did."

She laid a hand against my head and called for hot mulled ale. Then she sat down on a box and heard me out, asking many questions, and paused only to call for food for us both. At last she said, "I was a great lady in the world before retiring here; I have sat in judgment many times. Jommy, the world will think two things." She held up one slender, pale, wrinkled finger.

"First, that you have every right to avenge your wife and unborn child." She paused. "But, second"—another finger—"that the Falconers have every right to do as they please with their women and their children. So you are truly in a trap."

"Theirs, theirs, theirs!" I cried out. "How are we theirs? The wolf who raids the flocks doesn't think of them as his, does he?"

"He probably does," she said dryly. She made me finish the rest of the ale, then said briskly, "The women of Falconer Village have asked our aid in the name of Gunnora, and we will give it to them. Do you mind disguising yourself as a woman? No, I see not. Or riding with a witch of Estcarp?"

"Why should I? Elder mother," I said, exhausted, "what you say, I will do. But you know I have the Falconer madness now."

She laid a hand on my head again. "You were a boy pushed

beyond endurance. But see that killing does not become a habit."

After a safe but uneasy night's sleep and a good breakfast, I was dressed in ash-gray robes, ordered not to speak to anyone, and put in a wagon with two other women. As they drove out of the city, a guard who could have been the twin of the one I had seen yesterday asked with sober concern, "Where are you going, good Dames, with a mad killer on the loose?"

The tall, heavy one put her head down and said a little sadly, "To the Shrine in the Forest, to learn the discipline of silence." The guard shook his head, and with a faint smile waved us on. I all but cried to see the shrine of Gunnora, so calm and peaceful in the leaf-filtered sun.

I must live long enough to tell the village that I had killed. Even now I regretted that I had killed the wrong man more than I regretted the killing. Yet, I must also tell them that I had dared ask the abbess if the Falconers truly made men out of boys by beating them, and very dryly she had said, "That is the usual way men are made."

Or madmen? Yet, I was a killer, and nobody had ever hit me in all my fifteen years. Men said that boys were like mules; you must first hit them to get their attention. An unwelcome thought!

We came to the village after a long ride I remember little of, for my shame at being Falconer-mad. As the wagon entered our clearing, a girl ran off long-legged. She came back dancing ahead of my mother, who moved as slowly and painfully as an old woman. Lennis stood in front of the wagon, glowering at me. My mother cried out and kissed me.

I kissed her back, but then blurted out, "Mother, I killed a Falconer!" and heard the pride in my voice with horror, as Lennis stepped back in loathing and terror. The priestess and our three healers gathered around and the elders slowly came up as I told my tale, uncaring for anything but to get it all said. When I came to the beating of the boys, everyone began talking at once, all but one little girl who handed me a rag and said, "Jommy, don't cry!" I think she was one of Aunt Lorin's granddaughters.

"Mother," I said then in a low voice, "I cannot live among people anymore; but I cannot endure the outside. Let me live and weave apart from the others and watch for enemies I might have brought among you."

"Enough of this foolish talk," Aunt Lorin scolded me. "Your old room is ready for you; your mother and I and your foster-sisters have prepared as much of a party as we could with only a lookout's notice . . ." But her voice trailed off and she looked at me dubiously. My mother was weeping, heartbroken.

The priestess put her hand on my shoulder. "We cannot leave you completely alone, Jommy; that would truly make a mad-man and a monster of you. But in your wisdom you shall have your wish."

I slept in the back room of the healers' that night, with their old gray tomcat for company. In the morning we drove my mule and the wagon up a steep path in a hillside overlooking the river, the plains, and Falcon Crag, depending on which way you were looking. There was a cave in the hillside, and a little creek ran nearby. The land around the cave was wooded; there was enough room in front of it to set up a loom and even have a little garden.

I had all I needed: an upright loom and wool, some blankets, a water pot and a cooking pot and a firepot full of coals. Noriel the Blacksmith, my driver, took from her skirt pocket a small, long-necked pot with holes in the top, full of sweet grain seeds. She set up the loom, gathered wood for my first fire, and then surprised me with a quick kiss, saying, "Some of us think you did no more than keep a two-legged wolf from the flock. Is there anything more you want?"

I did not say "Jorra." Instead I asked for the blue and violet dayflower vines that follow the sun. She nodded and drove off, and so my second life began.

The wind came in from beyond the river, and the threads on my loom became a welcome windbreak. I huddled deep in my cave, blankets wrapped around me, feeding twigs to the firepot and roasting bread and cheese. It was my third week on the mountain, and the storm was a bad one for the season. I listened to the wind outside, but my thoughts went round and round like children in a ring-dance.

Laughter and tears flow freely in our village. I have had much sorrow, and have cried much. Men outside despise tears, though they laugh freely; and they fight like beasts. Falconers do none of these where others can see, but they are mad.

Women outside act toward men as children do toward elders; and the men act toward them as the big girls do the little ones they tend, but not so motherly. There were many things we do the women outside do not do, sometimes from pride, and sometimes in fear of a scolding. It was hard to tell which, or why.

My mistress, Elthea. I had not thought of her when I left, or when I came back, which was strange; I had spent most of my life working by her side. She was a silent woman, speaking only of the work at hand. Her days as a sheep herder? The rug I was weaving should be for her. Had she minded having a boy apprentice? She never said.

There were women outside who wore bright colors and talked freely among themselves; to men they talked like horse traders trying to sell a horse. One decided in all kindness to teach me how to start children when you are not lovers, but without Falconer brutality. Now she haunted my dreams, all mixed up with Jorra and Lennis and the dead Falconer and the man on the road.

I had a red cloth to hang outside the cave to cry for help. Would I need to do this when my food ran out? My garden would not be ready for some time. Would they bring me food, when I was doing nothing in return? And why?

They would come on the mule I have never called by name. This is not rudeness. She is stubborn, so I named her for a villager it would be unkind to make known; I think the name and say Mule.

Well, one moon cycle exactly from the day I came to the mountain, the oldest healer came to me, with fruit and vegetables, herbs for tea, and bread, but no meat. This is what you eat when you are seeking wisdom, so I understood. She said nothing to my questions about my mother, Aunt Lorin, and Elthea, but the next moon my mother came instead. It hurt that she had waited until the healer reported I was not mad, but she was my mother and I was her only child. I hugged her and let her cry and asked her to tell Elthea about the rug. We had little to say to each other but regrets.

In turn all of my family, and many of the women central to our lives, came. I grew my garden and watched the land and the stars, and chewed over my thoughts. I would deliver my weavings to whoever came, for whatever I pleased, and the village seemed to think the trade was fair. I was growing tall despite my twisted foot, but when hairs began to sprout on my face, I hid myself and tried to scrape them off with the edge of my knife. Many men outside had hairy faces, but being different was bad enough for me without adding ugliness to it.

One warm month my visitor was Noriel the Blacksmith, and she seemed shy about something. "There are other Jommys in the village now," she said. "One is blind, one is simple, but the other is whole. He's slender-built like you."

I was glad to hear it, and took her hand, not speaking. Then she looked at me and blushed like a girl with her first best friend.

"I have never been to the trailhead," she blurted out. "I feared the Falconers would dislike my strong arms and kill me. But I've always wanted a child and am still young enough to bear. Jommy, would you do this for me?"

She had been a good friend to me since Lennis tormented me on the trail so long ago. "If I can," I said, then had to admit, "The Falconer part of me does not always obey my will, but only its own."

"How like them," she said, and laughed. I remembered what the woman outside had shown me, and for all we were both awkward, I think we handled it well. It was a long time before I heard what came of this, but later from time to time others made the same request, and from time to time I heard news of other boys—they called them Jommys—and how they were doing.

From my hillside I could see the Falconers come down from the crag, and cry the warning. I could see the Dames coming by the forest trail and hoot the dove call. One year I saw great masses of riders moving across the plains, and, frightened, gave the vulture's cry. Later, one of the sheep herders, now armed with spear and sword, told me this was an army, which had burned down and looted a village less hidden. We took in those women and children who survived, and made them ours. I wondered how long they would tolerate the need to hide every year as we did.

That year and many more, the armies moved back and forth, the storms grew wilder and longer, and I heard tales of witches in our village. Not just women with some knowledge of herbs and spellcraft, but women of great power. I remembered then that I had returned with one such, and she had made alliance with our elders. Alone as I was, I heard only fragments of news, but kept up my duty to watch and warn, as well as weave.

(My mother told me that my storm blanket, with its streaks or reds and oranges, and its darkening grays, now hangs on the abbey wall as one of their treasures!)

At last came the great storm that shook even Falcon Crag, when lightnings played around the mountaintops, and wolves howled night-long. The land trembled like a woman in childbirth, and when it was over, the very face of the crag had changed beyond recognition. My next caller, Natha Lorin's-daughter, spoke of the witches doing great deeds as she sat beside me and braided my hair for me. But what I remember most is that the Falconers came no more. Never, ever again.

A hand and a half of years after the Falconers stopped coming, people were calling me the Wise Weaver of the Mountain. They would come to me with questions, as well as news, as if I were a priestess, and they often brought the Jommys when they came, or the boy-children of the people they had taken in. I was starting to think of going back, excessively tall and hairy though I was, and tainted with killing, when I heard a cry on the hillside.

Wounded men were nothing unusual these days. This one was short and wiry, with fair hair and gray eyes, and the look of a fighter by trade. I am no healer, but from the way he breathed, his lungs were hurt. I helped him up the mountain slowly and laid him on my rug. Cousin Natha had been there a few days before; I had plenty to offer him.

"Bandits," he said when I asked. "They grow bold. My brother was murdered years ago and his killer was never found." Speech came hard to him, but he spoke with a gentleness rare among men who lived by the sword. "I'm glad to see a shepherd lad on this hillside, and thank you."

I was feeding him from my pot of vegetable soup, and now offered him my old pain. "My sister-friend, Jorra, was murdered, too. A Falconer killed her, claiming she belonged to them, but she did not."

"If she had a name, she did not," the man said gently. "We don't give our females names. I'm amazed they can even talk, they hear a human voice so rarely." My mouth fell open; quietly he said, "We only speak to them in dire cases. It happened once in my lifetime, and I hope never to see it again."

"You're a Falconer?" I asked stupidly.

"Was. Falcon Crag has fallen." He lay back and closed his eyes, breathing harshly.

For other men I could call the healer, and send them on their way when they were well. A Falconer might recognize her, or the village. And he'd claim ownership for no other cause than a wolf's cause to own the flock he raided. He seemed a man of reason, but—great Jonkara! If he thought we couldn't even talk, the sound of our songs and stories, debates and decidings, might drive him back into a killing madness! Which was so absurd, and so probable, I strangled a laugh and a sob together.

He opened his eyes and said, still gently, "Our customs may seem strange to you, shepherd lad, but you have seen dogs go mad and turn against their masters. So with our women." He winced in pain. "Some still do. Then we must stamp it out, quickly. I had this to do once, and the creature was with child. I did so as humanely as possible. The gods grant I need never do it again!"

I set down the bowl and left, then, turning my face from him, I fled at a cripple's slow pace to the creek, tears coming from me in great gasps. I plunged my head in the icy running water as I cried. This was the man who had killed Jorra! A decent, kindly, reasonable man with beliefs so cruel they had twisted his actions as my foot was twisted, but left his mind untouched. What could I do now?

I should kill him as he slept, to avenge Jorra's murder. If I did not, all the village risked a cleansing and humane death at his hands. I would become no better than the Falconers, but what was that against my people's lives? But then, those who came after me might murder by my example; I could not risk that, either.

Could he be brought to see the truth? In time; but not before he ran mad and tried to kill us all.

I could do nothing, but tend him and let him go. He had a lung wound and would surely die, but that was in the Goddess's hands. I would have done nothing—like a little girl who puts another up to doing her mischief?

But I could not let our village be ravaged by a wolf whose madness masqueraded as reason and necessity. In fact, the Falconer was partly right! Surely we had driven them out as the old tale said because they had fancied themselves our masters, and they had not forgiven us this.

We and Jonkara, I realized then; and Jonkara met killing with killing. I knelt by the stream and prayed, "Gunnora, show me how to save my people without killing, please." Jonkara then cried, "Make him the village storyteller!"

Storyteller? I limped back to the cave. The Falconer waited for me, his face drawn with pain, but still concerned. "Are you all right, lad?" he asked.

"A griping of the bowels," I brushed it off, and refilled his bowl. "Falconer, I heard once of a village of such women as you speak of, but it vanished years ago. A very long time ago." I bit my lip. "If I raise this cloth, the healer woman will come, with help for your wounds and your lungs."

I have rarely seen such fear on anyone's face before, but he composed himself to obey and said, "Thank you, lad."

I would forestall the healer and together we would make up a tale that would misdirect the Falconer as the quail misdirects the mountain cats from her nest. I raised the cloth. Tears were running down my cheeks unashamed, for at last I could truly mourn Jorra without vengefulness or self-pity or fear for my soul, and I wept as I forgave her killer once and for all.

A falcon cried out overhead. The Falconer's body trembled and convulsed, and then lay still and white. I put my ear to his chest. His heart had stopped. He had died in fear of our healers! Jonkara cried out again and circled overhead as she left with the Falconer's soul. It seemed then that she smiled, and became Gunnora's dove even as she flew away. Down in the valley, I could hear the village women greet the day in song, and slowly, leaning on a stout stick, I made my way down there to join them.

Afterword

The rule of writing a good science fiction story, said one old master, is to construct a background faithfully—and then tell the tale of the day things were different. When it changed. So, "Falcon's Chick," a young boy reared in a women's world.

I was never happy with the early view of Falconer women as hapless dependents, hanging around between Falconer visits for their lords to tell them what to do. I'm Irish; I know how villagers regard absentee landlords. In fact, it seemed to me that every time a new situation arose, the women of the villages would test their limits further and further, until one woman, driven to the wall, would demand, "Why can't I keep my crippled son?"

The answer, to quote the prayer book of the faith I was reared to, is "envy, hatred, malice, and all other uncharitableness"; for Falconer women are people, just like you and me and Ivan and Jose, Jommy, and the witches of Estcarp themselves.

—Patricia Shaw Mathews

FORTUNE'S CHILDREN

by

Patricia A. McKillip

They named me Lyse, switching the letters of Ysledale, where I
was born, in a cow-barn at Yslekeep. No one claimed me, from
lord to stable-hand. My mother left me there in the straw; she
didn't linger to tell me who had fathered me. They found me
bellowing along with all the cows to be milked, with no legacy
but a pale, soft cloth and an odd, jagged bit of metal on a string
around my neck. The cowherd had taken pity on my mother,
let her in for the night. She didn't give her name. Years later,
when I was old enough to wonder about such things, I asked
him and he told me: She was a big-eyed, delicate, sweet-spoken
woman, he said; she gave him a silver coin for his silence and
his help, then she vanished, leaving me to him as well. He was
old and rheumy by then, and his memories were fading into
fantasy. No delicate gentlewoman could have born such a
rawboned gawk as I turned out to be.

I got my first tooth knocked out in a fistfight when I was six.
When I was ten, I battled in the long spring evenings among the
young boys, with wooden swords and blunt knives. The older
warriors laughed to see me chasing the boys around the yard,
yelling and whirling my weapon, with my feet bare and my skirt

stained with dirty dishwater. At sixteen, when I joined the
army that the lord of the keep raised against the siege of
Ysledale, no one laughed. That was the last I knew of home,
then, for our attackers had spilled over like a terrible spring
flood, seemingly out of nowhere—though we guessed, by their
blurred faces and odd, singing swords of light, that they had
come down from the northern mountains, out of the Waste.
Yslekeep burned; a handful of us escaped, ducking flames and
falling timber. We were beaten into Maryedale, and then into
Kylldale. The keeps were ruined; clans scattered into the hills;
farms, villages, and families decimated. Finally, after a bloody
spring and summer, we vanquished them. Or some say the
pounding autumn rains did them in, beat them down into the
earth. I don't know. When the smoke cleared, I was a blooded
warrior, a blank shield for hire, since I had no home; I had
nothing but a bit of metal on a string, an old, thin, finely woven
cloth I wore about my throat, and a reputation. I never even
bothered to hide my long hair. I was as tall as most men, strong
and tireless. The best learned to trust me; the worst learned to
leave me be.

So I wandered for a few years, through High Hallack, even
across the sea to Estcarp. I hired on a ship for a time, to guard
it from a fleet of pirates looting the traders' ships. The bitter
battles we fought cleared out the nest of marauders, but they
killed my love for open sea. Standing on a burning ship collapsing into itself, with nowhere to escape but down into a wet,
airless, alien world, made me long for land again. So I sailed
back to High Hallack, thinking to seek employment in the
south, as far from the Waste as I could get. But as soon as I set
foot on solid ground, I was seized by a sudden and overwhelming compulsion to find my mother.

It seemed very strange to me. I had thought of her, and then
turned my back on those thoughts years before. She was a
woman who had left her child unnamed in a cow-barn, to
starve, to get stepped on by a cow, to be raised, at best, to a life
of drudgery. No one was obligated to care if I lived or died, if I
learned to read, if I was loved or abused. I had made myself
what I was, with no help from her. I thought I had forgotten
her. Yet in an hour I became obsessed with her, furious with

her, curious about her. If she was alive, I would find her. If she was dead, I would trouble memories of her until, dead or alive, she gave me answers to my questions.

I bought a horse and gear at the dock where the traders and farmers and merchants were all dickering. I had money from my work on the trade-ship; I could live on that for some time. I bought some provisions at a nearby inn. Then I sat on my calm gray mare with the roads running north and south and west in front of me, and had no idea where to go.

In the end I rode north for three days, to the blackened ruins of Yslekeep. It was all I could think of doing.

There were sheep grazing on the green hillside among the fallen stones and broken walls. The cow-barn where I had been born existed only in my memory; wildflowers grew where it had stood. I sat on a stairway that had once run up the inner keep; now it climbed seven feet and stopped at open air. I ate bread and cheese and brooded over my past. The old cowherd who saw my mother was long dead; those who had known me best, from the kitchens, the training yard—all were dead or scattered. Where could I go to find her? Who could I ask? Something brushed my cheek: a windblown corner of the silky cloth my mother had left me. Why, I asked myself in sudden, impatient despair, had I bothered to keep it all these years? She had left me so little: that, and the odd piece of metal I wore now on a silver chain. Silvery gray, unornamented, thinner than a coin, the metal was like half an oval or half an eye, cut with a couple of graceful curves down the long center. It was meaningless, valueless. What kind of a woman would leave her child a cold, useless half moon of metal rather than a name?

But, I thought, this is all I have of her, the metal and the cloth. This is where I must begin.

The cloth teased my face again; I stroked it absently. It was light as breath. My hands tugged at it, pulled it loose. I dropped my face into its softness. I seemed to smell memories, then: threads running through it of old fires, the dust and bloody-iron of battles, briny sea winds, even the smell of the cow-barn. My life in those worn, delicate threads . . . I breathed more deeply: a fragrance of meadow grass, bread from the ovens, new-mown

hay, the scent of roses from the rose garden blowing over the
wall into the training yard on a long spring evening . . .

I smelled night through an open door . . . Cloth was
stretched on a loom, pale as bone, its threads silken, gleaming
in firelight. Hands, slender, delicate, workworn, moved a shut-
tle quickly across the loom . . . A bit of metal flashed from a
silver chain that swung free as the weaver bent over her
work . . .

I lifted my face out of the cloth, blinking. Had I dreamed a
moment?

Or had someone hidden in the woods and rolling hills of the
Dales sensed me searching for her, and sent a thought?

I stood up. The shadows had lengthened while I dreamed; it
was late afternoon. My mare was cropping beside the old
milkhouse wall. I descended the broken stairs, calling to her.
When my foot hit the grass I heard a sound out of a grave, out
of another life: the eerie, thrumming voices of the weapons that
had destroyed Yslekeep.

I leaped onto the mare's back and rode her hard down the
hill, feeling my unarmed back a target as wide as a corn field. I
didn't know if the sound was only another reverberation out of
my memory, or if the dark forces out of the Waste had roused
again and caught me there. I just ran. Later, I felt, was a good
time to find out which I ran from.

I spent that night in an inn. It was a dreary, thin-walled,
noisy place, but at least it was safe. I rode farther north the
next day and the next. I told myself I went north only because it
was as good a direction as any other; I could turn anytime, for
any reason. Yet even when I began to feel the strange, dreary
imminence of the Waste ahead of me, I continued north. For
no reason. The roads became narrower, rutted, overshadowed
by twisted trees. People seemed rougher, surlier; even the fields
had a miserly, stony look to them. It was as if a thin, malevolent breeze blew over this part of the Dales, causing the folk
here to begrudge a stranger a warm word, and to begrudge
even the night the light from their shuttered houses. I felt it
keep in me: a bitter, angry sorrow nagged at me, that I had no
real name, no home, that I had been unloved, abandoned—
when all my life I had made my home where I found myself,

and had never felt unwanted. Still, like spores of trouble blown out of the Waste, the bitterness and anger found soil and grew in me, until I barely recognized myself. One night, for the first time in years, I let myself be edged into a stupid, dangerous quarrel.

My challenger was a half-drunk boy, a guard in some local household. He had come into the tavern with a couple of friends, where I sat quietly in a corner, eating a watery stew. No one else in the place—farmers, a couple of merchants—had paid me much attention, even though since I had heard these singing swords again, I rode armed. I was very tired, depressed; the stew was not helping matters any. I raised my eyes at the wrong time and met the wandering gaze of the young guard. His eyes brightened; I recognized trouble, and my spirits sank to the soles of my boots. I had not had to prove myself or defend my reputation for years; I felt too weary to do it now. I simply wanted peace, and the easiest way to peace leaned, silver and deadly, on the wall beside me.

"What have we here?" the young man exclaimed. He joggled his companions for their attention, spilling ale on them. "A lady warrior?" I chewed stolidly on a bit of leathery meat, ignoring him, but he pulled his friends across the room. "What household do you fight for, lady? A house full of women? What house?" He leaned over the table, nearly falling into my bowl. "What house?"

I looked at him finally. "I have fought for Yslekeep and for the Sulcar traders," I said evenly.

"And now?" he persisted.

"I am not for hire."

"Not for any hire?" he asked with a boy's leer. I ignored it, taking another bite of stew and swallowing with difficulty. He seated himself on the edge of my table. His friends flanked him, grinning; the farmers watched expressionlessly. I felt his hand slide down my hair, then loosen the strip of linen that tied it back. "Tell the truth. You are too pretty to be a fighter. You fight best when the battle is over, and being refought in words around the fire. But who would care? I'm sure you entertain quite well . . . Did you steal this sword from some fallen warrior?"

He lifted his hand from my hair, ran his fingers down the long sheathed sword with the same light caress. Something went dark behind my eyes. When I could see again, I was standing with the unsheathed blade in my hand. The young guard had his back to the wall; I saw the muscles of his throat move as he swallowed beneath the tip of the blade slanted upward to drive through his mouth, into his feeble brain. I was talking; both my voice and my hand shook with rage.

"This sword was forged for me in the armory of Yslekeep, and given to me by the last lord of Yslekeep himself. I fought my first battle when I was younger than you. I have been a warrior for ten years, in High Hallack and on the sea, and I have never in any moment of all those ten years wanted to kill so much as I do now."

His face was dead white; his friends were noiseless as mice. I would have murdered him for any reason: a wrong word, a creaky door, a spoon clattering into a bowl. I didn't care. Someone at my shoulder murmured, "Excuse me," in such a polite, reasonable tone that it eased around my fury. In that moment, a ham-sized fist caught the drunken warrior on the side of his head, and he crumpled away from my blade to the floor.

The same voice spoke again, the same hand moved busily, collecting my sheath, my cloak. "Is that your mare in the yard, lady?" I nodded, speechless. "I know a quieter place for supper. The food here is pig swill. Come."

His voice was like the best of the voices I had taken orders from in my life: I suppose I followed him because of that. When I reached the yard, I began to tremble again, not from anger, but from how appallingly close I had come to killing in such a silly quarrel.

I tried to mount, then gave up and leaned wearily against the gray mare's side. "What is the matter with me?" I wondered, and my rescuer answered:

"It's this place."

I looked at him finally. He was around my age, burly as the biggest farmer I had ever seen. He towered over me by a head. His barley-colored hair fell lankly to his brows; his nose matched his size; his eyes, like his voice and expression, were

clear, good-tempered. He added, as I stared at him, "I thought
you might regret killing."

I drew breath and nodded; I saw the flicker of relief in his
eyes, and realized I still held my unsheathed sword. I took the
sheath from him. "Yes. Thank you." I sheathed the sword and
took my cloak. I mounted, and his eyes changed again.

"Wait! I thought—could we share a meal?"

"I'm not hungry now," I said desultorily, "and I have a long
way to go. I think. I am very grateful to you, though. I have
never killed anyone in a tavern before."

"It gets messy," he said.

"You might think I get pushed into quarrels often."

"No. I don't."

"But I don't. It's been so long, in fact, that I've forgotten
how to dance around them." I lifted the reins; his voice stopped
me again.

"But who are you?" he asked baldly. "Where are you
going?"

I looked down at him, surprised, recognizing the impulse in
him that considered my business his business. I found I liked
looking at his big, young face, with the fair stubble on it like a
mown field. I didn't mind giving him a bit of truth. "I am Lyse,
born in a cow-barn at Yslekeep. I decided it is time for me to
find my mother."

His eyebrows rose to vanish under his hair. "Why?" he asked
with reason. "If that's where she left you?"

"I don't know. It's not a thing I have to understand, just
something I must do." I pulled the shard of metal from under
my shirt, to prove to him that she had given me—not much—
but something. The metal glowed strangely, moon-colored in
the twilight. "She left this on a string around my neck. And she
wrapped me in this cloth."

He stared at the metal. His hand reached toward it impulsively, dropped: a small gesture that made me catch my
breath. "You know what it is."

"No. But I know where it came from."

"Where?"

But, shrewd as a trader, he bargained for that "where." He
would not tell me where; I could not go alone, it was dan-

gerous; anyway, the directions were too complicated. He had no great wish to go there himself; I could tell that by the lines of uneasiness and distaste that formed beside his mouth. But for some reason, he was reluctant to let me go out of his life as haphazardly as I had entered it.

"All right," I said finally. "Take me there." And he smiled, his face flushing as if he had won some great victory instead of a ride into uncertain danger.

We had meant to find an inn for the night, but there were none along the path he chose. So we spent a night among the trees, sharing our supplies. He had dried meat and dates and brandywine; I had dried apples and salty, blue-veined cheese. As we ate, I felt my spirits revive a little, enough to finally wonder about him.

"Who are you?" I asked, and realized that the courteous and prudent time to ask that had long passed. But he refrained from laughing at me. He stretched out on the ground, his face, half moonlit, half firelit, looking content with bracken for a bed and a pillow of stone.

"I am a bastard son of the lord of Hollowkeep," he said. My eyes widened in the dark, for Hollowkeep was a story, a fable, a mythical place of grim poverty and eerie ways. To be a child of Hollowkeep was to be a child of chancy fortune; to be a bastard of Hollowkeep was a threadbare destiny indeed.

"You seem cheerful enough in spite of it," I commented.

"Odd things happen to me." He nudged a branch onto the fire. "I've grown used to it."

"Like what?"

"I found a woman lying on a roadside once. I thought she had fainted from weariness and hunger, so I stopped and fed her all I had. It turned out she was a witch, she had just come back from a journey into the Waste. She looked into a midnight-blue jewel she had found there, and read my future."

"What did she see?"

"She said I was a child of Hollowkeep." He chuckled. "Then she gave me the jewel to sell and went on her mysterious way. I bought a horse and sword, since I had lost both in a battle at Maryekeep, and I joined the army in Kylldale in time to get hit by a flying weapon during the—"

"You fought in those battles for the three keeps, too?"

"I mostly did not fight since I was hurt. It was strange . . . I never saw what hit me, and I never bled much. It was as if an ice flow had entered my veins, slowed my blood, my thoughts. I saw things: our world like a dream out of our enemies' eyes. They were alien eyes. They could not see color, they could see heat and cold. Especially cold . . . When autumn came, and the rains turned everything wet and cold, they grew confused."

"What did they want?" I whispered.

"I saw that, too. They were oddly drawn by a bit of metal."

I swallowed. My throat was so dry beneath the touch of the metal I could barely speak. "This?"

"You left Ysledale after the final battle, didn't you? You disappeared for a long time."

"Yes." I drank brandy, shifted closer to the fire, as cold as if the icy vision flowed through me. "I went south, then I went to sea."

"And now," he said very softly, "you are back."

"Aren't you afraid?" I whispered. "Of me? I am."

He rolled upright, sat looking at me. "You are not the danger. Neither is that piece of metal. They are."

"But—"

"Do you want to take it off, bury it somewhere?"

I nodded. "But how would my mother know me?" I was silent then for a very long time. His voice came out of the firelight, speaking my thoughts.

"Who is your mother that she would leave that with a child?"

"The ruin of three keeps." A tear slid down my cheek, startling me. I brushed at it furtively, huddled over myself. "So," I whispered. "Son of Hollowkeep. Where are you taking me?"

"I have led you down a road and into a story," he said. "Now I must follow you."

"When you were hurt, dreaming, did you see anything more about this metal?" All the words I spoke had jagged edges, hurting my throat. I could not see the man's face; it was lowered as he listened to me. I saw his pale hair move as he shook his head. I swallowed, but the words still burned. "Who are you? What is your true name?"

"Jaryl," he said. "I am the only living child, bastard or otherwise, of the lord of Maryekeep." He leaned across our dwindling fire; his big hand stroked away the tears on my face. Then he roused the fire again. "My mother was the abbess of Seely Shrine, who broke her faith and vows to love. So you see, being the bastard son of a ruined father and a foresworn mother, I truly am a child of Hollowkeep. At least I know them both, and that they loved. At least I could fight a little for my father before he died."

"He was a strong, kind man, I heard."

"I heard tales of you, as we fought that war."

"Did you recognize me at the tavern?"

"Yes, the moment you drew your sword. You had us all transfixed. Even the hearth flames stopped moving." That made me smile. He reached across the fire again, slipped his hand behind my head. I saw his eyes, firelit, smiling, and I let him drift toward me. But he caught his breath sharply and loosed me to beat at the tongues of fire along his sleeve.

I laughed immoderately while he put himself out. "I'm sorry," I gasped. "I'm sorry."

He sighed. "Even for me that was clumsy. I'm sorry, too." We sat there uncertainly, the fire still between us, idling innocently within a log. I had not been kissed for a hundred years, it seemed. Did he desire me, or my legend, I wondered; he, on his side, did not seem to know either.

"Are you hurt?" I asked cautiously; he said at the same time, once again, "I'm sorry." We stopped speaking, waited for each other's voices. He cleared his throat.

"I'll find more wood for the fire."

"It's a warm night."

"I know," he said simply. I heard him walk away. And then my whole body chilled again as I realized what he was thinking: The last peaceful spring night at Yslekeep was much like this.

I lay back on the soft ground, feeling the metal like a death-blade at my own throat.

But nothing troubled us that night. When dawn came, we rode again, through thick, dark woods where no birds sang, and then through a pass between steep cliffs. In the late afternoon we rode out of the pass onto a vast, rocky plain edged with purple-gray mountains, the barren southern boundary of the Waste.

Here the plain still had life to it. Small dark streams cut through lichen and stone; solitary trees, twisted and stunted by wind, broke the misty horizon. But among the stones and mossy streams the grass grew pallid, sour; not even mountain sheep could live on it. The air smelled of dust and of rain that never fell. Here and there great dark-weathered stones rose above the ground, wanderers like ourselves, trudging across the plain to an uncertain destiny.

It was there, as I stared at the harsh, bleak landscape, that I had another vision.

Somewhere across the plain rocks gathered themselves out of the embrace of water and moss and cold ground. They built themselves into a tiny cottage . . . Within the shadows of the cottage, something gleamed, swinging gently in and out of darkness. Something quite small, something . . .

I came back to myself. Jaryl's hand was on my shoulder. I held the metal at my breast so tightly it had cut into my hand. I had made a sound, or he had; some voice echoed in the air.

He loosened my hand gently from the metal. It was no gentlewoman's palm he opened, scarred and callused and newly bleeding. He dismounted, searched among the mosses beside a stream, and pulled up a handful of something purple. He pressed it against my palm; the throbbing died away.

"I lived for a while with an old woman who knew every tree-leaf and herb, mushroom and moss in these old hills," he said while he bound my hand. "I was a child then. I had run away from another place . . . She found me curled up asleep among some yarrow, naked and starving, she said, a wild thing. I don't remember that. She took me home and fed me, and taught me how to find things for her. I loved her. When she died, I threw myself into a bog, I was that wild . . ." He gave a small chuckle. I stared at him.

"How did—"

"Oh, a man came along and pulled me out. I fought him, wanting to die. He made a bargain with me: that if I came with him for five years and learned to be a warrior, at the end of those five years we would fight again, he and I, and if I won, I could throw myself back into the bog. I was young—not twelve—but big even then, and he liked my strength. He took me to Maryekeep. Five years later I met the lord of Maryekeep

by accident on a stairway. He looked me in the eye, I looked
him in the eye, and we both knew what we saw. He saw the
abbess of Seely Shrine, I saw my father. He was still married,
my mother had died long before, he had never known what
happened to me until I appeared in front of him on his stairs,
wearing the colors of his household . . ."

"What did he say?" I asked, entranced. Jaryl smiled.

"He said nothing; he just looked at me, and I saw how he
must have loved my mother. Then he kissed me on the cheek
and went on down. I sat on the stairs in a daze until someone
came along and rousted me. He never spoke of the matter—he
always was a stiff-tongued man—but he came sometimes to the
training yard and taught me himself. I think in time he would
have gotten around to speaking. But two years was not time
enough. Maryekeep fell and he died, and fighting for Kyllkeep,
I was wounded, and then Kyllkeep fell . . . and that was the
end of my family life."

"Then what did you do?" I asked.

"Like you, what I had to." He mounted again, gazing across
the plain. His gear nudged at my attention; for the first time I
noticed its incongruity.

"You don't carry a sword."

He looked at me. Again for the first time, I noticed the color
of his eyes: a light blue that hid nothing. He smiled, amused.

"I never did like fighting much." Then he touched me lightly,
as if guiding me back to some path. "What did you see when
you stopped just then?"

"A house." I drew breath, remembering. "A tiny stone
house, somewhere ahead of us. And inside the house . . ." My
hand reached again for the metal, as if by gripping it I could see
more clearly. Jaryl took it from me before I hurt myself again.
"This."

He grunted. An evening wind came from the east across the
plain, a thin, mean, threadbare wind that crept into clothes like
a pickpocket. I shivered. Jaryl, his head close to mine, studied
the metal in his palm. I studied the shades of wheat and barley
in his hair, the muscles in the back of his neck. He started suddenly, his whole body tightening, as if he had been struck, and
I wheeled my horse away from him, my throat swelling with

fear and anger. I drew my sword, scanning the pass behind us, sure that our talk of the old battles had brought the attackers with their singing weapons upon us once again.

Jaryl turned his mount also, glancing around us a little wildly. "What is it?"

I looked at him a moment. Then I sighed and sheathed my sword. "Why did you jump like that? You scared me."

"You scared me," he said. He rode close again, lifted the metal. "Look."

"So? It's blood from my hand," I said wearily. My body was still settling itself down after its false alarm.

"No," he said. "Yes. You bled on it. Now look at it."

I did. I saw what he saw, then, and my breath stopped. Beneath the thin film of blood from my hand, a strange language had appeared, etched into the metal in tiny rows that ran the width of the metal and then were broken off.

"No," I whispered. "Not broken, cut. But what language is it? What does it say? Can you read it?"

"No." His voice sounded very distant. "I've never seen anything like it. But it's very simple to explain why it was cut in two."

"Well," I said after a moment. "Explain it. Simply."

He raised his head finally. All the humor was gone from his face. He seemed older suddenly, and beneath his warrior's build and competence I finally glimpsed the other man I didn't know so easily: the one who picked herbs, recognized odd languages. He said, "Two halves make a whole; the whole is very dangerous. Your mother was not able to destroy it years ago, so she cut it and separated the halves. Yet it still must be destroyed, or she would have buried it, flung it into deep water, anything, rather than leave half of it around the neck of her newborn child. She has the other half. You are bringing her the whole."

For the first time in my life, I felt very small on that vast, windy plain, and very vulnerable. "She's bringing me," I said, and shivered. "Jaryl. We don't know her. How do we know what she will use this for?"

"How would you stop yourself from going to her?" he asked,

and I knew he was right. I couldn't stop. Nothing could stop me.

"But how," I asked impatiently, "can I find one tiny stone cottage on this plain?"

He considered it. Somewhere in his piecemeal past he had stumbled into experience of such matters. "Have you had other visions?"

I told him of the daydream I had had sitting among the blacked ruins of Yslekeep. I didn't tell him of the deadly singing I heard out of the past; there was enough in front of us to make us edgy. He made an absent noise, musing.

"Try the cloth," he said at last. "Threads weave, so do lives . . . Perhaps she wove a path in it for you."

So, trying to draw one tiny stone cottage out of this great stony plain, I gathered the cloth in one hand, held it against my face. We rode in silence into evening. We passed dark jutting stones that the earth had thrust out of itself in a mysterious quarter-moon pattern. I watched a black raven land on a stone covered with pink moss, the first living creature I had seen on the plain. Later I watched a long black snake wind along our path awhile and then slither out of sight. A corner of the shawl blew across my nose and mouth. I moved my head to breathe, and a strand of my hair whipped darkly across my eyes.

The dark shadows of the cottage within the open door . . . What vague light fell across the threshold revealed a hard earth floor. The half oval of metal turned in the shadows, caught light, glinted, turned. Someone stood in the shadows, held the metal by its chain. Turning, glinting, the metal beckoned. The stones of the house, the land itself beckoned. This place, they said. This place.

And in the vision I saw a shadow arching out of the earth, bridging earth and air like a black rainbow above the house.

This place. This place.

When I could see the world again, I said, "East. We ride east."

We slid off our horses then, for night was falling fast. Sucked into that vision, I couldn't speak much; I could scarcely think. Jaryl, too, ate silently, preoccupied. But I felt his eyes on my face now and then. Once he reached out, brushed a crumb from the side of my mouth. That turned my attention; with the same odd, drugged intensity, I regarded him as if he were at once very far away and very close, at once a stranger and a friend.

I felt him kiss me gently; that too was very far away.

It took us four days to cross that wild, empty plain. The day skies were gray, sultry by noon, too cool by evening. But at night the stars seemed to rain down on us, and the wind sang the alien runes. I still spoke very little; all my thoughts were concentrated on one tiny, turning speck of light. But one night as we lay beside the fire, restless on the rough ground, I felt the stars pour into my eyes, and I heard my voice again, "How beautiful they are, all the secret worlds."

"Yes," Jaryl said, but his voice held other words: no, and perhaps, and yes but beware, beware.

In the late afternoon of the fourth day, I saw the black rainbow.

I pulled at my reins, startled, and realized I was free again. Jaryl, murmuring in surprise, had stopped as abruptly. Two enormous, massive black stones had sagged together to form the apex of a triangle. And between them . . . a gray stone house.

Staring at it, I felt chilled without knowing why. The stones were melted into one another by time and weather; they must have fallen together thousands of years ago. It was not such a strange place to build a cottage. Yet something seemed wrong, distorted: the tiny house in the middle of nowhere, the stones themselves . . .

They were alive. As we watched, strands of blue fire spat from the apex of the stones, wove down their sides into the earth.

I saw a gleam of metal within the open cottage door, like a scratch of sudden light upon the shadows. I put one cold hand against my mouth. This was a place of magic, mystery, no place for a plain swordswoman. Then I thought: Lyse of Yslekeep, lady of the cow-barn, you have nothing in this world but courage, and if you lose that you will have nothing at all.

She came outside then: a tiny figure in the distance with the great black stones above her head. She waited for us.

She blinked a little when she saw me: a big-boned, broad-shouldered woman wearing fighter's garb, with a sword at her side. The old cowherd had remembered well: she herself was slight, her dark hair barely beginning to gray, her hands the fragile, workworn hands of my dream. Her metal-piece hung on the chain in her hand, flashing now and then with its own pale light.

I dismounted. We gazed at each other, mute. She said at last, wonderingly, "You kept the cloth."

Her voice was as delicate as the rest of her. I swept my hair out of my face. I had lost the tie somewhere, and now it kept weaving dark webs in front of my eyes. I said, "Who are you? Who was my father, that you got such a giant for a daughter?"

But her eyes had gone past me to Jaryl.

I felt a sudden hurt anger that I had come so far to find her, and she had forgotten me already. I didn't, I reminded myself, need a mother. I never had. This one did not even look proba-ble. Then I heard her say to Jaryl, "You are the child of Hol-lowkeep," and my anger turned to wonder.

He had a look on his face to match my wonder. "You are the witch out of the Waste I found on the roadside. I fed you my last dry bread and moldy cheese."

"I gave you a blue jewel. Now you have brought me my child."

I found my tongue finally. "You are of Estcarp."

She nodded, sighing. "I would be in Estcarp, if I hadn't found this to keep me here."

"You have been on this plain."

"Since you were born."

She changed under my eyes, then: fragile as she looked, she had a great warrior's strength. "But why?" I whispered. "Why?"

She turned her head to look up at the stones overshadowing her. "I have been guarding this Gate. The strange army out of the Waste that attacked Ysledale ten years ago has been on this world for a thousand years, but their homeworld lies elsewhere. Someone of great power made a key long ago, that locked this Gate against others of their world trying to enter. I found the key in the Waste before you were born, and deciphered it. But

I couldn't destroy it. I divided it, left half of it with you, partly so we could identify each other if fortune were that kind to us, partly to hide it from the alien army, whom I stole it from. But somehow they sensed it in Ysledale, and came searching for it. Me they could not find: the Power in this Gate overwhelms the Power of the key. The runes on the key would tell them how to lock and unlock the Gate at their bidding. And they have an army striving to get in."

"How can you tell?"

She glanced at the stones again: the blue fire washed over them swiftly, silently, vanished. "You can see their Power."

I felt another moment's panic. It seemed a very silly place for the three of us to be, in the Gateway on an empty plain, with a darkness out of the stars about to pour through it.

"You have both pieces again," I said. "Can you destroy it now?"

She nodded. "Yes. I have learned how."

"Then do it! I waited for twenty-six years to meet you, and you have been for twenty-six years on this benighted plain—that's long enough for both of us."

She opened her mouth to answer, then didn't. She smiled at me instead, and my heart turned over suddenly, that she had the right to smile at me like that, as if she had accidentally made something pleasing to her. So for a moment I forgot about the Gate.

"Estcarp." She nodded again, silent, waiting. "What brought you across the sea?"

"I felt something dangerous stirring in this part of the world. I was driven to find it. You came with me inadvertently."

"It does not take nine months to get from Estcarp to High Hallack. Normally."

"No."

"So—"

"You were conceived across the sea." She paused; this time I waited. "I walked alone out of this plain, across the Dales, searching for a home for you when I knew you were coming. When I reached Yslekeep I could walk no farther and I sensed it was a tranquil place. A good place. I couldn't keep you on the plain. I had nothing to give you, nothing to help you grow

in the world among people. I made the cloth for you out of
threads that worms spin on the plain near dawn. It was all I
could give you. All I had." She smiled again, though I saw tears
glisten in her eyes. "And look at you. You survived without
me, you grew strong, gifted, intelligent, you even kept the
things I gave you, when you must have hated me sometimes.
You heard me when I called, you came here. None of this I
expected. But all of it I hoped for. What did—what did they
call you?"

"Lyse," I said. "The cook named me." I added gruffly, because, mother or no, it was not easy to question a witch of
Estcarp. "And you? Can— Do you have a name you can give
me?"

"Oh, my dear." She crossed the distance between us, held
my rough, scarred hands. "I am Chace. Your father was—"

And then the ground shook under us so hard it threw even
Jaryl off his feet.

He had been holding the horses' reins as we spoke; falling, he
kept his grip on them. As soon as I could get my balance, I
drew my sword from where it hung on my saddle. Jaryl found
time to ask, "What do you think you can do with that?"

"I don't care," I said tersely. "I want it. What is happening?"
I asked my mother as she tugged at the chain around my neck.

"They have grown more powerful," she said breathlessly. "I
must get through—" The chain tangled in my hair. Impatiently
I pulled it, broke it, and pushed the metal into her hand. And
then I felt as bewildered as if I had given her all of my past, and
that the next moment was the true beginning—or more probably the end—of my life.

Light flowed continuously down the flanks of the Gate; it began to arch from stone to stone, weave a web within the triangle. A strand of light broke free suddenly. It streaked
through the air toward me, and licked my sword. The force
numbed my arm from fingers to shoulder; the sword, blackened, pitted, clattered to the ground. I stared at it. Then I lifted
my head, watched my mother fit the pieces of the metal—her
life and mine—together.

The light within the Gate vanished. A darkness swallowed it,
swallowed the cottage, swallowed the world framed by the

stones. There was an eerie silence, and then the long, long sigh of wind coming from another place, or perhaps the sound of time itself traveling between worlds. Stars appeared within the Gate. World after shining world, and webs of light with new stars cradled in them. I stood spellbound again, feeling as if I were the Gate itself and whoever traveled into this world's time must come first through my eyes.

And one came: a dark, faceless rider on a strange beast, with a blade of blue light blazing in his hand. He rippled out of the night, so close to Jaryl that the horses pulled from his hand in terror and fled. Jaryl stared up at the rider, still entranced himself; in that moment, as he stood with his marveling, defenseless face upturned to death, I picked up my poor blackened sword and threw it.

It struck the rider just as his light-sword swung into Jaryl's face. Jaryl had flung up his arm; my sword hit the alien rider; the light-sword descended, and then there was a great explosion of light within my mother's hands. The earth reeled again; I stumbled, blind. When I could see again, I saw:

A pair of black stones toppled together, with a tiny gray cottage between them. An alien beast fleeing in one direction across the plain, our horses fleeing in another. A headless shadow on the ground.

Nothing else. I picked myself up, staring. I retrieved my sword, wondered briefly at the odd metallic gleams within the alien's open neck. I went to the cottage door, saw a dirt floor, a loom with shining, half-worked cloth. I backed out, scanned the plain.

No one. I shivered, my skin prickling. I stepped back from the cottage to stare up again between the dark, weary stones, where moments ago night and the stars had hung.

I whispered, "Jaryl? Mother?"

And then the wedge of daylight winked black again, and a giant spilled out of it, trailing stars.

I screamed, raising my sad blade. Then I lowered it, panting. Jaryl stood before me, looking stunned. The Gate cleared again one final time.

"Where did you go?" I whispered.

"I don't know. She—" He stopped, drew breath. "She took

me with her." He came to my side, dropped his arm heavily across my shoulders. "She saw I might be killed in that instant, so she pulled me through. Then she sent me back."

"Where is she?"

He shook his head. "Somewhere. Some world. She sealed the Gate against them, but she still must destroy the key. She said she would return when she could."

"But, Jaryl—" I found myself blinking away tears. "I just found her!"

"I know."

"How do we know what time does in other places? Or what she will do there? She spent half her life on this lonely plain. If I were her, I would find another Gate, and then another, and then another, just to taste freedom for a while."

He kissed my hair. I gazed upward at the great doorway, envisioning her path.

"There's no way—"

"No. My heart, she took the key with her. There is no way for you to follow."

I sighed, dropped my head against his shoulder. "Then I'll never know who my father was."

"We are fortune's children," he said simply, and loosed me, after another kiss, to call the horses back.

Afterword

I remember encountering Andre Norton's Witch World as a teenager; what lingered through the decades long after I had read of it was the eerie, wonderful mingling of science fiction and fantasy. Details escaped me: I had to read to write "Fortune's Children," study the maps and the notes. Things caught at my imagination as I researched: the mercenary without a home, the Waste (wastelands fascinate me because they only seem barren, empty; they are always sources of enormous, untapped power), witchcraft, the strong position of women in various types of societies. True fantasy worlds remain in the memory like countries once lived in: it was a pleasure to return to this one, even though I had to find my own way into it.

—Patricia A. McKillip

GODRON'S DAUGHTER

by

Ann Miller

and

Karen E. Rigley

How many times have I heard the story of my birth retold? About how my mother and father, though no older than I am now, pledged their sworn troth; how Godron, servant of the Dark, kidnapped my mother while I still grew inside her to corrupt me to serve his own evil plans; of her rescue and the purification of my birth at an ancient place of Power. Yet, each time I listen closely, as if hearing it anew, hoping I might catch something heretofore missed; something that would explain this growing restlessness inside.

Ah, a poor choice of words, perhaps, as it seems more of a seeking than restlessness. I only know I'm being drawn toward . . . something? Somewhere? And soon must accept this compulsion to go forth and find answers to questions I do not know how to ask.

"Silistia?"

Upon hearing my cousin Reldo call to me, I put away

my journal and left my cozy window seat to walk outside into the early spring sunshine. As I emerged from the house, Reldo lifted his hand to motion me over to 'the stock pen. I quickened my steps, guessing he intended to show me the first foal of spring, an arrival eagerly awaited by us both.

I stepped up on the bottom board of the pen to peer over at the gangly, staggering newborn, then swapped delighted grins with Reldo. Even though he stood on the ground and I on the board, I still had to look up at him. At a year younger than I, Reldo, just past his sixteenth birthday, was over half a head taller, having grown remarkably during this past winter. My mother and his father, both of the Old Race, are double first cousins, and Reldo had the typical dark hair color of that lineage, as did I. But his eyes were the same light ginger hue of his outworld mother's, while mine are the clear gray of the Old Ones.

My father, Gunnal, knelt beside the shaky foal as Lenil, Reldo's father, stroked and complimented the mare.

"At least she had the decency to birth her foal in the morning hours," Lenil said with a laugh. "And not drag us from our beds at midnight."

"Perhaps we should ask her to speak to the other mares," Father suggested, obviously lighthearted at the successful foaling. The winter had proved a hard one and more than a few of our animals had succumbed to its icy harshness. Each new foal would serve to replenish our depleted stock.

Animals were not the only thing lost this past bitter winter. At that thought, my gaze went to the little hillock at the far eastern corner of our hold where my small brother lay at rest beneath his cairn of stones. After losing him, I doubted my mother would ever agree to send me for training in my awakening Talent. However, grief for my baby brother overshadowed disappointment and I could feel a sting of tears behind my eyes. He'd had the light brown curls and blue eyes of our father, and I recalled the merriment sparkling in those blue depths as he extended his chubby arms and flexed his stubby fingers, teasing me to pick him up. And I would, laughing and swinging him high . . .

I wondered, Had I know how to use the Power growing within me, could I have saved him?

Reldo's touch on my shoulder made me jump. "Riatha calls you," he said, studying me.

I looked quickly at the house to avert my face from his scrutiny and saw my mother standing in the doorway. "She must need my help to prepare our noon meal," I chattered breathlessly. I hurried to the house. I tried not to display my grief; since my mother acted so bravely I felt I could do no less. My father had wept long and bitterly the night he held his dead son in his arms, but Mother had borne up stoically, steadying us with her strength. But since the initial shock wore off, she clung to me with determined fright.

Spring events continued to distract her, and the rest of us, from our loss. Our old sow birthed her litter that afternoon, and five survived.

"More than I expected, Gunnal," Lenil said as we took our places around the table for our evening meal.

My father grunted agreement as we passed around bowls to help our plates.

"Spring seems to have actually arrived," said Varela, Reldo's outworld mother. "The ranni vines are budding out, and they're usually weather-wise." She handed a piece of buttered bread to Jenli, Reldo's younger sister. I looked at the little girl who favored me more than she did her own brother, with her ash-dark hair and gray eyes of the Old Race, inherited from her father's side. Would the Talent of the Old Ones bloom in her also, as it did in me? She was young yet. That question might not be answered for some years. Feeling my gaze, Jenli turned to me and crossed her eyes and stuck out her tongue.

"Jenli!" Lenil admonished her, not seeing my responding funny-face. Jenli giggled into her hand.

"Never mind scolding her, Lenil," said my father with a lifted brow in my direction. "Silistia encouraged her, I'm sure."

I concentrated on my food, letting the murmur of conversation flow around me, until I heard my name spoken.

"Silistia is seventeen now," Lenil was saying. "Well of an age for training her Talent. She needs—"

"Why?" Mother demanded, cutting off her cousin midsentence. "She can wed, bear children, live a normal life. She doesn't need to develop her Talent. It can be a curse. You know that, Lenil! Even these days Old Ones are viewed with suspicion and distrust."

"Yes, until a wise woman or witch is needed to solve someone's problems," my father pointed out.

"I won't have it," Mother stated firmly. "She will not leave this hold."

It angered me for them to speak of me as if I weren't there or could not speak for myself, but I held my tongue, seeing the tight lines around my mother's mouth. Perhaps when the death of my brother was no longer such a raw wound she would relent. For I longed to exercise my Talent, to learn how to control it, use it for good. Especially since my little brother . . .

I forced such thoughts from my mind and finished my food. Useless, useless. I could only go forward, not change what was past.

Again, I dreamed—someone calling me from deep within the mists of the forest. My mother forbids me to speak of my dreams. She claims they are nonsense, but I can see the fear in her eyes. Something she will not tell me. What is she hiding? Why should it frighten her? This is more than her desire to keep me within the hold by her side.

Reldo laughs at me. He teases that a dream-lover is calling me and asks if I will tell my lover to find a girl for him. I wish it were a lover's voice to gladden my heart, rather than this strange calling that places such a burden upon it. I know I cannot resist much longer seeking out what calls me. The pull grows more powerful each day.

Tomorrow I shall go into the forest to seek out my dream-caller. I must keep my quest secret or Mother will prevent my leaving. Reldo wants to accompany me. He suggests we tell our parents we are going to the Festival of the Young in Emerald Cove. This would please them. My true mission would not.

We must prepare for our journey. Supplies for food, warmth, and survival, for our travels may be lengthy and will take us into primitive territory; deep within the forest where we are forbidden to go. Though it saddens me to defy Mother, I am

compelled to discover my dream-caller. Need burns within my
soul like a white-hot flame.

Morning dawned bright, soft dew kissing the meadowlands.
Reldo bounded in and greeted everyone at breakfast, announcing our wish to attend the festival.

"No," Mother said immediately.

"They are of an age, Riatha," Father said. "You cannot keep
her behind your skirt forever."

Mother opened her mouth but before she could speak,
Varela rested a hand on her arm. "Riatha, let them go. Reldo
can take care of Silistia, just like Lenil used to watch out for
you—" She flashed a smile at her husband. "Still does."

Mother's gaze sought Lenil's hoping for an ally. He smiled
gently. "It'll be all right. Emerald Cove is an easy journey for
young strong legs."

Mother turned to look at me, her eyes bright with unshed
tears. I nearly gave in, feeling her painful fear as though it were
my own, but knew my compulsion would allow me no rest. I
gazed at her pleadingly.

"Very well," she whispered, looking down at her plate.

"I want to go, too!" Jenli piped up, giving me a bad turn
before Varela said, "No, Jenli. You're too young."

Father laughed saying, "Don't worry, little one, your turn
will come." He looked at Reldo and me. "You children must
hurry if you plan to reach Emerald Cove before the festival
opens."

Mother's gray eyes, so like my own, still looked troubled, but
she smiled, shaking her head as if to shoo away lingering cob-
webs of doubt. "Go and have fun, but don't speak to strangers.
Take care of each other."

Our eagerness was understandable so we didn't need to conceal it, quickly finishing our breakfast and rushing to gather our
things.

Impatient, I wanted to head north to the forest; yet forced
my feet to travel east across the meadow until we disappeared
from view of the hold. At the top of the second hill, we glanced
back, satisfied it would be safe to alter our direction. We began
to zigzag down the hillside, then Reldo broke into a run north

toward the forest. I followed him with abandon, enjoying the breeze flinging my hair and the scent of crushed ranni blossoms as we trampled the blue flowers underfoot. I passed my cousin before we entered the forest. Suddenly a shiver shot through me that I blamed on leaving warm sunshine for shade. Evergreens towered over newly budding butron trees, stretching eerie branches up to the heavens. My pack slapped against my back as I halted to wait for Reldo.

He reached me, panting. "You're a swift one, Silistia. Remind me not to race you on a wager." He gazed around the dark forest. "It's like a different world, isn't it?"

Again, a shiver. The fragrance of pine and moss mingled with a sharp repellent odor, the gentle meadow breeze gusted into a chilly wind, and trees blocked out the sunlight so completely it looked like twilight instead of midmorning. The screech of a golden hawk echoed somewhere above us. A sign? But of what, I could not say.

"Silistia?" Reldo sounded dubious. I turned to look at him. "Are you sure we should do this?"

I gazed into his ginger eyes. Perhaps I had erred in allowing him to accompany me. After all, this was my quest, not his. The call tortured me, not him. I could be leading him into mortal danger. "Reldo, you go on to the festival. I must do this. I don't know why, I just must. But you can attend the festival, tell me what it was like so we will never have to confess to our parents—"

"No!" He shook his head vigorously. "Never. I shall not leave you to pursue this—this dream alone. I know I am male, and half outworld, and have no Talent, but I can protect you from beasts and other dangers. No, Silistia. We both turn back or we both go on together."

"Oh, Reldo, you are my best friend as well as my cousin. I only wish I could ignore this calling."

He gave me a crooked smile and I turned to hurry on, pushing through the thickening woods. The siren's call sounded louder in my head, leading me true, though we followed no visible path.

Time ceased to exist in the strange twilight world. No sun passed overhead to mark the hours, hidden behind a translucent silvery overcast. I felt tireless, without hunger, and pressed on through the forest until Reldo's call halted me.

"I'm hungry," he said. "I'm sure it's noon. Aren't you tired?"

I shook my head. "I've acted thoughtlessly. I feel nothing but the desire to continue. Of course, we shall eat and refresh ourselves."

I tried not to rush, but somehow I felt that my goal lay nearby, that soon I would have answers to the questions plaguing me for so long. We set out again.

Cresting a hill, we saw a meadow sloping away toward a forbidding stone tower. I stopped, frozen by the sight—I knew this was my destination.

Reldo stopped beside me, standing close, resting a hand on my shoulder. "What's wrong, Silistia?"

"Here . . ." I breathed, ". . . this place . . ."

A light shudder rippled through his body and I quickly looked at him. "Do you sense anything?"

"I—I'm not sure. I do know the forest is rumored to contain places of Power of the Old Ones . . . perhaps this is one such place."

"Yes. It is a place of Power." But I sensed no warm benevolence. The Dark lurked here. Though fear kindled within me, I knew I must push on, enter those looming premises, seek the one who called me. As we crossed the meadow, I noticed the plants and grasses didn't appear normal and healthy, as if the force emanating from the structure had twisted and deformed them.

Why? Why? The question echoed in my head as we drew close; why would this place—a place of evil, of the Dark—call to me? I wanted to turn and flee but a force caught me securely. My feet made their way as if following outside directions past the outer stone wall on toward the inner castle.

"This looks like an abandoned hold," Reldo said as we stepped up to the gaping doorway. "Not like a place of Power."

"I doubt, cousin, you would know any more than I what a place of Power should look like, since our travels have been confined to occasional trips to Emerald Cove with our parents and visits to our grandparents' hold." I spoke with a bravado I didn't feel. I sensed Reldo's fear mingling with my own. Had I brought him to his doom?

We dropped our packs and stepped inside. A dank chill enveloped us as though we had passed through an invisible curtain. Pale light filtered down from above and I looked up, seeking its source. Several tall, narrow windows placed around the top of the tower allowed the sickly light to enter. I looked at the steep, narrow stone steps winding up the wall of the tower and tentatively approached them with the idea of climbing them. However, within a few steps I realized my goal did not lie this way. I stopped, feeling Reldo bump into me.

"Not here," I said, my voice strangely muted to my own ears.

Without comment he turned to precede me back down, then await my next move. He seemed to know that only I could solve the riddle that beleaguered my mind. I stood in the center of the tower, turning slowly as I examined the dusty stone walls, unbroken by any doorways. Knowing it must be here, I closed my eyes and allowed my mind to seek.

There! It struck me with such force I fell to my knees with a gasp.

"Silistia!" Reldo cried, kneeling to seize me by the shoulders.

Crossing my arms, I placed my hands on his, drawing in deep breaths. "I know . . ." I gasped, ". . . look there . . ."

A doorway appeared where we'd seen none before, and I rose, moving toward it as though pulled by unseen ropes, Reldo right behind me. I halted, suddenly fearing for my cousin, knowing I confronted something here truly of the Dark; something that could—and would—bring harm to us both. Did I have the right to expose him to such danger?

"You must wait here for me," I whispered, and at his protest I insisted, "To keep guard! Would you have me attacked from behind?"

The doubt flitting across his young face told of the war within him my words caused.

"But what awaits before you, Silistia? It's unwise to allow you to go on without me. I will not permit it. I promise to keep a close watch on our backs."

I relented, ashamed of my relief to have Reldo with me as we descended the winding tunnel toward darkness. However, a pale ghostly light seemed to move ever ahead of us, showing us only enough so we would not stumble on the uneven paving stones. Our steps thudded in a hollow echo that the stone walls swallowed up, as though feeding on the sound.

A pressure entered my mind, flowing down to fill my chest with foreboding. Yet I could not stop. In fact my pace quickened in spite of my fear. I hurried forward seeing the end of the tunnel beckoning. Here, I knew, lay my answers. I no longer felt sure I wanted them, but such a choice did not remain for me to make.

The tunnel spilled into a great chamber that arched away into darkness. Runes etched the walls, glowing scarlet, lending a bloody cast to the pale light that had accompanied us and now flickered weakly in the huge vaulted cavern in which we stood.

An ebony stone altar, so black it seemed to trap light within its mysterious depths and absorb without reflection, stood in the center of the chamber. Red glowing runes covered the pedestal it rested upon, throbbing in sequence with their counterparts on the walls. What message did they attempt to convey? I shook my head in frustration, peering frantically at them, failing to decipher their meaning. It seemed to hover just beyond my grasp, tantalizing me.

"You've come at last."

I jumped, startled, at the voice that sounded as if it came from within my head rather than to my ears. I glanced quickly at Reldo for his reaction; he appeared deaf to the voice.

"Only you can hear me, Silistia."

Instinctively, I looked back at the altar. Something wavered above it, something not quite formed. My heart thudded in my chest. "Who are you?" I whispered—or rather, it felt as if I did—perhaps I, too, spoke only with my mind.

"I am your father."

"I don't understand."

Reldo turned to me. "What don't you understand, Silistia?"

I looked at him. "You don't hear the voice?"

"What voice?"

"Can you see what is attempting to form above the altar?"

"I see no visions. What does it look like?"

At his question, I turned back to gaze at the altar. As I stared the vapors took on the form of a man, though it remained ethereal.

"Silistia, I have waited long to claim what is mine. I lost my mortal life in a battle for you. I shall not lose you this time."

"What battle? You speak to me of things I do not know."

"I am Godron, your father. It is for my purpose that you were born."

"I have heard the story of you, of your Power corrupted to the Dark, and of my mother's abduction. But you are not my father. Gunnal is my father."

"Do you seek the truth? If so, I will show it to you. Open your mind."

Visions flooded me: I saw Godron seizing my mother, his Werebeasts slaughtering her guards. I saw him bring her to this very hold and force himself upon her; Mother's screams resounded through my head, punctuated by Godron's brutal laughter. I saw my mother swollen with child and knew it was me growing inside her. I saw her desperate rescue where Gunnal nearly sacrificed himself, receiving a grave wound, allowing Lenil the opportunity to spirit her away. I saw Godron's attempt to recapture her, foiled when Varela happened by to join the fray. I saw Lenil and Varela gaining the place of ancient Power with my mother so that my birth might be purified. I saw then the battle of which Godron spoke; of his disdain of me after the purification rites, his attempt to slice my throat, thwarted by Varela's toss of her dagger.

The horror of his visions so engulfed me that I felt it strike a crippling blow to my core, to my very essence. How could I accept myself as the spawn of this evil Darkness?

In desperation, my mind cried out, "Mother, help me. Is this true?"

I now tried to shut out his invading presence, and found myself unable to do so. "Mother, what's happening?" I cried again.

But I stood alone. Realizing his plan to make me his vessel, I knew I must summon my untrained Talent to eject him. I gathered my strength within me, attempting to protect myself from further invasion, focusing my mind to force him out.

His apparition wavered at my rally. A power I did not know I possessed welled to repel his invasion. I felt his joy at my unexpected display, and realized he intended to harness my power to his command.

I could not let that happen! His capacity for evil could become unconquerable as it drew upon my latent Talent, making it his own. I redoubled my efforts to prevent it.

If only I knew what to do! The runes on the walls and pedestal writhed like snakes and instinctively I stretched out my hands before me, feeling a strange tingling rush to my fingertips. As though in a trance, I sketched a sign in the air and it lingered bluely for a long moment. The runes on the wall seemed to pulse in response and I heard Godron's laughter taunting me, as if urging me to fight my best fight. A wind surrounded me, standing my hair out to swirl around my head wildly, and the crimson glow of the runes flowed toward me as if to engulf me. I traced a circle before me, blue fire sparking where the force from the runes touched it, but it held, shielding me.

No longer amused, Godron sent a mental bolt hurtling into my mind. I fell to my knees with an audible gasp. Through a haze of pain, I saw Reldo leap between me and the altar in an attempt to rescue me from an adversary he could not see.

"No!" I cried, afraid for his life. What protection did he have from Godron's evil?

Too late, I tried to shield his mind. I felt his mental scream; his consciousness retreated from the onslaught. He possessed no mental barriers to protect himself. The desperate flight of his mind would end in complete withdrawal leading to death unless I could save him.

But how?

Frantically, I followed him with a lance of questing thought horrified at the emptiness I found, realizing I had to catch him quickly.

As I divided my energies, Godron increased his efforts to invade my mind and my resistance wavered. I sensed Reldo, caught his wounded consciousness, and held fast, knowing I mustn't let him go. I would have no other chance. To release him now and concentrate on my defense would mean to lose him forever. That I could not bear.

Sickness washed over me in waves, pounding me with agony, burning my mind. I felt Godron's evil absorbing me, yet I held fast to Reldo.

Stay with me, stay with me . . .

I knew I could not withstand this alone. Godron's power was proving too great for my untrained Talent.

Suddenly an outside source of strength poured into me, coalescing my scattered senses and aiming them in ways they must go. Now, *now* I knew what to do; how to direct my mind, holding Reldo while shoring up my resistance to Godron.

I grew aware of the presence of others—was this real? Yes! I felt hands clasping mine, saw my mother raising a slim dagger with a handle of brilliant blue stone that pulsed bursts of crackling bolts of light that encircled the chamber, lashing the walls, exploding chunks off the altar. The wind intensified, roaring with the sound of a thousand mountains collapsing. Clouds of dust billowed from the crumbling walls.

The bolts concentrated on the writhing, transparent figure above the altar, encompassing it.

"Nooooo . . ."

I took my hand from Mother's grasp and joined it with hers that held the dagger. Lenil's hand covered mine.

The pressure that had tortured my mind, my soul, began to retreat and I chased it to purge it from me completely. I felt as if I grew, expanding outside myself, and I knew that to expel Godron was not sufficient to vanquish him. He must be destroyed utterly so he could never again poison our world with his Dark evil.

Gunnal and Varela drew closer, lending their strength though they possessed no Talent, and I saw Reldo stir, rise, and come to us. He no longer needed me, allowing me to devote my undivided Power to Godron's destruction.

An earthquake heaved the floor beneath us, buckling it, as slabs of stone crashed from the ceiling. I knew we must escape soon, but dared not leave until I saw Godron's shriveling essence completely dissolve.

The pulsing bloody light from the remaining runes washed to blue and with a thunderous roar the altar collapsed, taking with it the last vestiges of Godron's spirit. The knife handle turned dark and we spun to flee from the maelstrom erupting around us. We raced up the buckling tunnel. The entire hold appeared to be collapsing and I could feel our collective fear that we might not escape. Pushing down panic, I drew on my newfound strength to hold back the stones until we passed.

As we ran beneath the tower it swayed above us and I sent forth my thoughts to stay it. The effort drained me physically and I stumbled. Young strong hands clasped me—Reldo. Sweeping me into his arms, he charged outside behind our family to tumble to safety as the tower crashed down, bringing the walls of the castle with it, leaving nothing remaining but a pile of ruins and dust.

My loved ones hovered over me and I gave myself up to blessed unconsciousness.

A second foal was birthed this morning though not at such a convenient hour as the first. My father—Gunnal—and Lenil were asleep, exhausted but pleased with the new addition.

Voices? Ah, yes. Looking out from my window seat I could see Reldo and Jenli walking hand in hand toward the stock pen, Jenli chattering and skipping. Reldo smiling tolerantly down at his little sister.

Varela gave me her own journal to read, the one she has kept since becoming marooned on our world while exploring. It contains an account of my origins and birth, and to read it written by a loving hand instead of having it poured into my mind with hate helps me view the events with a better perspective.

I think of Gunnal as my father, for he truly is. He shared in my mother's rescue, then wed her, raising and loving me as his own, though he knew from whose seed I sprung.

I'm preparing to journey for my training, now that Mother's fear has been assuaged by Godron's true death. She no longer feels she must protect and shield me from evil. Fortunately, her Talent, though dormant, allowed her to receive my call. She told me afterward how she knew, upon hearing my mental cry, where we had gone, for it was there Godron had taken her those many years ago, the reason the forest had been forbidden to us. She has given me the dagger—this very dagger resting beside me as I write—that played such a vital part in the purification of my birth, then pierced Godron's throat, ending his physical life.

How humbling to discover I am blessed with a Talent so great that its limits have not yet been tested. I shall endeavor to learn my lessons well so that I may channel my Power for the good of our people and our world.

Afterword

When Andre Norton asked for a second Witch World story I immediately called my cowriter, Karen Rigley. She reminded me how we had speculated on the future of that very special baby born in "Stones of Sharnon" (Tales of the Witch World Volume 2), and we knew that child's fate would become our story.

After collaborating long distance for two years, for the first time we actually wrote while together in the same place. I shall always remember sitting side by side at Karen's typewriter while Silistia unfolded her tale to us, and the thrill we both felt when Andre accepted "Godron's Daughter" as is.

By first showing me the way to the stars, awakening in me the dream of becoming a writer, Andre indirectly brought Karen and me together. We're proud our efforts are worthy of her approval.

Ad astra.

—Ann Miller

Afterword

Andre Norton not only opened up fantastic new worlds for me, she gave me my writing partner, Ann Miller. Ann freely admits that Andre Norton changed her life and inspired her to become a writer. Without Andre the team of Miller and Rigley would not exist. The Grand Master of science fiction has influenced our work from the briefest article to the most intricate novel. When she accepted "Godron's Daughter" without requesting a rewrite or suggesting any changes, we felt as honored as if we'd won the Pulitzer Prize or an Academy Award.

—Karen E. Rigley

A QUESTION OF MAGIC

by

Marta Randall

I

The hedge magician had set up his tent in the field behind the potter's shed. Jora, Imrie's best friend, spent all day talking about it as they worked in the fields, until Imrie thought she would go mad from her chatter.

"I'll bet he's been everywhere," Jora said, pulling damp hair from her forehead. She refilled her seed basket from the sack. "Across the ocean and everything. And they say he can even tell what you're thinking," she continued. She shivered, scared and delighted. Imrie merely grunted.

"I heard my mother tell my aunt that he could talk with the Old Ones." Jora stopped all pretense of work. "And my father said he could make rain, too. Even lightning!"

"Nonsense," Imrie said. "The rain comes or goes, the lightning happens or not, and that's all there is to it. Talk to the Old Ones—humph." She pulled her damp shirt away from her body—it was hot today, and sticky.

"Come on, Imrie," Jora said. "Aren't you excited, just a little bit? I'll bet he's even seen dragons, and flying ships, and all sorts of stuff."

"Have *you* ever seen a dragon? Or a flying ship?" Imrie said, planting her hands on her hips. "Or talked to anyone who's seen one? No, it's always someone knew someone knew someone who heard that someone else's aunt saw one. Or the Old Ones, have you ever seen one? Or heard one? Or felt one?" She glared at the other girl. "Well, have you?"

"Your problem," Jora said angrily, "is that you have no imagination." She took her seed basket and marched away between the furrows, leaving Imrie to finish filling her own basket alone. A vagrant breeze pulled dark hair from her headband, and she swiped it away from her neck. Magician—charlatan, rather, she thought impatiently.

At dinner, Imrie's cousin Tib bubbled with childish speculation about the magician's upcoming performance, while Uncle Rosin pulled his beard and made pronouncements. Aunt Melia nodded, silent as always. Imrie watched her as she helped her aunt clear away the meal and prepare to go out. Melia was her mother's sister, a survivor of the raids in Menasdale, to the north, that had killed Imrie's parents. Like Harkensdale, Menasdale lay in the clutter of small valleys that dotted this part of High Hallack, save that while Harkensdale abutted the great sea, Menasdale shared a border with the Waste, that desolate and unknown land inhabited by scavengers, outlaws, and the ghosts of the Old Ones. The raid, in a larger Dale, would have been minor; mounted outlaws sweeping into the valley with sword and fire, another skirmish in the constant border disputes. Save that tiny Menasdale had no adequate defenses against a force that large, and within the course of a day the Dale's small holdings lay in ruins. As far as Imrie knew, only she and Melia had escaped the slaughter.

Imrie sometimes wondered if her mother would have become like Melia: silent, tired, and gray. She remembered her parents only vaguely, as laughing, loving people who filled her world with light and happiness. Melia she remembered as a young woman, pretty and quick with laughter. Melia had saved a few relics of Menasdale, keeping them in a tiny wooden box on the mantelpiece. Her aunt never touched the box anymore, but to

Imrie it was a key into a lost and better world. Sometimes, late at night, she lifted her mother's amulet from the box and took it to bed with her, holding it close and pretending that she and Melia were still back in Menasdale, that Melia still laughed and flirted with the young men, that Imrie's parents held her and told her silly riddles. Then, silently, she would cry herself to sleep.

That night, after dinner, she reluctantly accompanied her family to the field behind the potter's shed, but only because Tib had teased her unmercifully throughout the meal. The magician's tent, gaudy with flags and banners, sat on a rough platform and the magician's boy sat on the platform's edge and kicked his legs, watching the crowd with a bored, superior expression. The sleeves of his overtunic dragged on the wooden platform beside him. It seemed that everyone in Colmera had come. Rosin and Melia stopped to talk with Set, the village headman. Imrie expected more nonsense about the magician, but instead Set scratched under his worn blue cap and gestured to the east.

"Trouble brewing," he said quietly. "Down to the coast. War talk."

Rosin tugged his beard. "Any weight to it?"

"Maybe. Maybe." Set frowned. "Halle from Norrisdale came by last night." Norrisdale was the next Dale over, as tiny as Harkensdale and, although landbound, near one of the main trading roads that braved the rough hills of High Hallack. Imrie felt surprised. Usually, no one left home in the spring, not until the fields were safely planted.

"Didn't hear of it," Rosin said.

"Came quiet. Lord Betry had people up to his castle, asking help. They want troops. He's come to see Lord Harken. Since we're on the coast."

"Any word who they're fighting?"

"Outlanders. Come across the sea."

Rosin looked surprised. "Across the sea?"

"Unlikely. Might just be wind-talk, always something after a winter. Harken'll tell, if there's anything to it."

Rosin grunted an agreement, and Set moved off in search of the other elders. Imrie shivered and crossed her arms, tucking her hands against her sides.

"Uncle Rosin?" she said.

"Just wind-talk," her uncle replied. "You get on, watch the show. Happens every spring, talk of one wild thing or another. Set loves it, it makes him feel important. Go on, find your friends, have a good time. And keep an eye on Tib."

"I don't need her," Tib said rebelliously, but at a look from his father he took Imrie's hand and dragged her through the crowd. Jora spotted her and made her way over.

"I knew you couldn't stay away," she said. "Come on, my sister's saving us a place up close."

Tib cheered and towed Imrie after him, following Jora to the front of the crowd. Imrie sighed.

Soon the magician appeared, a shabby man with a straggly gray beard and sleeves even longer than his apprentice's. After a long oration promising all sorts of wonders, he proceeded to toss various powders into the air, create a number of obnoxious stinks, and flail about in the center of a plume of smoke. When the smoke started, a number of people screamed and covered their heads, and the man standing behind Imrie swore the way men do when they're afraid but aren't willing to show it. The magician's boy shrieked prayers and disappeared into the crowd as though seeking safety; Tib buried his face in Imrie's skirt and howled. Imrie shook her head, squinting, but all she could see was dark smoke, and the hedge magician writhing about inside it like a man with pepper in his underclothes. She poked Jora sharply with her elbow.

"What is it?" she demanded. "What do you see?"

"Monsters," Jora gasped. "O great Mother, save us, they're eating the magician!" She howled in terror. Her sister buried her head in her arms and wept with fear.

The magician gave a fierce, triumphant cry and leaped out of the smoke, leaving it in tatters. Everyone cheered, and Tib bounced enthusiastically. The smoke blew away, the magician bowed, and the magician's boy went through the crowd with a bowl collecting pennies. Jora tossed coins into the bowl, but Imrie merely scowled at him. The boy thumbed his nose at her and passed by.

All that night, the villagers could talk of nothing but the magician's deadly battle with the smoke monsters, until Imrie pulled the blankets over her ears and pretended to sleep. Even

Set's talk of trouble was forgotten—and probably, Imrie thought, for good reason; the trouble was nothing more substantial than the magician's illusions. But it bothered her—even her hardheaded Uncle Rosin had seen the smoke monsters, and Uncle Rosin didn't believe in anything he couldn't plant, harvest, chew, or swallow. Imrie bit her lip, staring over the top of the blanket at the hut's wattle wall. Maybe Jora was right, she thought. Maybe she didn't have any imagination.

She turned over. Her aunt and uncle snored on their pallet, and Tib muttered in his sleep. Well, maybe she didn't have any imagination, she thought, but that didn't stop her from knowing what her life would be like, and it didn't stop her from disliking it. She was fifteen—ripe for marriage, Uncle Rosin said, and Imrie thought that she'd be married to Posten, who worked the neighboring fields—or, if she was very lucky, to Met, the smith's son. She snorted. Met was squat, loud, and drank too much ale at the village celebrations. But whoever she married, she knew that all too soon she, too, would be tired and quiet like Aunt Melia, spending her life cleaning, cooking, weaving, mending, working in the fields, drawing water, bearing children, while the moments of her life passed away into grayness, and the grayness darkened into death.

I have enough imagination to imagine that, Imrie thought unhappily. Maybe Jora can stand it because she has enough imagination to imagine dragons, too.

Then, impatient, she punched the pile of straw under her head and closed her eyes. Imagination or no, the magician was a fraud and that was all there was to it. Holding this thought close like a prayer, she eventually fell asleep.

The magician left the next morning—gone, it was rumored, to entertain at the castle near the Dale's head. Imrie just shrugged when Jora told her this breathtaking news. She had seen the Harkens riding out a few times, the lord heavy in his saddle, his wife almost invisible under her finery, and the young lord brave and bright and obviously proud of it. They would probably be just as taken in as the village folk, Imrie decided, and lugged her heavy seed basket back to her set of furrows.

The hot weather broke at sunset, just as they finished planting; the skies darkened and a fine, small rain began to fall. Imrie opened her arms to it, glorying in its reality, in the cool drops running down her neck, the soft, sweet breeze, the aroma of damp, fertile earth. Lightning flickered to the east and Jora, standing beside her, gasped and pointed.

"It's from the castle," she said positively. "It's the magician—he didn't make lightning for *us*."

"I wish," Imrie said, "that you'd forget about that forsaken magician and start talking about boys again—at least there are more of them."

Jora glared at her and stomped away. Imrie looked at the lightning appraisingly. It certainly looked like regular spring lightning, nothing special really—except that the weather usually came from the east, not the west, and this lightning seemed to be centered over the Dale's head, and not moving despite the breeze that tossed the clouds. She shook her head impatiently, hunched her shoulders, and marched toward the village. Nonsense, she thought. Just arrant nonsense.

As the night wore on, the lightning grew stronger, sending bright white flashes through the sky above the village—bright enough, Uncle Rosin said, to count the seeds in their furrows. He and Set talked at length and with worry about a possible spring flood, their seeds washed away, crop ruined, while Aunt Melia kept the ale cups filled. Whenever the thunder rumbled, she jumped a little. Even Tib was, for once, silent.

Imrie finished cleaning the supper dishes, then, infected by the tension in the room, took her small wooden box from the mantelpiece. Still watching Uncle Rosin and Set, she opened the box and groped among the trinkets. Her eyes widened and, sitting quickly, she emptied the box into her lap. Her mother's battered amulet was missing. The amulet was an old sphere of metal, smooth with years of wearing; certainly nothing valuable save for its memories. Unbelieving, she counted through the trinkets again.

"Aunt Melia!"

"What is it, child?" her aunt said, coming over to her.

Imrie showed her the box. "The amulet's gone, Mother's amulet—"

"Hush." Melia frowned at her. "I'm not surprised, it always

did get away from folk. Save your mother, and you. It's probably in your bed, you'll find it soon enough. Quiet, now, your
uncle and Set are very worried. Put those away and take this."
She held out a trencher of guest bread.

Imrie refilled the box and put it away, lay the bread on the
table, and retreated to her corner, where she proceeded to take
her bed apart. She found two buttons, a missing ribbon, and
any number of fluff-balls, but no amulet. Melia, watching her,
shook her head in warning. Imrie remade the bed and sat on it
unhappily, her plain cloak pulled tight around her shoulders.
She'd find the amulet in the morning, she told herself firmly; it
had to be somewhere in the hut. She certainly wasn't going to
cry about it. At least, not yet. She put her shoulders back and
listened to the men talking. A spring flood would spell disaster
and possibly famine, and the gloom thickened. Neither of them
mentioned the magician, although from the way Set kept making the sign against evil, she knew that magic was on their
minds.

But, she told herself firmly, the magician had no more magic
than she had—just the ability to make people believe in him.
Just powders and stinks and smoke, nothing more—he certainly was not responsible for either the rain or the lightning, or
the booming thunder that accompanied it.

Although he probably had enough magic to distract people
while his apprentice burglarized their houses, she thought suddenly. She jumped to her feet. Aunt Melia frowned and Uncle
Rosin, rising to see Set to the door, shook his head. Imrie sat
back down again. It was only, she thought, a suspicion, and a
paltry one beside the possibility of flood and famine.

"Uncle Rosin," Imrie said as soon as Set left.

"Not tonight, child," Rosin said wearily. "Whatever it is, it
can wait till morning."

The family went to bed, but Imrie lay rigid, thinking about
the amulet and about the storm until both merged in her mind,
one as dire as the other. A louder blast of thunder shook the
hut, and Imrie leaped off her pallet, fumbling for her cloak,
pulling on her boots, shoving an unlit torch under her belt.
Moving rapidly, she threw half a loaf of bread into her belt
pouch, along with her spark-striker and a dried apple. Then,

still moving with silent, desperate speed, she rushed out into the night.

Magicians were stuff and nonsense, and no doubt about it—but if the magician was making all this racket, she could make him stop, make him return her amulet. She didn't know how she'd do that, against someone who might, after all, control the heavens, but she knew she had to try. Imrie pulled her hood tight around her cheeks and set out, almost running, along the path leading east to the Dale's castle.

After a while, she noticed that the small rain continued to fall, as gently as a benison, then drifted into a fine mist, and that into dryness. No danger of a spring flood, then—but the lightning still clove the sky, the thunder shook the ground beneath her feet, and she never thought of going back.

II

Ryle Harken drummed his fingers impatiently on the tabletop, while the acrobats spun and stretched and tossed one another about. A stupid waste of time, Ryle thought; the banquet, the speeches, the entertainment, everything. Across the table, his uncle Betry, lord of Norrisdale, frowned and picked at his beard. Betry had come over from Norrisdale two days ago, bearing news of a possible invasion that caused Lord Josich, Ryle's father, much amusement.

"Come now, Betry," Lord Josich Harken had said, his wine cup supported comfortably on his great belly, "you know better than to come traipsing over the hills with wild rumors. An invasion from the sea is ridiculous just on the face of it—there's nothing out there, cousin, and everyone knows it."

Lord Betry, a thin, anxious man, fluttered his hands. "But, Josich," he said, almost squeaking, "listen—"

"Besides, Harkensdale's tiny, very tiny," Lord Josich said genially. Late afternoon sunlight spilled through the room, illuminating the cushioned chairs and unassuming tapestries. "The size of a sneeze, Betry, just a sneeze-worth of farms and a sin-

gle fishing village. And so, for that matter, is Norrisdale. If anyone did come from the sea, they'd probably miss us entirely.
Now, now, stop your fussing and enjoy yourself—we know you
just wanted an excuse to visit with your sister."

Betry had reluctantly allowed himself to be dragged off to
admire Lady Kora's flower beds, while Lord Josich smiled and
called for more wine.

The trouble, Ryle now thought, was that his father might be
right. An acrobat somersaulted before him, the firelight golden
on her damp skin. She stood on her hands, almost losing her
balance, almost losing her performer's grin. Harkensdale had
been at peace for decades, too tiny to attract much notice, neither very rich nor very poor, snuggled into a tiny valley between the sea and the tall western hills that marked the
beginning of Norrisdale. To the north, rugged hills and forests
protected the valley from Menasdale, from which nothing had
been heard for a good ten years. Harsh granite mountains,
rumored to contain places of great, dark magic, maintained a
wall between Harkensdale and the south. Isolated, quiet, and,
Ryle thought angrily, boring, where the best entertainment
they could provide a visiting lord were this troupe of awkward
acrobats and the tattered hedge magician waiting in the
kitchen. The songsmiths, Ryle thought, would find nothing but
comedy in Harkensdale.

The acrobats finished in a trembling, sweaty heap before the
great fireplace. Lady Kora clapped enthusiastically, her round
face flushed, while Josich banged his wine cup in approval and
Lord Betry continued picking at his beard. Ryle shifted impatiently in his seat.

"Wonderful," his mother said in her little-girl voice. "Don't
you think so, Betry? Weren't they wonderful?"

"Wonderful," Lord Betry echoed dutifully.

Ryle covered his face with one hand. He'd spend his entire
life like this, he thought with despair. Tied to this boring Dale,
surrounded by farmers and fishers, never too rich or too poor,
tiny beyond history's notice. If he were lord of Harkensdale, he
thought, he'd fortify Pessik, the fishing village at the castle's
foot; stockpile food and water, empty the castle's modest armory, conscript men from the fields. He had said as much to his
father, after Uncle Betry disappeared toward the gardens.

"You would, would you?" his father had said, signaling for more wine. "Fortify ten stone huts—with what, pray? Seaweed and dreams? And you might remember that it's barely spring—there's very little to stockpile unless we levy the villages, and then what are the people to eat? And I wouldn't think of a conscription, not during planting. Unless you expect us to eat twigs and bushes next winter. You haven't developed a fondness for bushes, have you? I hope not—it would upset your mother."

"I don't think it's something to joke about," Ryle said angrily. "If Betry's right, if there is an invasion, you won't have to worry about what to eat next winter, because we won't be around to eat anything."

"But Betry isn't right," Lord Josich said patiently. "He's all a-flutter because of a rumor he heard from some trader on the road, who heard it from another trader, who heard it from heaven only knows where. Last summer, it was outlaws marching out of the Waste, and the spring before it was something equally silly. Betry gets bored, that's all. After a long winter, everyone gets bored."

"And you don't?" Ryle said rudely.

"Me?" His father laughed. "With everything I have to do? Don't be silly, boy." He had waved Ryle away, and ten minutes later was in the fields behind the castle, deep in conversation with the beekeeper.

Servants rolled up the acrobats' rush mats and dragged them out, while others brought in the magician's paraphernalia. Lady Kora pried family gossip from her brother, and the magician came in. He bowed to the head table, shook back his long sleeves, and produced a dozen gray doves from the air. They flew toward the rafters, Lady Kora clapped, and the magician presented her with a bouquet of roses that he also plucked from the air. His assistant set up a brazier.

The show, Ryle had to admit, was really quite good, especially the smoke monsters. They filled the hall, coiling around themselves, eyes gleaming, claws extended, huge wings cupping as they danced through the air, menacing the magician. The magician battled them fiercely, while his boy did a very professional job of looking terrified. This was more like it, Ryle thought, leaning forward. Monsters, dragons, great battles, danger and daring—that was what life should be about. The magician struck the monsters, shouting magic words. After a stirring fight, the monsters screamed in defeat and dissolved, and tatters of smoke fled through the windows. Lady Kora gasped and applauded, Lord Betry uncovered his eyes, and Lord Josich bellowed his approval and invited the magician to their table. Ryle scooted over to make room as a servant set a chair beside him. The magician sank into it, wiping his forehead, and smiled modestly at Lord Josich's praise.

Of course he had seen such monsters, he said in answer to Ryle's barrage of questions. He had battled monsters in the wilds of the outlands, forcing their magic secrets from them before he destroyed them utterly. Certainly the Old Ones respected his powers, for the evil ones left him in peace, while the others eased his travels with good hunting and shelter. He had been all over the Dale lands, north to south, east to west, and had seen all there was to see; he had performed before the great lords in their sumptuous palaces and, he implied, been fittingly rewarded by lord and lady both. He had been offered positions of power and wealth, but, he said, he preferred his life as a traveling magician and would not trade the danger and adventure for any number of rewards or sinecures.

"When I was a little girl in Norrisdale," Lady Kora said dreamily, "a magician came through who made lightning for us. It was so pretty—can you do that? Make lightning, I mean?"

The hedge magician smiled. "Of course," he said lightly. "Even an apprentice can make lightning—there is very little mystery to it."

"Really?" Lady Kora said breathlessly. "Could you make some for us? Now?"

The magician frowned. "Naturally, your ladyship—but we would have to go outside. And it is raining."

"A little rain never hurt anyone," Lord Josich boomed, pushing back his chair.

"I only meant," the magician said hastily, "that it really would be much too easy, with the rain falling—no art to it at all. Besides, you might think the lightning natural, with the rain and all. Much better to make it on a clear day, your lordship—a clear, bright day with not a cloud in sight."

"Perhaps," Lord Josich said, scooping up his wine cup. "But if I know anything about the weather, it's going to rain for another two or three days, and you'll be gone by then. So come along, Master Magician. Let's see your lightning, rain or no rain. And I promise to believe in it—those aren't storm clouds overhead, you know, just simple, quiet rain. My dear," he said, offering his arm. Lady Kora tittered and put her hands around his huge forearm. Betry dithered for a moment, then accepted his cloak from a servant and followed the lord and lady from the room. Ryle, trying to look sophisticated and bored, walked with the magician, while the magician's apprentice brought up the rear. The magician, Ryle noticed, did not look very happy.

"It's all right," Ryle whispered. "It really isn't a storm rain, so we'll believe your lightning, I promise."

The magician's lips pinched down.

Lord Josich led them to the castle's roof. A light breeze brought the rain to their faces. Ryle peered west, where sunset gilded Pessik's thatched roofs. Long spits of granite reached into the sea, almost joined at the mouth of Harkensdale's tiny harbor, and the waters were empty and calm. Disappointed, Ryle turned back to the magician.

The magician, arms crossed and gray beard fluttering in the breeze, stared with concentration toward the north, while his apprentice watched him with a peculiar expression on his face. The castle folk maintained a respectful distance, letting him take his time. After a while, the magician suddenly flung his arms wide, tilted his face into the rain, and began shouting magic words. Ryle's skin prickled and he clenched his hands. Nothing happened.

"The skies are confused," the magician explained, rubbing his sleeve across his face. "I shall have to bend them to my will."

"My goodness," Lady Kora said. "Is that safe?"

"Your ladyship, all magic is fraught with danger," the magician said sternly, and called to his boy. They conferred briefly, then the boy retreated and the magician resumed his cross-arm contemplation of the sky. Josich drew his family farther away from the magician—Lord Betry was already at a distance, ready to bolt down the stairs. The sky darkened further. The magician began flinging his arms about, describing vague but undoubtedly magical shapes in the air, then again shouted at the clouds. Again, nothing happened.

The magician turned to Lord Josich, shaking his head. "My lord," he said, "there seems to be some disturbance in—"

The sky flashed white, throwing stark shadows along the rooftop, and the castle rocked with thunder, flinging them all down. The magician looked astounded. Lady Kora screamed, and after a shocked moment, Lord Josich said firmly, "Very impressive, Magician—now turn it off."

Lightning flashed again, and thunder bellowed, and Lord Betry fled down the stairs. Ryle had landed almost head to head with the magician, across the roof from his parents. He peered with great excitement at the skies.

"That's *wonderful*," he said. "That's really wonderful."

The magician muttered.

"Beg pardon?" Ryle said, turning his head to look at the magician. The skies lit, and the magician's face looked stricken. Before the thunder could finish, lightning struck the castle roof, rocking the stone, and the sound deafened him. Ryle yelled, frightened and blinded. Someone grabbed his shoulder and tried to drag him away.

"Get going," the magician shouted. "Come on, you fool, do you want to die? *Move!*"

Ryle pushed the hand away and sat up, blinking. For a moment the darkness remained, then cleared. Ryle shook his head, and screamed—the other part of the castle roof was gone, tumbled into fragments of stone and wood, and his parents had disappeared. The magician pushed him toward the stairs.

"My mother," Ryle yelled, trying to pull away. "Father!" The magician pushed him again, and Ryle spun to face him. "You've killed them! You've—"

"You idiot, I can't make lightning," the magician shouted. "I didn't do it—come on!" He ran down the stairs. Ryle stood rooted, staring at the broken roof, while another bolt of lightning struck at Pessik by the sea. Startled, he looked east.

An immense, dark shape filled the mouth of the harbor. Light streaked from it, and a moment later the entire fishing village disappeared in a burst of heat and noise.

Horrified, Ryle fled down the stairs. The castle rocked and groaned around him; screams echoed from the servants' quarters, and the main hall, directly under the roof, was a shambles of broken stone and splintered furniture. Valon, the captain of the castle's small guard, caught him up as he streaked from the stairwell; in his other arm, he held the magician. The magician's boy cowered behind them. Valon had come to Harkensdale years ago, a blank shield retired, he said, from fighting outlaws in the western Dales, but for all his age his arms held both magician and boy immovable.

"What is it?" Valon demanded. "What has this one done?" He shook the magician like a rag.

"Nothing," the magician howled. "I tell you, I didn't do it—"

"There's something in the harbor," Ryle gasped. "Pessik's gone—we have to get out of here, they're destroying the castle!"

Valon shook him, too. "Who is?" he demanded. "Where's Lord Josich?"

"The roof," Ryle said, faltering. "Lightning hit the roof, and—my father—" He couldn't make his mouth say the words, and Valon, peering into his face, widened his eyes.

"By the Flame," he whispered. The castle shook again, and the stairwell crumbled. Valon released them. "Come, then. And quickly." He strode from the room. Ryle, the magician, and the apprentice crowded at his heels.

The guardroom had suffered a hit, for the outer wall was gone, and dead men lay across the floor like broken puppets. Valon grabbed weapons from the rack, thrust them at Ryle and the magician, and led them, running, back through the great hall and into Lord Josich's council room. He pushed aside a curtain, revealing the dark mouth of a tunnel. The magician stopped.

"What's that?" he demanded suspiciously.

"Just go," Valon said, shoving him. He snatched an unlit torch from a bracket. "It'll take us out of the castle."

Ryle hesitated, looking behind him.

"You too," Valon said, pushing the apprentice through. "Come on, your lordship—you can do nothing for them now."

Choking back a sob, Ryle followed the magician into the darkness.

III

The low arm of a hill separated Colmera from Harken Castle and the bay. Imrie had been over it a thousand times, but tonight lightning flared and thunder shook the ground under her feet as she crested the hill and froze, staring at the ruins of Harken Castle. Harsh white flashes struck again and again, pounding the land between the castle and the sea. Not lightning, she thought numbly. Magic, perhaps, but a magic fearsome and more evil than any hedge magician could command. Tatters of cloud blew away, leaving a fat white moon riding the sky. A flash struck the base of the hill and the trees in the copse below caught fire. She flung herself on her belly and scuttled backward through mud until the coast dropped from sight, then she stood and ran toward a granite outcrop. She didn't think the granite would protect her, not after what she had seen of Harken Castle, but perhaps the magic could not reach this side of the hill. Diving headlong into a gap in the rock, she wrapped her arms around her middle and prayed as she had never prayed before.

When someone touched her arm, she screamed and leaped to her feet, ready to flee. A hand closed over her shoulder and another hand, large but gentle, covered her mouth.

"Hush, lass, I won't hurt you. I'm Valon, of Harken Castle." The voice paused. "When there was a Harken Castle." Imrie stopped struggling and the hand moved away from her face. "Who are you?"

"Imrie, Imrie Rosinsniece, of Colmera, I came up, the noise, Aunt Melia was frightened, I saw the castle—what *happened*?" she finished, panting, as three other figures emerged from the darkness of the granite cleft. She recognized one of them.

"You!" Imrie yelled, furious, and charged the hedge magician. A tall, young man stood between them; she bowled him over. "Where's my amulet, you thief!"

The magician, waving his sleeves about, skipped back and collided with his apprentice. Both went down in a tangle of sleeves. Grunting with triumph, Imrie sat on the magician's stomach and grabbed his beard. Behind her, the tall, young man howled curses, the apprentice sniggered, and Valon grabbed both Imrie and the magician and held them in the air, shaking them.

"Quiet, then!" he demanded in a voice that brooked no disobedience. Everyone stopped shouting, and in the silence Imrie heard another silence; the thunder had stopped. Valon's expression told her that this was not of itself good.

"They'll come ashore now," the captain whispered, almost to himself. "They'll come to take Harkensdale."

"Who?" Imrie whispered back. Valon released her, but kept his grip on the magician.

"I demand—" the magician squeaked, and Valon shook him again. Something clattered to the ground. The young man, bending down, retrieved a necklace and a small box.

"It's Mother's," he said, holding the box to the moonlight. It glittered. "It's Mother's powder box—" He sobbed suddenly and turned on the magician as Imrie snatched the chain from his hands.

"That's mine," she yelled. "Where's my amulet?"

"Enough, Ryle!" Valon said firmly, and added as an afterthought, "Your lordship." The young man stopped crying. Valon set the magician down. "I need to see what's at the coast—we'll deal with this one later. Perhaps your lordship would guard him? And his boy?"

Ryle shifted his grip on the sword and spread his feet. He looked like he knew how to handle the sword; the magician, muttering quietly, sat down.

"Your lordship?" Imrie said weakly.

"And you, lass, you come with me," Valon said. "I'm not leaving both of you alone with the magician, he'd be dog meat in a minute. Now!"

She scampered after him, biting her lip against the questions

she wanted to ask. When he dropped to the ground, she did
likewise, and together they slithered over the crest.

Beyond the pall of smoke from the burning trees, Pessik
glowed like coals in a grate; the castle was a dark ruin. Flames
ate at the small fishing fleet, and farther out a dark bulk filled
the harbor. Lights glowed along it, and a line of large shapes
moved toward the land. When they reached the beach, they
kept going; square, determined sea monsters invading the
coast. Imrie gasped. Very distantly, she heard a sound like
rocks rubbing together.

The monsters reached Pessik and pushed through the stone
ruins as though through grass. One of them shot flame toward a
hut; the hut disintegrated. A few minutes later some had
reached the base of Harken Castle, while others started on the
road to Colmera. Valon cursed and crawled backward; Imrie
followed.

"What is it?" she whispered as they stood and rushed toward
the outcrop.

"I don't know," he said, and cursed again.

Ryle had done an efficient job of tying both magician and
apprentice up in their own sleeves; beside them, he had accumulated a pile of combs, earrings, embroidered pouches, and
other petty thievings. He looked remarkably pleased with himself, Imrie thought warily, remembering how she had knocked
him down. Valon frowned.

"Pick them up," he ordered. "Damn it, boy, the enemy will
find those and be on us immediately. Your lordship."

Ryle drew his shoulders back. "I think you ought to be more
respectful," he said. "I'm Lord Ryle now."

"Lad, if you don't hurry you'll be Lord Crowmeat," Valon
replied. "Whatever destroyed the castle and Pessik is coming
this way, and fast. Pick up that litter, we have to hide."

"Hide?" Ryle echoed.

"It's terrible," Imrie said. "Big sea monsters that swim and
crawl too, all by themselves, and shoot fire and knock down
buildings and they're heading toward—" she stopped, her
stomach cold. "Toward Colmera," she said, and turned to run.
Valon caught her up, wrapping his arms around her.

"Hush," he said. "Listen."

The sound of monsters grew suddenly louder. Imrie had time to see one crest the hill, blocking out the sky, before Valon carried her, running, deeper into the granite. She clawed at him and yelled, and he clapped his hand over her mouth. The tunnel turned sharply and even the faint light disappeared. The monster sound died away.

"You can't help Colmera," Valon said as he ran, his breath hot against her neck. "Lass, we can't help any of them."

After what seemed a long time, Valon halted and let her down. Imrie thought of Aunt Melia's tired smile, of Tib's bright laughter. She leaned against cold, damp rock, holding her arms around her middle, while the others came up to them. Ryle and Valon conferred in whispers. Occasionally the earth shook.

"Imrie," someone said. She tried to move away, lost in a grief so deep she could not even cry. An arm circled her shoulders.

"Imrie," the voice said again. "Lady Kora—my mother died in—my father . . ."

Then Imrie turned toward him, and they held each other and wept in the dark belly of the earth.

Even though Valon carried an unlit torch, and Imrie had both a torch and her spark-striker, the captain decreed that there would be no light. "We don't need it now," he had said, "and we're sure to need it later." So they huddled in the darkness, speaking in whispers. The rock shook slightly, as though giants marched over their heads.

"There are men in the moving boxes," Valon said. "Or something that looks much like men—I saw their heads, when the monster came over the hill. And that means they'll be afoot, when they think it safe. And *that* means that they'll find the tunnel, so we'd best be gone as soon as we can."

"And how, pray tell, are we to do that?" the magician said. He and his apprentice were still bound together, despite his bitter complaints.

"Tunnels," Ryle said. "I used to play in some of them. My father—" His voice trembled and he paused, then continued resolutely. "My father said that the Old Ones mined these hills, and the tunnels remain. Some go to the coast, to the cliffs beyond Pessik—"

"No good," Valon said. "The enemy has the seacoast, and the fishing fleet's burned. We have to strike inland, get to Norrisdale and warn them."

"I think not," the magician said quickly. "Menasdale's much closer, isn't it? We should certainly head north, it would be much safer there, I'm sure."

Imrie heard Valon's snort. "What, strike over the mountains? During the melt? No, Norrisdale is where they'll head next, and Norrisdale's where we'll go. What worries you, Magician? Did they catch you thieving in Norrisdale?"

The magician was silent, but his apprentice sniggered again. Imrie's hands curled into fists.

"Charlatan," she said. "Making stinks and smokes so that folk won't know you're robbing them—"

"He did make good smoke monsters," Ryle said. "Everyone saw them."

"Well, I didn't," Imrie replied. "All I saw was black smoke, and this one jumping around in it and shouting like a madman and scaring people, scaring Tib . . ." Her throat ached. Valon took her hand.

"Courage, lass," he said. "I had a woman in Pessik—we've all lost someone."

"Except the fraud," Imrie said bitterly. "He took my amulet, my mother's amulet, and I want it back. Now!"

"Lass, put it behind you," he said. "And perhaps your family escaped—Colmera had warning, as Pessik didn't. But we have to get out of here—Ryle, what else about the tunnels?"

"What about my amulet?"

Valon gave her a stern look as he rose, and she bit her lip.

"Well," Ryle said slowly, "there is one that goes toward the hills behind Colmera, it branches off from this one. But my— my father said it wasn't safe. He told me not to use it, but he never said why, exactly."

"Still, it's our only chance," Valon said. "Whatever's wrong with it, it can't be worse than what's outside in Harkensdale. Lass, I need your torch now, and the spark-striker." Imrie handed them over.

"I won't go," the magician said. "If Old Ones mined these hills, there's no telling what they've left behind."

"Fine," Valon said. Sparks flew in the darkness. "Ryle, untie them. They can try to make it out on their own."

"Now wait a minute," the magician said hastily. "You can't leave us here, unprotected."

"Oh, yes?" Valon said. The tinder ignited, and he nursed the flame onto the torch. It sputtered and caught.

Imrie blinked against the dim light. They were a sorry-looking bunch, tattered and mud-stained. She glared at the magician and his apprentice. The apprentice glared back; there was a bulge under his tunic.

"Captain," Imrie said. "The boy's hiding something."

"I am not," the magician's boy said, but Ryle held him down and extracted a sack from his clothes. It held a loaf, a slab of dried meat, and a flagon of wine. The Harken crest gleamed from the flagon's side.

"More thievings," Ryle said.

"These, at least, we can eat." Valon stamped out the tinder and put the remains in his belt pouch, along with the spark-striker.

"I have some bread," Imrie said. "And an apple."

"Not much, but altogether it will do for three," Valon replied.

"Three!" The magician struggled to his feet, arms still bound. "Three! You can't go without us—I can help you, protect you against the Old Ones. I know how to deal with them, they're sure to have left something in these forsaken tunnels, you'll be sorry if I'm not along."

"That's doubtful," Valon said, looking at him coldly. "Still, it's better than the risk that you'd find your way out, and bring the enemy down on us—"

"I wouldn't! How dare you—"

"Shut up, thief," Ryle said, poking the magician with his sword. "Valon, I could just kill them now—"

"No. There's been too much death this day already," the captain said. "And he may be useful to us. Come." He handed the torch to Ryle and lifted his sword. The magician cowered, but Valon merely slit his sleeves, freeing him and the boy. More thievings fell to the floor, and Imrie grabbed one up.

"My amulet!"

"Leave that be, you stupid child." The magician tried to snatch it back, and Imrie skipped away from him and behind the captain. "Give it back, you don't even know what it is."

"Oh, yes?" Imrie said tauntingly, safe behind Valon's bulk. "You think it's valuable, don't you? It's worth more to me than it is to you."

The magician glowered. "I'll buy it from you," he said. "For more money than you can imagine—just give it back, before you hurt yourself."

"Hurt myself? Why?"

"Give it to me," the magician said cunningly. "I'll show you—" Imrie shook her head, clutching the amulet. "You stupid fool!" He lunged for it.

"Silence!" Valon said, lifting his sword again. "We haven't time to bicker—the lass keeps it, it was hers to begin with. Another word out of you, Magician, and I will split you, and slowly."

The magician stepped back, mouthing silently at Imrie. She stuck her tongue out at him, and Valon frowned at her, too, before turning back to Ryle.

"Your lordship, you know the way?"

"Yes." Ryle lifted the torch and set off down the tunnel. At Valon's gesture, the magician and his apprentice followed, while Valon and Imrie fell into place behind them. She slipped the amulet into her pouch; it felt smooth and comforting beneath her fingers. The torch flickered against the dark rock walls.

IV

Ryle held the torch higher, and repressed a shudder. The rock corridor before him was even and wide, sloping down gently. Perfectly ordinary, he told himself, save that the skin on his nape prickled uncomfortably, and he could not tell why.

Behind came the footsteps of the others: the magician's nervous patter, his apprentice's shuffle, the solid, comforting ring of Valon's boots. The girl's footsteps were so quiet he could not hear them over the others, and he thought about her while he walked, in an effort to ignore his discomfort. He didn't remember seeing her before, although he must have if she came from Colmera; there were no other villages in Harkensdale. She claimed the magician to be a fraud, said she hadn't seen anything in his magical display—which was patently nonsense, Ryle decided. He had certainly seen the smoke monsters, and for that matter, so had his father. He put that thought away quickly, afraid that it would lead to tears. And tears, he decided resolutely, were not the proper thing for a young man confronting enemies and great danger in the world.

The tunnel narrowed slightly and angled to the left. Ryle examined it minutely, trying to remember the map his father had once shown him, then shrugged and proceeded. Until the tunnel branched, there was nothing to do but follow it.

The girl—Imrie, her name was. Pretty eyes, for a peasant. And a young man in the world needed someone to rescue, all the best songs included a helpless maiden in dire need, and she would have to do, for the nonce. Of course, she wasn't properly helpless—her journey toward Harken Castle certainly seemed to indicate some courage, but peasants were hopelessly coarse when it came to the finer points of chivalry. Still, she'd have to do.

"Ryle, halt," Valon whispered. Ryle jumped, unsheathed his sword, and spun around.

"What is it? Enemies?" he demanded. The magician and the apprentice plastered themselves against the walls of the tunnel; Valon shook his head, and the girl, beside him, looked at Ryle curiously. Mud stained the front of her plain gown.

"No. You missed a tunnel," the captain said, indicating the wall. A second tunnel branched at right angles from the first.

"Oh," Ryle said, embarrassed. "Well, I did notice it, but—well." He bustled to the side tunnel and thrust his torch forward so that it shone into this new darkness. Damp walls glimmered back at him.

"What are we waiting for?" the magician said testily. "Let's get going."

"Patience, charlatan," Imrie muttered. "Does this go seaward or landward, do you think?"

While Ryle frowned, trying to remember the map, Valon knelt and, with the tip of his finger, drew lines in the fine dust.

"The mouth faced west," he said. "The first tunnel angled east and north, toward Harken Castle, and we're going back along it, so this new tunnel—this tunnel must head west, west and slightly north again, I think. Landward, toward Norrisdale."

His words seemed to free a corner of Ryle's mind, for he could suddenly see his father's map before him, as clear as if it lay real beneath his fingers.

"Yes," he said, excited. "And from it branches another tunnel, heading toward the sea—just about here." He squatted and jabbed his finger at Valon's quick sketch. He drew in other lines, rapidly and confidently, then rocked back. "That's the map," he said. "I know it."

Valon looked at him, and nodded. "Magician, do you have paper?"

The magician spread his hands, then looked from Valon to Ryle and, obviously thinking better of any protest, delved into his voluminous robes and produced Uncle Betry's tooled Book of Days and Ryle's own stylus. The apprentice sniggered again.

"I'm growing tired of that noise, boy," Valon remarked. "Do it again and I won't leave you a nose to make it with. Lass, your hands are free—can you draw?"

"I know my letters," Imrie replied, as though insulted, and took book and stylus from the magician. Kneeling, she quickly copied the map into the book, then held it out to Ryle. She smelled of spring, damp earth, and flowers.

"I remember it," he said, standing and moving a step away from her. She turned, hands still outstretched, toward the captain.

"No, lass, you keep it. Our hands are full enough already," the captain said. The girl tucked book and stylus into her pouch, and Ryle began walking down the new tunnel.

Within a very little time it began twisting on itself, the floor grew uneven and pick-marks scored the walls. The prickling at Ryle's neck intensified, until even thoughts of derring-do did not serve to hide it. His pace faltered and he stopped, his heart beating hard.

"You feel it too, do you, boy?" the magician said. "Evil here, something very old, and very wrong." He made a quick gesture of protection.

"Don't call me boy," Ryle said angrily. The magician seemed to leer at him in the uneven torchlight. "I am Lord Ryle to you, and you'll remember it."

"Oh, of course, my lord," the magician replied, bowing. Ryle peered at him, suspecting sarcasm. "I only meant, my lord, that I sense a presence here, an old and evil presence, beyond the ken of man—dangerous, my lord, greatly dangerous. And hungry."

Ryle shuddered, and Valon looked nervous.

"Bunk," Imrie said clearly. "Great and immediate nonsense, thief. Captain, do you feel such a thing?"

Valon frowned at her. "I feel something, lass, something uneasy, like the night before battle, against a superior force. I do not like it."

"It's like facing the sea rocks on a dark night," Ryle added, referring to the fanged stones that guarded the entrance to Harkensdale's harbor. "In a high tide, or in a storm."

"Well, I feel nothing," Imrie said. "But I know that whatever is behind us is a greater danger than nervous willies in the dark. I say we go on. Now." She paused. "My lord," she added.

"A stupid child," the magician said angrily. "She alone does not feel the Power—but we do, Captain, and we are men of the world. If we press ahead, you will need me, for I alone know the ways of these beings, and can bring us to safety."

Imrie snorted, but Ryle and the captain were nodding, albeit reluctantly.

"Very well," Valon said. "Ryle, give him the torch."

"No! I mean, that's not necessary, I can sense the presence without having to see it," the magician said. "You go ahead, my lord—your young eyes are sharper than my old ones. I will feel for this Power, this Old One, in other ways." The magician screwed his eyes closed and adopted an expression of great con-

centration, raising his spread hands as though fingering the air
before him. Valon rested his hand on the pommel of his sword,
Ryle braced his shoulders, and the group proceeded, the apprentice guiding his master.

The tunnel narrowed farther, its roof bending toward them.
Ryle unsheathed his sword. The corridor angled sharply to the
right, then to the left again and opened suddenly into a large
chamber filled with a pulsing green glow. Ryle stopped suddenly as the others crowded behind him. For a moment he saw
the cavern empty, and the tunnel continuing at its far side; then
the glow twisted upon itself to become waves as tall as cliffs.
Demons rode the crests, their voices shrill with menace, bran-
dishing barbed lances and evilly notched swords. As Ryle cried
out the first wave crashed to the sand, the demons springing
free to rush upon him.

"Ware demons!" young Lord Ryle screamed, casting the
torch aside and grasping his sword with both hands. He slashed
out, but for every demon left dead and smoking on the ground,
two others took its place. Valon appeared beside him, the captain's great sword cutting wide swathes in the demonic ranks,
then Ryle was too busy to notice anything save the endless
waves of enemies ready to engulf them.

V

"Ware demons!"

Imrie, still in the tunnel, caught the torch as it arced through
the air. She held it high as Valon leaped past her, sword out.

"Wastelanders!" the captain yelled. "Guard yourselves!"

The magician and his apprentice, skipping to either side of
the swordsmen, scooped and hurled rocks from the floor. Heart
beating hard, Imrie approached.

"Stay back, lass," Valon commanded grimly. She hesitated,
biting her lip. The dim green light of the cavern barely outlined
the battling men. They formed a flying wedge before her,
Valon's and Ryle's swords flashing and spinning like scythes at

reaping. The magician, looking terrified, flung stone after stone and his apprentice ducked and wove as though avoiding something very deadly. Imrie shook her head sharply and held the torch aloft, squinting.

"They don't stop coming!" Ryle called, his voice catching.

Imrie saw nothing save mail-clad backs and a shine of moving blades.

"Magician, do something!" the captain commanded. "Lass, replace him."

Imrie grasped the torch with both hands and jumped forward, almost singeing the magician as he leaped back. He grabbed at her pouch.

"Give it to me," he shouted.

Imrie shoved him away; giving her a wild look, he raised his hands. "If we die, it's your fault," he said, and began incanting furiously, waving his sleeves like tattered flags. Torch braced like a club, Imrie turned toward the cave and searched for the enemy.

And found none. Before her, the bare cavern widened and narrowed again to the tunnel; in its center stood a small rock, no bigger than a loaf of bread, from which emanated the unpleasant green light. Imrie blinked, lowering her torch.

"Defend yourself!" Ryle shouted with a curse, and swung his blade so close before her that she jumped back.

"But there's nothing there," she said. The men, shouting and battling, ignored her, and the magician set up a cloud of spells and sleeves.

"I don't think this is very funny," she added. "And you're not going to frighten me, so stop it."

The one-sided battle continued, as though she had not spoken. Imrie took a deep breath and walked forward.

"They've captured Imrie!" Ryle yelled. She ignored him.

An unseen force pressed against her skin, as though the air thickened as she neared the green rock; the torch fluttered and dimmed, until it barely gave light at all, and Imrie could no longer force her way forward. Reluctantly, she moved back until the torch flared again.

"She's escaped them!" Valon cried. "Good lass, get behind me."

Imrie glanced at him and shook her head. She started around
the side of the cavern. Here the air maintained a constant, but
pierceable, thickness; when Imrie was half way around the
cave, she paused, chewing her lip, and turned to look at her
companions. They looked comical, until she noticed that Valon
and Ryle had turned more toward each other, that at any moment their swords would engage; that the danger came not
from invisible enemies, but from their own weapons. She
rushed back to them.

"My lord! Captain! They—they fear the torch!" she yelled
with sudden inspiration. "They fear fire! Follow me!"

Valon glanced at her, surprised, and in that instant one of the
apprentice's stones struck his right shoulder. The captain
grunted and Ryle raised his sword against him.

"Lord Ryle!" Imrie screamed. "Ware behind you! Apprentice, guard the magician!"

Ryle spun away from the captain, his face white and slick
with sweat.

"This way!" she yelled. "See them drop back before me?
Follow, Captain. My lord, the path is clear behind you! Retreat!"

Valon threw the sword to his left hand and turned toward
Ryle.

"Captain! To your right!" Imrie shouted, and as he turned
she grabbed his cloak, tugging him backward. "Magician! Follow!"

At that moment a pall of thick black smoke emanated from
the magician's swirling form, greeted by the others with glad
cries.

"Come!" Imrie shouted. "This way!"

Urging, shouting, discovering enemies just in time to keep
her companions from killing one another, Imrie led them along
the sides of the cavern, skirting the green rock. The smoke hurt
her throat but she did not stop yelling until the cavern narrowed and the tunnel twisted. Both the green light and the
heaviness disappeared, and Imrie sighed with relief, then noticed that the others were still behind her, battling and yelling.
She ran back, grabbed Ryle's shirt, and jerked him backward.
He stumbled, yelled, then looked about him, blinking. She did

the same for the captain, made sure he and Ryle were not attacking each other, and reached for the magician. He tumbled into Ryle, sending both to the floor. Valon bent to lift them up, and as Imrie turned to fetch the apprentice, light exploded before her, followed immediately by the dark.

"You needn't have thrown a rock at her," someone was saying as she woke up. The world jounced rhythmically, and with each bounce, her head threatened to split. She groaned.

"I thought she was a . . ." The apprentice's voice trailed away.

A what? Imrie thought fuzzily. She opened her eyes, saw mud-stained blue just before her nose, and closed her eyes again.

"Stop," she said.

"Ah!" Valon halted and swung her gently to the ground. Imrie groaned again and buried her head in her arms. Her stomach felt queasy.

"Give it a moment, lass," the captain said. "It won't kill you, much as it feels like it."

"Here," Ryle's voice said. "Sip this."

She smelled spirits, turned over carefully, and sat up. To her astonishment, her head remained in place. The liquor tasted sharp and burned her throat, but she immediately felt better. Ryle, kneeling beside her, beamed. The magician turned ostentatiously away, and Imrie groped in her pouch, closing her fingers around the amulet.

"Some rescue, huh?" Ryle said. "It was close there, but I got you out in one piece."

"You rescued *me*?" Imrie said, incredulous. Ryle looked offended.

"Of course I did," he said. "Oh, you must not remember, after that blow on your head. Sure, back in the cavern, when you were surrounded by demons. I brought you out," he added proudly.

Behind him, Valon's lips quirked. "Well, lass, we all rescued you," he said gently. "Of course, my lord Ryle did the most of it, naturally—"

"They had you," the apprentice said suddenly. "We had to fight our way to you—"

"Then we had you surrounded," Ryle interrupted, glaring at the apprentice. "And we were almost out, but they snatched you again, and I pulled you loose, and that one stumbled in right after you."

"I was doing my share," the apprentice said stoutly. The magician cuffed him.

"None of you would have won free, if not for my spells," the magician announced. "It was the smoke monster who routed them; without that, we'd be in there still, fighting or dead. If I had that idiot girl's charm, I could have destroyed them all."

"You colossal fools," Imrie shouted. "I rescued you, every last one of you—I led you out of there!"

"Well, well, in a way, lass," Valon said.

"In a way! There you all were, hacking away at the air and almost hacking away at each other! You, Captain, what happened to your shoulder?"

Valon grimaced, touching his right shoulder. "One of them got through my guard," he said grimly.

"One of what, Captain?"

"Why, a Wastelander, of course," the captain replied.

Imrie grunted. "And you," she said. "My lord. You saw demons, did you not?"

"How can you doubt it?" Ryle said, frowning at the captain. "They were demons, Valon, great fanged ones with claws like green daggers—surely you saw them."

"I saw Wastelanders, boy," the captain said testily. "Men, not demons, though for the way they fight they could be demons, I'll grant you that."

"And you," Imrie said, turning on the magician and his boy. "What did you see? Townsfolk come with pitch and pig-slops to run you out of town?"

"Nothing of the sort," the magician said, looking indignant. "It's not safe to stay here, my lord, we should move on."

"And you, lass?" Valon said.

"I saw a cavern with a big green rock within it, and the closer I got to the rock, the denser the air became. I saw the four of you hacking and shouting and prancing about and almost killing one another, and I told you that they were afraid of fire, and I led you out."

"That's absolute nonsense," Ryle said angrily, leaping to his feet. "Magician, you're right. Let's be moving." He stalked off, holding the torch before him, with the magician and the boy on his heels. Valon reached down to help Imrie to her feet.

"Well, Captain?" Imrie said.

"I don't know, lass," the captain said, his face disappearing as the torchlight moved farther ahead. "I'll have to think on it." They started to walk after the others.

"Perhaps," the captain said after a while, "we none of us saw the truth, in there. There are places where men—where people see what they wish to see. Yet you saw nothing, lass. I do not understand it."

"I didn't see that charlatan's smoke monsters, either," Imrie said, and hurried to march ahead of him. No imagination, she thought. Well, if it leads to Wastelanders and demons, I'm just as glad I lack it. She put her hand in her pouch and curled her fingers around the amulet, finding some comfort in its worn shape.

By the time they grew hungry for supper, the companions had agreed to disagree on the inhabitants of the cavern, and spoke no more of it, although Imrie nursed a core of indignant anger at what she saw as the belittling of her victory.

Valon called a halt and they squatted on the rocky floor, sharing a niggardly meal of bread and apple slivers, washed down with a sip of wine.

"We'll rest, try to get some sleep," the captain ordered. "I'll take the first watch, then Ryle, then . . ." He looked at the magician doubtfully, and said, "Then we'll move on again. We should be near the end of this tunnel, unless we're lost."

"I don't think so," Ryle said. "We followed the map—unless my father's map was incomplete, but I doubt it. It was a very, very old map."

Valon grunted and extinguished the torch. "We'll see on the morrow," he remarked. "By the Flame, I think I'd prefer those sea-going monsters to more of this rock. Sleep, your lordship, I'll wake you for your watch."

Imrie brushed small stones away, smoothing the tunnel floor.

The tunnel was so dark that it didn't seem to matter whether her eyes were closed or opened. She quietly took the amulet from her pouch, slid the chain through it, and hung it around her neck, then lay back, feeling a little better. The magician wouldn't dare steal it now—would he? She pulled her cloak over her shoulders and lay down, turned over, pulled the cloak over her head, pushed it back down again, turned onto her back, stretched, curled up again, and finally sat.

"Trouble sleeping, lass?" Valon's voice whispered. "Then come share a watch with me."

She groped her way toward his voice, almost stepping on the apprentice, and settled beside him. He smelled of leather, and sweat, and metal, a comforting scent. The air was very still.

After a while, metal grated softly as Valon moved. "You're not from Harkensdale, are you, lass?" he whispered.

Imrie shook her head, then said, "No, Captain. From Menasdale—we came here after the raids."

"We?"

"My aunt—" She paused, her throat suddenly tight. "Aunt Melia. My mother's sister. She brought me here."

"To Colmera. Take heart, lassie. They had warning, they may have escaped."

Imrie didn't reply, her mind busy with unwelcome images of the great sea monsters and their unnatural lightning. She shifted quickly. "What are we watching for?"

"Anything. Another—thing, like that in the cavern. We won't see it, but we'll feel it. Save that you won't, will you?"

"I guess not," Imrie said. "Jora—my friend Jora, in Colmera . . ." She had to stop again, and Valon found her hand and patted it. Imrie took a deep breath. "Jora says I have no imagination, that's why I couldn't see the smoke monsters."

"Or the demons, or Wastelanders, or whatever," Valon said. "But you saw a rock, true? A green rock."

"And I felt something—like heavy air, that wouldn't let me get close to it," Imrie said. "When I tried, it was like—like walking through syrup, until I couldn't move forward at all."

"So you did feel something," the captain said slowly. "And what you saw was probably true, Imrie—we saw illusions, made by that rock, that Old One, to confuse us—to draw on whatever we most fear." He chuckled suddenly. "So either you have no imagination, lass, or you have no fear."

"No," Imrie said. "There's lots of things I fear, like the sea monsters, or cutting myself with a scythe at harvest, or growing up to marry Posten or Met Smithsson and getting old and tired and gray like my aunt. If that thing just wanted to scare me, it should have shown me ten thousand farmers, come with marriage on their minds."

Valon chuckled again. "It may be a blessing, lass, that you have no imagination. Perhaps you did rescue all of us, while we were battling imaginary enemies."

"Me, and not the magician?" Imrie said sarcastically.

"Don't be too harsh on him," Valon replied. "I spent years on the borders, riding against outlaws from the Waste—after a while, we learned that a bit of Power is not to be scorned, especially if it's on our side. That's why I retired here, to Harkensdale—far enough away from everything so that Power is not treated with fear, as it is in the rest of High Hallack. Not that I have any," he added. "I just respect it. And I suspect, lass, that if you ever meet true Power, you'll see it as plain as we do. Plainer, perhaps. Until then, remember that the magician may yet have his uses, for all that he's a thief."

Imrie fingered her talisman. "Why does he want my mother's amulet so much? I mean, it's important to me, but why to him?"

"I don't know, lass. Magicians are strange folk." The captain was silent for a moment. "Is it—odd? Does it do anything?"

Imrie thought. "No," she said finally. "I feel good when I have it, and bad when I don't—but I think it's because it was my mother's, it's all I have of hers. And Tib—Tib didn't like it, he said it tried to run away from him. But Tib was—is—he's just a baby, he makes things up."

Valon snorted. "Well, leave it be, then. We've enough problems to solve now, that one can wait." He busied himself with something, then touched Imrie's hand again.

"Here, lass, use this as a pillow and get yourself some sleep. It's been a long day, and perhaps a longer one tomorrow."

Imrie obediently lay down, pillowing herself on Valon's

rolled cloak. She heard his soft breathing nearby and, comforted, fell into a dreamless sleep.

VI

It began to seem to Ryle as though they had been underground forever when, ahead, he spotted a radiance so dim that, at first, he thought his eyes must be tired. Then, catching his breath, he wondered if another cavern lay ahead, with monsters for him to battle and for Imrie to complain about. He stopped, and Valon came up beside him.

"I see," the captain said quietly. "Stay here, lad, let me take a look."

Valon moved along the tunnel's side toward the light, and Imrie came to stand beside Ryle. He resisted the urge to move away. She still smelled of flowers and sunlight, and she was still pretty, but it didn't help—she was, he thought, a complete failure when it came to being a damsel in distress. Imrie squinted at the light.

"At least," she whispered, "it isn't green. I don't think I could take another such battle . . ."

That was more like it, Ryle thought.

"With a straight face," Imrie added.

Furious, Ryle moved two paces ahead, his nape prickling. Valon returned, striding down the tunnel's center.

"We're out," he announced quietly. "Somewhere in the hills—the tunnel opens above the valley, and we'll have to scout before we leave it. Put out the torch, and come. And not a sound, remember—we don't know where the enemy is."

Ryle's stomach tightened as he remembered the huge monsters stalking the valley, the deadly lightning and the thunder that tumbled castles. Then, resolutely, he put his shoulders back and followed the captain.

The tunnel opened into a dense growth of bushes and trees, part of the thick forest covering the hills. Valon led them to a rocky outcrop a few paces away, and they blinked against the bright sunlight. Ryle looked at his companions. They were even more tattered than he had suspected, their clothes and faces so streaked with dirt that even the symbols on the magician's sleeves had disappeared into a uniform muddy brown. Valon left them again. The Dale was silent and Ryle realized uneasily that even the birds were quiet.

Valon returned, his expression hard to read, and gestured that they should move west, higher into the hills. Ryle shook his head.

"It's my valley," he whispered. "I want to see."

"Lad, don't do it," Valon replied as quietly.

"I do, too," Imrie said. "My family—"

Valon sighed. "Go, then, the both of you," he whispered. "You have a right. But stay beneath the stones, they may have scouts close by. I'll stay with these two."

The magician grimaced and looked away, offended; his boy curled up in the forest duff and napped. Ryle and Imrie followed the faint track Valon had left, through the dense copse and up a chimney in the rocks. The chimney opened to a ledge, which they crept along until Ryle, in the lead, put his hand up. After a moment, they both raised their heads.

At first Ryle thought they had come clear through the mountains and found a different valley; then, throat tight, he recognized the curve of the hills. The village of Colmera had disappeared, replaced by a burned and ruined waste; the newly planted fields were churned to mud, the woods reduced to smoking twigs. A dark pall of smoke hung over the valley, and the sea monsters crawled everywhere, leaving destruction behind them. Men moved amid the wreckage, wearing strange uniforms; men and monsters clustered at the top of the hill between Colmera and the sea, where they seemed to have established a camp. Of the people he saw no trace until he noticed a field just behind the blackened stables, where arms, and legs, poked through the earth. Ryle felt sick, and glanced at Imrie to see his own shock mirrored in her face. He touched her shoulder, and she turned quickly and buried her face in his tunic, her body shaking silently. Ryle hesitated, then held her close.

No songsmith had ever described a battlefield more terrible, a slaughter more complete, and it came to Ryle that there were things worse in the world than monsters, and dragons, and magic. There was no glory, he thought, in taking sword against monsters that breathed lightning and ate entire valleys—only foolishness, and the promise of a swift, ignoble death. Then he saw movement beyond a tumbled wall, and a moment later a column of soldiers emerged. They surrounded one of the monsters while two of their number scaled its sides; they wriggled into the monster, feet first. Ryle touched Imrie's shoulder, and she raised her head to look. The monster started jerkily; a huge hollow pipe atop it swung left and stopped. The other monsters came to life, rumbling down the Dale toward the Norrisdale road. Imrie and Ryle glanced at each other, amazed, then scooted backward down the rock, until they could not see the valley; together they scrambled back to Valon.

"The monsters aren't monsters," Ryle said, his voice low and angry.

"Aye," Valon said. "I saw men within them, before we entered the tunnel, and again by Colmera. But if not monsters—"

"I don't think they're alive. They're like—like—I don't know *what* they're like, but if men control them, they can be stopped. And we have to do it." Valon shook his head, but Ryle put his hand up. "No, listen to me. They're gathering at the foot of the hills—they've found the road to Norrisdale. We can't let them—there must be *something* we can do—"

"Not me," the magician said loudly.

"Quiet, you idiot." Valon clapped a hand over his mouth. "Do you want us all killed?"

The magician pushed Valon's hand away. "You stop them," he whispered. "The boy and I will rush to Norrisdale, and warn them."

"They'd catch you," Imrie said. "And you'd tell them all about us before they gut you."

"Stop!" Valon whispered furiously. "We'll all be caught with this noise. We move higher up, first, away from them, then talk about it."

Within a few moments they were moving, Ryle in the lead. He had hunted these hills often, and found the thin tracks of deer, the sudden watercourses, which took them higher and to the south, until the valley dropped well behind them. It was late evening by the time they entered a small copse, and Valon decided they had come far enough. The night was sharp and cold and they huddled without a fire, for fear of drawing the enemy to them.

"Valon, we must do something," Ryle said as the captain parceled out the food. "If they make it to Norrisdale, they'll reach the main trade road—"

"Lad, I've thought on it," Valon said around a mouthful of bread. He swallowed. "I agree, but what are the five of us to do, against a force that large? With that sort of weaponry? You saw the Dale, what's left of it—there's no way we can fight them. Our best hope is to reach Norrisdale before they do, and hope that Betry kept his armsmen prepared."

"I doubt it," Ryle said. "Besides, it takes three days to reach Norris Castle, even if we run. How fast do you think those monsters are? They'd be there right behind us, if they didn't get there first."

"Why not head beyond Norrisdale?" the magician said. "We could outrun them—"

"And leave every Dale in the area in ruins?" Ryle said. "No, we have to stop them here, in Harkensdale. Even if it takes a miracle to do it."

"Perhaps not a miracle," Imrie said slowly. "Perhaps all we need is magic."

"Magic!" the magician said sarcastically. "More of my stinks and powders, little girl? I thought you didn't believe in that."

"I just don't believe in you," Imrie retorted. "Captain, your lordship, listen a minute. Last night, Captain, you said that you believed me, about the cavern, and the green rock. No, wait, let me go on. Suppose the stone I saw really was making illusions, convincing each of you that you saw what you most fear—you all did see different things, didn't you?"

Ryle nodded reluctantly, as did the others. Imrie took a deep breath.

"I think, maybe, that if the stone did that to you, it could do that to the enemy, too—and maybe they'd start fighting one another, as you almost did. Then we wouldn't need an army, all we'd need is the rock."

"Supposing all of this to be true," the magician said, "I suppose you have a plan to lure the enemy into the mine tunnels? Sea monsters and all? I wish you luck, child, but I'll have no part of it."

"We could bring the rock out," Imrie said. "It's not very big, and—"

"Bring it out!" The magician snorted and crossed his arms. "That's not a pebble in there, girl. That's an Old One. I suppose you're powerful enough to deal with an Old One?"

"Even if such a plan would work," Valon said, "you told me you couldn't get near the stone. And *we* certainly couldn't do it, we'd just meet our demons, or Wastelanders, again. A good thought, lass, but not, I think, one that we can use."

Imrie bit her lip. Ryle stared thoughtfully at the magician.

"Perhaps we can still use magic," he said. "Magician, if you made a smoke monster in their midst—"

The magician frowned, then his expression shifted. "Perhaps I could, my lord," he said slowly. "But I wouldn't help—unless I can borrow a bit more Power. Then, I think, I could do it."

"Borrow Power?" Ryle repeated. "From where?"

"From her," the magician said, pointing at Imrie. She stared at him. "From that amulet of hers. The stupid child doesn't know what she has, and wouldn't be able to use it anyway—but I can, and with it, I can save us, and Norrisdale, and everything."

Everyone started talking at once, until Valon silenced them with a slash of his hand.

"One thing at a time," he said firmly. "Magician, you'd best tell what you know about that amulet, and now. And I'll have the truth this time."

"But he can't have it back," Imrie said quickly.

"It's just a trinket," the magician said, spreading his hands. Valon lifted his sword a little from its scabbard, and the magician made a face. "Very well, it's more than a trinket. It comes from the Waste, a leftover from the Old Ones. Oh, a good thing, no evil in it, Captain, but it does focus Power—if one has Power to begin with, as I do and she does not. It's wasted on her—"

"*How* does it focus Power?" Imrie said, but the captain interrupted her.

"Tell me about your Power, Magician," he demanded.

The magician eyed Valon's sword unhappily.

"Very well, but you're not to hold it against me," he said. "I grew up in the Waste, my parents were scavengers. My mother dabbled a bit in magic—nothing serious, you understand, just enough to learn a little, and teach it to me. It's not an easy life, out there, and when I was old enough to come into the Dales with my father, to sell the metal he found, well, life just looked easier here, that's all. So I stayed. And I had to do something to make a living, so I became a magician. See, it's all very simple, really. Very innocent."

"And how many Dales were you run out of?" Valon said. "They don't take kindly to magic in the rest of High Hallack, especially magic with a man behind it."

"I know," the magician agreed. "That's when I developed my—my other skills. But I do have Power, you know, and if I had something to help me focus it, something like the amulet—"

"You'd be even more greedy and unscrupulous than you are now," Ryle said.

"Wait," Imrie said, leaping to her feet. "How do you know that I don't have Power? The green rock didn't affect me, did it? It couldn't make me see illusions, maybe that's Power, too. How do you know that it isn't?"

The magician made a gesture of disgust. Ryle put his hand up.

"Maybe she's right," he said slowly. "There seems to be a lot of stuff that the songs don't talk about—maybe this is one of them."

"And if my Power is that I don't get taken in by magic, then if the amulet helps me, not the magician, I should be able to get the rock out of the tunnel," Imrie said. "Captain, your lordship, it's certainly worth a try. It's better than any other plan, and if it doesn't work, then we're no worse off."

"And no better," Valon replied. "Lass, let me see the charm."

The sun had almost set, and the companions squinted in the dusk as Imrie reluctantly pulled the amulet over her head, and dropped it in the captain's hand. It immediately slid through his fingers and onto the dirt. Imrie snatched it up.

"I didn't drop it, lass," the captain said, his voice soft. "It moved."

"Let me try," Ryle said eagerly. Imrie carefully put the amulet in his cupped palm, and he watched with amazement as it slid up the curve of his hand and over the side.

"Aunt Melia said it was slippery," Imrie said, a hint of apology in her voice. She took it back, and it rested solidly in her hand.

The magician stretched out his hand. "I can hold it," he said confidently. Imrie's fingers clenched around the charm. "And if I can, Captain, then I'm the one to use it, you'll agree to that. It's like putting a sword in the hands of a child, or in the hands of an armsman. Who would *you* rather have defending you?"

"Lass," Valon said, "he's right. I know it pains you, but you must give it to him."

Imrie blinked, and Ryle saw her suddenly as a young girl, dirty and tired, as bereft as he himself and ordered to lose the one memento she had of a happier time. He leaned forward impulsively and touched her cheek.

"You'll get it back, Imrie," he said. "After all of this is over, if we live—I promise you, I'll see that it returns to you."

The girl looked at him, tears pooling in her pretty eyes, then tightened her lips and opened her hand.

The amulet hesitated for a moment before sliding free, and the magician twisted his hand quickly, catching the charm by its worn chain. He closed his other hand around the amulet.

"Aha!" he said. "You see!"

"He's *not* holding it," Imrie said hotly. "He's got it by the chain, that's probably how they managed to steal it. Make him do it right."

"I'm getting tired of threatening you," Valon said. "Release the chain, Magician, and consider the threats already made."

Muttering curses, the magician slid the chain from his fingers. A peculiar expression crossed his face, then he yelled suddenly and his hand flew open. The amulet fell and the magician tried to stuff his hand into his mouth. Imrie grabbed the talisman and clutched it against her breast.

"Mine," she said. "Unless you want the apprentice to try it, too."

The magician took his hand out of his mouth and examined it. "It never did that before," he whispered.

Imrie grunted and waved the amulet at the apprentice, who shook his head, stuffing his hands into the remains of his sleeves. Ryle looked at the others. He could barely see their faces, then the last of the sunlight disappeared. The waning moon cast a dim glow over the group.

"Captain?" Imrie said. "Your lordship? Do we try my idea?"

"We try it," Ryle said firmly. "We've run enough, and I won't have the songsmiths say that Harkensdale fell without a sound. Captain, are you with me?"

"I'm with you," Valon said, standing. "By the Flame, it will be good to do something to strike back."

"Good." Ryle turned and led the way back down the hillside.

VII

"Wait," the magician said. Their second torch was almost burned down, and Imrie glanced back at him, impatient. Ahead, a pale green glow suffused the corridor. The magician moved up beside her, and she took a step away.

"I know you don't trust me," he said. "But we seem to be stuck with this, and I, at least, want to survive it. Can we call a truce?"

Imrie studied the magician. He looked tired, and old, and friendly, and her lips pinched down. "Why?" she said rudely.

"I do have some Power, child, more than you—and I know some of its ways. It's not easy to use the Power, even for those with practice. If we are going to do this, you'll have to let me help you."

"How?" Imrie clutched her amulet tightly.

The magician sighed. "Using Power is exhausting, especially for a novice. And if you try to harness a Power greater than your Talent can hold, it can overwhelm you, overwhelm all of us. If we blend our Talents, perhaps we can be strong enough to do this thing. Will you let me try?"

"It's a good idea, lass," Valon said, even as Imrie was thinking the same thing. "We can't afford to turn down help."

Imrie nodded. They had already agreed that if she could move the stone, they would place it high in the pass above Colmera, where the road ran through a natural cut in the stone hills. But it would take most of the night to reach the cut, even if they took the stone on their first try, and they were already tired. What the magician said made sense, and Imrie tried to quench her dislike. He examined her face for a moment, then pushed his sleeves back.

"First," he said, "you must cleanse your mind, put everything aside so that the Power has room to move within you. Second, you must concentrate on the task, to direct the Power, and for this you must know precisely what the task is. Do you know what that is?"

Imrie thought a moment. "I must be able to get close to the stone, to pick it up, and to carry it to the cut."

"Yes, that's what you mean to do, but that is not the task," the magician said. "Think again."

Imrie frowned. "The task is—is to hold back the stone's influence, to contain it, so that I can hold the stone."

"And so that the rest of us are not beset with demons," Ryle added. Imrie agreed.

"Third," the magician said, raising his finger, "we must try to insure that the Power you evoke will be something that you can handle, and we have no way of knowing that, because you have never done this before, never even come close to Power."

"Then that makes all the other stuff pretty useless, doesn't it?" Imrie demanded, but the magician was shaking his head.

"No. If we can link together, we can merge our Powers, you borrowing mine. It may not be enough, but it's the best we can do. And the amulet will help us."

Under his direction, Imrie wrapped the amulet's chain around her wrist and around his, so that she held the talisman in her hand, and he cupped her hand with his own. The amulet seemed content to stay in place. She glanced at Ryle, Valon, and the apprentice, then closed her eyes.

"Picture a cup of water," the magician said softly. Imrie visualized one of Aunt Melia's worn pottery cups, with water sparkling within it. She felt thirsty and pushed the thirst aside.

"There is nothing, save for the cup, and the water," the magician continued. "And now the cup fades, slowly, very slowly, until you can see through it, see the water, water in the shape of a cup, for now the cup is gone and there is only water, water by itself, alone. Now the water, too, fades, so slowly, growing lighter, growing fainter, and now the water, too, is gone.

"Now," the magician's quiet voice said, "behind the nothingness there is the green stone, but it is held, enclosed, captured in a wall of nothingness, and it is still, the nothingness holds in its light. And now the nothingness folds, like an invisible cloth, until the rock is covered, sealed tight, until its light cannot escape, and all you see is an envelope of nothingness holding a green rock, just a small green rock, and it is harmless. Can you see it, that nothingness?"

"Yes," Imrie whispered.

"Then open your eyes and walk to it, and we will pick it up," the magician said.

Imrie opened her eyes and walked forward, and it seemed that nothing existed save for the small green glow before her; she barely felt the magician's hand, clasped over hers. The cavern opened up before her, and she walked straight to the stone, and bent. The magician gasped, a distant, meaningless sound. One-handed, she spread her cloak over the ground. Something seemed to push at her, trying to force her back. Quickly, ignoring the magician's groans, she wrapped her fingers around the stone and levered it onto the cloak. The pushing grew stronger, like hard hands thrusting at her. She leaned into them, panting, and twitched one end of the cloak over the stone. A wave of pressure moved against her, and she closed her eyes suddenly.

Old One, she thought, *Old One, I will not harm you. I need your help, Old One, against great evil—I beg you, Old One, let me through.*

The pressure faltered for a bare moment, and in that instant she flipped the cloak entirely over the stone and tumbled forward through the suddenly passive air, taking the magician with her. She cried out; the green light had disappeared, and they were alone in the dark.

"We did it!" the magician shouted, and to her immense astonishment, he flung his free arm about her and kissed her cheek. A moment later the others ran up to them, almost dancing with excitement and bringing the dim light of Valon's torch.

"It's going to work," Ryle said. "By the Flame, Imrie, I think it's going to work!"

"I hope so," she said, gasping. She felt as though she'd just run, nonstop, from Colmera to the sea. Her ribs hurt. "I don't think I could do that again."

"Let's hope you don't have to," Valon said. "We don't have much time—they'll start moving at sunrise."

The magician slid his hand free of the chain and rose, brushing his robes, while Ryle handed Imrie his belt and she bound stone and cloak together.

"Keep the amulet around your neck," the magician said. "You'll have to carry the stone yourself—we'll need my strength later, and I don't want to be too weary."

Imrie opened her mouth, thought better of it, and pressed her lips tight. She picked up the stone.

"If you feel anything strange," the magician added, "call me at once." He strode to the tunnel and waited, his back turned.

To her relief, the stone was fairly light, but as she held it a strange emotion came over her, as though the rock demanded her protection, her care, as much as an infant.

Sleep, Old One, she thought. *I'll guard you—sleep.* The sense of demand faded slightly. "All right," she said to Valon. "Let's go."

He looked at her dubiously, then nodded and moved away. Imrie held the stone close, took a deep breath, and followed him from the cavern. Her foot struck something, and she glanced down to see a skull roll out of the sputtering torchlight. Ryle, falling into step beside her, shuddered quickly.

"That was very brave of you," he said. She didn't reply. "I'm sorry I was rude to you before—about seeing things back there. Is it—is it very heavy? You can lean on me, if you want."

"All right," Imrie said again, still trying to catch her breath. *He's not so bad,* she thought. The torch flickered ahead, and they hurried to catch up.

                    *   *   *

The moon had set, leaving only dim starlight. Ryle had long since extinguished what remained of the torch. Imrie leaned against his shoulder.

"Just a little longer," he whispered. "Here, sit down."

The captain had left them a few moments ago, to scout the way into the cut on the Norrisdale road. Imrie gratefully sank to the ground. They were well above the tree line and she felt that she had walked for days amid granite fields, around great boulders the size of houses, while the green stone grew heavier and heavier in her arms. She settled the stone in her lap and leaned against a boulder, eyes closed.

They had formulated a plan of attack—not, as Valon said ruefully, the best in the world, and fraught with danger, but it would have to do. Once half the enemy force had passed through the cut, they would set the green stone on the road itself, and hope that its effect was both quick and strong enough to panic the soldiers. Placing the stone was the one great question remaining, and Valon had gone to seek a place where they might hide beside the road, safe from the enemy, until the time came. Imrie refused to think about the long hours they would have to spend waiting, while sea monsters and soldiers marched by; her concentration had narrowed to carrying the rock safely. She heard voices nearby, speaking in whispers.

"She shouldn't be this tired," Ryle said uneasily. "We haven't come that far."

"It's the stone," the magician said. "She has more Power than I thought, or she wouldn't have been able to touch the rock at all. But for all that, her Power is scarcely enough. The stone is draining her."

"Well, make it stop." Ryle sounded angry and frightened. "Can't she just put it down for a while? Wouldn't that help?"

"Oh, surely it would help her," the magician said. "But what of us? Only the girl prevents the stone from filling us with images of demons, or whatever. Do you, my lord, think you have the fortitude to ignore a legion of monsters?"

Ryle was silent. Imrie's limbs felt heavy, made of stone themselves, and the rock in her lap seemed to pin her to the ground below. Eyes, lips, tongue, everything was dense, immovable, and even sound became a distant, ponderous thing. She disappeared into a great and weary silence.

A noise like leaves rustling in a small breeze, but there were no trees here, she remembered. She listened to it, vaguely wondering what it was. The sound sharpened a little; she recognized the magician's voice, and his boy's, conferring together. Only a few words came clearly to her: escape, and amulet, and weapons, and the captain's name. Ryle must be asleep, she realized distantly, almost falling into silence again. They're frightened—they're planning to run away. The thought came to her unbidden, and she examined it as though it were a novel idea, something to be played with but not, really, important, not a thing of moment. They're going to leave, and take the weapons, and take the food, and take—the amulet. An uneasy feeling grew within her; she felt the weight of the talisman against her chest, and the whispering came clear again.

"Yes you can," the magician said, cajoling. "It's weak, too—she doesn't have the Power to keep it strong. Just take it, boy, just lift it off and take it. You'll be safe, I promise you."

The words were sharp and clear and dangerous, and she fought against her lethargy, still unable to move. Without the amulet, her Power would disappear and the Old One's influence blossom not against the destroyers below, but against themselves.

Old One, she thought, *help me—help me now, or we are both lost. By all that lives in light, let me move.* Slowly and with struggle, her hand rose toward the amulet around her neck.

Footsteps approached quietly over the rock, creeping closer. She fought the lethargy, her muscles almost cramping with tension; a rock rattled in the cut below them and the footsteps stopped.

After a moment, the magician whispered, "Go on, you fool, hurry!" but in that moment's grace Imrie's hand had found and touched the amulet. The heaviness abated just a little bit, enough for her eyes to slit open, and her free hand to twitch upon the covered rock. If only Ryle would wake up! Her fingers picked at the bound cloak. The quiet footsteps resumed; she could see the apprentice's shape as a darkness against the starlit rocks, and beyond him a taller darkness that was the ma-

gician himself. Ryle snored steadily. The apprentice knelt
slowly and reached a hand toward Imrie's throat, and in that
instant her fingers touched the stone itself, and she pushed a
corner of the cloak aside.

Her hand flew away from the rock as though pushed by the
beam of sharp green light that shot from the stone, momentarily illuminating the apprentice's startled face and the magician behind him. Then the apprentice screamed, flinging his
arms over his face; the magician yelled, Ryle cursed and leaped
to his feet, sword drawn, and the green light spread, a pulsing
glow rapidly filling the small stone hollow in which they lay.

Like a beacon, Imrie thought, and did the only thing she
could think of. Hand clenched tight around the amulet, she
pitched forward, throwing her body over the bright green
stone.

VIII

The light disappeared as quickly as it had come, but not before Ryle had grabbed the magician and thrown him to the
ground. The magician lay rigid as Ryle rested his sword against
the mage's throat.

"She did it," the magician said, gasping. "The girl, she released the rock, she wanted to kill us all—"

"Shut up," Ryle said fiercely. He turned the magician over
and, planting a foot on his back, bound his sleeves together
before turning toward Imrie and the apprentice. The girl lay
collapsed over the bundled rock, and the apprentice, his face
etched with horror, lay on the ground beside her. Ryle touched
the boy's throat, but no pulse beat. Then, fearfully, he reached
out a hand toward Imrie.

He couldn't touch her. An Imrie-shaped force pushed his
hand away, no matter what angle he tried, so that it seemed the
girl was captured within an invisible shell a bare hairbreadth
larger than herself. He remembered Imrie's version of their first
meeting with the stone in the cavern, of the pressure that had

kept her away. Now, it seemed, whatever force protected the rock protected, or ensorceled, Imrie, too—he could not even tell if she still lived.

Pebbles rattled as Valon ran up, bare sword in hand, and stood for a moment staring. Ryle gestured wearily and rose.

"I don't know what happened," he told the captain. "The magician says Imrie tried to release the rock, but I don't believe him. The boy is dead. And Imrie—" He stopped, his throat tight, and turned away while Valon bent over the girl. After a while the captain touched his shoulder.

"She's alive, lad. You can see her back move as she breathes."

"No thanks to this one," Ryle said bitterly, and raised his sword to kill the magician. Valon barely stopped him.

"If she's captured in magic, we'll need magic to free her, no matter what its source," he said. "Listen, I've found a cleft leading down into the cut, almost midway through it. There's another cleft across from it, narrow enough to hide us."

"It won't do you much good," the magician said. He had rolled himself over and now lay on his back. "You can't touch the girl, which means you can't touch the rock. Or perhaps you're planning to roll girl and rock together into the road? The soldiers will be amused by that."

"Not half as amused at finding a trussed magician in the road," Valon said. "Would they gut you, or let their sea monsters squash you? Because, unless you shut up and cooperate, that's all you have to worry about, in the few hours left you." He spat and turned back to Ryle.

"My lord, we can die here, or we can die on the road to Norrisdale. On the road, at least we have a chance to strike back, puny as it may be. If I can, I'll carry the girl down. You follow with the magician, at sword's point. And you, charlatan, you had best think to your Power, and how to use it to release the girl. It is your only guarantee of life, I promise you."

Ryle pressed his lips together, nodding, and levered the magician to his feet while Valon sheathed his sword and bent to the girl. She seemed to make a rigid bundle, but he was able to slip a hand beneath her knees and another around her shoulders, and raised her up.

"What about my apprentice?" the magician said suddenly. "We can't leave him here, unburied, for the crows to eat."

"The crows may yet eat all of us," Ryle said. "If we live, I'll return and bury him. Which is more than I'll do for you." Poking the magician with the tip of his sword, he urged him after the captain.

The trip down the cleft was a nightmare in stony darkness, for the pallid starlight did not reach here, and of the three, only the magician was free to use both hands. The cleft opened into a tumbled slope of scree, which they slid down to reach the road. The sky paled slightly. Valon led them quickly to a cleft on the other side. A boulder at the cleft's mouth offered minimal concealment, but, Ryle thought, it was the best they could do. Valon set Imrie down on her side, gently stroking the invisible field above her arm. Distantly, a bird sang. A more ominous noise followed it; the far clangor of an army preparing to march.

Ryle raised his sword until its tip touched the magician's throat. "Magic," he whispered. "Now."

The magician, looking unhappy, set to work. The problem, Ryle thought, was that he had no idea what the magician was doing, could not tell if he worked for good or for ill, and there was not a thing he could do about it, either. He stood uncomfortably as the magician took various implements from his robe. One was a wand, with which he drew a large geometric shape encompassing himself, Imrie, and Ryle. Next he produced a number of herbs and performed various actions upon them, all the time muttering incantations almost silently. Ryle glanced at the captain, and they both shrugged. The sound of the army drew closer, and under it came the stone-on-stone noise of the moving monsters.

Eventually, content with his preparations, the magician stood up and traced various patterns in the air; his finger left a glowing line behind it, until the line solidified into a complex pattern Ryle did not recognize. He raised his hand to make the sign against evil, but froze at the magician's quick shake of the head, and lowered his hand again. Valon, outside the magic shape, crept to the head of the cleft, ventured a look out, and returned, his face grim. Now Ryle could hear the distinct sound of marching feet. The first wave of soldiers passed the cleft, singing a hoarse, unpleasant song in an unfamiliar language. Ryle held his breath, but no alarm was raised. He glared at the magician, who frowned back and sent more glowing patterns into the air. The rock beneath them shook gently as one of the sea monsters rumbled by.

Imrie stirred, the barest motion of her shoulders. Ryle dropped to his knees beside her, his hand extended, but could not touch her skin. The magician knelt on her other side, staring at her hand.

"If she releases the stone, grab it and throw it immediately," the magician said, his voice hushed and hoarse with effort. Then he closed his eyes and swayed with the force of his incantations, and Imrie slowly rolled onto her back, her body still clenched around the stone. Ryle could see a side of it under her arm; the belt seemed to have worked loose from the cloak that covered it, but the rock was quiet. Her lips opened, as though she sighed or groaned, but he could not hear the sound. Beyond the cleft, more sea monsters rolled by, drowning the soldier's song.

Suddenly the magician flung his arms above his head while bands of light flared from his fingertips, and in that moment Imrie's body relaxed. Ryle grabbed the stone, not giving himself time to think; it resisted, then came easily to his hands and he almost drowned in a world of hatred, swords and lances flashing toward his body, a sea monster directly before him lowering its deadly snout toward his belly. Gasping, he staggered to his feet.

"Now!" the magician shrieked. "By the Flame, now!"

Ryle rushed blindly toward the sea monster, through it, through a phalanx of leering demons until he caromed from the boulder guarding the cleft. With all his might, he pitched the stone into the center of the Norrisdale road. The cloak blew free of it, and the soldiers yelled in confusion as it landed in their midst. Then Valon's hand grabbed his collar and jerked him back into the cleft, and the demons disappeared.

The sounds of surprise turned quickly into shouts of fear and outrage; weapons clashed and men screamed. Within the cleft, the magician sprawled limply over Imrie's legs, and she lay pallid and as still as death. Ryle moved toward her, but Valon's hand clamped hard upon his arm.

"We have to get out," the captain shouted. He tossed the magician over his shoulder, caught his balance, and moved quickly down the cleft. Ryle swore and put his hands to Imrie's body; it was soft and warm, and he thought a brief prayer of thanks as he slung her over his shoulder and followed the captain. She didn't smell of summer now, just of sharp sweat and dirt.

Although it twisted and turned, this cleft was slightly broader than the other, and the slope more gentle. Ryle staggered onward, one arm clasping Imrie and the other grasping the hilt of his sword. The noise of battle was deafening, and clouds of dust billowed into the air. Ryle blinked against the grit in his eyes, and almost ran into Valon.

It seemed the very mountain had turned against them, for the cleft took a final twist and opened higher up on the Norrisdale road, where soldiers screamed and fought downhill against their own. One soldier saw Valon and shouted; he and his fellows, turning, multiplied, until a horde of screaming fighters rushed forward. Ryle let Imrie slide to the ground behind him and braced his feet, swinging his sword and thinking only briefly of death.

His sword bit into the first soldier and slid through the second as though through air. Beside him, Valon cursed.

"The stone!" the captain shouted. "Some are illusion, lord, but which?"

There was no way to tell, and a wrong guess would be instantly fatal. A sword swung through his guard, slicing through his arm without leaving a trace; his own sword jolted against an enemy's armor.

"My lord!"

He swung, missed, swung, connected.

"Ryle! There are three of them!" Imrie's voice, harsh and shrill, screamed over the sound of battle. "To your left, Ryle! Captain, before you!"

The soldier in front of Ryle leered and raised his axe, and Ryle spun away from him and struck at the man to his left. The sword bit into flesh, just as the first soldier's axe hacked at Ryle's head, and disappeared.

"Captain, another behind you! They also fight illusions!"

At that moment, the second soldier swung furiously at the air, and Ryle's sword slid through his guard and through his armor. The man collapsed, and did not disappear.

"Ryle! Your right, the man with the axe fighting Valon!"

Ryle strode through legions of illusory enemies, impaling nothingness on his sword, until the sword touched solidity and he drove it through the soldier's back. Together he and Valon dispatched the remaining warrior, and looked at each other wildly.

"Back!" Imrie shouted. "Before others come, quickly!"

She staggered upright. Grabbing the magician by his arms, Valon and Ryle retreated after her into the cleft again, away from the road and the stone. As soon as the illusions stopped, Imrie pulled the magician from them, drew her arm back, and slapped his face as hard as she could.

"You're not asleep," she cried. "Get up and do something useful!"

The magician opened his eyes. "What?" he demanded. "If we're to be killed, I'd rather go quietly, thank you."

Imrie hit him again. "Make a smoke monster, you fool," she said. "The enemy won't come through it, only illusions will. We can follow it out of here."

The magician blinked at her and sat up quickly. "By the Flame," he muttered, delving into his robes. "By the Flame, girl!"

Ryle, leaning against the rock face and panting, stared at them. "A smoke monster?" he echoed.

"Do you have any better ideas?" Imrie retorted. "I may have been under the rock's spell, but I wasn't asleep, and I'm not stupid. Come on, thief, hurry up, hurry up!" She rocked back. "Ryle, Valon, all you have to do is remember that the illusions can't hurt you—only your fear can harm you, and that's what the stone feeds on. If you have no fear, it has nothing to throw back at you."

"Aye, easy to contemplate, and harder to do," the captain said. "You propose that we walk through an army of warriors and sea monsters, and not feel fear?"

"Yes," Imrie said. She rose. "Blindfolded, if necessary. I can lead you. We have to head for Norrisdale—there's nothing left behind us, and we must give warning. The sea monsters haven't started making lightning yet—I don't think they're ready, or alive, or whatever it is that gets them going. Captain, I don't think we have a choice, and I don't think we have much time. Once we get beyond this, is there a break in the cut?"

"Yes," Valon said. "About fifty paces up—but the stone's between us and it."

"Good," Imrie said. "Hurry," she said to the magician, and offered to hit him again.

Ryle closed his eyes. "I thought you were dead," he said.

"No, my lord," she said gently. "Just removed—and fed my Power back and my strength, as though it had been borrowed and returned twofold. I don't know why. And we don't, I think, have time to talk about it. Charlatan?"

"Hah!" the magician said. He shook back his sleeves, arranged a pile of supplies on the ground, and produced a smoke monster. It lunged into the air, eyes glowing and claws extended. Ryle looked at it dubiously.

"Do you see it?" he demanded of Imrie.

"I see a bunch of black smoke," she said impatiently. "Do you want a blindfold?"

Ryle shook his head, then reached out and grabbed her hand. She turned to him, surprised, and he looked for a moment into her pretty, grubby face, before bending and kissing her swiftly.

"That's just in case," he whispered, and turned to go.

If anything, the walk on the Norrisdale road was even more horrifying than the earlier battle. The smoke monster surrounded them, belching fire, and around them screams and the clash of metal filled the air; dead and dying men lay underfoot, the ground slippery with their blood. Ryle kept his eyes fastened on Imrie, ignoring the legions of enemies that attacked his sides, only to vanish the moment they touched his skin. Beside him, Valon kept up a steady stream of curses, and the magician walked just ahead, guiding the smoke monster with his hands and glancing nervously over his shoulder.

In the midst of it all, to his astonishment, Imrie paused and knelt. She reached to touch the smooth green stone lying in the roadbed, passing her palm over its surface gently and murmuring. Then she rose and led them on, at a faster pace. Light flared and thunder shook the mountain; the sea monsters were finally awake.

"Here, lass!" Valon shouted, and they ducked into yet another cleft. Imrie immediately started to run and they followed her up piles of talus and a narrow chimney in the rock, leaving the sounds of battle farther behind. Small rockfalls struck at them as the sea monsters loosed lightning on the road below; Ryle's hands, slick with sweat, slipped again and again on the rock, and the muscles in his arms cramped. He fought the cramps grimly, his world narrowing to touch upon dark rock, sounds of screams, bright unnatural flashes that hurt his eyes, the rocking of stone against deep thunder. The chimney went up forever, then it stopped and hands gripped his wrists, levering him into starlight.

"No resting," the captain ordered, panting. "Remember Harken Castle."

Ryle shuddered, gasping clean, cold air, and stood. The companions staggered on, grabbing one another, legs weak and barely able to see; and of a sudden the entire mountain writhed beneath them, tumbling them to the ground. Ryle clutched at the moving stone, eyes closed; it seemed that the world was ending, and a new, more terrible one begun. Thunder and the shuddering of the earth, again and again, until with a final, cataclysmic movement the mountain stilled. He held his breath, fingers aching against the rock, and gradually realized that a silence had fallen, in which even the sound of wind over rock had died. Cautiously, he raised his head and looked.

The sun shone through a haze of dust. He turned his head slowly to see Imrie, beside him, staring into the distance, and he followed her gaze. A pale, rectangular cloud of dust rose above the Norrisdale road, and after a moment the earth shuddered one final time as a peak slid into itself and down, leaving a jagged fang against the horizon. Ryle pushed himself up and looked back. A few paces beyond his feet, a new chasm had opened in the land, and below it lay Harkensdale, desolate and still. The Norrisdale road had disappeared.

"I think the earth herself cried out," Imrie murmured. Ryle

turned back to look at her. She sat, shaking her head; dark hair tumbled around her shoulders, shining in the sun. She glanced at him, and behind her he saw Valon and the magician come, blinking, to their knees to see what the earth had wrought. Ryle stood, using his sword as a crutch, and Imrie came to stand beside him.

"It's not over," he said as Imrie rested her head against his shoulder.

"No. High Hallack will see change greater than we can imagine," she said. "By the Flame, Ryle, I am tired."

He put his arm around her, and all his visions of chivalry, of high-born maidens in romantic distress, faded forever as he held Imrie close, savoring the sharp tang of her, the unkempt hair, the feel of Power and of promise in her weary body. Valon and the magician came up beside them, and without speaking they turned together to face away from Harkensdale, toward the rest of High Hallack's many Dales.

"We'll rest, my lady," Ryle said. "We deserve a rest. As someday, my lady, I hope to deserve you."

Imrie snorted, a tired, loving sound, and after a moment he realized that she was asleep, upright against his body. Valon laughed.

"And who, my lord, has a better right?" he said.

Ryle laughed with him and, wrapping his cloak around the sleeping girl, lowered himself and her together to the quiet earth.

Afterword

When Andre Norton asked me to write a novella for one of her Witch World anthologies, I was both flattered and dubious. You see, I don't believe in magic. Oh, I like reading stories that include magic, and have no trouble suspending my disbelief—unless it's a story of mine, in which case I can't suspend my disbelief at all. But I sat at the computer, announced to my characters that despite the opinions of the management, they were going to believe in magic, and started writing.

I should have known better. They didn't believe in magic any more than I do. Something magical happened, they made skeptical noises, and then they all stood around and refused to move, or talk, or think, or anything.

Does this all sound more than a little nuts to you? I mean, these are only characters, right? They exist only in my own imagination, correct? They have to do what I want them to do, no matter what.

Well, tell it to them. It would certainly make my job a lot easier if these imaginary folk understood that they live at my whim—but they don't believe it for a moment, and neither, really, do I. No, my characters treat me the same way that certain primitive tribes treat their gods—if the god doesn't provide rain, or good harvests, or a successful hunt, they beat it with sticks, and if it still doesn't shape up, they unceremoniously toss it out and get a god who delivers.

Then I remembered a sterling piece of advice that Chelsea Quinn Yarbro once gave me, when I was stuck in the last third of a novel and disgusted with the entire business. Quinn *suggested that I introduce a character who was as disgusted with the proceedings as I was, and see if that broke through the block. This strategy worked splendidly, and I determined to try it again now.*

And suddenly there was Imrie, her feet planted in the mud and her hands planted on her hips, announcing to all and sundry that magic was a lot of bunkum and she didn't believe it for a minute. And, in the back of my head, a small voice suggested that perhaps not being able to see magic, not believing in it, could be as powerful a charm as any wizard could provide.

From that point, the story just flew along. I sat at my computer trying madly to keep up with all these "imaginary" people as they spun out their story, not caring that I was getting hungry and tired and was in desperate need of the bathroom. Characters are an ungrateful lot, all in all—but when they get their steam up and start moving, I wouldn't try to stop them for the world—even if I could.

—Marta Randall

STRAIT OF STORMS

by

K. L. Roberts

Four times a day riptides churned and twisted through the Strait of Storms from the Gulf of Hilarion to Oceax Bay and back again. Where passage through the strait was narrowest, a cluster of small islands, like spikes of iron, rose precipitantly from the sea. Owing to the tides, to the wide skirts of jagged coral surrounding the islands, and to their barrenness, they were uninhabited, save for a single young woman. Though she had not abided there long, her body might have been framed of the cherts and obsidian of the islands themselves, so bleak and flinty was her aspect. She clung to life by hatred and by guile, using an old charm to encourage the fish and marine iguana to regard her fingers as fat worms—worms that, at the last moment, snatched their prey from the water and dashed them upon the rocks. Often, however, she forwent eating, and her body had become gaunt; even her breasts had begun to dwindle. Soon she would go nude, for her frock, once a heavy, tapestried garment, was disintegrating a few threads at a time.

Each morning she climbed a spire of rock, central to the islands, that commanded a view of the strait from shore to shore. With her was a small, silent child, as gaunt as she, to whom she spoke in conspiratorial tones as she searched the sea for ships. But the child never responded, nor, for that matter, did she remark upon any event whatever. At times vessels did dare to navigate the strait, and on those occasions one might have thought the child's silence to be born of terror, for the woman was such a sight as even a grown man might not look upon willingly. Glaring across the strait with almost inhuman malice, her body would grow rigid, and her lips draw back in an awful grimace. Then, with ability beyond her years, she would raise her fists far above her head and draw to them a writhing nimbus of force . . .

Duke Chastain, in his prime, had been a man of imposing proportions, but affairs of office had long blunted the edge of his vitality and he tended now to corpulence. Within the limitations of his imagination and of his ability, his reign had been a capable one. He had sent scribes to copy the moldering manuscripts of the Old Race in far western Lormt; he had initiated curbs on his own authority; and he had led expeditions to destroy the strongholds of the Sarn Riders. Now, however, he was more preoccupied with his digestion and with music. Recent events, unfortunately, had ruined the former and afforded him little time for the latter, and he sat in chamber in a foul temper, wishing he had been born a swineherd.

His chamberlain, Gestin Crabtree, was as sensitive as a wife to his moods. Since the death of the duchess, he was, in fact, the real backbone of the tiny duchy, inasmuch as he alone retained any ability to direct his lord's flagging attention to matters of importance. It was he who had arranged this morning's audience with a young man who, he judged, would do nothing to improve the duke's digestion.

The visitor arrived at the appointed hour, was announced, and approached the throne, halting at a respectful distance. The lad could hardly have seemed less certain of himself and was, Crabtree surmised, little more than fifteen or sixteen years of age, most likely an apprentice in his second year of sea duty. The duke studied him from head to foot for a long moment with evident reluctance to hear what he had to say.

"Well, fellow, what are you called?" he finally asked.

"Gar . . . er . . . Garth, lord," the young man quavered.

"Do I understand, Garth, that you have been witness to events of some moment?"

The brow of the young man wrinkled in perplexity at the unfamiliar words and usage. "Lord?"

"You saw something, something important?"

"Uh . . . yes, lord—that is, something—something terrible." He hesitated, evidently uncertain as to how to proceed.

Chastain frowned. "Well? Speak, lad, speak!"

Garth flushed. "Yes, lord. Well, uh . . . we was making passage through the Strait of Storms, all hands a-deck. We was looking for rocks, you see. It's shallow, and the rocks, you see, ain't always the same place twice. And we're going along and the boatswain shouts, he says, 'Look!' and he points at Merfay Island. And I looks, and I sees . . . uh . . ." The jaw of the apprentice seemed to lock, and he flushed again.

"Yes?" prompted the duke, somewhat intrigued now, despite himself.

"Well, I sees a woman, a lady, lord, with golden hair. Only she hasn't no clothes on . . ." A faraway look came to the eyes of the apprentice.

"Yes, well, I believe we've all seen women unclothed."

"Yes, lord. Well, Rolf looks too, and he sees, well, I guess he sees something like gold and gems and such as that; but the only lady he sees is ugly, with black hair, and skinny. But he sure sees gold. And the captain, he looks too, and he sees . . . well, I don't know what he sees, but he tells the helmsman, 'Hard a-port!' and the helmsman went quick to it! Well, the rocks, you know, was still there; but we forgot about those somehow, and there's a noise, a terrible noise! And the *Lucky Wind,* she ships water; and, you know, there's yelling, and we lets down the lifeboat, only the current is too strong and it keeps pulling the boat, back and forth, and only a few gets on. And the captain, he swears at the helmsman, only the helmsman fell into the water, and he don't hear nothing! Because the water pulled him under." He stopped for a moment. "That was Osbrey, lord. He was my friend . . . Well, the *Lucky Wind,* she founders, and I fall in, only I get hold of a spar, and I ties myself on with rigging. And . . . well, I walks back, you know, and I . . . uh, steals some food, only a little bit that nobody wants, with mold, and all that . . . and, uh . . . well, I guess that's all."

The duke frowned meditatively. "Merfay Island, eh?"

"Yes, lord."

"You didn't note other ships? Wrecks, that is?"

"No, lord. But . . . well, the currents, you know, they wouldn't leave nothing grounded there for long."

"Mmm. I suppose not. No. And you say you saw a temptress, but Rolf saw a hag?"

"Yes, lord. Skinny, with black hair."

"Mmm. There's witchcraft in that, lad."

The apprentice gave what he hoped would be a wise-seeming nod. "My thought, exactly, sir."

"No doubt. No doubt. Well." Chastain studied the vaulting timbers above him abstractedly. "Lord Chamberlain, take young Garth here to the steward, see you that he has new clothing, and have him arrange an apprenticeship on a worthy craft—mind you, a tight ship, not a rotting bit of sea wrack like the *Lucky Wind*. We must discuss this matter when you've returned."

"Yes, lord."

The apprentice attempted a dignified bow. "Thank you, lord."

"Mmm."

Crabtree wasted no time seeing through this task and returned as quickly as possible, to find that the duke had made use of the interval to slip into a doze. The chamberlain took in the slack features of his lord resignedly, and after a moment forcefully cleared his throat.

Chastain blinked. "Eh? Wasn't sleeping. Must consider all aspects of this matter. Mustn't overreact."

"Yes, lord. Have you reached any conclusions?"

"Eh? Well, no. But the lad's story lends support to Grenwall's report . . . Did he have any luck in making out who this hag might be?"

"Perhaps, lord. In Es he heard a sad and rather strange tale of a young woman whose luck turned bad. It seems she was taken in training by the wise women, having had an unusual talent for the Power almost from the first. But they were ambitious, and they pushed her too far, too hastily. She broke in both spirit and body, utterly exhausted, and was given up by the witches as useless. Grenwall discovered that she wandered overmountain and was taken in by the Green People. They set her to work in a garden and there, after some months of weeding, hoeing, and such she seemed near recovery. She was noticed by a man of the Old Race shortly thereafter, and left with him. Grenwall was unable to discover where next they went, except that they traveled east, downriver; but she is described as being dark-haired."

The duke nodded thoughtfully. "That would establish her ability, and place her nearby—though that proves nothing. Still . . ."

After a time he heaved himself to his feet and slowly strode to the windows of the sunny eastern end of the chamber. Crabtree eyed him hopefully: this action he knew to be characteristic of Chastain at his most enterprising. After some time the duke turned and seated himself on the window ledge. "It's a pretty problem, Crabtree. We're effectively cut off, with half the fishing vessels stranded at sea and half the merchants trapped in port. We should have cut a channel to Merfay and fortified it to forestall just such an imbroglio."

"Easy to say now, lord, but it would have been a difficult and costly venture at best."

"Indeed, but hardly more costly than this affair has already proven. However 'should haves' never won the day—the question is, what do we do now? Do we assault the island?"

Crabtree shook his head. "I should think the cost in lives would be considerable. We cannot expect to approach undetected, and we possess no weapon with sufficient range to attack from shore. However, I have consulted in this matter with Grenwall, and he has put forward a proposal that I believe has some merit."

Chastain snorted. "I might have expected as much. I have never known the rogue to be in want of a proposal where some profit to himself might be garnered. What will this latest 'proposal' cost me?"

"Less, I believe, than any alternative. Consider this." He

handed the duke a watercolor that depicted a creature roughly human in form with, however, webbed hands and feet, gill slits, and glossy, mottled flesh.

The duke looked up, handed the picture back with distaste. "Sea-Krogan? Fah! They will not assist. They are still offended by our trafficking in Oceax Bay."

"Indeed, they will not, lord. I have already spoken to them and matters stand as you say. However, this was not what Grenwall had in mind."

"No? Then just what has our dear Grenwall hatched in that pregnant imagination of his?"

Crabtree studied the watercolor carefully. "He proposes a true shape-changing, lord. In such form he could swim to Merfay in the dead of night and be upon the hag before she knew what struck her."

Chastain stroked his white-streaked beard with fleshy fingers and considered the suggestion. "Ingenious, but the currents there are treacherous, and beneath the water it will be dark as a closet at night. I have no great liking for the man, yet I would not send him to his death. Can we do no better than this?"

"What would you propose, lord? I have considered the construction of a great ballista . . . but I am told that its fashioning would require more than a fortnight of toil, and there is nothing to say the hag could not destroy it. Or we might try to pit witch against witch, if we could find such to try; but that would entail greater danger than Grenwall proposes to risk." Crabtree shrugged. "No. On balance, I believe that what he suggests is best. True, he must needs watch the tides carefully. But, as for the other, Sea-Krogan are said to see the night as day."

Chastain returned to his throne and seated himself wearily. "And again I say, what will this cost me? Grenwall drives a notoriously hard bargain."

"He asks for the land from which he drove the Gray Ones—"

"What! That's the sweetest land in the duchy. I planned to build fish ponds there!"

"—and for Merthe's dowry," Crabtree concluded impassively.

The duke stared in mute disbelief. "My daughter doesn't

even know Grenwall . . . what am I saying? He is not even a noble. No, thrice horn the man, it's beyond reason!"

"Lord, Grenwall is a resourceful man. He has been trysting with your daughter for many months. She loves him. And where the risks are great, so must the rewards be. Remember, it is possible, entirely possible, that he will not return to human form. Think you: the man would remain half fish the rest of his days, with none but Sea-Krogan for company. Offer rewards to others of the nobility. If none will accept the risk, give Grenwall scope. This is my counsel."

Chastain studied his chamberlain for a long moment. "Grenwall is an opportunistic dog," he said bitterly. "Not half good enough for Merthe."

Crabtree sighed. "Perhaps, but at least his ability has been proved time and again, more than can be said of your other retainers. And Merthe . . . Merthe is Merthe. Even Grenwall will have his hands full, as you will admit if you think on it."

Chastain looked away, through the window, to the forest, and to the hills beyond. "You take me too lightly, Crabtree. You ruin my sleep and digestion, you counsel me to hateful action and insult my daughter, and you stand and blink and expect me to concur like some great, stupid eunuch." He stood. "Go from me now, Crabtree; I have much to consider. I could wish that I were not duke, and yet I am."

In the end Crabtree's advice prevailed, as the nobility little cared to risk what it already had, and Grenwall was selected for the task. He asked for, and was granted, various implements and a day in which to set his affairs in order. As he lived a simple life, however, the time needed was but a few hours.

Kenten Grenwall was a short, stocky man, with coal-black hair and brows, dark eyes, and a smile many women had found comely. As a child he had been rather slight of build, the butt of much taunting and bullying; in consequence he had learned to fight. Like his mates, he had been ignorant and superstitious; unlike them, he had somehow educated himself. And his parents, like the parents of his friends, had been poor. He had determined not to be, however, and fully expected events to work in his favor in this as well.

He rode now for a small fishing village in eastern Escore known as Coelwyn where there lived a wise woman of middle years who was well regarded and a healer of ability. Traveling the northern strand of the Gulf of Hilarion, Grenwall made good time and avoided the Sarn Riders who were preying once again upon the sole trade road. Here and there he was even able to supplement his provisions with sea-quasfi and occasional fish; but he was glad nonetheless to see, as he rode one morning, the quays and fishing boats of Coelwyn. As he drew nearer, a stiff salt breeze swept away the stench of the town, and the small but sturdy homes and stout little fishing vessels took on a certain charm. Grenwall knew, however, that life here was characterized by unceasing labor, discomfort, and, above all, interminable boredom. It was a matter of some wonder, even to him, who did not often wonder at human foibles, that Twyx, the healer, would choose such a town in which to live. He found her at home on the outskirts of Coelwyn in a tidy structure of dark timber and slate shingles. He was met at the doorway, as if expected.

"Ah, Kenten." She smiled. "I see that you have come after all. You had a safe trip, I trust?"

Grenwall smiled in return. "I did, lady. And I bring good news. The duke has charged me with undoing the hag."

The witch peered at him soberly for a moment from under her dark, arched brows. "Good news, Kenten? That it may be—or mayn't. You were able to bring that which I asked for?"

"Yes, everything. And the duke has agreed to the financing of aught else you may need."

Twyx motioned him within the house. "A resourceful man you are indeed. Anything I need, is it?" She shook her head. "Well, come in, sir, sit—a stew I'm making, with rabbit. We must eat and talk. More of the hag have I learned."

Grenwall seated himself on a squat wooden stool that sat before a short table of unvarnished beams. "Oh, yes? Tell me."

Twyx knelt before a black, round-bellied pot suspended above a small slate hearth, and stirred the bubbling contents. She looked up at him, then back to the pot. "A queer story it makes, Kenten, most queer, all in all." She tasted the stew. "Quite done, I think. Well, after you lost the trail in Green

Valley I took it up in my own fashion. She and her man of the Old Race took a boat east to Maddoc, where they wedded."

"Man and witch?"

"Aye, man to witch. But like Jaelith of old, she lost not the Power, though she little cared to use it. She begot a child, Drotha, whom she loved dearly; and for some years the three of them prospered, for her husband had secured Torgian stallions and mares, and their issue was much in demand.

"But there came a time when they made a holiday of delivering a gelding and mare downriver. And there was one aboard the boat who looked and listened, and noted their prosperity.

"One night, as they slept, this one came to their cabin, and when he left her husband was dead. Drotha had been struck in the head, and could not be awakened. The witch also was cruelly wounded, but she recovered and learned that this man who had done them so ill was a sailor—a sailor of your duchy, Kenten." She ladled his stew out upon a wooden plate. "I must own, enough fish have I eaten here for this lifetime and the next."

Grenwall took the plate from her. "That I can well believe." He took a tentative bite and found it better than anything he had eaten in weeks. "Truly, I can't understand why you have elected to live here, so far from Es."

She smiled and shrugged. "My needs are few, Kenten, and do not include an appetite for intrigue. Would you hear the rest?"

"Yes, please, go on."

"The woman took Drotha to many healers—that is where I got the story—but they could do naught. One day mother and child disappeared, and when they returned Drotha had the semblance of life, but not the substance. She never spoke, and responded only to commands. It was rumored that the woman had bargained with the Dark Ones to attain this half life for Drotha, and had paid a terrible price. The people of Maddoc began to shun her, and even the horses grew skittish. One day she seemed to go mad, and then the both of them disappeared, not to be heard from again."

Kenten chewed in silence for a moment. "A strange tale indeed. I have seen this Drotha in the distance-lenses . . . she never moved. Tell me, has this woman a name?"

"Aye, Miriel."

"Miriel . . ." Grenwall ate methodically until the stew was gone, then pushed back from the table. "You know, Twyx, it occurs to me that we have never settled the matter of your fee."

She pursed her lips in amusement and pulled her hair back from her face. "True, Kenten, true. Somehow I had imagined we would settle that, and other matters, before you accepted any commission from the duke."

Kenten studied her features closely, suspicion flickering alive within him. "You have a reputation for fair dealing, my dear Twyx. I took your goodwill for granted."

"Truly? So astute a man as yourself? I would have thought you took nothing for granted."

She is amused, thought Grenwall, *but does she jest*? "Well then, out with it. What is this hideous fee of yours?"

"Fee? There is none. I said only that we did not discuss any such. But I am not certain you understand the Power, Kenten. I can guarantee you nothing, neither a true shape-changing nor return to your present form. Did you represent these facts to the duke?"

"You underrate me, Twyx. I well understand the risk entailed, as does the duke."

"I am glad to hear that your grasp of the nature of the Power is so profound," she said wryly. "You also understand, then, why I do not use it for either personal gain, my own or another's, or in the service of unworthy causes?"

Grenwall's eyes narrowed. "The Power recoils against any who employ it in such fashion. But my cause is worthy enough: I would clear the strait so that husbands might return to wives and trade resume."

"Would you, indeed? It is well that this is the cause uppermost in your mind. And what of the girl, possibly bereft of reason, knowing not what she does? What would you do with her?"

Grenwall frowned. "I—I see. Perhaps . . . yes, just let me think for a moment." He stood and crossed the room to a narrow window opening toward the sea. Well, what *had* he thought to do with the girl? To cut her down, he realized, as he would a Sarn Rider or Gray One. But if, in her madness, she were innocent of guilt, the backlash of the Power might indeed prove unpredictable. He would simply have to immobilize this Miriel woman somehow—she was a mere bag of bones, after all. And . . .

What else had Twyx implied? That personal gain was uppermost in his mind. . . ? Grenwall fingered his chin uneasily. Twyx received a modest recompense for her services, he knew. Evidently the Power did not begrudge her some sort of gain. Was it then a question of motive—of using others purely as means to ends? Grenwall began to realize dimly that he far more often acted upon his intentions than he appraised them. Still, he *did* care about the people of the duchy, and he even felt a certain tenuous sympathy for the girl and her child. *No,* he decided, *my motives are not by any means entirely selfish.* He turned from the window decisively.

"I am anxious to begin, Twyx. If we ride now, we might arrive at the strait by eventide, and I can spend the morrow studying the currents."

Twyx folded her arms, searched his face. "So . . ." she said with some surprise. "I must own, I thought you might change your mind. Still, if you are quite certain what you do, I am prepared to leave at any time. By all means, lead on, Kenten."

Though Grenwall was weary of riding, they made good time and arrived at the strait at dusk. He encamped with the practiced assurance of a mercenary, ate hurriedly, and took distance-lenses to the jagged lip of a bluff overlooking the shoreline. Here he squatted, a warm breeze from the sea stirring his hair, and scrutinized Merfay Island carefully.

Though he had once before seen the island, its wild and utterly forbidding appearance struck him forcefully. Nothing grew on the island, or on any of the others nearby, save thornwort; and nothing within sight moved, save the currents and an occasional, brooding marine iguana. Sharp-edged spires of rock, like the blades of so many broken knives, thrust against the sky. None of the islands appeared to have inlets or beaches of any kind, aside from narrow banks of scree. Grenwall shook his head slightly, then turned the lenses on the currents of the strait itself. He immediately received an impression of tremendous, uncontrolled power. Great twisting sheets of water shouldered over and boiled around black spurs of rock everywhere he looked. Although he could not drown in Sea-Krogan form, to be hurled against stone here would be to risk being either killed or knocked senseless.

"Have you seen Miriel yet?" Twyx asked.

Grenwall put aside the distance-lenses and looked across at the witch. "No, but then I did not expect to. When last I came, her daughter kept watch by night; and in any event, there are many places to conceal oneself on Merfay."

The sea breeze blew Twyx's hair into a shimmering cloud about her face. "Can you do this thing, Kenten?"

He shrugged. "I have done more difficult things and have failed to do lesser. There is an element of luck and of the unforeseen in every venture."

"There is indeed." She folded her arms across her bodice. "At least, when you put on Krogan flesh, the water will become your element, and your strength will be the greater."

"A boon for which I shall, no doubt, be grateful." Grenwall stood. "I would sleep now. I will need my wits about me on the morrow."

"As will I," said Twyx.

Grenwall awoke slowly, the shrieks of sea birds and the sounds of rushing water in his ears. The smell of food was in the air, and he realized that he was hungry. Pushing aside the flaps of his tent, he found Twyx cooking breakfast.

"Up so late, Kenten? One might almost suppose you preferred sleep to the day's work."

He combed his hair with his fingers drowsily. "I *do* prefer sleep to this day's work. However, I prefer breakfast even to sleep. It would seem your magic extends even to cooking, lady."

She smiled. "In truth, it would seem the work ranks a poor third, if not lower."

They ate in leisurely fashion, and then Grenwall set himself in earnest to the study of the strait. He rode for some distance up and down the lightly wooded shoreline, stopping often to study the turbulent waters with the distance-lenses. Twice he risked observation by loosing arrows he had painted white, the better to observe their passage down current. As late afternoon

wore toward evening he took an axe in hand and notched a tree
adjacent to the strait on its shoreward side. With a few more
blows it would topple and slide into the water.

Twyx looked upon his labors with interest. "Would you ride
it downstream to the island?"

"Perhaps." He wiped sweat from his brow with the back of
his wrist. "Twice today, however, have boles gone past with
such momentum as to make me doubt that they can readily be
guided. Still, it may be worth trying. I will wait for the lull
between tides." He rested his axe against the tree. "Tell me,
Twyx, would I have anything to fear from this woman if she
were bound and gagged?"

The witch shrugged. "That will depend upon how accomplished she is. Some with the gift of mind-touch can compel
others against their will, and need not move or speak to do so,
while others can weave illusions. Then again, she may be weakened, and if she has been stripped of her jewel she may be less
effectual than otherwise."

"And if she acts against me in this fashion, can you be of any
assistance?"

"Count not upon that, Kenten Grenwall. True shape-changing is no mean task, and I am not so young as once I was. I may
well not have strength enough after your transformation to
help."

"I see. You are nothing if not candid, Twyx."

She raised an eyebrow. "And that is ordinarily counted a virtue, sir."

He eyed her vexedly for a moment, reflecting that she had
not once had a word of encouragement for him. "Then truly
there must be few women so virtuous as yourself." He looked
out upon the darkening silhouette of Merfay Island. "We must
soon begin. I will need some time to accustom myself to the
Krogan-form."

"As you say," she said coolly. "I am ready when you are."

They returned to camp, where Grenwall took a light meal.
He felt restive, though he could not have said why, and he
found himself wondering what he would do if compelled to
spend the rest of his life as an amphibian. He watched the witch
for a moment. "How often have you done this, Twyx?"

"What? Accomplished a transformation?"

"Yes."

"Perhaps a half-dozen times."

"And how many returned to human form?"

She laughed. "Why, they all did."

He stroked his chin uneasily. "Hmm. Well then, let us be about it."

The witch gathered various implements, and they rode to the spot where he had hewn the tree. Grenwall tethered their horses a good distance away and returned to find Twyx drawing a pentagram in the sand with a silver rod. He watched in silence as she unwrapped five small tripods and positioned them at each of the points of her diagram. From each hung a small censer that she lit with a tallow wick, one after another. When she was done, she took his hand. "Come, Kenten. It is time."

Twyx led him to the center of the pentagram, and then drew away a few feet. She closed her eyes and stood quietly for a few moments, and then, while smoke from the censers began to wreathe about him, she began to croon a singsong chant in a tongue unknown to him. As the smoke twisted higher, Grenwall suddenly realized he could no longer see his body. There came, slowly at first, but then more rapidly, the impression that his very bones had become fluid and insubstantial. He tried to speak, to move, but found he could do neither; and then he felt his body altering—stretching, bending, flowing. If he could have cried out then, he would have; but, abruptly, it was over. He had become flesh and bone again. Grenwall felt certain, however, that this was not the flesh he had worn before. It was—different, peculiarly different, and—he couldn't breathe!

He gulped and choked convulsively for a moment, and then his body seemed to take over of its own initiative, using muscles he hadn't known he had. He drew air into lungs that had been empty; and he blinked and found he had an inner eyelid that moved sideways. Grenwall discovered that he could see well in the dimness of twilight, and realized now that Twyx had collapsed, though she was breathing normally. He shuffled awkwardly to her on webbed feet, and turned her over with a hand that also was webbed.

"Trrrggs," he said thickly. "Trrrggs . . ."

She blinked up at him wearily. "I am perfectly well . . . Kenten. How are you?"

He held his hand up before his eyes and flexed the strange-looking fingers.

"Geels . . . geels gunny."

She closed her eyes. "You will grow accustomed to it soon enough. Perhaps you should practice swimming—and breathing water."

"Brrging errtr . . ." The odd phrase startled him, and he reflected that he could now remain underwater indefinitely, and could go places few men had dreamed of going before. "Yeggs."

He stood and tried to get the feel of his new anatomy, swinging his arms, stamping his feet. When he felt more confident, he went to the bank overlooking the strait and climbed to the narrow shore below. Here the water would be shallow, the current readily negotiable. He waded into the dark, shifting water slowly, then held his breath and submerged. Uncertain as to how to proceed, he drew the water into his mouth and found once again that his body proceeded on its own, squeezing the liquid back over his gills effortlessly. He found that his sense of taste had become far more acute than he had ever dreamed possible.

Grenwall opened his eyes, his protective third eyelid sliding into place, and found that his vision readily pierced the shadows, though the color had been leached from everything. He could see the pebbles beneath his feet and, farther away, a number of fish. Launching himself from the bottom, he swam gracefully almost from the first stroke. As Twyx had promised, he was indeed stronger than he had been; and he found himself sliding through the water with surprising speed and ability. Grenwall began to feel that his task was perhaps not so formidable after all.

After some time he returned to shore and climbed up the bank. Twyx had wrapped herself in a blanket and rested her head on a bundle. "You must leave soon, Kenten," she said. "The lull in the tides has come."

"Yeggs," he said briefly, finding it strange to have air in his lungs once again. Taking his axe in hand, he finished felling the tree and noted with satisfaction that most of its length had dropped into the water. He quickly strapped around his waist a bundle he had made up, and then turned to the shoreline.

"Kenten!"

"Yeggs?"

Twyx smiled wanly. "Good fortune!"

"Taggs."

With some difficulty Grenwall worked the fallen tree fully into the water, and then, clinging to it, kicked out into deeper water. As he had thought, it proved difficult to maneuver; but it would help him to conserve his strength and avoid underwater obstacles. At first there was no appreciable current; but he knew that the water was always turbulent, even between tides, and as he made his way into deeper water this was borne out. His tree shifted so that its bole pointed down current, and he clung to branches in the crown, finding it increasingly difficult to steer. As the tree gained speed its bole began to glance off of upthrusting rocks, and the sound of rushing water grew loud in his ears. His makeshift vehicle was drawn ever closer to the fastest part of the current, and he could see ahead the froth and spume of white water.

Judging it folly to remain longer with the tree, Grenwall pushed off and swam strongly across current. Something hard and unseen struck him a sharp blow in the rib cage, and he gasped in pain. Had he not been able to breathe water, he would have drawn it into his throat or lungs instead. As it was, he swam underwater for all he was worth, gulping and expelling the cold water frantically to keep pace with his desperate need for air. He soon noticed that the deeper he swam, the less the force of the current, and he quickly dropped to the bottom. Here even his dark-adapted eyes could hardly penetrate the gloom. The water was gritty and odd-tasting, but he was able to get back his breath and assess his injury. His side bled freely, and he would have a sizable bruise, but nothing seemed broken. He swam on more slowly for some time, coming now and again to an anchor or a trangled mass of rigging or a stove. Twice he saw enormous, armor-plated fish in the distance, hugging the bottom after his own fashion. After the second sighting he began to look over his shoulder as he swam, uncertain what effect his still-bleeding wound would have upon them.

Grenwall long went on in this fashion, and then the water began to grow more shallow. Finally he risked rising to the surface to get his bearings and found himself near the jagged coral skirt of the islet adjacent to Merfay. If he bore to his left, hugging the coast of the islet, he would soon be upon his destination.

He resubmerged, hugging the bottom again, enormous coral heads visible in the shallower water to his right. As he passed a pitted outcropping of rock something shot forward toward him with tremendous speed. Grenwall spun to face it, his hand to his sole weapon, a long-knife. It closed quickly: he saw great, saw-toothed jaws gape wide, glimpsed its fleshy, hideously ugly head. He twisted to one side at the last possible moment, striking into the baggy belly of the thing as it passed. A dark cloud of blood spilled into the water immediately, but he was able to see that it was some species of eel, more than three times his own body length. The thing doubled back upon itself with incredible fluidity to strike at him a second time; but now Grewwall was above it, and he opened a second gaping wound along its back.

If it had struck at him a third time he could probably not have eluded it, but now it thrashed about insanely, coiling back upon itself and biting its own back. He pushed off from it convulsively and back-pedaled with all speed toward the surface. Fortunately, the animal showed no interest in pursuing him, and continued to thrash about in clouds of its own blood. Grenwall spotted one of the armor-plated fish moving in, and he swam as strongly as he was able toward Merfay.

During low tide Grenwall had observed but a single gap in the ring of coral surrounding the island. This was now his destination, for to approach the island from any other point would slow him, and force him to risk repeated laceration. He moved cautiously, fearing another eel or some other hungering denizen of the reef. Several times he did spot peculiar creatures, the like of which he had never seen in fish market or net; but none sought to deter him, and he came at last to the gap. This he swam through to shallower waters, where he fastened ill-fitting sandals to his feet and thence furtively waded ashore.

Lying behind a scrubby patch of thornwort he surveyed the island carefully. Narrow banks of scree shouldered up against the steep slopes of the nearest spire, and thickets of thornwort crowded its fissures. The rock underfoot and above was unnaturally dark and unreflective, like coal, while his flesh was glossy and mottled. Grenwall reflected that he would have to make careful use of cover. Neither the witch nor her daughter was within his view, though he watched carefully for several minutes. Nevertheless, he already felt uneasy. His injury drove sharp spikes of pain into his side with each breath, and much of his strength had been used in merely getting to the island.

When finally he broke cover, Grenwall made for the shadows at the foot of the spire, not for the heights. He could, he reasoned, climb once he sighted the witch. This, however, proved unexpectedly difficult. Though Merfay was not a large island, he could not explore it quickly without risk of disclosing his presence. The loose scree tended to slip out from underfoot and rattle away, and the spiny thornwort obstructed his passage everywhere. After some time, the landscape suddenly began to look familiar, and he realized that he had completely encircled the island. Had the two perished, or moved to another island, or did they perhaps wait in hiding, forewarned of his presence? He frowned, recalling that he had not seen the witch since his arrival. It now seemed that there was no alternative to climbing, and this, too, made him frown, for in circling the island he had discovered that his webbed feet and makeshift sandals were poorly suited to that purpose. Too, he had had to reenter the water to keep his gills from drying. The higher he went, the farther behind he left the water.

What choice, he thought, *what choice*? He reentered the strait briefly, and slowly began to make the ascent.

Long before he reached the summit, he discovered why he had not been able to see the pair: they were concealed in a depression on the highest spire of Merfay. Though they did not seem to note his presence, Grenwall doubted now that he could approach at all closely without alerting them: there was simply not enough cover. The sole possibility seemed to lie in ascending the sheerest side of the spire and dropping upon them from above. He doubted that this could be done in his present form, but decided to descend and at least examine the side in question. When he reached bottom, a faint sound came to his ears, rising and falling, disappearing, to rise and fall again. He paused to listen more closely, and then realized that what he heard was the witch conversing with her daughter. Few complete sentences came to him, but what little he could hear was a kind of strange, incoherent stew of words. For the first time Grenwall became truly and uncomfortably aware that the woman whom he hoped to detain was deranged.

He moved toward her voice, then, almost too late, realized that she and her daughter were slowly descending. Dropping to one knee behind an outcropping of rock, he studied the broken terrain between himself and the woman, trying to decide which way she would come. He thought to detect a faint trail passing within a short distance of himself and, using what cover was available, worked his way closer.

Crouching tensely in his jagged pool of shadow, Grenwall listened as the voice of the witch drew nearer and nearer, its weird cadences and the strangeness of the thought it expressed unnerving him by degrees. Then, from somewhere nearby in the darkness, there came the hammering of wings followed by a sudden and complete silence.

Grenwall stirred uneasily, wondering what had happened, more certain with each passing moment that he had been seen. When he was no longer able to bear the tension he slowly peered around the edge of the outcropping that concealed him—and came nearly face-to-face with the witch. She recoiled, spitting maledictions, while Grenwall hesitated, paralyzed. Regaining himself, he sprang forward and grabbed the skinny arm of the woman. An instant later he held something else altogether: the limb of a flabby abomination such as he had never glimpsed in all the length and breadth of Escore. It fought and twisted in his arms with terrible strength, and he lost his grip on its gummy, fetid flesh. The creature twisted away, its cockroachlike mouth parts working furiously, then struck forward with a rock. Grenwall ducked and, bobbing upward again, clouted the thing's skinny jaw with all the force in his arm. His blow sent it reeling, and it collapsed to the ground, a woman once again.

Grenwall drew a ragged breath, and then something made

him look up. He found himself staring into the hollow eyes of the girl, Drotha, who stood, watching, a few feet behind her fallen mother. He started forward, not quite knowing what to expect, but the girl neither spoke nor moved as he approached. He reached out hesitantly to stroke her hair; but her forehead and cheeks were cold as snow, and nearly as white, and he jerked his hand away as if he had touched something unclean. Once—twice—before he had seen such a creature, and knew it for a sickly simulacrum of something living. "Please . . ." she said dully, with the appearance of having made a terrific, draining effort, "please . . . end . . . this."

Grenwall stared in horror for a long moment, and then reached for his knife, but his hand never reached its hilt. Something bat-winged and glossy hurtled out of the night, its razorlike talons stroking his jaw. He struck at it, but only fanned the air; and a moment later it was back, tearing at his scalp. This time he succeeded in slapping it away, and saw it long enough to know it for what it was: a familiar. He was bending over to pick up a rock to hurl after it when something clamped down upon his will with such force that he gasped. Though he fought as hard as he could, he found himself straightening against any intention of his own, and his right hand dropped to the hilt of his long-knife, grasping it firmly. Guessing what that other will would force him to do with the weapon, he abruptly shifted from fighting the pressure to acceding to it, and succeeded in throwing the blade a few feet from himself. He realized at once, however, that the ruse had only purchased seconds for him, as he was already being forced to retrieve the weapon. Opposing the pressure with all the powers of concentration he possessed, Grenwall was able to slow, but not stop, his involuntary movement; and he realized with sinking despair that unless he found some defense against this mind-meddling he would be dead within moments.

As his body jerked and hopped like a puppet on strings, he thought frantically; but he had no talent for the Power, and he danced onward, unimpeded, toward his doom. As his hand closed once more around the hilt of the long-knife, he tried to send forth a mental entreaty to Twyx—and there was a response, though it seemed faint. Now, however, there were three minds locked in struggle, and Grenwall found that his own will was not so completely overmastered. Sensing that this was his last chance, he bent every effort toward turning about, and slowly succeeded in doing so. He could see the witch now, and her malevolent gaze locked with his. Though he felt as though he opposed the force of some powerful gale, he took step after difficult step toward her, and suddenly she broke, voicing an inarticulate wail of despair. For the first time, Grenwall realized that she probably expected the worst from himself; and indeed, in Krogan-form, with dried blood caking his side, and wounds about his head, he was a horrific sight.

Forcing her to the ground, he discovered that she still possessed a witch's jewel. He had supposed that she would have been stripped of it when the wise women had done with her; but, apparently, she had engaged in an act of theft or subterfuge. He quickly pulled it from about her neck, hoping that would serve to protect him from further attacks, and bound and gagged the woman. As an additional precaution, he took a vial from his packet and held it under her nose until she was forced to breathe the drugging vapors. This accomplished, he searched the bleak landscape for her familiar, but was unable to discover its location. It was only then that he realized that he was quivering with exhaustion. To attempt to return to shore across current this night would be madness, and very much against his inclinations, he set the idea aside.

Grenwall became aware that his gills felt dry and raw, and he waded a few yards out into the strait and submerged himself in the ice-cold water. *I've done it,* he thought dully, *it's done. Thank you, Twyx.* He surfaced and looked across the currents to the shore. There was no way to know what the effort of assisting him had cost her, but he knew the price could have been high. *Thank you,* he thought again, but there was no response. Was she dead or dying, or merely exhausted? There was no way to discover that this night.

Grenwall slowly waded ashore, and once again faced the girl, Drotha. She looked at him wordlessly, an expression of terrible weariness on her face. He shook his head, as if to clear it of his disinclinations, then drew his long-knife and did quickly what had to be done. Though giddy with exhaustion, he made a small cairn for her wasted body with rock from the banks of scree.

Dropping heavily to the ground, he carefully wrapped the witch's jewel in a square of cloth from his packet. Using that as a pillow, his last glimpse of the world before the onset of sleep was of the witch, still lying facedown where he had left her among the rocks.

Far into the night, he awoke suddenly, knowing something was wrong. But what? He opened one eyelid a crack and found himself looking almost in the face of a small, but nightmarish, creature of glossy black pelt. He watched for a moment to see what it would do, and then realized that it must be searching among his scant possessions for the witch's jewel. When it turned away from him for a moment, he thrust forth a hand and grabbed the creature by the nape of its neck. It screamed and chattered like some tiny black imp, its glossy bat-wings beating furiously at the air. He bound it with twine from his kit, not without receiving a few shallow wounds, and then returned, muttering, to sleep.

Grenwall awoke slowly in the morning, stiff in every joint, his side one long aching pain. The familiar, he saw at once, was trying to bite through its bonds, and had almost succeeded. Suddenly it became aware that it was being observed, and glared up at Grenwall with one black, beady eye.

"What ugly Krogan scum do with Malef?" the thing asked in a tinny voice.

He stared at in for a moment in surprise, then shook his wounded hand at it angrily. "I'm going to gut gyou up and geed gyou to gyour mistress, gyou wretched little blagg maggot!"

The thing cackled gleefully, but made no further inquiry regarding its fate. It had, however, raised an important question in Grenwall's mind. What was he going to do with the witch? After a moment he shook his head resignedly. There was really only one thing to do: wait for another lull between tides and swim down current with her. He got more twine and went to retie the familiar; but when he picked it up, it bit him again and slipped loose of its bonds. Winging into the air, it circled him once, cackling. "Malef bite smelly Krogan scum!" it jeered. "Good Malef! Strong Malef!" As it veered off and flapped swiftly out to sea, Grenwall picked up a stone and threw it after the creature.

"Malef a turd!" he shouted.

He secured his packet, making certain he still had the gem, and then waded into the water, searching for quasfi and eating them raw, until the lull between tides came. He then approached the witch cautiously. She was making an effort to get at his mind, of that he was certain; but it seemed that, without the jewel, her powers truly were dim and unfocused. He untied her bony ankles and helped her to her feet. She glared angrily at him; and after his experience with Malef, he decided to leave her gag in place.

"I mean gyou no garm," he said. "Do gyou understand? We must now swim to shore."

Her eyes slid toward the funeral cairn. She could not have seen what happened between Grenwall and Drotha, but perhaps she had surmised something of the course of events.

"She was . . . tired," Grenwall said softly. "She was not meant gor living death . . . or gor this place."

Perhaps he reached some spark of reason within her, or perhaps not. Tears dropped from her eyes to the stony ground, but she said nothing.

"Gome," Grenwall said. "We must go."

He was hampered by the necessity of supporting the witch and of swimming near the surface. On the other hand, however, he needed no concealment and did not have to make for any particular point on shore, and so he returned about as readily as he had come. As he waded into the shallows with his prisoner, he scanned the low bluffs for some sign of Twyx, but saw nothing promising. They walked a way along the narrow, stony beach, then, at a point of advantage, climbed to the summit above. Still there was no sign of Twyx, and they trudged on. At last they arrived at Grenwall's makeshift camp, and he pushed aside the flaps of Twyx's tent. An unmoving body lay inside, and he shook its shoulder gingerly.

"I am perfectly well, Kenten," the witch said, yawning. "No need to pull off my arm." She rolled to her knees and studied his companion. "You have made captive your victim, I see." Her eyes moved to his frame. "And she has made so much chowder of you, it seems."

"Spare me gurther gongratulations," Grenwall muttered. "I would eat."

"A worthwhile suggestion," she agreed. "But first you must give me the jewel."

"What jewel?"

She held out her hand. "You know very well what jewel. It is no mere bauble for you to bargain away or toy with. Women have given their lives that its like not fall into grasping hands."

Grenwall grimaced and fished it out. "Take it, then. I have had my gill of witches and witchery."

Her hand closed about it. "Thank you. Now . . . I will see to breakfast, and then . . . I must make a man of you again."

Grenwall muttered something a younger woman might have colored to hear, retied the ankles of his prisoner, and disappeared into his tent.

After eating, Twyx drew her pentagram in the soil again, and Grenwall attended to Miriel, drugging her once more to prevent any interference in the proceedings.

"Well, Kenten," Twyx said, "you make such a handsome Krogan it seems a shame to change you back . . . still, I suppose I would have to listen to your tiresome objections, so let us be about it."

"Let us indeed." He stepped into the pentagram and crossed his arms. "Please proceed."

Twyx lit her censers, and Grenwall reexperienced the dissolution of his body, but this time the experience was subtly different. Everything seemed to take longer, to proceed more grudgingly, and he sensed that the witch was fighting hard to keep the transformation on course. He felt his flesh congealing oddly, like once-molten metal that had cooled too far to be properly worked, and then the transformation was over. Twyx looked at him in tired dismay. "Oh, Kenten . . . I'm—I'm so very sorry. I tried so hard . . . but something was wrong from the start."

Grenwall looked down at himself, a sick feeling in the pit of his stomach. Everything looked normal except—except his right foot, the toes of which were still webbed and—he felt his face. All was nearly normal there, except . . .

"Give me a mirror," he said hoarsely.

Twyx stood looking at him for a moment longer, then slowly

entered her tent. She reappeared with a small dish of polished metal and handed it to him silently. He examined his reflection grimly, and saw that the upper left half of his face and one eye had not transformed, had instead remained Krogan-flesh. The effect was unnerving.

"What happened?"

"I don't know, Kenten. Sometimes the Power simply fails . . . sometimes, sometimes it recoils against those who use it improperly."

He handed the dish back. "You think I abused it," he said accusingly, "don't you? You doubted my motives from the outset."

She frowned and looked away, and Grenwall suddenly realized that she was trembling with exhaustion or with anger, or both. "I *considered* them from the outset, Kenten Grenwall, carefully. Did you?"

He started to frame an acrid response, but stopped. Harsh words would not restore normalcy to his appearance.

"Can you not try it again?" he asked.

Twyx sighed. "I can, but when such has been tried in the past, it has as often made matters worse as it has made them better. I do not advise it."

He turned away bitterly. "So be it."

"Kenten?"

"Yes?"

She came to him and put her hand on his shoulder. "There is this: I can give you the appearance of normality. The time would come when the illusion would break down, but it would give you, and those you know, time to make the best of it. And there is also this." She gestured at the young witch. "Greater or lesser misfortune comes into every life at some time. Compared to this woman, yours is the lesser. I do not know that I can restore her mind to her, or if she will have any enjoyment of life if I can. Tell me, what did you do with her daughter?"

Grenwall shrugged. "What mercy required."

"I see. Perhaps I can create some healing illusion for Miriel also. And now, what do you say?"

He thought for a moment. "Perhaps it would be best," he finally said. "I would not care to greet Merthe looking like this."

* * *

Seasons came and passed, and with their passage the Sarn Riders grew bolder in their raids upon the northern trade road. The question arose as to how best to deal with them; and as it was evident that the duke would lead no further raids, his chamberlain's thoughts turned once again to Grenwall. Crabtree rode out to his new estate personally to sound him out, and in due time returned. He encountered the duke in the stables as he was mounting for the hunt.

"Ah, Crabtree," said the duke. "Back from your mission so soon? What does Grenwall ask for this time? Stardust?"

"I believe some fee was mentioned," Crabtree said vaguely, "but come, put away your falcon, and I will tell you what was said."

Chastain frowned for a moment, but handed his bird down to his astringer. "Oh, very well. Let us stroll, it is a fine day."

Crabtree raised an eyebrow in surprise. "Certainly."

They passed through iron gates into a small garden. "Grenwall's estate is beginning to prosper, lord. He acquired Torgian horses from the relatives of his new bride, and their issue is well thought of. He asked, by the by, if Merthe thought much about him."

Chastain grunted. "You lied, I hope."

"Yes, lord. I said she asked often about him."

"Hmm. A bit thick, Crabtree. I doubt if Grenwall is so gullible as all that. I must say, I never thought the witch would recover, let alone wed—let alone wed Grenwall. It seems an odd pairing."

Crabtree shrugged. "Perhaps, perhaps. They seem happy enough. He still walks with a cane, but he seems to have made peace with his looks."

"Mmm. Good. Good. I thought for some time that he might ruin his mind, what with all that racking his brain about motives. But enough of this. What did he say to your proposal?"

"Yes . . . well, he agreed to accept the commission. But . . . shall we say, he seems not unduly obsessed with motives these days."

Chastain scowled. "You refer to his fee? Well, out with it, Crabtree. What is it the scoundrel wants now?"

The chamberlain rubbed his bald spot, choosing his words
carefully. "You recall the fish ponds you intended to build on
Grenwall's land? Well, he has built them, and they brim with
fish—quite tasty, by the way. We made several meals of them. I
doubt if better can be had."

"Yes, tasty, go on."

"Well, it seems Grenwall wants you to buy them."

"Buy them? All of them? Buy the confounded fish the man is
hatching on the property he cheated me out of in the first
place?"

"Yes, lord. I should say there are several thousand."

Chastain's face reddened. "Thrice horn the man!"

Afterword

Andre Norton administered an addictive dose of enchantment to me some time about 1964 when I discovered a copy of Galactic Derelict *in the local library. Although I was only ten at the time, I knew immediately that I had stumbled onto the good stuff, and launched myself immediately on a reading campaign. I soon exhausted the resources of the library and began indulging in the work of other science fiction authors. One thing led to another, and with the encouragement of an elementary schoolteacher I undertook to write my first "novel."*

About the time I graduated to collecting rejection slips from Analog, *Andre appeared at the Orlando Public Library. I have three recollections from this first meeting: first, as rumor had it, Andre indeed proved to be a woman; second, she seemed to have read absolutely all the science fiction and fantasy worth reading; and, finally, she graciously autographed all of my battered Ace editions of her works, and I owned most of them.*

Many years later Mary Hanson-Roberts and I met Andre at a local convention, and we struck up a friendship that had a substantial element of pixie dust for Mary and myself. Andre's invitation not long afterward to submit a story for her Witch World *anthology more or less stunned me: she hadn't read anything I'd written, the* Witch World *novels struck me as landmarks of adult fantasy, and some of the other submissions were from very capable writers indeed. Really, though, I should have known that any author kind enough to get writer's cramp for a fourteen-year-old had to be nice to the bone.*

—K. L. Roberts

CANDLETRAP

by

Mary H. Schaub

Parven stared, terrified, at the unyielding stone floor spread out more than a tall man's height below him. His mind screamed that he was falling, that any second he must be dashed against the figured slabs. He would have cried out or shut his eyes to block the horrid sight, but he had lost all bodily sensations, as if he had plunged into frigid water. Suspended in midair perilously high above the magician's floor, Parven was reduced to only one conscious function: thought. He tried to shrink back from the yammering hysteria that threatened to overwhelm him. Perhaps if he concentrated on one thing or one person. He had heard that there were rare people who could direct their thoughts to others. In all his reading and gathering of scraps of forgotten lore, Parven had never discovered any spell or chant to enable an ordinary person to converse mind to mind. If only he had! Parven ran through a mental inventory of the amulets and protective charms tucked in his pockets or secured around his neck or wrists. Even though he could not touch or feel any of them, he knew they were there, and whatever powers they possessed should still be working in his favor. Not enough, he reflected ruefully, to ward him from this unexpected suspension spell, but he was conscious and he might yet think of something constructive.

Time also seemed suspended in this chamber deep beneath the ruined castle. Parven's immobility prevented him from seeing anything not within his limited field of view. At first, he thought he might get some idea of time's passage from the two candles he could barely glimpse on the side table, but he soon saw that they were no longer burning as ordinary candles. Their flames continued to emit a dusky light, but they were static, and the substance of the candles did not diminish. Parven belatedly deduced that the candles must be part of the entrapment spell he had carelessly set in motion. He had not expected to be trapped; he knew that there might be dangers associated with pursuing ancient lore, but somehow he never thought that he could be so easily overwhelmed. He felt a surge of resentment that his amulets had proved so futile, followed by an equally fervent conviction that his being alive at all might well be due to those very amulets. They might not have preserved his freedom to move, but they were probably responsible for his still being himself. Parven shuddered mentally, recalling tales of hapless souls transferred into animals' bodies, or, worse, dispersed like morning mist rising above a lake.

The image of a mountain lake brought with it a poignant memory of his mother. She had been a scholarly, gentle lady totally out of place in his father's rough foothills holding. Although she had died when Parven was a small child, he cherished a glowing vision of her gathering flowers on the lake bank beside their upland meadow. Parven had been a shy, sickly only son. His father, not knowing what to do with him and encouraged by his forceful second wife, had dispatched the boy to be apprenticed to Halvard the trader. A shrewd man, Halvard had immediately discerned Parven's retiring nature and had set him to work learning to read and write. As soon as he was proficient, Parven had been directed to handle records received from scouts and travelers and to search the archives for hints of possible new trade goods and curiosities.

It was while he was sifting through a clutter of musty travelers' notes that Parven first encountered the description of a curious, remote mountain valley always cloud-bound, as if the

mists were drawn there to conceal the place. Intrigued, Parven
sought out other reports on the same area, but the little he
found was discouragingly brief. Those mountains were omi-
nously near the edge of the Waste, so few sensible folk ever
ventured there on purpose. One intrepid scout called the valley
"forbidding and chill," and another traveler, lost after a storm,
said his horses had refused to stay hobbled there, fretting and
pulling at their tethers until he had moved his camp outside the
valley. Parven diligently sorted through all of Halvard's precious maps. On one very old fragment, he was just able to decipher a faded warning scrawl: "Valley of Kulp—fog—ruins—
AVOID." The more he thought about it, the more interested
he became, until he traced every connection he could find relat-
ing to the valley. In those heights, natural accidents were a
common danger to man and beast, so no general alarms seemed
to have been circulated. Parven decided that there must be a
treasure there—why else the persistent, unnatural fog and the
repellent reputation of the place? Something valuable was
likely to be at the center of it all, and the shrouding fog suggested that it was spell-guarded. Parven began at once to seek
out charms and amulets warranted to guard against all sorts of
nefarious spells. When Halvard announced that he was leaving
on an extensive buying trip, threading through the populated
parts of the Dales and culminating at the Fyndale Fair, Parven
asked to pursue on his own some rumors of a trove of old
manuscripts. Halvard frowned and said he supposed they could
spare Parven during this trip, but only if he discovered some
worthwhile information. His harassed assistant, Fulch, responsible for converting Halvard's orders into action, reluctantly organized an extra horse and supplies for Parven before he was
swept off amid the usual chaos accompanying Halvard.

Parven set out on his own, too quiet and nondescript a traveler to attract unwanted attention. Days of hard riding brought
him to the isolated, ramshackle inn where the single rough road
and two merging trails degraded into barely passable footpaths
threading on into the wild. Parven asked for any available
guide, but the only man claiming to know the territory demanded so steep a price that Parven had to decline his help.
Not knowing whether he could find any useful information or

goods for Halvard, Parven felt that he couldn't waste Halvard's silver on what was truly his own fancy and might well lead to nothing. He had his copied maps, and left the inn the next morning as quietly and unremarked as he had come.

Three days later, in the afternoon, Parven glimpsed an opaque fog bank spilling across the crude shepherd's track that seemed the only route in these mountains. He was certain it must be the valley of Kulp when his horse shied at the rise and refused to advance. Sensibly deciding that he should wait for daylight before entering the misty area, Parven camped in a nearby clearing where his horse consented to be tethered. Parven was too excited for some time to be able to sleep, but when he dozed at last, his dreams were ominous and troubling. He roused abruptly to find himself on his feet edging slowly toward the valley. Frightened—for he was never one to walk in his sleep—Parven hastily unpacked his most potent amulets. Further inspired by a thought of what the practical Fulch might do under such conditions, Parven also prudently tied his left wrist to his saddle. He awakened just before dawn, uncomfortably cramped, but still safely confined within his camp. Choking down a dry journeycake, he impatiently waited for the rising sun to lift the fog, but the cloudy mass stubbornly puddled in the hollows and lost only ribbons of its substance to the light breeze.

Parven finally concluded that he could wait no longer. The foresighted Fulch had packed a number of torches in case Parven might have to venture into dark cellars or caves. Not expecting to need one, Parven chose to be prepared, and marched into the fog bank, unlit torch in hand. He initially despaired of finding any ruins when he tripped over a broken paving stone. His excitement was short-lived, for the ruins seemed to be disappointingly bare, with not even any interesting animal tracks to mar the wind-drifted silt. As he peered closer, Parven discerned a pattern in the courtyard paving, an extended set of curves that nagged at his mind. He traced the pattern into the roofless remnant of the great hall, and found it became progressively more decorated, like an embellished spiral. The back wall where doors would have opened into the mountainside had been totally buried by a massive rockfall.

He spent the humid afternoon shifting stones and sweeping away loose soil with an improvised conifer-branch broom. His efforts eventually disclosed a metal-bound door once secured by an ornate but now-shattered lock. Behind the door, steep stairs descended, their narrow treads decorated with the dark red spiral pattern set into the stone. Parven took a stern grip on his natural inclination to rush down the steps. He sniffed the air cautiously, but it smelled only of damp stone and stillness. He then hurried back to his camp to make sure that his tethered horse had ample grazing and water in easy-reaching distance. From his array of charms and amulets, he chose the best ones to secure firmly around neck and wrists, and as an afterthought, Parven slipped the excess in his pockets before returning to the ruins.

Feeling uncharacteristically adventurous, Parven kindled one of Fulch's torches and kicked aside the last rubble cluttering the top step. After descending Parven's height, the narrow stairway abruptly turned at a sharper angle into the mountain. With his attention focused on the downward passage, Parven failed to notice the slow, silent closure of the outside door. The flickering torch obscured any awareness of the loss of outdoor light reflecting down the stairs. Parven progressed steadily down, quite soon losing any sense of direction amid the turns and counterturns. The walls remained unbroken by doors or side passages. He suddenly emerged into a much larger space with shadowed furniture bulking against the walls, whose stone expanse was muffled by great fabric wall hangings. A deeply carved high-backed chair provided a makeshift socket for his torch, and while wedging it securely, Parven saw some candles scattered on a narrow table nearby. Thinking to save his torch for the long return climb, Parven mounted five candles in a heavy metal holder, then quenched his torch with Fulch's leather snuffer thriftily tied to the butt. The candles, the same dusky red color as the spiral inlay on the floor, burned with a spicy, slightly musty scent. The room was too large for the odor to be immediately oppressive, but Parven left the holder on the table, and carried with him just one tall free candle to light his way. Its fumes made him dizzy, so he held it well away from his body while he examined the floor.

A great intricate spiral spangled across the stones, with twists and embellishments lacing every block. Parven felt compelled to trace the main pattern. The farther he followed the sinuous red lines, the more abstracted he became. He did not observe that his candle was not burning down; instead, the flames on his candle and the five on the table were all getting smokier. In the still air, the smoke threads rose and broadened into ripple-edged fans that spread until they touched. The corners of the room were gradually obscured, leaving only two illuminated areas—the sultry glow at the table, muffled in barely drifting veils of smoke, and the ruddy sphere around Parven's candle. He was nearing the center of the pattern when his foot rolled across something uneven on the paving. Parven shook himself; he had almost forgotten that he was supposed to be searching for treasure. He bent down to pick up the obstacle and erupted in a fit of coughing. A heavy layer of smoke pooled near the floor. Parven was surprised that he could scarcely distinguish the table's outline. He had never seen ordinary candles produce so much smoke, nor had he seen it pour over the edge of the table like a silent flood of dark cream. Faintly alarmed, Parven was again distracted by his boot's jarring against the obstacle. Snatching it up, he fumbled with a handful of golden squares linked into a chain. Something cylindrical was tangled in the chain. As he extracted it, Parven's heart pounded and he threw the object down in sudden dismay. It was a bone, the right size and scale to be human. His agitated movements swirled the smoke layers up all around him. Stifled, Parven belatedly scrabbled in his pockets for his amulets. Touching them seemed to clear his head a bit. What was it he had been doing—treasure hunting? No, surely the vital task was to trace that fascinating red spiral, which was almost ready to enter the broad medallion design at the center of the floor. Parven absently scuffed aside more bones and jewelry as he proceeded along the bloodred track. The design absorbed his total concentration so much that he was not immediately aware of a startling development: he was walking a finger's width above the floor. Tendrils of smoke were eddying *under* his feet, between his boots and the stone paving. Parven was abruptly jolted to see the pattern on the floor *through* his feet. That shock finally shattered his unnatural

placidity. It forcefully occurred to Parven that he was ensnared
in high magic, far beyond the level of his amulets. He intended
to stop moving along the last tight spiral into the central
medallion, but found that his semitransparent body was no
longer obeying his mind. He suspected, in rueful retrospect,
that his will was not truly free from the instant that he descended the castle stairway.

His brain was now finally clear. His last voluntary action was
to drop his candle and grasp an amulet in each hand. They were
clearly visible through his glasslike fingers, although Parven felt
neither the cold silver of one nor the polished wood of the
other. All of his normal bodily sensations were cut off, as if his
mind were swathed in thick wool, remote from the rest of him.
Then he was suddenly *there,* at the center of the pattern, but
suspended farther above the surface than before. Parven took a
brief glance at the torturous symbols writhing in the medallion,
and wrenched his attention away, terrified that he would be
riveted forever, gazing at what no mortal soul should ever see.

As he hung in space, Parven sensed a throbbing, not in the
air, but in the power web sustaining the spell that had trapped
him. It was oddly tentative, almost hesitant. In a burst of insight, Parven perceived that the original purpose of this awful
chamber must have been to translate the adept elsewhere. Over
long years of disuse, the spell was corrupted by distortions. It
was almost like an intricate piece of machinery. Parven visualized a great windlass designed to raise massive weights. When
first made, its parts all meshed smoothly and performed their
separate tasks, but time brought friction and creeping slippage.
Wood could swell or dry out, metal would rust despite the finest
oils. Something similar, he supposed, must have affected this
activating spell—perhaps even the presence of his multiple
amulets—for Parven failed to be translated. He was instead
frozen in space, a span above the ensorceled floor, like a
shadow suspended in a mirror's smoky glass. Parven flickered,
then hung motionless. The candles, he could see from the corner of his eye, were also frozen, their flames static. The room
was completely still. Unable to breathe, unaware of his body,
Parven hung, his only link with reality was his mind, churning
with fears and frantic plans for escape. Even had he known the

proper words to release himself, he could not speak them. At first his thoughts raced in an incoherent babble; then as he grasped the full extent of his predicament, Parven settled on the only action he could take: calling soundlessly for help. He had no specific person to be the focus for his pleas, but he hoped that some sensitive mind somewhere might notice and respond. He was right. He did reach another mind—Merreth's.

She was harried out of a sound sleep by a gnawing sense of distress and unease. There was an almost unbearable urgency pressing upon her, but no matter how she tried, Merreth was unable to discern any articulate warning or message. Clutching the inadequate bedclothes around her, she sat up, staring into the darkness as if she might somehow find a visual sign respon-sible for her disturbance. The shabby room was unchanged, as mean and cold as always. Sighing, Merreth stood up and dared to splash a little of the basin's freezing water on her face in an effort to rouse herself fully. She wrapped her one heavy cloak around her shivering shoulders and went to the narrow window overlooking the back courtyard. There was no bustle of unex-pected travelers seeking Meadowvale Abbey's hospitality. Mer-reth realized that whatever awakened her came from within, not from the outside world. It was a troubling thought, but at least she had one friend to whom she could confide her strange story—Willow.

Merreth had herself been something of an unexpected trav-eler, for nearly eighteen years earlier, at the turn of the Year of the Crowned Swan, she had been a foundling abandoned at the Abbey's door. The Dames found a silver locket around her neck with the name "Merreth" written inside on a scrap of fine white leather. A modest amount of silver coins wrapped in with her blankets insured a fair level of care for the child. The Ab-bess at that time might have known or suspected something about Merreth's origins, but she died of a fever when the child was about a year old, and left no instructions other than that Merreth was to be cared for. Without a substantial dowry, Mer-reth was unlikely to marry well. Being a quietly practical child, Merreth soon determined that she would have to make her own way in the world, possibly being an Abbey resident for the rest of her life. Meadowdale Abbey was not one of the more fervent establishments, and she was not pressed to take vows, but she felt obligated to repay the Dames for their care of her, perfunctory though it was. As she grew, Merreth considered mastering herb and plant lore, but none of the Dames were truly skilled in that field until Willow arrived.

Merreth was about fifteen on the winter day that the old blind wise woman appeared at the Abbey's side gate, alone except for an equally elderly horse and a few hampers of dried herbs and parchments. The current Abbess was not overly impressed by the prospective guest's decidedly modest trappings, but she was also too shrewd to turn away what might be an able, possibly skillful wise woman. Two small ground-floor rooms were set aside, and Merreth, as an unattached general helper, was sent to attend the new resident. From initial shyness, Merreth soon relaxed into a growing respect and affection for the older woman. Willow was living alone in a secluded valley with one apprentice who was recently called home to Norstead and her family. With the winter looming, the wise woman decided that she must seek a safer home for herself. She welcomed Merreth's request to learn about plants. Her blindness caused some difficulties in conveying her knowledge, but Merreth learned to bring samples that Willow could identify by touch or scent while Merreth made notes on their appearance, location, and uses.

As soon as she worked through her morning tasks, Merreth hurried to Willow's sitting room to explain her disturbing dream experience. Willow listened attentively, then prompted Merreth to recall every detail she could.

"It sounds to me, child, as if you have received the impression of a thought link. Not the substance, mind—you are not trained for such linkages—but for some reason, you are aware of a sending, and an urgent one, it would seem."

"But what am I to do?" Merreth asked. "I don't know where to go or even who is . . . calling me, but I feel that I must do something about it."

Willow took her hand in reassurance. "Indeed you must. I shall send word for an audience with the Abbess. I have little experience in such high matters, but I do know that callings cannot be ignored. You must listen with all your attention, with your mind as well as your ears. You will know which direction you must travel." She shook her head, frowning. "This is no time to be setting out on a journey, and I fear that the Abbess will spare you only the barest assistance, but you are a strong, able woman now, and you may be aided on your way. As you know, I am not one who can foresee the future, but I feel that your path will not be totally solitary. Here." Willow probed deep into the recesses of a hamper she kept by her bed. "Take this silver bracelet—no, do not refuse. I earned it for curing a rich man's son of a particularly nasty wound. The silly goose should have known better than to put a dirty poultice on a wound, but few pay note to such things. Let me arrange to speak with the Abbess, and do you come back before you depart. It is fitting that we should ask Gunnora's blessing upon your venture." Willow instantly sensed Merreth's discomfiture. "No, I do not mean a formal invocation service by the whole company of Dames; I suggest a quiet prayer by the two of us. It is my believe that Gunnora will hear an individual plea as well as a chorus, especially if the supplicant be sincere."

The Abbess gave her most reluctant permission for Merreth's trip, along with scanty supplies and a horse so old that Merreth felt she should be carrying it. Merreth's sense of urgency drove her to depart as soon as she could, so the next few days whirled by. The weather fortunately stayed clear, although bitterly cold. Merreth reached the nearest inn on the very last of her poor mount's strength. She traded Willow's bracelet for a sturdy mountain horse and a better stock of food. Trying to follow Willow's suggestion, Merreth paused several times each day, holding her mind open for any directional guidance from her internal imperative. At first, her efforts were fruitless. It was only when she turned the horse in frustration and started back toward the abbey that she had a clear impulse to race back the opposite way, deeper into the mountain country. As the cold, weary days passed, Merreth felt increasingly certain that she was right. Her sense of being desperately needed grew with every ridge and valley that she crossed.

When she finally reached the decrepit inn where Parven stayed, she was dismayed to find that there were no more established trails farther into the wilderness. The little money she had left was not sufficient to hire a guide. A stable lad who looked less villainous, although a bit dirtier than the others in the yard, saw her hesitate as she took stock of her remaining supplies.

"Be you going farther on, lady?" he asked.

"I have still a way to go, yes," Merreth replied. The lad had a pleasant face and shrewd brown eyes beneath a sun-bleached thatch of hair. She decided to be frank. "I need a guide, but I have only a certain amount of silver. Would you know a reliable man I might hire?"

The boy grinned. "No reliable man here, lady. This be a bad place to seek help without a sword to hand and a friend to guard your back." Seeing her obvious disappointment, he hastened to add, "But if you would allow, I know most tracks hereabouts. And I have my own pony, so you'd not supply one for me."

Merreth took a moment to think. The boy couldn't have been much over twelve years, although he was stocky and seemed healthy, as best she could judge beneath the grime.

He thought her pause doubt. "It is my pony, lady," he asserted. "I saved the foal when its dam died."

"I'm sure it is your pony. I couldn't ask you to leave your work here. I don't know how long my trip may take. It could be many days."

"I make my own way, lady. The innkeeper lets me bide for helping in his stables, but I can leave when I will."

"Surely your parents," Merreth began, but the lad interrupted.

"I have naught, lady. Just my pony."

"We are alike, then, you and I," Merreth said, struck by their similar isolation, "for I know of no family of my own."

"You be a lady," the lad said firmly. "I be Rymple."

"My name is Merreth. I have come from the abbey of Dames in Meadowdale, where I have lived all my life. If you can guide me into the mountains, to the place I must go, I will pay you five silver pieces." She hoped that was a fair fee.

Rymple seemed cheerfully willing to go anywhere, possibly for no pay at all. "That be generous, lady. Bark—my pony—be ready to leave this midday, if you want. They say a journey that starts in sun will go the warmer."

Merreth shivered as an icy breeze penetrated her worn cloak. "Then by all means, let us begin in sun, for I would welcome any warming."

They were scrambling along a narrow track scarcely visible to Merreth's eye as the sun dipped behind the higher peaks. Rymple had approved of her riding style soon after they set out. "I can see you know horses, lady."

Merreth thought wryly of the weary hours she'd spent riding the paths around the abbey grounds with sour-faced Dame Katherilda correcting every lapse. By necessity, Merreth had mastered a light but firm touch on the reins and an effortlessly erect seat. "You could say that we are well acquainted, Rymple, although this is the longest journey I have ever undertaken."

Rymple coaxed his shaggy pony down a steep incline. Merreth could see why he'd named the animal "Bark"—its rough hair closely resembled the dun trunks of the tenacious mountain evergreens clinging to the rocky ground. "They say, lady, that a journey is only as long as you make it. Some go fast, some slow."

"Rymple," Merreth accused, "I begin to suspect that you are the source of all of these 'they say's."

The lad looked back at her with a happy smile. "Sometimes, lady, there ought to be a saying, and if you don't know one from hearing it, you can guess what it should be."

They camped twice more, each time in wilder and more desolate country. The wordless calling that Merreth had come to think of as her summons grew stronger and more desperate. It was Bark who first alerted them just before Merreth saw the bank of mist seeping across the track ahead.

"Bark's likely smelled another horse," Rymple suggested. "That's the sound he makes for such. Let me search ahead a way, lady, in case you might not care to meet the rider."

Merreth prudently reined in to wait behind a concealing boulder. Rymple returned shortly looking concerned. "Was a horse hereabouts. I found where it was tethered. It ate all the nearby food and pulled free some days ago by the signs."

"Is there no trace of its owner?" Merreth asked.

"No, lady, but he left his camp ready to come back to."

"Can you tell where he might have gone?"

Rymple hesitated, then made up his mind. "You may as well come along, lady. It be not safe to leave you here."

They rode slowly into the clearing where Parven's modest belongings were tidily secured. Dismounting, Rymple and Merreth pursued Parven's tracks, leaving their own animals tethered at the deserted camp.

Rymple paced uneasily when they found the ruins. "They say, lady, a wise man never sleeps where old stones are broken."

Merreth gingerly touched one of the broken blocks and drew back. "These stones certainly give no sense of welcome," she agreed. In fact, the longer she examined the site, the more clearly she sensed a cold, implacable menace. Spurred by her summons, Merreth urged Rymple to keep searching for the missing horseman. She had explained to Rymple on the trail how she didn't know exactly where she was being drawn, but that she was responding to an urgent plea for help. Now Merreth had to weigh the forbidding impulses from the ruins against her worry at the recent weakening in her internal call, as if the caller were losing strength.

Rymple soon noticed the area that Parven had cleared in front of the closed door. He glanced about nervously. "Lady, there be the smell of magic here. We had best guard our backs and go wary."

Merreth fervently agreed with him. It took a conscious effort for her to reach out to the door, which swung open easily enough. "If it opens that freely," Merreth reasoned aloud, "it may also close freely. Do you watch to see it stays open while I go within."

Rymple stretched out a restraining hand. "Wait, lady. Best we brace it open. There be plenty of rocks here. Strong winds do spring up in these mountains, and should we need to hurry out, we'll want the way free."

Once the door was securely wedged open to Rymple's satisfaction, he ran back to Parven's camp to fetch two torches. It was obvious that he intended to accompany Merreth wherever she went. Peering into the dimness beyond the door, Merreth was glad of his presence. They descended the stairs slowly, watching for any signs that another had recently passed that

way. The marks that Parven's boots had made in the gritty dust
on the stairs stood out clearly in the torchlight. Merreth's sense
of urgency pricked at her, so that she edged past Rymple on a
tiny landing and took the lead despite his objections.

She was the first to enter the ensorceled room, where the
static candle flames instantly resumed burning. Coughing from
the fumes, Merreth hurried to the table and snuffed out all the
candles with fingers tucked in a fold of her cloak. A current of
clear, cold air poured down the staircase, quickly thinning out
the suffocating smoke. Merreth held up her torch to survey the
room. Somehow, she felt reluctant to step out on the patterned
floor. She could see the odd tangles of glinting metal scattered
on the shadowed surface, and above the floor, just barely visible, as if half seen from the corner of an eye, something was
suspended.

Merreth gripped Rymple's arm with her free hand. "Rymple,
do you see it? Near the center of the floor, a span above that
great dark knot in the pattern."

Rymple dutifully peered where she directed. "See what,
lady?"

Merreth fumbled for words. "It's like—like a fish deep underwater, or something reflected in an old dusty mirror. Don't
you see it?"

Rymple shook his head. "No, lady. There is naught there
that I can see."

Merreth shut her eyes briefly and concentrated. This had to
be the source of her calling. The plea was frantic now, but
faint, and it was definitely emanating from the center of this
room. She could feel where it was located. When she opened
her eyes, the dim disturbance in the air did seem a trifle more
substantial. "I believe that I have found the source of my summons, Rymple," she said. "The difficulty is that magic must be
preventing you from seeing it. And," she added, "to be honest,
I cannot see it all that well myself, but I *know* it is there . . .
that *he* is there." She was suddenly convinced that her identi-
fication was correct. "Rymple, we have found the man from the
deserted camp. He has been trapped here for all these days of
our travel, and before."

"Then we must free him, lady." The boy shared her excitement, but his basic practicality steadied him. "But how can we free a man we can't even see?"

Frustrated, Merreth stamped her foot. "If only we had one of those charms so common in the old songs and tales. Heroes are forever waving them about to open locked gates and such."

To her surprise, Rymple said, "But we do have one, lady." He reached inside his tunic and extracted a small metal pendant suspended around his neck on a rawhide thong. Pulling it off over his head, he handed it to her.

Merreth turned the object in her fingers. "It looks as if it is made of . . ."

"Horseshoe nails," Rymple completed her thought. "Aye, so it is, but not made by me. That takes fine work and lore to be said over it during the making. A smith at Groff gave it to me, and I have always worn it since."

Merreth could see that what she had initially taken to be a crude lattice of nails hammered together was actually a carefully crafted piece, with the metal strands laced over and under one another and smoothed on all edges. "Thank you, Rymple," she said, slipping the cord over her head. "I have heard that forged iron has great virtue against evil magic."

Rymple looked pleased, but turned his attention back to the challenge at hand. "It may be my eyes, lady, but I think I see bones out on that floor. Could be wiser not to step on those red lines, in case they be part of the magic."

"I agree," Merreth replied, "but how else can I reach the center of the floor? That table is not long enough to push out and walk upon, and even if we moved the two chairs, we would still lack the full distance."

Rymple scanned the wall above the table. Jumping up, he seized a section of the nearest hanging tapestry and jerked until it fell away into his arms. "Here, lady, touch my amulet to this. If it be good honest cloth, it should not be harmed."

Merreth bent toward the dark red material and pressed Rymple's amulet against the cloth. There was no reaction. Rymple at once turned to pull down more lengths. "We can walk on this, lady," he observed triumphantly. "It should spread out fair across the floor." He busied himself finding the best ways to fold the cloth so that Merreth could push it ahead of her while carrying her torch with one hand. As Rymple experimented, Merreth stood thinking, scarcely aware of his bustling figure. She didn't want to be left alone in this dangerous place, but she also didn't want to risk Rymple's life any more than she already had. "Rymple, can you see the man hanging in the air now?"

Puzzled, Rymple looked again. "No, lady. It be empty air to me."

"Then I believe it is better for me to try to reach him alone while you return to guard the door. No," Merreth forestalled Rymple's protests. "I know you want to help, but I have thought on this matter, and as you say, there is very strong magic here. If that door should close, we would also be trapped. Better that you make certain our exit is safe. Now that you have provided this clever way for me to walk out to the poor man, I should have little trouble. Do go on, for we want to be outside and away before nightfall."

Rymple was reluctant to leave, but had to admit the sense of what she said. He showed her how to push the folded tapestry bundles across the floor to provide a path, then wedged his torch above the table and took the old torch that Parven had left there.

When Rymple had climbed out of sight up the stairs, Merreth gathered her courage and stepped out on the first tapestry section. Instantly, she felt two contrasting sensations—a coolness at her throat and a more muffled warmth on her chest. The source of the warmth was obvious at once. Parven's amulet hanging outside her gown was as warm as if it had been heating near a forge. The sharper coolness was higher. Merreth plucked out her silver locket on its thin chain and was astonished to see the metal glowing softly in the dimness. Neither object was painful to touch, but both evidently represented unsuspected Power. Encouraged to think that she might have some form of magic at work on her behalf to pit against that force ensnaring this chamber, Merreth proceeded cautiously, unfolding and pushing ahead of her more lengths of tapestry as she neared the central medallion. She had quickly learned not to look at the design on the floor after one curious glance sent her mind reeling. Reaching the medallion's edge, Merreth could at last straighten up, torch in one hand, to concentrate on her goal.

She could distinguish the suspended figure of a dark-haired young man, but he was hazy and partially transparent. To her dismay, when she stretched up tentatively to touch his boot, her hand passed right through the space. "Oh!" she exclaimed. "You seem to be here, yet you are not." For a moment she stood immobilized by frustration, then she tried to think more clearly. "If I shut my eyes," she said, "perhaps I can sense you better."

With her eyes shut, Merreth could definitely place the mass above her. The link in her mind was so faint that she almost ignored it, but abruptly she realized that she was at last communicating with the source of her summons.

The message was like the ghost of a whisper. *"Help me! Help me!"*

"Who are you?" Merreth thought back, straining to achieve a stronger link.

The reply was stronger. *"Parven. I am Parven. Help me, please!"*

"I am Merreth. I have come in answer to your call, and want to help you get away from this dreadful place, but how are we to proceed? I cannot touch you to pull you down." Merreth opened her eyes. Parven seemed a bit more solid. She slid a piece of tapestry around so that she could look up at his face, and so that he in turn could presumably see her better, for it was evident that he could not move by himself.

"I cannot move," Parven confirmed. *"Have you any amulets?"*

"Yes, I seem to have two." Merreth glanced down and saw that Rymple's lattice had turned a glowing gold. *"One is iron, although it now looks gold. The other is my silver locket. I never knew before that it had any power, but in this room, at least, it has a light of its own."*

"I brought many charms with me," thought Parven ruefully, *"but they were not sufficient to free me. Perhaps yours may turn the balance if only you could reach them up to me."*

Merreth estimated the distance between them. "I shall need to climb upon a chair," she decided, and retreated warily to fetch one. Using a tapestry strip, she lashed her torch securely to a cross-brace in the chair's back so the torch extended safely parallel to the floor, allowing her to climb on the seat. She also brought back more cloth to spread beneath Parven and added her cloak to the layers in case he should fall directly to the floor. Her preparations made, she tucked up her riding skirt and climbed onto the carved wooden seat. *"I believe I can reach you from here,"* Merreth said. *"I can still feel your presence better than I can see you, so I shall shut my eyes when I reach. Wait—let me bind an amulet to each hand. That might help me touch you."* A few twists of her silver chain secured her locket in her right palm, and Rymple's thong was ample to bind his lattice to her left hand. Both amulets continued to glow. *"You must think of yourself as solid,"* Merreth suggested to Parven, *"and I shall do the same."*

"I am ready," Parven whispered in her mind.

Shutting her eyes tightly, Merreth focused her directional sense, mentally groping for Parven. Of course he was there—she was keenly aware of him hanging above her. She suddenly realized that the spangle of bright sparks that she sensed against his mass had to be his amulets. It was strange to sense light sources with her eyes closed, but there were two even brighter glows in her mind, one silver and one gold. As she raised her hands, those glows also elevated as she lunged for Parven. For a sickening instant, her grasp closed on empty air, then she felt a peculiar shifting of space, and her hands brushed against rough fabric. With an elated cry, Merreth clung to Parven's legs and leaned too far, losing her footing on the chair. Together, she and Parven sprawled onto the cold floor with an impact that quite took Merreth's breath away. It was Parven's real voice that recalled her to the present.

"Merreth! Your skirt—it's afire!"

Horrified, Merreth saw that part of her riding skirt had fallen beyond the tapestry protection onto the patterned floor. Sullen little flames were flickering along the smoldering cloth. Her mind racing, Merreth snatched her skirt off the floor. As Parven helped her beat out the fire, she reasoned that the tapestry would probably also have burned had it not been so long immersed in the magic permeating this evil room. Breathing hard, Merreth leaned against Parven while both of them recovered from their exertions.

Parven was feeling severely shaken by his experiences, his limbs trembling as his nerves slowly regained their control over his muscles. He was startled to realize that his shaking was not wholly accounted for by his immense relief at being free. "Merreth," he exclaimed, "the floor is moving!"

Clutching each other, they fled back across the tapestry path to the safer edge of the room. It soon appeared that nowhere in the room was secure, for the tremors were grinding the stone blocks against one another, and cracks were webbing across the paving.

"The stairs," Parven called above the rising din. "Run!"

A gust of cold air pressed Merreth's skirt against her legs, slowing her frantic effort to move. As the draft rapidly grew to a blast of wind, Parven pulled Merreth along. "This is not normal wind," he shouted. "It must be part of the trapping spell, to keep us here." He threw aside the now-useless torch, its flame blown out.

In the shrieking darkness, clinging to the side walls, Merreth and Parven fought their way upward step by step against the gale that threatened to dash them back down into the chaotic room below. Merreth squeezed her eyes shut to keep out the stinging dust and rock chips. When her outstretched hand seized something rough but snakelike, she cried out and nearly fell. Closer touch identified it as a rope extending from above. Blessing Rymple, Merreth called out, "Rope!" and passed its free end back to Parven. Steadied by the rope, they made faster progress until, as she rounded a corner, Merreth felt a strong, upward pull and saw Rymple's figure silhouetted against a dim light. He was guiding the rope, trying to keep it from fraying against the turn in the stairwell.

Seeing the struggling pair below, Rymple shouted over his shoulder, "Bark—pull!" The pony hauled to such good effect that Merreth and Parven were virtually jerked up the final stairs. As they stumbled into the open at a breathless trot, a last vindictive burst of wind raged from the door, bringing down an avalanche of rocks and debris and burying the passageway.

All three people dropped to the ground a safe distance away, whooping for breath amid the swirling dust. When the air cleared, Merreth introduced Parven to Rymple, then she hastened to pat the stolid Bark.

"Had you not lowered that rope," gasped Parven, "we should never have emerged in time."

Rymple flushed with pleasure. "Always carry a bit of rope," he admitted shyly. "Never know when it be handy."

"Let us move away from this wicked place," said Merreth, shuddering. "That wind has blown me cold, and in our hurry, I forgot to bring my cloak."

"We had scant time to pack," Parven said. "Never mind. I have a spare cloak at my camp—if it is still there," he added. "I have no idea how long I have been trapped."

"I have traveled nine days," said Merreth, "and I received your call two days before that."

Parven stared at her, amazed. "No wonder I am starving."

"There be bread and cheese with the packs," Rymple pointed out. When they reached the camp, he kindled a fire against the twilight chill. Merreth gratefully wrapped herself in Parven's spare cloak while Rymple set out a simple meal.

As he reached for another piece of hard cheese, Parven declared, "I never thought bread and cheese could taste so good." He sighed wistfully. "I had journeyed here hoping to find treasure, or at least some old documents. I fear that I shall have nothing to show my master as excuse for my folly."

Rymple emitted an apologetic cough. "I fancied you were too busy, lady, to have time for the gathering, so I did it."

Merreth looked at him blankly. "Gathering?"

"Aye. There was a fair lot of plunder on that marked-up floor. I picked up a bit while seeing how best to fold those cloth strips for you." Rymple turned out his belt scrip, shaking loose a heap of gold and silver chains, ornate bracelets, brooches, and rings. Parven and Merreth stared, quite bereft of speech, then Merreth hugged the surprised Rymple before he could evade her. "Rymple," she said, "*you* are the treasure."

"Nay, lady—anyone would have done the same."

Parven, whose wariness had been sharply heightened by his ordeal, poked at the glittering heap with a stick. "Do you suppose these are spellbound?" he asked in a low, nervous voice.

Arrested by the thought, they all pulled back, then Merreth suggested, "Rymple's amulet should guide us." She had quickly unbound both charms from her hands as soon as she had emerged from the staircase, and had given Rymple his lattice back on their walk back to camp. Rymple now slipped it off and touched each piece of jewelry to the lattice, which had resumed its usual appearance of ordinary iron nails. To their mutual relief, there were no adverse signs. The friends passed around the items, exclaiming at the jewels and the workmanship.

"They seem to be just as they are," observed Parven, "the spoils of that evil trap."

"Except this," said Rymple hesitantly, holding out a blackened ring of intricately woven metal. It had a strangely unclean patina, and Rymple prudently gripped it in a fold of his tunic rather than touch it bare-skinned. "It was caught on one of the chains," he explained, "or I would not have brought it. It be dire."

Merreth peered at it only long enough to discern part of the familiar, harrowing spiral design from the castle floor. "This ring must have belonged to the sorcerer who bewitched that room," she ventured.

Rymple dropped the ring on a flat rock. "They say, lady, that like calls to like."

"In this case, Rymple," Merreth replied, "I believe that what they say is most definitely true. Something dark clings to that ring, and if we carry it away with us, I fear that taint would mark our trail."

Parven shivered despite the warmth of the fire. "Then let us bury it here, where no one is likely ever to find it. I should have been forewarned by my study of old lore, but I let my desire for treasure blind me to the dangers of this place. You will have heard, I expect, that long ago the Old Ones warred among themselves, and some were banished or driven away, while others clung to scattered bases of power, often in the Waste or near to it. I now see that this Valley of Kulp, as the old map names it, must have been such a base for an Old One of the evil path. He used that vile room of spells as a door or gate through which he escaped, but he must have intended to return since traces of his Power still endure, as we found to our cost. I know that I should not care to draw the attention of such a one should he ever become aware of our intrusion. I must confess that this ring frightens me. The old lore assures us that such objects can retain links to their owners, even after great lapses of time."

"There be an old dry well off to one side of the ruins," said Rymple. "I found it while looking for water for the horses. Not likely that any traveler would search such a place."

Taking torches, the party at once investigated and agreed that Rymple's idea was sound. He dropped the suspect ring down the shaft and they heard it rebound against the stones as it fell. Feeling as if a lingering threat had been safely disposed of, they returned to Parven's camp to make their own travel plans.

"I suppose we must go back," said Parven with obvious regret.

Merreth sat erect. "Not I. I have more than repaid the Dames for their care of me, and I will not return to waste my days in that barren place." Her fierce expression softened as she added, "I would like to send a message to my one friend at the abbey, Willow the wise woman, for she is the only one there who truly cares for me."

"But where will you live?" asked Rymple, practical as always.

"Wherever in the Dales I can find a holding that will accept me," said Merreth decisively, "or I shall live beside my horse."

"You need better shelter than that against the winter," Parven objected. "Halvard, my master, has ample space. If I asked him, he might allow us all three to settle in one of his empty storage houses."

Merreth's face was set in stubborn determination. "These last days I have known freedom and companionship, and I will not return to confinement and bondage." She touched Parven's sleeve lightly and smiled. "Dear Parven. I do thank you for your kind offer. Besides Willow, no one has ever cared before what might happen to me."

"Or me," Rymple inserted. "I stay with you, lady. Where you go, I go, and Bark, too."

Somewhat dismayed by this sudden acquisition of a mounted retainer, Merreth exclaimed, "But, Rymple, I cannot pay you."

"Don't you think," Parven suggested diffidently, "we should all share equally in the jewelry from the castle? From the little I have seen of such goods in Master Halvard's trade, there should be value enough to sustain us all for some time."

Rymple had been marking idly in the dirt with a twig. "There be holdings in these mountains left long ago. Might be we could find one and settle there for the winter."

Parven leaned forward eagerly. "I passed just such a place on my way here! The house had fallen in somewhat, but if we could patch the roof—and there was still some fruit in the side orchard, and some grain gone wild in the field."

"Now who is being fanciful?" accused Merreth, but she also felt a rising excitement. "We could at least examine the place," she conceded.

Parven could scarcely plan fast enough. "I could send a message to Master Halvard. The first winter storms may well come before I could return to speak to him myself."

"Where be this holding you saw, master?" asked Rymple.

"Two valleys beyond that churlish inn—I trust you stopped there?"

"I met Rymple there," said Merreth, "for which good fortune I forgive them their churlishness, if not the outrageous amounts they charged."

"There is a fine stream close by the holding," Parven rushed on with enthusiasm, "and the nearby slopes are not steep enough to threaten avalanche."

Rymple seemed unusually interested. "Be there a twisted tree by that stream? And a big dark rock an arrow's flight from the house?"

Distracted, Parven considered. "Yes, now that you mention it, I did notice such a tree, and I remember several large rocks in the vicinity."

Rymple nodded, satisfied. "'Tis Juspel's Holding, then."

Merreth's concern had been increasing during the exchange. "Rymple," she demanded, "what is amiss at Juspel's Holding?"

"They say it is accursed, lady," Rymple replied cheerfully. "That is why no one goes there since Juspel fled."

"But why is it cursed?" Merreth pursued.

Rymple shrugged. "Never heard to be certain, but some say Juspel offended the Old Ones and could stay on the land no longer." As when Parven had first mentioned the Old Ones, Rymple's hand moved again to touch his amulet.

"You don't seem frightened," Parven pointed out.

"Nay, master. So long as I have my amulet, I fear no magic."

Parven took a deep, steadying breath. "I, too, have my amulets, and Merreth has hers, for which I shall always be most thankful. Surely we need not be turned aside by mere reputation. I shall write to Master Halvard at once. We can send the message from the inn on our way to Juspel's Holding. I must also send Master Halvard most of my share of the treasure as well. He is a fair man and should willingly let me go my way, for he has many other scribes far better versed in trade than I."

"And I can send my message to Willow," said Merreth, and paused. "Is there anyone you need to write to, Rymple?"

The boy stared into the fire. "Nay, lady. I have no one, and besides, I have not the skill of writing or reading."

"That's easily remedied," said Parven. "I can teach you. It is one of the few things I do really well."

Rymple was temporarily speechless, then he babbled, "Me? You could show me how to read? And write?"

"Of course. It might take a while, but there will be plenty of time for us indoors during the winter storms."

Merreth shook a finger at Parven in mock severity. "Have a care, Parven. You have already heard a few of Rymple's They say's. Should he learn to read, we should also be treated to an endless store of It be written's, mark my words."

At first abashed, Parven joined in the laughter. He had never before felt that he had truly belonged anywhere, in any company. Now suddenly he did belong, with these friends. "I accept the challenge," he announced. "We might as well start at once with a few letters. Here, Rymple, sit by me nearer the fire where the ground is flat. Take this stick and see how the marks are made."

Merreth watched them for a while, then settled herself to sleep. They would be rising early to begin their journey to a new home, the first real home that any of them had ever had. They would want a new name for the place, she thought drowsily. If it hadn't been for Parven's being trapped, and Rymple's cleverly bringing the rope, and her own unexpected discovery of her locket's power, they would not have escaped from the dreadful room with its fuming candles. Candles. Candletrap—they would call it Candletrap Holding. She would suggest it in the morning as a reminder of their adventure. As she drifted into sleep, Merreth was smiling.

Afterword

For this second of my writing forays into the Witch World, I am indebted to a dream fragment and a double reverse coincidence. The visual impression of a terrified mind suspended above an ensorceled stone floor occurred to me one night in a dream (fortunately in color, so I could detect the red spiral pattern set into the stones). Subsequently, in writing to Andre Norton, I remarked that so many tales had men rushing to rescue imperiled damsels, it would be a welcome change to see the reverse tack: a young woman striving to rescue a young man. After I had suggested a brief action outline, Miss Norton then dealt me the double reverse, inviting me to write the tale, setting it in the Witch World.

When I considered my notes, Parven, in his severely suspended predicament, demanded an immediate introduction; then Merreth emerged, shy but determined; and suddenly, there was Rymple, diffidently offering any number of useful sayings. Once the rescue attempt was set in motion, I had only to describe it. I have wondered since how the trio fared the rest of that snowy winter at Candletrap Holding. I suspect that Rymple found ample opportunities to invent even more "they say"s.

—Mary H. Schaub

WHISPERING CANE

by

Carol Severance

Sionna remained silent throughout the long funeral. She watched dry-eyed as her newborn daughter was lowered into the ground. Not even the setting of a mourning spell over the small grave caused her to reveal her tightly suppressed rage. The men guarding her murmured when the priestess Tammon's touch brought a flicker of light, then the faint green shadow of newly sprouting grass across the mound, but at their warlord's order, they did nothing to stop the harmless locking spell.

They could have, Sionna knew, for their leader, Keron, a man who had once been a trusted neighbor, was now partnered with a great evil. Whether the source of his Power had come from within his own lands in Rimsdale or from somewhere in the Waste beyond, Sionna did not know, but it counteracted easily the various light spells her own people employed. Even the new grass that now sealed her daughter's grave seemed stunted and dry.

Sionna brushed her fingers across her lips in the sign of farewell and remained silent.

When the ceremony was finished, she left the others and walked alone into the sugarcane fields. The guards let her go,

341

they were that certain of her loyalty to Lelanin, and of their own ability to stop her should she try to leave the valley. The only exit was by sea.

She slipped through the cane until she reached a small clearing not far from the road. It was silent except for the ceaseless rustling of the cane. Sionna loosed her long black hair, then knelt and dug a hole in the loose, porous soil, scooping out dirt until the opening was as deep as her arms could reach. She leaned across the hole—and screamed.

Again and again Sionna screamed, emptying into the hole all the pain and torment of her daughter's birth and the incredible horror of her death so soon after. She thought of the baby's father, her beloved Tersan, dead now at the Alizonians' hands, and her father and brother, and so many of the men from Lelanin Valley. She screamed her hatred into the ground, then wept when she thought again of her child.

She forced herself to hear again the baby's first cries, watch as the tiny eyes blinked open, then squeezed shut against the light. She stiffened as she felt again the sudden terror as the strain of afterbirth began. It was as if she were giving birth a second time, the force was so intense. Terror wrapped around her like a living thing, and she felt as if her soul were being torn from her.

The baby wailed and Sionna tried to reach out to her, but the air turned gray all around and she couldn't breathe. She gasped and the gray turned to dark. When she was at last able to move and see again, she remembered that she was at the mourning hole, not back in the birthing room where Tammon and the midwife and Keron's guard, whom he had insisted be present, had stood staring dazedly at her daughter. The babe had been blue and shriveled, as empty of life as if she'd never known it.

"Stillborn," the guard had whispered, and he had made a warding sign and run from the room.

"She was alive!" Sionna screamed into the ground. "My daughter was alive and she was murdered!" She cried out her rage and her hatred of Keron and his outlaw invaders, for she knew that only the most evil of warborn sorcery could have entered that birthing room. The children of her family were Lelanin itself, protected by their trace of the Old Ones' blood, they were always born with strength and good health.

Sionna screamed until her voice cracked and her throat was raw, until no sound would come. Then she wept, sobbing against the cool ground so that her tears, too, could sink into the fertile soil.

When her mind was dulled and empty, when she felt nothing but her fury's finely honed edge, Sionna refilled the hole. She worked quickly, scooping with both hands until the ground was level again. Leaning forward, she blew softly across the burial site to set a proper mourning spell and seal her grief underground. She waited until the shadow of new grass had spread across the freshly dug earth, then pulled one of the tall cane stalks down. She broke the tassel from its tip and pressed it into the loose soil.

"I am Lelanin," she whispered. Her breathless voice was indistinguishable from the rustling cane, but she was sure that the Guardians heard.

Sionna pointedly ignored Keron's men posted along the road back to the village, although more than one of them sniggered and commented rudely on the dirt that smeared her hands and clothing. She glanced instead toward the charred remains of small family shrines standing on hillocks throughout the valley. Keron had ordered them all destroyed, even after she'd sworn that the places were not repositories of magic, only sites where the Lelanin people honored their dead.

Tammon met her at the village gate. "You should be abed," she said. The elderly priestess had cared for Sionna since she was a child and had she been allowed her way, Sionna would still be secluded in the birthing house. Sionna merely shook her head and accepted the old woman's supporting arm. Her legs felt as if they were made of cane syrup, thick and heavy, soft enough to melt into the ground. It was beyond belief that they had carried both her and the child just two days before.

"There is no need for you to be about this soon. The valley people would understand," Tammon said.

Sionna sighed. Tammon's words were true, but she knew she could not hide away. She must continue performing her traditional duties or risk losing the small advantage her status currently provided. And there was still the funeral supper to endure.

She bathed and changed, and rested for a time, then walked

to the village hall where the valley nobles had already gathered. On this night of mourning, the nobles had each worn their clans' colors to honor the last of their valley's heirs to carry full Lelanin blood. Sionna nodded her thanks as she entered and touched her lips in silent greeting.

Keron sat with three of his outlaw-warriors at the head table. He wore the feathered crest that proclaimed him a high chieftain, and Sionna wished for an instant that she had taken the time to don her own elaborate headpiece. Then she decided that in this company, she was better off without it. Keron's crest made it appear he needed to prove his rank, while there was no question of hers. Even Keron's men stood as she passed, though only the valley folk touched their lips in response to her greeting.

Keron, too, rose from his bench, surprising Sionna with his adherence to local custom. He surprised her again by offering her her rightful place as Lelanin's liege. She hated him even more for giving her reason to hate him less.

Keron had publicly demanded that Sionna wed him and bear him a child as soon as she was able, so that Keron could legally wear the Lelanin crest. It would establish him as the seat of power in these far southern lands, for Lelanin provided the source of the vital seed stock for the sugarcane trade.

For centuries, Lelanin had traded peacefully with Keron's forebears in Rimsdale, shipping cane from the hidden valley through a sea passage known only to the Rimsdale and Lelanin lords. It was a pact made by the first dwellers in these isolated lands, those who had lived together here for a time with the Old Ones. Even the Sulcar traders who bought the cane from Rimsdale did not know the secret entrance to Lelanin Bay.

But after his father and elder brother had died, Keron had broken that ages-old trust, taking advantage of Lelanin's weakness with so many of her own men lost. The Dales had never been ruled by any one lord and with so much land now in chaos, it had been easy for Keron to gather an army of outlaws and criminals, deserters and men who had no other lord to follow. Some, it was rumored, had joined him from their homes in the Waste.

Keron had killed any Rimsdale man who spoke against his

plans of conquest before he and the most bloodthirsty of his followers slipped into Lelanin Bay. Accepting guest right from Sionna, he established a hold upon the keep before revealing his evil plans to her. Fighting off what small resistance there was from old men and women and children, his men took over the cane fleet and sent it back through the passage for the rest of his invading army. Sionna wished to weep at the thought of what those evil men would do when they arrived.

"Why doesn't the lady speak?" one of Keron's men asked as the funeral meal neared its end. "They say she's not made a sound since the child was born dead two days ago, not even to weep."

"The valley people share their grief with the soil that feeds them," Tammon said. "They don't waste it on strangers."

"A stupid custom," a second warrior murmured, "burying your grief. Better to get out in the open and be rid of it."

"Better not to have it at all," the third warrior said with a laugh.

"Is it true, Priestess," Keron asked, "that your people believe that incessant rustling in the cane fields is their ancestors' voices whispering ancient troubles from their graves?"

His words brought a sudden stinging to Sionna's eyes. Was her own pain now whispering among the cane? She wondered if that last tiny cry of her child had found a place among the wind-blown leaves. She lowered her gaze quickly and felt the thin fabric of her mourning shawl split under the strain of her clenched hands.

"Do not mock her grief," Tammon snapped. She touched Sionna, a brush of gnarled fingers across smooth skin. It added to the pain, though Sionna knew the old woman meant to offer comfort.

"She'd best deal with her grief soon, old woman," Keron said. "My army will arrive tomorrow and I want her decision by then."

"Decision, Warlord?" Tammon spat across her shoulder, narrowly missing the edge of the warlord's cape. "She must marry you and produce a legal heir or be raped to achieve the same end. What kind of decision is that?"

Keron stared at the spittle for a moment, eyes narrowing.

"There's another choice, old woman." He pulled a broad sword from the scabbard on his back. A stone, red as spilt blood, gleamed on its hilt. "I can simply destroy the entire valley and all within it."

"It doesn't take much courage to murder old women and newborn babies," Tammon said.

Keron lifted the sword, held it crosswise between them, and blew a puff of air across the blade. Tammon staggered back in her seat, cried out in choking pain. Her gnarled hands lifted in useless defense.

Keron laughed and lowered the sword.

"You think that you're safe because your ancestors made a pact with the Old Ones," he said. "Well, Priestess, the Old Ones are long gone from this land, and I have made a pact with forces far greater than your simple magic can control." The stone on his sword grew brighter. "Try me again, Priestess. Let me show you just what I can do."

"Aunt, do not provoke him," Sionna said before Tammon could respond. "Your anger is better spent in the fields."

She turned on the warlord.

"If you can't control yourself better than this, Keron, you might as well lay waste to the valley right now. Lelanin under such childish rule would be chaos. The cane will die without the people to care for it, and without the cane, even the Sulcars would have no use for this part of the coast. You would be lord over a dead and useless land."

Keron lifted his sword again, but when Sionna made no move to protect herself, he cursed and dropped the blade back into its scabbard.

"This is a night for mourning, not playing with swords and insults," Sionna said. "I declare the meal finished." She stood, took Tammon's trembling hand in her own, and left the hall.

"I have already lost a daughter to that butcher, Aunt, and a father and brothers to the Alizonians," she said when they were alone in her chambers. "I do not wish to lose you as well."

"He must be stopped," Tammon said. She sat on the wide bed, leaning heavily against the bedpost. She had still not entirely caught her breath.

"Goading him into killing you will not accomplish that end,"

Sionna said. She walked to a window overlooking the cane fields. Outside the windblown tassels shimmered like seawater in the moonlight. The sweet smell of fertile soil and night-blooming ginger drifted on the warm air. Lifting a long, thin knife from beside a fruit-filled bowl, Sionna thrust it through the woven dust mats into the solid wooden sill. She took a deep breath and spoke again.

"We cannot face Keron's army with cane knives and pitchforks, though the people have offered to try. And our magic, based as it is on peaceful interactions with the gods, is useless against Keron's Shadow-based sorcery. That horror draws on all the hatred and pain of each of his warrior's years of violence and only grows stronger as his conquests continue. You saw the red stone in his sword?"

Tammon nodded, her face twisted in remembered pain. "That's no ordinary gem. I could almost smell its evil the moment he unsheathed the sword. He boasted of making a pact with some dark force. That must be the talisman of his alliance."

Sionna shifted her gaze from the place where her child was buried to that where her grief was interred. Tammon joined her at the window. She caught at her niece's hand.

"There is only one way to stop that kind of power."

There were tears in Sionna's eyes when she turned back. "We can't defend the valley without help and there is none outside to offer us aid. Had my daughter lived, we might have . . ." She shook her head, swiped angrily at the tears. "Lelanin won't last a year under Keron's rule. The land itself will be destroyed."

She turned again toward the shimmering cane fields. "And we are the land, Aunt. You and I. It is the gift and the trust the Old Ones left us. We are Lelanin and we must defend the valley."

Tammon touched her hand. "There is a thousand years of buried pain out there in those fields," the priestess said. "A thousand years of Lelanin sorrows, great and small. If you free that force, there could be chaos."

Sionna met her aunt's troubled stare. "Better a chaos of our own making than one born of Keron's evil. Will you help me?"

Tammon's chin lifted. A slow, rueful smile spread across her aged features. "With cane knives and pitchforks if I must, Niece."

By midmorning the following day the village was nearly empty. Sionna explained to Keron that the prime upland fields were ripe for harvest and even the children were needed to help cut and haul the cane. The minor priests and priestesses were seeing to the last of the funeral rites, so only she and Tammon were free to dine with their guest.

Keron grunted and straightened his shoulders, visibly pleased to have been referred to as "guest." He sat between the two women on a hillock overlooking the bay. Two guards stood some way off, not included in this private luncheon.

"I assume that you have reached a suitable decision?" he said.

"I have," she replied. She dropped her gaze to her plate and selected a last bit of meat. Chewing it slowly, she shifted her gaze to the sunlit sea.

Tammon speared a ripe lichee with the point of her knife and lifted it from the low table. She peeled the leathery skin and bit into the juicy white pulp. When she was finished, she laid the knife beside her plate. "So," she said, leaning to one side so the juice could drip on the ground, "when do you expect your fleet, mighty warrior?"

"You have the tongue of an eel, Priestess," Keron replied dryly.

Tammon licked her fingers calmly.

"They have come," Sionna said. She pointed seaward, where a ship could be seen rounding the northern tip of the bay. Keron jumped up just as the cry came from below that the fleet had been sighted. He stood, fists on his hips, grinning, as the cane barges, filled with his men, worked their way into the sheltered waters of Lelanin Bay. Tammon glanced at Sionna, passed her the knife, then rose to stand beside the warlord.

"It is an impressive sight," Tammon said. She moved to Keron's opposite side and asked him about his men and their origins. As Keron boasted of his warriors' bloody past, Tammon wandered slowly about, circling the warlord twice over. When she had completed the third circuit, she nodded to

Sionna, and in that instant, Sionna felt the warding spell settle softly into place. She rose and slipped silently away.

As soon as she was free of the hillock, Sionna raced for the place where she had cried the afternoon before. It was not far off, they had chosen their luncheon site with care. She pushed through the rustling cane, growing more and more conscious of the indistinct voices whispering among the wind-tossed leaves. The voices seemed louder, more powerful, than she remembered, as if they were eager for what was to come.

A small fire, cradled carefully in a stone-lined depression, awaited her at the clearing. It had been laid that morning by a kinsman on his way to another such place known only to those of true Lelanin blood.

Sionna lifted a torch from beside the fire and set its oily tip into the heat. She waited until the flames whooshed, then burned strong and steady. Then she turned back to the burial site.

Sionna knew her next move would mean her own death before this day was finished. Only a female of the ruling line could unseal the ground and call forth the ancestors. And when her work was complete, the one who had opened the ground must lead them back to the fields and join them underground.

"I do not wish to die," she whispered to the rustling cane. "But Keron must be stopped before he destroys this land. We have lived in peace for many centuries because we remain hidden to all but our nearest neighbors, and we care for the land according to the wishes of our ancestors. We bury all that is hateful and harmful to us, seal it under the ground where its strength can be used by the Guardians to nourish the soil and provide the seed stock upon which we depend."

Sionna wept to think that those who survived this day, if any did, would have to establish a new ruling family line for the valley—a family line that would no longer carry any trace of the Old Ones' blood in its veins. Only her aged aunt would remain. Sionna plucked a strand of her hair—it was ebony, shiny and smooth, her legacy from that ancient and inexplicable past— and held it up to the wind. She took comfort in knowing that at least the family chosen to take the place of her own would carry no Keron blood. She loosed the hair and it drifted away to tangle in the cane.

She brushed away her tears, then brushed away the crushed cane tassel that she had pressed into the soil the day before. She spat upon the place where it had been. "Open," she said, as simply as if she were preparing a grave for one of Lelanin's dead. Instantly, the grass began to shrivel. It quickly turned brown and brittle, dead and as cold as her infant daughter lying beneath her own seal of grass. There was a hush in the cane.

Sionna stood and pulled the knife from her belt. Holding the hilt in both hands, she lifted the blade high into the air.

"I am Lelanin!" she cried as loud as she could. The voices in the cane remained still for a moment more, then rustled again as she cried out a second time.

"I am Lelanin. Be free Lelanin, aid me in defending this land."

She swung her blade down, sliced it deeply into the ground. It slid through the fine, rich soil as easily as if it were cutting through flesh. The earth shivered, the air wavered. Sionna called out again and struck the earth a second blow. The voices in the cane grew louder.

Soil as red as blood began bubbling from the cuts. Sionna slashed her long, thin blade through the earth again and again, until the ground was afroth with roiling soil. Then she jumped back, grabbed the firebrand, and began torching the cane.

The flames licked eagerly at the dry leaves, thick black smoke billowed upward with the same turbulent motion as the soil. Sionna stabbed her knife into the ground once more, very deeply, then pulled the blade free. Glancing to her right, then her left, she saw other patches of smoke lifting from fields all across the valley. Her own fire had been the signal for other families to open their fields. The defense of Lelanin had begun.

As she raced back through the shivering cane, she saw a thin tendril of pale smoke rising from the site of her daughter's grave. She frowned, wondering who might have lit that unexpected fire. Behind her, she heard her ancestors cackle and begin to roar.

Keron's fleet was anchoring by the time Sionna reached the hillock where she had left Tammon and the Rimsdale lord.

Many of the ship's small boats had been beached and their crews milled like maggots around the edges of the village. Two houses were already in flames. Sionna brushed her fingers across her lips at Tammon's questioning look. Tammon stepped away from Keron, then sat cross-legged on the pile of mats. Sionna dropped the knife into her aunt's eager hands.

Suddenly Keron blinked and shook his head, freed from the warding spell he'd not known was upon him. It had been a calculated risk, he could have broken the spell easily had he realized his entire attention was being kept on his fleet by unnatural means. But the ruse had worked. He was not aware that Sionna had left the hillock, though he looked somewhat confused at Tammon's position on the mat.

"You said the village would be spared," Sionna said to divert him.

"You can't expect my soldiers to come ashore without a ripple, lady," he said. "They've been waiting for many weeks and looking forward to battle all that time. They deserve a bit of fun."

"At the expense of my people," Sionna said.

"*Our* people," Keron replied with a grin.

"Ah, the fabled Rimsdale manners," Tammon said, drawing his attention away from both Sionna and the thin tendrils of smoke that had begun to drift seaward from the cane fields. If the warlord looked behind him now, he would realize that not all the smoke in the air was coming from the houses his warriors had torched. Great pillars of inky black were rising all across the valley. The air was filling with the cloying smell of burning sugar. Tammon ran her fingers along the knife blade. Scratches and nicks appeared under her touch and she held it up as if to inspect the damage closer.

"That's a sorry weapon you carry, Priestess," Keron said.

"It's a Rimsdale blade," she said sourly. "I had it made at your father's forge not a year ago."

"That's no . . ."

But the blade did indeed suddenly appear to be wider and double-edged as was the Rimsdale style.

"What are you—?" The warlord coughed. "Damn this

smoke!" He turned, caught sight of the black pall that now covered the entire upper end of the valley.

"It's only the cane fields," Sionna said quickly. Her voice was strained though she faced the warlord calmly enough. She could feel the forces gathering within her, waiting for her to focus them according to her will. "It's a harvest day. They're burning off the stubble to kill any harmful pests."

"Lelanin's had trouble with pests lately," Tammon said.

Keron threw her a disgusted look and sent his guards into the village. "Tell the men to spread out and find the villagers," he ordered. "Gather them in one place where they can be watched—kill them if necessary." Sionna lifted a hand to her mouth and a puff of smoke circled the warlord. He coughed again.

"What are you up to, woman?" he growled, turning back to her. "Some damn Lelanin magic, no doubt." She lifted her hand to her mouth again. He stopped, coughing so hard he had to bend over in the effort to clear his lungs. Straightening suddenly, he yanked his sword from its place on his back. The crimson stone gleamed.

"It won't work," he rasped. "No sweet-smelling Lelanin magic can withstand my war curse." He whirled his sword in the air and uttered a series of sharp, shrill notes. Instantly, his warriors picked up the cry and the valley suddenly echoed with the shrill ululation. The smoke that had settled around the warlord hesitated, thickened, then lifted sullenly and slid back toward the cane fields. The tendrils that had reached the war fleet began drifting away on the natural lines of the sea wind.

Keron laughed. "You see, lady? You have no defense. There is no way you can overcome my strength. I'd have thought you would have learned that in the birthing room. This valley is mine!"

Sionna lifted her hands before her face and screamed.

"I am Lelanin!" she cried. "Be free Lelanin, aid me in defending this land."

Tammon, too, lifted her hands and echoed Sionna's words. All across the valley, voices were suddenly raised, faint at first, almost indistinguishable above the sound of Keron's booming laughter. But the voices grew in number and then in volume, until the sounds of endless anguished men and women and children billowed from the cane fields like the smoke before them. The voices slid through the heavy air like sharks seeking prey.

Keron's men cried out in confusion as the voices multiplied, as the sounds separated into screams and shrieks of deafening intensity. The warriors drew their weapons, but as a thousand and more years of buried pain struck their souls, they dropped their swords and knives and began screaming themselves.

Proud warriors pressed their hands over their ears and fell to their knees. Tears sprang into their eyes as their souls were filled with the pain and agony of generations of Lelanin people. It was not the depth of evil in the pain, for many of the warriors had caused and witnessed things far worse in their lifetimes than any valley dweller ever had. They were undone by sheer volume, by the seething accumulated agony of hundreds, thousands of Lelanin souls, freed at last from the carefully nurtured fields of the Old Ones.

Men tore at their hair and scratched their own skin trying to escape the terrible despair. One pulled his dagger and thrust it into his eye to end the chilling horror. A few, those whose souls were already dead from a lifetime of rape and murder, clung to their swords and fought with the old men and the women and the children who appeared suddenly and silently among them. Pitchforks and cane knives took a deadly toll.

Keron watched the destruction of his troops in shock. He tried to stop the onslaught with his shrill war curse, but his warriors could not hear his call and failed to join him in fighting the unseen enemy. Keron called on all the gods he knew, directed spell after spell into the carnage below, and still his warriors died.

Finally, he turned in fury to the two women who shared the hillock. The priestess had sunk to the ground as if she too were being attacked by the screaming voices. But Sionna stood in rigid concentration, her fingers lightly covering her opened lips. Power streaked like living flames from her hands to the carnage below.

"I will kill you!" Keron shrieked. He lifted his blade.

"You'll have to kill me first," Tammon cried. She pushed herself up and threw herself at the warlord. The knife she held

was long and thin again, without blemish save for a light dusting
of valley soil.

Keron cursed and swung at her. His blade sliced through her
shoulder, but her knife slid along his wrist as she fell.

Sionna turned then and lifted one hand toward the warlord.
He glanced at his wrist, shook it as if it stung, then gasped as
Sionna's wave of anguish struck him. He lifted the sword,
shouted one of his foul war spells, and fought the heartbreaking
pain back. Sionna flinched, then straightened and lifted a second hand. She opened her soul and flung at him all the hatred
and fear and grief that his very existence had brought into her
life. Still he twisted away from her mental grasp, ripping at her
horror and thrusting it back upon her doubled.

In desperation, Sionna called again upon her ancestors. "I
am Lelanin!" she screamed, and they answered with screeching
rage. Keron staggered back, lifted his flaring sword, and
shouted yet another of his counterspells. Sionna was thrown to
the ground by its force. She knew then that the battle was lost,
that he would kill her and all her people, for nothing in
Lelanin's history had created enough horror and pain to match
this man's evil soul and that of the Power with which he was
allied.

Suddenly Sionna saw a thin, pale tendril of smoke approach
the warlord. She heard a soft cry, the tiny wail of a newborn
infant. She reached for the sound, wanting desperately to lock
that one remembered moment of joy into her heart. But the
child's wail slipped from her grasp. It grew and swelled as it
circled the warlord. Around, and around, and around. It
trapped Keron in its innocent fury, crushed him with the pain
of its own ensorceled death. It was the cry of a child who had
wanted to live.

Keron slipped to his knees and tried to block the sound by
covering his ears with his hands. The red stone flickered, darkened. The child wailed on and the stone turned muddy black
and dripped from the weapon's hilt like the blood of one
damned. The sword fell useless at Keron's side.

A tremendous quiet settled across the valley. Only the warlord's ragged breathing and the shrill wail of the child could be
heard. And then only an infant's soft whimper as Tammon
thrust her thin knife into Keron's side.

Sionna shuddered and sank to the ground. She covered her mouth and then her eyes with her hands. *Let the horror end,* she prayed. *Lady Gunnora, let it end. Let me go now so that I may lead the dead back to the fields, and the living may go on with their lives.*

The silence continued.

At last, she looked up. Near the shoreline, villagers were moving among Keron's fallen men, slitting the throats of those few who still lived. Already the beached boats were afire and swimmers were approaching the ships at anchor. It was clear that no resistance would be met there. Smoke from the burning boats was drifting upland to join that from the smoldering sugarcane fields.

Tammon moaned and Sionna crawled stiffly to her side.

"Is he dead?" the priestess asked.

"Aye, Aunt," Sionna whispered.

Tammon sighed and sagged under Sionna's hands. Her thin lips were turning blue and her age-spotted skin lay flaccid along her high cheekbones. Blood soaked her shoulder.

"I am going now to lead the ancestors back to the fields," Tammon said.

"But it was I who freed them," Sionna cried. "I unsealed the ground and called them forth."

"No," Tammon said. "You only called them forth. I unsealed the ground when I saw to the digging of your daughter's grave. If you had not been so torn by grief you would have seen that I never laid a proper mourning spell to seal the site."

Sionna remembered suddenly the stunted, dry grass that had appeared over her daughter's burial mound. And later the strange pale smoke that had lifted from there. Her aunt had known this thing must be done, and her child had lain waiting all that time.

"You must bear another child," Tammon whispered. "Many children so that the Old Ones can live on in those of Lelanin blood." She relaxed further, her eyelids closed. "You are Lelanin."

Sionna lifted a trembling hand to offer thanks, but the

priestess was already dead. The lady of the valley moved gently instead to close her aunt's shrunken blue lips.

Sionna placed a hand over her own mouth then and waited in silence until others came to care for Tammon. Then she walked alone into the sugarcane fields. Sheltered by smoldering, whispering cane, she buried her grief in a deep hole, and sealed the wound with a carpet of perfect green.

Afterword

If you walk quietly through the sugarcane fields in Hawaii, you will hear a ceaseless rustling whisper. It sounds like many soft voices conversing all at once. Some say they hear only the windblown leaves brushing one against the other. Others claim to hear the voices of early immigrant field-workers, some of whom are said to have buried their sorrows and pain in the ground just as Sionna did.

I began this tale believing that Sionna's story was one of revenge. Her child, surely her most precious possession, had been destroyed by the most evil of sorcery. Yet, as Sionna poured her grief into the fertile valley soil and later spoke with Keron at the funeral supper, I began to realize that the child was only a symbol. It was the land itself, a precious piece of Witch World, that was being stolen. Suddenly the story took on a much deeper meaning.

Like so many others, I began my fantasy reading career with Andre Norton's wonderful tales and I continue to enjoy them today. I am honored to have had the privilege of helping Sionna save this one small piece of Andre's world. And I acknowledge the whispering cane for providing me with the means.

—Carol Severance

GUNNORA'S GIFT

by

Elisabeth Waters

I'm going to Gunnora's shrine because I haven't borne a child in eight years of marriage, but I'm certainly not going to tell you that, Kyria thought, smiling politely at the innkeeper. She returned a noncommittal reply to what he had no doubt intended as a civil question, then set about the business of arranging for food and a night's lodging for herself, her pony, her dog, and her hawk. The innkeeper insisted, however, that all the animals sleep in the stables, pointing out that the dog was almost as big as the pony anyhow.

Kyria acquiesced with a sigh. She would have been glad of the dog's company—she slept with her at home when her husband was gone; that way she didn't wake up freezing in the middle of the night. Still, this was the last inn before she reached the shrine; for the next few days they would all be camping out together and could make what sleeping arrangements they pleased.

The inn was not crowded, so she had a room to herself. But, as she had feared, she woke up in the dark time before dawn, shivering violently. She doubled the blankets up at the foot of the bed and scrunched down under them, pulling the pillow

358

with her to stop the drafts around her neck. She wouldn't be able to sleep much in this position, but at least it was a bit warmer. She would really have preferred to be asleep; for now there was nothing for her to do but think, and her thoughts these days were not pleasant.

Harne would not send her away for her failure to bear him a child; she knew that. Even if he didn't care for her, and she had reason to think he did—he had always been kind to her, ever since she was turned over to him as a nervous fifteen-year-old-bride—she was the key to his possession of her father's hold. But her father had certainly not been happy that her mother bore him no child save this one daughter, and she certainly didn't think that Harne would be content forever with no child of his body to be his heir.

And now she knew that it was her fault. Last week, while riding out past one of the tenant cottages, she had felt someone watching her and turned to see a boy, about nine years old, staring at her with Harne's peculiar gray-green eyes. While she stared back in astonishment a woman had come out of the cottage, looked from her to the boy, and hastily dragged him inside. For a moment Kyria had considered following, to ask what this meant, but the woman had looked terrified, and Kyria had always been reluctant to make anyone unhappy. At the time she had been a bit in shock, and she had always hated awkward scenes. This one promised to be very awkward indeed.

The boy was Harne's son; this much was sure. If it were merely a chance resemblance, the woman, presumably his mother, would have had no reason to be afraid of Kyria's seeing him. After all, he had clearly been born before Harne married Kyria. Past was past; Kyria had no right to complain about anything Harne had done before he married her. But why had the woman looked so frightened? Was Harne still seeing her? Were there other, younger children?

Stop it! Kyria told herself firmly. *You're being morbid; these are simply the kind of horrible ideas you get when you wake up in the dark. You know Harne wouldn't do that—he's an honorable man!*

But the sight of that boy had been enough to make Kyria

take the journey she had been considering for the past year—a
pilgrimage to Gunnora's shrine. Kyria had always wanted a
large family; she had been very lonely as an only child. And all
the time she was growing up, as she carefully learned everything her mother had to teach her, she had thought, *Someday
I'll be teaching all of this to my daughters*. Why couldn't she
have a child—even one? After all, her maidservants had babies
every year, and they didn't need them as much as she did; they
didn't have two holdings waiting for a child to inherit them. So
now Kyria journeyed to Gunnora's shrine, to ask the Goddess
to grant her a child.

As soon as the first glimmering of light showed in the sky
Kyria got up. It was still very cold, but anything was better than
huddling in bed with her thoughts running about her head like
small animals in a trap. She went to the stable, where Lara, her
dog, bounced excitedly about her for several minutes, as
though they had been parted for years, rather than hours. Once
Lara had calmed down and was willing to keep all four feet on
the ground again, Kyria went to saddle her pony and transfer
the hawk to the block on the front of the saddle. By this time
the light was stronger and the innkeeper was up and about,
enabling Kyria to get breakfast and make an early start.

Her day's journey was uneventful, but very tiring, being
largely uphill. She walked a good deal of it, leading the pony,
who was burdened with supplies—after all, he had to carry
himself and the food and bedding, it would be unkind to force
him to carry her on top of it all. In many places it would also
have been impossible; her legs would not have fit between his
sides and the rock walls of the trail they followed. Kyria was
quite thankful that it was late enough in the spring that there
was no snow, especially when it came time to camp for the
night. True, it was cold, but at least she didn't have to wade
through snow or sweep it away from her sleeping area. She
found a small indentation in the cliff wall, which might, if one
was very imaginative, be called a cave, and curled up there between the pony and Lara, while the hawk roosted on the saddle
block that was piled up with the rest of the gear. She slept the
night through, without dreams, and when she woke, the sun
was already high.

She ate quickly and got back on the trail, loosing the hawk to fly free and get some exercise. The hawk flew high above them as they continued up the trail, but Kyria was surprised when it dove suddenly downward—she hadn't thought there would be any game to interest a hawk this high up in the hills. Lara also took off in the direction where the hawk had dropped from sight, so Kyria went to see what they found so interesting.

It was a baby. Someone had apparently left it here, for it was placed in a sort of bowllike shelf in the cliff, high enough so that Lara had to put her front paws up on the rock to reach it and lick its face. It was wrapped in a black cloth and appeared to be about four months old. Kyria reached out and picked it up. As she did so, she heard a cawing noise overhead and looked up to see four crows flying away as if she had disturbed them. *Well, if they were planning on this baby for dinner,* Kyria thought indignantly, *they can't have it!*

The bundle in her arms felt decidedly damp, so Kyria shifted it to one arm and rooted around in her pack for something dry to put on it and something warm to wrap it in. While she changed the baby girl, she wondered who had left her there, and why. The black cloth around her wasn't warm enough to have kept her alive through the night, so she must have been put there that morning. But why would anyone do that? The Dales were not so thickly populated that anyone would want to throw a baby away—and surely here in the high hills a child would be even more valuable—wouldn't it?

Kyria wrapped the baby up snugly, improvised a sort of cradle by making a sling on the side of the saddle, and continued on her way. The baby quickly fell asleep, lulled by the rocking of the saddle, leaving Kyria free for other concerns, such as food. What was she going to feed her? Maybe she could find a house somewhere about and get some goat's milk. Maybe if she could find a house, they would know who the baby was and how she had gotten to where Kyria found her.

The sun was dropping noticeably when Kyria found a cottage. There were two goats wandering about it, so she stopped to ask if she could buy some milk. The woman who came in answer to her call looked old and worn, but two toddlers clung to her skirts. She looked at Kyria with resentful suspicion, even after Kyria politely explained what she wanted.

"And what would you be wanting milk for then?" The woman's tone was positively hostile, and the baby, which had been sleeping peacefully, chose this moment to wake up and start screaming.

"I found a baby on the trail this morning," Kyria said simply. "Do you know whose she is?"

The woman's glare became even more pronounced as she frowned at the baby. "She's Raidhan's! Best you put her back where you found her!"

Kyria stared in frank astonishment. "But how can the crone have a baby?"

"Young fool!" the woman spat at her. "You know nothing! Go on to Gunnora's shrine and pray—but be careful what you pray for, for you will certainly get it!"

Kyria's lips tightened. She didn't need to be mocked for her childlessness; it might be her fault but it certainly wasn't her doing! "About the milk," she began, but the woman interrupted her.

"You'll get nothing from me," she snarled. "Go your way, and never return here!" Voices floated down from the hills behind the cottage, a man's voice, mixed with those of several children. "Go on!" the woman snapped. "Go *now*, and never come this way again!"

Kyria went. There was something going on here that she didn't understand, but she was not at all sure that she wished to understand. She went a good deal farther on the trail before stopping for the night, this time in a small cave lit by the small sliver of a new moon. She broke bread into small pieces and soaked them in water, and the baby ate them hungrily. Tomorrow she would reach the shrine, and in less than a week she should be back among civilized people. The baby wouldn't die of starvation in only a few days.

She settled down to sleep with the baby cradled securely in her arms, tucked between her and Lara. But that night she dreamed.

Raidhan stood in the mouth of the cave. The hood of her dark, ragged cloak was thrown back, and her eyes were greedy as she stretched out her skeletal arms toward the baby. The long clawlike nails on her fingers seemed ready to rend the child to bits. Kyria clutched the baby more tightly. Even her hawk had not sought to lay claws to the child—was the crone less than a hawk? Lara was crouched on her haunches, growling softly at the crone.

"Give her to me," Raidhan demanded. "She's mine."

Kyria sat up, still clutching the baby protectively, and faced the crone. "How can she be yours? You don't bear children."

"Neither do you, my girl," Raidhan snarled back.

"I didn't say she was mine," Kyria said steadily. "I said that she was not yours. I say that she *is* not yours."

"And I agree." From the light shed by the thin sliver of crescent moon low in the sky, a figure appeared around the voice that spoke. Kyria recognized her at once, thought it had been many years since she had seen her. Dians, the Maiden Goddess, stood there, thin and silver as her moonlight. She wore a short tunic and was crowned with the crescent moon. "If this child belongs to the goddess, Raidhan, then surely she is mine. Even you cannot claim that a child this young is not a maid—or that she has chosen to serve you."

"Her mother chose, and her mother gave her to me!" Raidhan's voice was fierce. "Can you say that the woman is not capable of free choice—or do you hold that many years of Gunnora's 'blessings'"—she made the word a sneered curse—"have unsettled her wits so as to make her incapable of rational thought?"

"Any woman is free to choose for herself whom she will serve," Dians said calmly, "but she is not free to choose for another, whether her child or no. You know that, Raidhan. And if you claim this child to be one of Gunnora's 'blessings,' why then, let Gunnora decide whose she is." She turned to Kyria. "You served me once, Kyria, serve me now in this. Take the child to Gunnora's shrine. Tomorrow night we shall meet there and decide her fate."

Kyria bowed her head in assent, and when she looked up again, they were both gone and the moon had set.

* * *

She woke as the sun rose, and shuddered slightly as she remembered the dream. How could any mother give her child to
Raidhan? How could any woman even think of such a thing?

It was only a dream, she reminded herself. *No doubt it was
inspired by the odd behavior of that woman yesterday.*

And if it was a true calling?

What matter? You're going to the shrine in any case.

Kyria got up, changed the baby, fed her some more
moistened bread, and continued her journey.

It was evening when she arrived at the shrine. She fed the
animals and the baby, but did not eat herself, knowing that it
was easier to see the Goddess without food in one's stomach.
Food tied one too much to the material world.

Like the Moon Shrine where she had worshipped Dians when
she was a girl, this one had four pillars. But instead of being
carved with crescents, these had the circles of the full moon.
There was a pool beside it, where she bathed both herself and
the baby before entering between the pillars of the shrine and
kneeling before the plain stone table that was the altar. Although the sun was still up, the new moon was faintly visible
high above it in the western sky. Kyria knew that it would set
about two hours after full dark.

Kyria knelt there with the baby in her lap and thought about
Gunnora as the sun set. As it disappeared the Goddess appeared, golden with the color the sun had left behind. The amber pendants in the shape of sheaves of grain hung on her
breast and forehead and seemed to glow with their own light,
shedding it upon her dark hair and the deep yellow of her robe.
She stood across the altar from Kyria and smiled down at her.

"Be welcome, my daughters," The Lady said. "Why have
you come here?"

The question had the feel of a ritual challenge, and Kyria,
forgetting all the careful prayers she had formulated during the
past months, answered with the first words that came into her
head. "I have come to ask you for a child."

Gunnora laughed. "You have a child," she said.

"What do you mean?" Kyria stared at her in bewilderment.

"What is that you are holding?"

Kyria looked down at the baby in her lap. "But she's not mine."

"Really?" Gunnora still sounded amused. "Whose is she then? What makes a child 'yours'?"

Kyria sat in silence. That was a question she had never considered, beyond the obvious "a child of your body is your child."

The last traces of daylight were gone, and the moonlight made a pale pool to the left of the altar. Now Dians appeared in the moonlight and took form, as Raidhan moved from the darkness outside the shrine to stand to the right of the stone table.

Raidhan spoke first. "I have come to claim that which is mine," she said firmly.

"Which is?" Gunnora's voice was cold and even.

Raidhan's clawlike left hand, drooping from her bony arm, indicated the baby. "That child."

"No." Dians's voice was firm and sure. "That girl is a maiden, hence she is mine. For all maidens are mine unless they choose otherwise."

"Her mother gave her to me!" Raidhan shouted furiously. "She has had more than enough of Gunnora's 'blessings'—the annual baby that breaks the body and wears out the spirit—and she has prayed to me for release from these 'gifts.'"

"And offered her last-born child as payment for this great boon?" Dians asked sarcastically.

"Yes!" Raidhan snarled. "I wouldn't expect *you* to understand. What does a maiden know of the suffering children cause—of having your body torn apart by their births and your heart torn ever after? Of never having any place or time to call your own? Of being ever pulled by the demands of others, until such time as they abandon you altogether? What do you know of this, Dians?"

"Nothing," Dians said quietly. "As you say, Raidhan, this is not my path. But many do choose it, and seem not to regret their choosing."

"And it is my path," Gunnora said gently. "It is true that there are pains upon it, but there are many joys as well. With the demands come love, if you can only see and accept it. Can you never understand this, Raidhan, my sister? Will you always be blind to love?"

Raidhan drew her hood over her face and did not answer.

"The child." Dians spoke in the dispassionate tone of one long accustomed to reminding others what they had been discussing before their emotions had dragged the conversation elsewhere.

Gunnora smiled. "Yes, the child. Kyria, you have said nothing through all this; answer us now. Whose is the child?"

Kyria grasped the baby tightly as she looked at them; at Dians, standing calmly and watching her; at Gunnora, looking at her with the look of a mother willing her child to answer a question correctly; at Raidhan, a dark shadow with an unseen face.

"The child is mine," she said steadily. "I found her on the trail where her natural mother had left her, giving up all claim to her. But she had no right to give her to Raidhan; a child is not a piece of property to be disposed of as her parents wish. It is her choice as to whether she shall serve Dians, Gunnora, or Raidhan, and when she is old enough to understand the choice, she can choose. Until then, she is mine, to care for as I have done since the moment I found her."

"Well said," Gunnora spoke approvingly. "Take her as my gift, to teach and to care for."

"Agreed," Dians said shortly.

"Very well," Raidhan snarled from beneath her hood. "Take her for now, but remember, she'll come to me in the end."

"Perhaps," Kyria acknowledged. "I know not what lies ahead. But if she does come, it will be by her choice, not another's." She looked down tenderly at the baby and stroked her hair.

When she looked up again, she and the child were alone in the shrine, the moon had almost set, and it was cold. She hastily left the shrine and went to her baggage to bundle up the baby, dress herself, and start a fire. As she worked, the words of the woman at the cottage came back to her: "Be careful what you pray for, for you will certainly get it." *And so I did,* she thought in amusement, *but not at all the way I expected.*

Afterword

Andre Norton was the first fantasy writer I discovered, back when I was in grade school, and her books still occupy a good stretch of my ever-expanding library. (Did you ever notice that she has at least one book title beginning with each letter of the alphabet, including Q and Z?)

I find her books particularly helpful when I have to travel (I've gotten over the worst of it, but I still have some trouble with agoraphobia); not only are they absorbing enough so that I can get involved in them and ignore my surroundings, but she frequently writes about characters who are terrified by something in their environment yet go ahead and do what has to be done anyway, which encourages me to keep going even when I'm scared.

When Andre asked me to contribute a story to her first Witch World anthology, I was deeply honored. Unfortunately, however, I just couldn't come up with an idea for a Witch World story, much as I loved Andre and wanted to give her something in return for all she'd given me. So after months of fruitless struggle, I wrote to her and said, "I'm sorry, I know I promised you a story, and I tried, but I just can't do it." And Andre said that it was all right and she understood. A few years later, when she was doing a third volume of Witch World stories, she asked me again. This time I managed to write "Gunnora's Gift" and she liked it.

—Elisabeth Waters

WOLFHEAD

by

Michael D. Winkle

I

Throughout the Year of the Moss Wife did we Dalesmen hear of the Hounds of Alizon and their strange allies from across the sea. That they brought war was plain to all, like storm clouds upon the horizon, yet, though each Dale's lord saw to the storing of food and the training of men, they did not ally themselves to one another until nearly too late. We are a proud, stubborn, and independent breed, and such alliances are alien to our way of thinking.

Yet it chanced that Lord Torak of Ellskeep, my father, traveled south to the war front before the grudging Dales alliance. Ellsdale had known peace for many years, excepting minor skirmishes with outlaws of the Waste, and though most men long for such relative tranquility, it grated against the fiery temper of my father. There were Sulcarmen amongst his ancestors, as one could tell with a glance at his mighty physique and bronze skin, and this, mingling with his Dale heritage, produced a man who itched for action that no hunt or sword practice could provide. Thus it was, when the first reports of an invasion of High Hallack trickled north to the Dales, that Lord Torak gathered a small entourage of fighting men and readied himself to march.

He called me to his chamber a week before his departure, and I dared believe I was to ride with him. I entered his bedroom to find him standing before the window, the cold air of the Month of the Snow-Bird drifting in like fog.

"You summoned me, Father?"

He turned and looked upon me as if for the first time, like a stranger unaware that Wylona of Ellskeep had all her life preferred the jerkins and trousers of boys to the dresses of girls.

"Wylona," he began quietly, "in a sevennight we start our trek south."

My spirits rose as I heard these words, only to be crushed by his next utterance.

"Whilst I am gone, you will be the highest authority in Ellskeep."

"Oh," I said, then, quickly, "I am honored by your trust, my lord."

My father cocked his shaggy head, a lion questioning like a pup.

"You expected something else? To battle the Hounds of Alizon at my side, perhaps?"

I cast my eyes down in shame, but I looked up again as my father continued.

"Heed me; it is no light matter I tell you this day. I could easily claim to have foresight other Dale lords lack, but that would be a lie. I ride, perhaps, on a fool's errand, but I fear nothing else will quell the thirst that gnaws within me. A thirst to clash, steel to steel; a thirst to strike foemen down before me; a thirst to fight with shield brothers at my side. As some men seek gold or women, so must I seek war."

He turned to gaze at the portrait of Lady Amiell, my mother and his wife, dead these dozen years.

"Before I met your mother, I would disappear from Ellskeep for months on end, carrying the blank shield of a mercenary. But, then, both my elder brothers died of the Creeping Plague, and I met Amiell, and so I stayed in Ellsdale as I should. For seventeen years I have fought the desire for battle, and I fear I can stave it off no more.

"You have been both son and daughter to me, Wylona. I have had you instructed in swordsmanship and strategy as well as in the ways of the court ladies, and in my absence, the gentles and soldiers of the court shall obey you as their liege. And should it happen that I do not return . . ."

"Don't say such a thing, Father."

Torak lay his mighty hands upon my shoulders.

"I must. Should I not return, you shall be their liege in truth. We have no male relatives to challenge you, and few Dale lords truly desire Ellsdale, bordering as she does the Waste on the north and west. And even should a challenge arise, I know the Lady Wylona of Ellskeep shall face it and triumph."

I knelt before my father and thanked him for his trust and faith, and then he dismissed me. A few days more and he left, though the Month of the Frost Sprite had scarcely begun, and breaths still misted like dragon-smoke. He bade me take seriously the counsel of my elders, such as Kegan, the crusty old captain of the guard, and then he said farewell. Nevermore did I see him.

II

The Alizon invasion was no border skirmish. Ragged bands of refugees came up from the south, first a trickle, then a torrent. The rumors they passed on were scarcely believable, but we knew them to be true.

The Hounds bore with them weapons the like of which we had never dreamed. Their footmen carried strange devices that slew from afar, using only a beam of reddish light. From their ships came great, squat, clanking things of metal, which crawled inexorably across the land like monster tortoises, spewing streams of fire before them. Even if the men to the south withdrew into their keeps and behind their city walls, the metal monsters penetrated the barriers of stone with the ease of a mole digging through soil. How could any mortal men defeat unliving metal juggernauts?

As ever more tattered bands wandered north, however, we finally received good tidings amongst the stories of the Hounds' atrocities. It seemed the metal monsters were not indestructible, after all. They needed supplies from the Alizonian ships to keep moving, and the supply lines from monster to shore were harried as often as possible. Furthermore, there seemed to be a limited number of the juggernauts, for no more were delivered from the Hounds' vessels.

Such hope was stirred in our breasts that more and more Ellsmen marched away to the south, leaving our Dale severely undermanned. But so far were we from the war front that we blindly thought ourselves safe.

I lay abed one night, some months after the sealing of the alliance by the lords Imgry, Savron, and Wintof, wondering whether my father still lived, and whether our land would ever know again the peace it once took for granted. I heard shouts and running footsteps far below, and I was up by the time Captain Kegan pounded 'pon my door.

"Milady—milady! They come from the Waste!"

"They?" I repeated. I grabbed my mail shirt and worked it on over my head, then I opened the door to see the guard captain's worried face.

"One of the border posts began to fire-signal," he explained, "but there came a flash, as of lightning, and nothing more was seen. But now a rider has reached the keep, half dead, his skin charred as if he'd fallen into a smithy's furnace. He says the metal monsters of Alizon come—from the north!"

My blood grew as cold as the rings of my mail.

"How could this be?"

"The coast to the east of the Waste is not often visited anymore, save by scavengers. Perhaps the Hounds landed there unseen. The how does not matter. The question is, what shall we do?"

"There may be nothing we can do," I said, pulling on a boot.

"If the combined armies of High Hallack cannot stop the invaders, what chance have we? I fear it is our turn to be refugees."

Kegan stiffened. "You suggest we flee Ellskeep, like rabbits dug from a warren?"

"If it were merely men, even a great army, I would fight to the death at your side. But neither sword arm nor coping wall will halt the metal monsters."

I scooped up my helm, which sat upon my dresser where most ladies arrange face powders.

"We must sever their supply lines as our countrymen have done in the south. But to do that, we must first survive!"

Captain Kegan reluctantly agreed, and we descended the stairs to a court ruled by chaos. Men and women ran helter-skelter with half-filled packs and wallets while the warning bells above spelled out the code of invasion.

"Milady," said Kegan suddenly. "You should have packed your belongings!"

I glanced back at the stairwell. "There is no time."

I visited the man who had brought the news. Though Belita, our wise woman, attended him, I knew he lay on his deathbed. The left side of his face was blackened and cracked; his left eye was gone completely. But still could he speak.

There were at least three of the metal juggernauts, by now, a league or so from the keep. They were ponderous and slow, evidently relying on their far-reaching fire to strike down enemies. Foot- and horsemen accompanied the monsters, but these troops seemed reluctant to stray far from their vicinity. Such did I learn before the burnt sentry passed from our world.

After a moment of silence, I came to business.

"We should have time to send riders to the villages roundabout. Also, we must send word to the Dales south and east."

"I shall attend to it directly, milady," said Kegan.

"And no doubt the Hounds will want to demonstrate their power by attacking the keep. It must be evacuated."

"I believe that decision has been anticipated, Lady Wylona," the captain observed, glancing about. Then he smiled, for the first time in living memory, and left.

* * *

From a distant hilltop did we see the first of the Alizon monsters. It was a vast vehicle of dull gray, shaped like a horseshoe crab. It moved at a walking man's pace, but whether it crawled on legs or wheels, or even upon its belly like a snail, I could not tell. From its apex shot a thick, reddish column on occasion, and wheresoever the column passed, flames sprang up as from a grass fire.

As I watched, grinding my teeth in helplessness, the metallic vehicle crept up to the very walls of Ellskeep and then paused, like a fat beetle that has run into an obstacle and is too stupid to turn aside. Slowly—and I gasped at the thing's mute power—the monster began passing through the solid north wall, which gave no more resistance than bread dough to a cook's prodding finger.

The northwest tower, where all my possessions and memories lay, shuddered like a post hit by an axe. Then it crumbled thunderously into a mound of rubble.

"Ellskeep is no more," I said, turning away. "Now we must leave."

Of our party, there was, besides myself, Kegan and a score of soldiers; Belita; the ladies Nabora and Varda, my father's cousins; a handful of servants; and a few villagers from nearby Lormill. There were horses for myself and each solider, and burro-drawn wagons for the ladies and the wise woman. The others kept apace on foot.

We traveled southwest for a day, desiring a safe distance between ourselves and the Hounds before holding council. One of Kegan's men brought down a fat hill-buck with his arrows, so we ate well that night, at least. Afterward we discussed our options.

"I fear all the abbeys in High Hallack are filled to bursting already," said Kegan. "Besides, from what I've heard, the Hounds take no heed of the sanctity of the Dames, but crush abbeys beneath their juggernauts with the same ease they smash keeps."

"We dare not go any nearer the Waste," I began. "If the outlaw bands know of this northern Alizonian strike, they may grow bold and cross our borders, like jackals following lions. I think we should warn our neighboring Dales and join our meager forces to theirs."

"We are cut off from those of the east," Kegan pointed out, "but I sent several riders to warn them, so in that direction should the warning spread. The south seems our best hope—perhaps Ronansdale."

"Yes," I said. "For Lord Ghislain of Ronanskeep was long friendly to my father."

I put the question to the folk around us.

"What think you of Ronansdale?"

Everyone muttered in agreement.

"Ronansdale it is, then," I concluded.

III

I took my turn at watch a couple of hours before dawn, and afterward I walked past Belita's cart on the way back to my bedroll. To my surprise, she stepped out from behind it and asked how went the watch.

"Nothing to be seen or heard," I answered her, glancing to the north, "which I count as a blessing."

Belita stared off in the same direction, and after a moment of silence, she spoke.

"Well, Alvred and Leofric are on watch now, not we two."

"Aye." I looked at her again. "Tell me, what might you be doing up already? As you say, it is not your watch."

Belita smiled coquettishly. "I intended to wash a few items at the stream—myself included. I waited for you because I thought you might be wanting to divest yourself of your byrnie and helm for a while."

I frowned. "Leave the camp before daybreak?"

"Not to worry—Alvred's post overlooks the stream, and he promised to watch—"

I raised an eyebrow.

"—not *too* closely, of course."

Belita smirked, and I could scarcely keep from laughing aloud. There were older wise women who looked down upon Belita, for she could not completely control her emotions, a discipline necessary for the craft. She tried turning a harsh mask to the world, but time and again her feelings bubbled out like steam from under a kettle lid. And that this was a bad thing, I would never believe. I could not turn down her offer.

I did not bathe in the stream, but I stripped partially and scrubbed myself with Belita's soap. Without my armor and weapon I felt naked, but also light as a dandelion tuft. I glanced up on occasion at the silhouette of Alvred, black against the purple dawn.

Nearby, Belita washed her hair. I did likewise.

"Does your hair not get snagged in your mail?" my friend asked, through her own dripping tresses.

"I usually braid it beforehand, but there was hardly the opportunity the other night . . . It would be most practical to cut it, like a lad joining the guard, but—"

"But you are not a lad?" ventured Belita, pulling comb and brush from her pack.

"No. Sometimes I have to remind even myself that I am Lady, not Lord, Wylona."

"You've tried to be both, since Torak left. If you carry all the woes of Ellsdale and her people upon your shoulders, you'll be old and stooped before your years."

I straightened suddenly, my pride stung.

"I am the Lady Wylona of Ellsdale. It is my duty to accept her people's woes, problems, and ill luck, and take action to lessen them."

Belita approached me, comb and brush in hand.

"Right now you look like a pond-dunked farm maid with snags in her hair the Rats of Nore could nest in. Drying, grooming, and rest are the only actions you should take now."

"You are irreverent and incorrigible, Belita," I said, then I smiled and hugged her to my breast. "You are also my best friend. Don't ever change."

*   *   *

Belita had just begun brushing my hair when an eerie, quavering howl echoed out of the wilderness beyond the stream. We both froze, staring in the direction of the sound. There was nothing to be seen.

"What was that?" I asked. "A wolf?"

A second howl filled the air, closer this time.

"I know the calls of all the four-footed inhabitants of the Dale land," my friend answered slowly. "This is like that of a wolf, but—different."

We began dressing quickly, and suddenly we heard, not a howl, but the blare of our camp's warning trumpet. Belita sprinted up the gravelly shore, ignoring my call to wait. I fought my way into my byrnie and snatched up my scabbard and helm.

I heard now the pounding of hooves and the shouting of men. There was a slight rise between the stream and the camp; it was here Alvred had been patrolling. He was no longer to be seen. Belita disappeared over the rise, and moments later I crested it.

Kegan and his soldiers were scattered about, fighting a band of horsemen with steel and arrow. I saw the villagers and even the ladies fighting with what weapons were to hand; I grew proud of my people and rushed into the fray.

As I yanked my sword from its scabbard, one of the horsemen bore down upon me. I had no recourse save to hurl my helm at him. He raised his buckler to deflect the missile; I noted that only furs protected his midriff, and as he galloped by I swung my sword into the area between his shield and his hips. The blade shuddered deep into him and slid out wetly.

After he fell, I observed that buried amongst his furs were the round seals of several Dales—trophies collected over many years. These were outlaws, then, not foreign invaders.

Suddenly I heard a strange sizzling noise. I looked up to see a man on a horse, carrying something that resembled a crossbow made of gold and silver. A red streak shot like unkinked lightning from this object into our camp, setting one of our carts afire in the wink of an eye. I guessed this weapon to be one of the fire-throwers of the Alizonian invaders, but these men were not Hounds, of that I was sure. They were outlaws who had one of the Hounds' weapons. Had they successfully raided an Alizonian party? Were the Hounds and these wolfheads in league?

I could not wonder about this now, for another horsemen rode upon me. He pulled forth a strange rod, half again as long as my sword, made completely of glass or crystal save for a black handgrip. Bubbles of greenish light skittered up and down the crystalline shaft like fireflies trapped within.

He carried the rod in one hand like a sword, and as a sword I met it. I parried it with my blade, but some terrible force ran along the steel, into my arms and thence through my whole body, like the poison of the Basilisk. I collapsed onto my face and did not rise.

IV

A steady jostling shook me slowly awake. I opened my eyes warily to find that I sat upright, ahorse, but not by my own doing. My hands were bound before me, and a loop of rope stretched from my wrists around the neck of my mount. I tested my legs carefully; a rope passing under the horse's chest joined my ankles.

I was not alone on the horse. A weather-gnarled arm stretched by on either side of me to grip the reins. One of the murderous outlaws rode with me, supporting me like a lad his love.

My only impulse was to struggle like a wildcat; my only desire, to spit him upon my sword. But the first would accomplish nothing, and the second was beyond my capabilities for now. I had remained limp instinctively upon awakening, and I decided to continue my unconscious appearance. My eyes were open to observant slits, however.

I glimpsed other horses to the left and right. Each bore two riders, one outlaw and one Ellswoman. That meant these wolfheads raided us, not for food, riches, or the simple thrill of

378 Michael D. Winkle

killing, but for wives. I recognized the Lady Varda, her sister, and—Belita! Her precipitous flight back to camp had been a disastrous mistake.

With such weapons as the basilisk rod and the fire-thrower at the bandits' disposal, I feared that Kegan and his soldiers had been overwhelmed and slain to a man. After all, I saw no male captives. I vowed silently to avenge them.

I tilted my head carefully, to get a better look at our captors. They were an ugly lot, clad mostly in badly cured furs, and they had more than their share of scars, eye patches, and missing fingers.

One man—the leader, I guessed—particularly caught my eye. He had ridden somewhere ahead, but now he reined his horse in, allowing his fellows to pass by. He scrutinized the women as if they were horses up for sale. All of his accoutrements—cloak, trousers, shirt, boots—were made from gray-white wolf skins, and the fire-gun was slung over his shoulder.

When he came abreast of me, his gaze caught mine. I winced my eyes shut too late.

"Ho! The swordmaid awakes!"

I feigned senselessness a moment more, until he continued.

"Don't play the puff adder with me, girl! I know you hear and understand."

Very well, I thought. I opened my eyes and glared at him with all the hate I could muster.

"That's better," the outlaw said with a sneering tone. "More spunk than the rest combined, and not reeking of Power. Bittard was right—you are a valuable prize."

He matched his pace to mine, and he reached a hand toward me as if to stroke my cheek. I spat at him. He only sneered again.

"You we'll have to watch," said he of the many wolf pelts. "More than all these others put together. You are a schemer—a warrior—a leader—just like me."

"Not like you, murderer," I denied hotly.

The bandit leader guffawed. "You'll be trouble—but you'll be worth it."

"That depends on what price you set to your miserable life, Wolfhead."

The outlaw stared at me for a second, then laughed. So did the man behind me. Perhaps my threats were hollow, but I did not deem them *that* funny.

"You happened upon a private jest, I fear," said the outlaw leader at last.

"Jest, then, while you may," I advised coldly.

"If glares were daggers and words, darts, lady, would none of us be here. And nothing more shall you—"

He stiffened suddenly, the smirk on his face replaced by a mask of anger. The raiders now clopped along a natural pathway between two copses of trees. From far to the west there reverberated the same eerie howl Belita and I had heard twice at the stream. I straightened to see the horsemen glancing to and fro, their mounts blowing nervously.

"So!" cried the bandit leader. "Still he follows us! Well—let him bay all the night long. I shall send no more men out till we reach Dragonsback."

The bandit's reaction puzzled me. He seemed to hate this strange howling creature as he would a human foe. However, he had good reason to do so, as the next few moments proved.

The bandits' eyes were turned to the west, where the mournful call was repeated, and my eyes were jumping from one man to another. None of us turned our gaze to the east until a score of gray, white, and black forms burst from the nearby trees. They were wolves, sleek, swift, and uncannily silent.

The world around me blurred as my mount rose and pawed at the air. The man behind me squawked in surprise and slid off its rump. Bound as I was, I couldn't have fallen if I tried.

I heard yells of command and shrieks of pain. The wolves shot in and out amongst the men, tearing with their fangs and dodging sword blows, still unnervingly quiet.

My horse bolted from the outlaw caravan and crashed into the stunted forest. I tugged on the rope around its neck as I would the reins, but the slavering beast would not obey. I gritted my teeth and ducked the slashing branches of the trees, and I prayed it would avoid stepping in any holes.

After nearly a quarter hour of flight, the horse slowed its pace. It came upon a stream and lowered its head to drink. Afterward, it climbed a slight rise and began cropping the

stunted grass as though I didn't exist. I bent forward and
started the arduous process of untying my bonds with my teeth.

V

My teeth slipped off the thick rope and clacked painfully together for the twentieth time. I spat out the bits of fiber I'd torn
loose and swore. I'd been at this for an hour, and this knot of
rope still seemed like a knot of wood. I grew thirsty and tired. I
wished to relieve myself, and my legs were chafed from rubbing
against the horse's shoulders.

Suddenly the horse's head rose, ears perked. A vaguely human outline moved amongst the gnarled trees and menhirlike
rocks. Was it a traveler? A bandit? Worse?

The skittish manner in which the horse backed away from the
approaching silhouette made me fear the last possibility. Just as
it seemed ready to bolt again, however, a strange trilling noise
filled the air, apparently coming from the dark figure.

My mount whinnied softly. It hesitated, then it actually
started forward, as if attracted to the trilling.

When I could make out the details of what approached, a
cold thrill spread through me. Although it walked upright, it
was not human. Its legs and arms were long and spindly, and all
its body was covered with gray-white fur. A plumelike tail
swished into view from behind it, and its head was that of a
great wolf.

Wolfhead . . . A private jest . . .

Suddenly I knew I faced the howling thing that the bandit
leader hated. That it was his enemy, though, did not comfort
me.

"Gee-up!"

I yanked hard on the rope about the horse's neck. The horse,
which had been blind with terror only an hour earlier, clopped
fearlessly right up to the wolf-creature.

The creature, still trilling, patted the horse's muzzle with its

pawlike hand and took hold of the reins, like any human eques-
trian. I caught myself making half-choked gasps of terror, un-
dignified noises that stung my pride.

The creature's eyes were sapphire-blue, and they shifted
from the horse to me. I bit my lower lip and stared back. For a
full minute our gazes locked, as though we fought with
willpower instead of weapons. Finally, the wolf-thing snorted as
if bored and turned away.

The man-beast slipped its clawed fingers around the rope that
held my hands to the horse. It lifted the rope as far as it would
come from the animal's skin and bit it with its sharp, white
teeth. Once, twice, thrice the wolf-thing sawed at the cord, its
lupine fangs accomplishing in seconds what my human teeth
couldn't in an hour.

I straightened and worked my wrists apart. My hands had
become numb and purple, and the tingle of returning blood
made me gasp. The creature squatted by the horse's foreleg and
bit through the rope that held me to the animal.

My mind was awhirl with questions. Why was this being helping me? *What* was it? That it had intelligence like unto a human's, I could not deny. But could I speak with it?

"Wh-who are you?" I asked tremulously. "Can you understand me? Can you speak?"

If the man-beast comprehended, it made no sign. Its ears
perked like a dog's, and it stared off into the gnarled forest
from which I'd come. I heard the distant howling of wolves,
and suddenly the wolf-creature shot away. Sometimes it loped
on two legs, sometimes on all fours. I almost called out to it,
but I checked myself. I knew not what motivated the creature,
but I found it hard to believe that it could be sheer altruism.

I dismounted and caught the horse's reins. For the first time I
noticed a dart-gun stored in a holster that was built right onto
the saddle. I snatched it out and found there to be a nearly full
complement of darts, for which I thanked Sul.

Now; what to do? The bandit leader had mentioned Dragonsback, a jagged line of peaks to the north. That seemed as
good a goal as any, but first I had to rest up from my ordeal. I
was one against many, and I had no shield-brother to spell me

on watch. I tied the horse's reins to a stunted bush and stumbled down to the stream.

I rode uneasily along the streambed, which stretched northward toward Dragonsback. As I studied a small knoll to my left, the horse neighed and sidestepped as if it had nearly trod upon a serpent. I scanned the rocky path but saw nothing. When I looked up again, the wolf-creature's blue eyes stared back like two fireflies. It squatted on the knoll like a great chipmunk. It flinched as I yanked out the dart-gun, but I did not fire, and it remained where it crouched.

"Wolfheads," it said in a guttural voice. It felt strange to hear a recognizable word from its bestial muzzle.

"What?"

It looked away to the east.

"That is the term you use for such as *those,* is it not? Robbers, murderers, rapists—wolfheads."

"It is," I admitted warily. "What of it?"

The man-beast bent forward, fur bristling.

"I would merely inform you that amongst true wolves such crimes are unknown. They do not abandon their children or their mates; they do not wage war; they hunt, but not for sport; and they are loyal to their packs, more so, I'm sure, than many men are to their liege lords."

"That is so?" I asked. I felt suddenly defensive, as if I represented all humanity. "You quite suspiciously resemble a Gray One, my furry friend. They are most definitely of the Dark. Do you claim such nobility for them, as well?"

"I would have, once," the wolf-thing snarled. "They are not responsible for what they are today. They were created and used as vessels for the Dark—if not by men, then by those with a similar disregard for fellow living creatures!"

I snorted. "You cannot compare my kind to those ancients who held High Hallack before, man-wolf. I know not why you chose me to hear your exaltations of your lupine friends, but—"

I stopped and lifted my gun again, for the wolf-thing hunched its back, and I sensed it would pounce. Pounce it did, but aside, not forward, and my dart whizzed through empty air. For the rest of that night I neither heard nor glimpsed Wolfhead—as I christened the lupine being—though I kept alert for its return.

VI

I would fall out of the saddle if I did not sleep soon, I knew. I was wending my way through a maze of channels that crisscrossed the Waste, the peaks of Dragonsback my only compass. As I passed the mouth of one such channel, I noticed an azure glow—mist lit by some source hidden behind a twist in the rock walls.

I reined the horse around and started down the narrow gulch. Ruins of the Old Ones could be found even in the Dales, though most avoided them. Some held an atmosphere inimical to men, some were indifferent, and some were actually friendly. Belita had taught me that ruins of the last sort were built of glowing bluish stones. If this was such a place—

I rounded a sharp outcropping and found an anomalous expanse of lush greenery stretching from one rocky wall to the other. At the center sat a great circular dais, several rods wide and as high as my chest, and in the middle of the dais stood a small temple of turquoise stone.

There was a throb—no, a *feeling*—that permeated the air, a sense of well-being and safety, like my earliest shadow-memories of my mother. The horse's pace picked up noticeably; I believe it, too, felt the benevolent atmosphere.

I'd saved some of the rope that had bound me, and with it I hobbled the animal, though I thought it unlikely to wander from this oasis in the Waste. A stone stairway reached from the ground to the lip of the dais. I ascended warily, though with each step I was more certain than ever that nothing ill could befall me here.

I approached the small building. It had a simple arched entryway, without a door. From it came a glow slightly brighter than that of the dais or the temple's exterior. I stepped boldly through the opening.

There was only one room in the building, scarcely any larger than my bedchamber in fallen Ellskeep. There were two windows, one in the south wall and one in the north. Taking up the west wall was a shrine of sorts, built of more blue stone.

At the south end of the temple I noticed a small wooden table with a single chair beside it. In the north stood a cot mattressed with soft rushes, as green as though they'd been picked this morning.

A strange feeling washed over me, as if a door had been opened and a gust of wind had blown in. I turned to find utensils, a plate of steaming victuals, and a mug of dark red liquid on the table. No physical person could have brought them without my spotting him.

"For the welcome of this house, my thanks," I said aloud, looking slowly about at the corners of the ceiling. "For the feasting on the board, my pleasure and good wishes. To the— inhabitants of this house, fair fortune."

Afterward, I ate the meal provided from thin air, for I was famished. I could not identify the meat or the vegetables, but each bite melted on my tongue like butter. The strange drink, which was neither wine nor mead, sent warmth down my throat and outward through every limb.

Finished, I removed my boots and my mail shirt and stretched out on the cot with a sigh. I faded into a dreamless sleep before a single thought of Wolfheads human or otherwise crossed my brain.

I awoke fully in but a moment, completely refreshed. I sat up with a smile and slid my legs over the side of the cot.

"Good morning, dear lady. Your rest appears to have done you well."

Wolfhead sat on the chair at the other end of the room, one elbow propped upon the table, as if he were someone I commonly breakfasted with. I swept my hands over my mail shirt, where I'd set my dart-gun. It took me a moment to realize the man-beast held it.

"Weapons are unwelcome here, my lady. Tolerated, perhaps, but not to be used in this place."

Wolfhead stood up on his spindly lupine legs and approached me, holding out the gun butt first. I stood up as well and accepted the weapon hesitatingly.

"Wh-why are you here?" I demanded.

"I wished to apologize for any offense I may have given last evening," said the man-beast. "There are certain subjects on which I feel strongly . . . Also, we have common goals and common hatreds we should discuss." He glanced about the temple with drooping ears. "But not here. Anger and war do not belong to this place. I shall await you outside."

He turned to the doorway on his double-jointed legs. He walked with a strange grace, like a dancer on tiptoe. Also was his voice less guttural today, as if his growling speech was something he effected to impress people.

"Wait! Who—what are you?"

Wolfhead stared back for a moment. His eyes were of the same turquoise shade as the stones of the temple.

"That is a tale long in the telling, lady, perhaps better saved for later."

With that, he padded out the door. I pulled on my boots and byrnie and followed.

With each step I took down the stone stairway, the feeling of well-being diminished and the doubts of reality awakened again. How could I trust this creature? What did he want?

Wolfhead awaited me by my horse. He was trilling again, and the animal nudged his furry hand as if seeking a sweet therein. He stared down his long snout at my dart-gun, which I held prominently before me.

"You are still suspicious," he observed.

"Humans always treat the unknown with caution," I explained. "Especially in a land such as ours, where death can come in the form of man or beast, weapon or willpower."

"Fair enough."

Wolfhead quietly patted the horse's muzzle until I spoke again.

"Yesterday . . . There were wolves . . ."

"Gnarrel's pack."

"Gnarrel?"

"Their leader, when I am not around. They lost three of their number in yestermorn's attack, while Shekkar has two known dead and several badly mauled."

"Shekkar?"

"The outlaws' leader. The one who wears only wolf skins—and only of wolves shaded like me."

The wolf-creature slid one clawed hand over his fur. That of his chest and stomach formed a white band, like a narrow tabard.

"He does that to annoy me."

I lowered my gun and slipped it into my belt.

"He is the common hatred you mentioned?"

"Indeed. He will be making for his headquarters near Dragonsback. He goes there to meet with the outlanders."

"Why would this Shekkar seek the invaders?"

"He would be wanting more weapons like the guns that sear from afar. The outlanders want men to guide caravans to the distant sea and back."

"So there is an alliance between the outlaws and the Hounds!" I exclaimed. "If only I could warn Ronansdale and the lands beyond . . ."

"Your men who still survive shall sound a warning for those of the south. On foot, and with scores of injuries amongst them, they cannot hope to follow Shekkar."

"My men? Some live?" I asked excitedly.

"Four or five. Akria and her pack are watching over them."

"Akria?"

"Gnarrel's dam."

I frowned. "My men may misinterpret the attention of wolves."

"My four-footed cousins will patrol for enemies and predators, and perhaps supply them with a rabbit or two. They will flee any confrontations with your soldiers."

"The soldiers—was one old, silver-haired?"

"I do not know . . . My lady, you are full of questions this morn. We really should move on. Tonight, perhaps, I can answer you more fully."

"You are right, of course."

"I must gather my four-footed brethren. We shall await you at the entrance of the canyon."

Wolfhead dropped to all fours and loped away at a startling pace. I had already started thinking of him as "he" rather than "it," but it was hard to distinguish him from the forest beasts when he ran as they.

I wondered at the wisdom of entering into an alliance with this mysterious man-beast. But . . . I glanced back at the Blue Temple. Were Wolfhead malevolent, he could not have set foot upon the dais. I was certain of that.

VII

Wolfhead ranged ahead of my horse throughout the day, as Dragonsback towered higher before us. The wolves loped along just out of sight, but I heard them call to their strange leader. Toward evening, they led me down a narrow valley to the east, in the foothills of Dragonsback. Now I could see the wolves, a score or so, all about. They sauntered along as if weightless, slapping their paws to earth only to propel themselves forward. By now, my horse seemed unconcerned even if one crossed closely in front of it.

Far ahead, the man-beast rose onto two legs before a bleak cliff face. I saw at the base of the cliff a small building near-completely tumbled, abutting its stony surface. There was a single entrance, cleared of debris, large enough for two horsemen to enter side by side.

"What is this place?" I queried.

"A good shelter for the night," the wolf-man answered. "There are stores within, and well water."

The wolves disappeared into the arid terrain around us as I dismounted. I hobbled the horse and followed the man-beast in. There was a main corridor that ran straight back from the entrance into the depths of the cliff. Along the walls were numerous other entryways, radiating out from the main hall, and also statuettes and busts covered with the dust of ages. These figurines were of men and legendary semihumans, like Satyrs and Mer-Maids.

"Here," said my lupine guide, pointing at an opening on the left.

I entered after him and saw a wide, calm pool of sparkling, blue, fluorescent water. The pool illuminated the room well enough to make things out.

On the far side of the room were stacks of smoked meat, bags of grain, and clay jars of obvious Dale make. I wondered how the man-beast had obtained them and transported them out here. On the left was a hearth or oven and, next to that, a pile of kindling. On the right the room receded into darkness.

"You have been quite industrious here," I commented. "Is this your home?"

"Near enough. It is my birthplace."

I lay on a pallet of dry rushes the man-beast had found in the darkness. He stretched out on a woven rug several feet away. The fire crackled brightly in its corner alcove, its light flickering on the floor between us. I had just finished a piece of dry meat as my lupine companion spoke.

"This was a beautiful land, once. The earth was rich and fertile, the beasts roamed peacefully through the woods, and the birds sang at one's request. Yet there existed people then, as now, who did not find nature's variety enough. They manipulated living creatures as a sculptor molds clay, and they produced beings previously unknown. Some served as ambassadors between the people and the creatures of the wild. Some spread the ways of the elder folk across the land and sea, and to places they themselves could not colonize—in the waters there are Krogan, in the air Flannen, and beneath the earth Thas. And some were no more than living portraits, expressions of others' imaginations."

"You speak as if you were there," I said softly.

"I was."

I started. "But that would make you so—old!"

The man-wolf's toothy grin glinted in the firelight.

"In one manner, I am very old. In another, I am not. Please have a little patience, and you will hear. Patience is a virtue most humans lack—as did not a few of those almost-human Old Ones long ago. All the universe holds—and more—would have been revealed unto them eventually, but many could not wait.

"Dark Powers and entities were summoned, only to escape and spread across the land like a forest fire. The Shadow touched upon people, animals, and in-between creatures like me, and war broke out, utilizing weapons to put the outlanders' fire-guns to shame. Mountains tumbled like a child's blocks. Seas dried or ran to other beds. The beautiful land became the Waste.

"There remained a wise man, Gwart, who thought a chosen few should leap out of the stream of life until matters were settled in the land. He picked a number of his followers—including such as I, for he judged us not by our outward form—and we went with him to a hidden vault. Then, we slept."

"Slept?"

"A near enough word."

Wolfhead rolled onto his back. He seemed to study the ceiling.

"Finally, I awoke—alone. Everyone but me was dead and dust or gone altogether. My mind and memory were like a new-born cub's; if the others had been as I, they may have simply perished in the Waste.

"I crawled from chamber to chamber, scenting nothing save dust and centuries-old bones. I finally found Gwart in his compartment, looking whole, if dormant. But when I touched him, he crumbled away. This reached through my clouded mind, and I howled for him."

The Gray One paused for a moment. I sensed his sorrow, and I wondered again at the dichotomy between his bestial exterior and his engaging personality. If ever he left the Waste for the lands of men, he'd be slain on sight, I knew, and my choler quickened at the unfairness of it.

Wolfhead continued:

"I heard the questioning calls of men, stirred by my mourning. I staggered onto two legs and followed the sound. Thus did I come upon Shekkar's band.

"The outlaws had entered the sanctuary, for what purpose I

never did learn. I suspect their intrusion had something to do with my awakening . . . At any rate, the bandits' first impulse was to slay me, and I was virtually helpless. But Shekkar was quite irreverent where it concerned the Old Ones. He ordered me captured instead, an easy enough command.

"He did not know why my mind was stunted, but he saw an interesting possibility in me. I was at first treated like a favored dog, and as my mind grew clearer I came to accept Shekkar as my master."

Wolfhead crossed his spindly arms over his chest, and his lips curled up to reveal his fangs.

"Some men have fighting dogs or war-horses for which they are envied. But who could boast of an obedient Gray One?

"Let me say only that I grew displeased with my lot over the next few months, as my memory returned, and that I fled into the Waste during a raiding foray. The true wolves of the wilderness accepted me quickly—that was why my kind had been created, after all. Since then we have harassed Shekkar and his band . . ."

The fire crackled for a moment or two.

"That has become difficult since the coming of the outlanders. Shekkar must not get more of their terrible weapons."

"You have my full cooperation, of course," I said. "But even together, what chance have we to defeat the Hounds and their fire-spitters?"

Wolfhead rolled onto his side, facing me. His eyes glinted in the darkness like two bright opals. He put a single clawed finger to his lips, as though shushing me.

"Ah, my lady, their defeat we must leave to your countrymen. Our task is smaller. If we each take half the pack and strive to our utmost, I think we might cause enough confusion to allow you to free your people."

"I take half the pack? How could I tell them what to do?"

"They will know, dear lady, trust me."

"But shouldn't we spy out their camp? Know the placement of their guards?"

"Indeed, indeed," Wolfhead interrupted. "But let us save that work for tomorrow. For now, we must sleep—though I've had enough for many lifetimes."

The man-beast smiled, and it occurred to me that two days ago I would have considered his toothy grin a frightful spectacle. How fast things could change! A week ago I doubt I would have believed such as Wolfhead could even exist, much less that he'd be my ally.

The man-wolf noticed my lingering eyes and sat up.

"If my presence disturbs you, my lady, I could find another room in which to sleep . . ."

"No, no," I spoke up hastily. "I wouldn't hear of it! I was merely thinking about the recent turn of events . . . It is not for me to turn you out . . . even if I so desired."

The Gray One lay gingerly down again. "As you wish, dear lady."

In the morning the man-wolf greeted me with two dusty satchels in his paws. He set them carefully onto the floor and opened one, then he reached in and lifted out an oval stone set into a bracelet. The stone was of the same turquoise-blue as the Old Ones' temple.

"What is this?" I asked.

"A form of protection," the Gray One explained. "Put it on."

I obeyed, and the man-wolf continued: "There are a dozen more such stones within. It is very important that you get your fellow women to wear these as soon as possible. And you must keep them on until you are well away from the outlaws' camp."

I sat silently for a moment, examining the blue stone. A feeling of security seemed to emanate from it, as from the temple.

"From what will they protect us?"

Wolfhead grinned, picking up the second satchel.

"This contains some things of Gwart's," he answered, slipping its strap over his lupine head. "I learned much from him in my youth—enough to prepare a surprise for our adversaries."

"You shall use Old Ones' magic against them?" I ventured.

The man-beast nodded, then he exclaimed, "Oh! There is also this!"

He reached into the first satchel again and pulled out a dagger in a sheath. The pommel of the weapon was wrought, appropriately enough, in the shape of a wolf's head.

"Not always did we fight with tooth and claw," the Gray One explained. "For now, I think you need it more than I."

I thanked him for the blade.

"Now, dear lady," he continued, "I believe we should prepare to depart."

VIII

The sky was so overcast, I could scarcely tell night from day, but this morning the dark clouds were a blessing. We traveled as we had yesterday, I on horseback, the wolves roundabout, and Wolfhead ranging between us. An hour or so before nooning, the Gray One bade me dismount and wait at the base of a rocky hill as he scouted ahead. When he returned, he announced that beyond the hill, in a shallow valley, our enemies lurked. We then climbed the prominence together.

Like the ancient building in which we spent the night, the bandits' hideout seemed to grow out of a cliff face, but there were so many balconies, windows, and turrets that one could imagine an entire cliff-city. Stretched out before it were tents, horses, dogs, crates, and one of the Hounds' metal juggernauts. I knew the bandits by their crude furs, but mixed amongst them were men wearing uniforms and crested helms. The Hounds of Alizon!

"The captives are held in the great tent on the north edge of camp," explained Wolfhead. "So much has Gnarrel sniffed out for me."

"Why would they leave them outside? That cliff-castle seems impregnable to attack."

"Yon structure is not truly held by Shekkar," Wolfhead continued. "Oh, he and his men occupy a few chambers. But that is a stronghold of the Shadow, where Dark Old Ones dwelt in the days of my cubhood, and their malevolent influence still permeates the air. It is too malignant in the deeper recesses even for the likes of Shekkar, but it is so impressive a hold that he will suffer the majority of the space to be held by Darkness. There is simply no room for a dungeon."

"Hmm . . . What about flight?"

The man-beast pointed out the tent-prison in question.

"There are horses brought by the outlanders tied off to the left. The outlanders fear the dark hold and keep their possessions far from it. While they and the outlaws are distracted, you can escape on the Alizon mounts."

We slid back from the hill's crest.

"Not even a hundred wolves would occupy the attention of all those men. And you say half the wolves will be with me?"

The Gray One studied me as one might look upon a backward child.

"The evil men below will be otherwise disposed when you come, my lady. With Gwart's help, that is," he added, patting the satchel around his neck. "Now, I think the time has come to get to our positions."

I fidgeted anxiously amongst the rocks near the Alizon bandit camp, a dozen wolves waiting with me. I was to move in as the animals did, I was not to lead them. The outlaw Shekkar had named me a schemer and a leader, yet I had been deferring to the Gray One's judgment ever since we joined forces. But, I reasoned, these beasts were his soldiers, this was his land, and even the bandits we opposed had been his enemies longer than they'd been mine.

Even if I successfully freed my people, the bandits would certainly give chase, unless Wolfhead's "surprise" took care of the lot of them. But if such Power was at his disposal, why had he not struck such a blow before?

Belita had taught me that each use of Power has its price, on mind, body, and spirit. For lesser manifestations, you merely gave up some stamina—you felt drained, as if you'd been working or marching all day. But legend told of the Power the Old Ones wielded, Power to move mountains or slay armies. Such great magic carried a far greater price . . .

A benevolent Gray One was a freak in the contemporary world. He could not join his own kind, nor could he live in the

Dales, where men feared the slightest departure from the norm. Perhaps he did not fear to pay a great price . . .

Far away I heard angry shouts. Wolfhead's assault had begun. A wavering howl came to me over the pounding of hooves and the sizzle of fire-guns. The wolves shot forth without a sound, and I followed as soon as I could put spur to horse.

Most of the bandits and Hounds were watching the commotion to the south, and some were running or riding to join the fray. Others, however, had enough sense to remain scattered along the camp's northern perimeter—and these were now being harried by my wolves.

I rode hard toward the prison-tent. Since my saddle and reins were of the outlaws' design, I was not immediately marked. I circled behind the tent and dismounted, my dart-gun and wolf-dagger ready as I crept toward the entrance.

I spotted two guards at the flap. One turned as if to speak to the other and spied me. I fired and watched a crimson flower blossom in his throat. His companion dove to the ground within the tent, then his hand reached out, a dart-gun of his own clenched in it. He pulled the trigger blindly, and a wasp-sting of pain burned into my left arm.

I cried out, and the two nearest wolves pricked their ears and disengaged themselves from their opponents. They charged into the tent, and I heard the second guard scream. I followed, pausing only to pick up the first guard's sword, though the pain in my arm pulsed with each step.

"L-Lady Wylona!"

Belita, Varda, and the others stared wide-eyed at me, the wolves, and the dead guards. The animals seemed shy of the attention and loped out the way they'd come.

"No time for talk," I said. I opened the bag at my hip and began hauling out the blue stones Wolfhead had given me.

"Put these on," I commanded. I watched to make sure the prisoners obeyed.

"What are they for?" asked Belita.

"Protection," I answered.

"Indeed," she agreed, "but normally against forces neither Hound nor outlaw wields. Where did you get them?"

"From a friend. Now we must go."

                            *   *   *

I peeked through the tent flap and saw no one, though I still
heard hoofbeats and cries. I crept to the corner of the tent and
spotted the tethered horses, but before we could reach them
the shouts of Hound and outlaw rose into screams of unmistak-
able terror, accompanied by horses' whinnies and dogs' howls. I
peered across the encampment and received my first glimpse of
Wolfhead's "surprise."

Out of a dozen windows and turrets of the cliff-keep there
billowed—smoke? The thickest smoke from a forest fire was
never so black as this. 'Twas like a river of oil flowing out onto the
surface of a lake, swirling, spreading, and polluting everywhere.

"Dear Gunnora," I gasped, "what has he done?"

Belita came up beside me. "Your friend?"

"I fear—yes."

The wise woman frowned. "His cure may well be worse than
the disease!"

A putrid gust of wind from the direction of the cloud hit us. I
held my wristlet up to Belita's face.

"He gave me these. Will they protect us?" I had to shout to
be heard.

"Perhaps," my friend answered. "I do not think it prudent to
test them, however."

Varda and the others had gathered at our backs, watching the
loathsome cloud as we did. I shooed them like chickens toward
the Alizonian horses. The horses snorted and stamped, but as
we untied them, they settled considerably. I can only think the
proximity of the magic stones calmed them.

Men, horses, and the narrow-headed canines of the outlanders fled past us unheeding. I looked out over the shallow valley,
searching for the man-wolf. The inky Darkness blotted out the
light more effectively than the thick clouds above; however, I
could see tiny figures running in its shadow—and, near the entrance of the cliff-keep, one figure upright but unmoving.

I noticed many tools and weapons strewn upon the ground
roundabouts, including a farseeing lens. I picked it up and
trained it on the unmoving object. It was, indeed, the Gray
One, standing stock still, his head thrown back as if howling. In

his paws he carried a small black pot, from which curled a
streamer of red smoke, a streak of blood against the Darkness.

Around Wolfhead lay several men, dead or alive I could not
tell. Also there were pale, indistinct moving things that gathered about the fallen like vultures. In a ditch near the cliff-keep
such a grouping incurred a swath of red beams—someone with
a fire-gun was still alive out there.

The Gray One collapsed, the black pot rolling from his paws.
The ghostly shapes around him crept closer. Even at this distance, I should have been able to see the blue glow of a brace-
let-talisman. I saw none, however.

"The foolish creature!" I exclaimed. "Hasn't he one of the
wristlets?"

"The Dark Powers of that place would have ignored his petition with such a charm nearby," said Belita, again popping up
at my side. "Who is 'he,' anyway?"

I glanced back. My horse had not bolted, but it danced about
nervously. I had three blue stones left in my pouch, besides the
one on my wrist.

"I'll introduce you after I fetch him," I promised, heading for
my mount.

"Are you mad? You cannot go out there!"

"We owe our freedom to him," I said, grabbing the horse's
reins. "I shall not desert him! Besides, he may know how to
stop what he has unleashed. You must ride after the others to
make sure they don't get lost in the Waste!"

I climbed into the saddle, wincing at the pain in my left arm,
and put spur to horse.

IX

There was a purple nimbus coating the tortured earth,
providing a vague illumination in the Darkness. Also did the
strange misty entities flittering about glow of themselves, and
once or twice, from the ditch near the cliff-keep, the red beams
of the fire-gun shot into the sky.

At first the mist-creatures ignored me, to gather still around the
camp's fallen. They did not tear into the bodies like scavengers; I
did not think they were solid enough—yet. There were loathsome

spiderlike things, bounding along with a speed unlikely for their
bloated forms. There were humanoid entities, a ghastly combina-
tion of man, lizard, and praying mantis, with skinny, slick limbs,
reptile heads, and fly eyes. And there were wattled bat-creatures
as well, with bulging eyes like those of a newly hatched chick.

The spider-things were becoming aggressive. I fired a few
darts into them, and they burst like ticks trodden underfoot.
My horse was getting harder to manage, blue stones or no. I'd
have to dismount soon, and I feared the animal would bolt the
moment I did.

Suddenly the beat of galloping hooves drew near. Behind me
I heard Belita's voice.

"Above you!"

I looked up and realized with horror that the Darkness had
thrown out lengths of itself like squid arms casting about for
prey. Belita reined in at my side and sketched something in the
air with her forefinger. For a second a strange symbol burned
above her, the same bluish shade as the magic stones, then the
tentacles of Darkness pulled away like so many fingers singed
by a stove.

"Thank you, Belita," I gasped. Then, "I thought I told you
to go after the others."

"Did you? The wind must have carried your words away,"
she lied. "But as long as I am here, perhaps I can be of service."

She drew another symbol, aimed, it appeared, at my horse's
head. The lathering animal calmed, as did the wise woman's
own. We rode the last few yards to Wolfhead's prone form and
dismounted.

"Great Gunnora!" exclaimed Belita. "This is a Gray One!"

"In form only, Belita!" I cried, kneeling at the man-beast's
side. "He is a creature of Light, not Dark!"

"Yet, he caused this!" she accused, spreading her arms wide.

The Darkness had replaced the sky, and its tentacles lapped
at the rim of the valley. The earth glowed with the sickly light
of fungi, and the disgusting Shadow creatures capered but a few
yards away. The wind howled over us, filled with a stomach-
turning stench of decay.

"Perhaps he can also put an end to it!" I yelled. I slipped one of the bracelets over Wolfhead's wrist and pulled him to a sitting position. He refused to stir.

I turned to Belita. "He won't wake up!"

Belita reached into a pouch at her waist and pulled out a bone vial. She shook a pile of crystals into her hand and cupped it to Wolfhead's snout. The Gray One snorted, winced, and opened his turquoise eyes.

"My lady!" he gasped. "You shouldn't have come!"

"I do not forsake my comrades," I answered him. "Now, come, before the Darkness claims us all!"

"I cannot," the man-beast cried.

"Are you mad, wolfling?" I asked, glancing up. The palpable Shadow seemed to press massively closer. I could swear a great whirlpool was forming directly above, a maelstrom in the sky.

"Not mad," sighed Wolfhead. "The evil in yon place demands its due for the routing of the outlanders and the bandits. It shan't retreat until paid."

"And that payment is—?" demanded Belita.

"Me," said the man-wolf.

I was stunned for a moment, though I'd half suspected he might try such a thing. The Gray One rolled weakly onto all fours.

"The bowl . . . Where is the bowl?"

From a depression nearby a trickle of red smoke emerged, to be whipped away by the wind. Wolfhead crawled slowly toward it. Meanwhile, a new volley of crimson beams shot out of the ditch near the cliff-keep. The Shadow creatures fled from the assault, now making audible squeals.

Suddenly Belita leaped past the man-beast and squatted by the trickle of smoke.

"Hold you place, Gray One! Wylona—come here!"

Her voice carried such authority that we both obeyed. I squatted beside her and stared at the black pot I'd seen earlier in Wolfhead's paws.

"Don't touch it with your bare flesh," she warned. She tore loose part of her tattered skirt and used it as a pot holder.

"Ah! Look at the effigy within! It gives me an idea to save this strange friend of yours."

I peered into the pot. The red smoke had finally dissipated; I could not identify its source, for within there was only a crude, unscorched doll, wrapped with wolf fur.

"What is this?" I asked.

"The Gray One's representation of himself," Belita replied. "A focus for the Dark Powers. He is not much of an artist, and this very fact may save him."

"How so?" I asked, looking up. It was not my imagination. There was a maelstrom in the Darkness, and the ceiling of its hateful substance was itself descending toward us.

Belita tilted the pot toward me. "Who does this remind you of?"

"Wolfhead—the Gray One, of course."

"Who else?"

Who else? There was no one else one could mistake for a Gray One. But—this was not Wolfhead, it was a very crude doll clothed in wolf skin . . .

I gasped, finally catching the wise woman's meaning.

"You understand," she said. "Good. The Darkness does not see and hear as you or I. It has only such tools as these to focus on our world. And the tools of magic tend to be somewhat symbolic. There is one other that this effigy might represent . . ."

We both glanced at the ditch, where another red streak split the Shadow.

"The Hounds fear all Powers, Dark, Light, or Gray," Belita continued. "They kept themselves, and their fire-guns, as far from the dark keep as possible. There was only one other, to my knowledge, who possessed such a weapon . . ."

"All he must do is touch it?" I queried.

"Yes. For one so resembling the effigy, it would not even have to meet his bare skin. Touching it to his clothing would suffice."

I grinned wickedly. "I shall fetch my horse. You'll have to hand the pot up to me."

"Wylona—your arm—"

"Belita," I hissed. Our eyes locked for a moment.

"Very well, my liege," she finally said.

Belita drew her horse-calming symbol once more over my mount, but the beast's muscles still quivered beneath me. The wise woman handed up the black pot, wrapped in her torn skirt, and I cradled it before me. Wolfhead watched us with horror.

"My lady—what do you intend?"

"I'm saving your shaggy hide," I called. Then I was off.

I galloped past overturned carts, sagging tents, and flapping banners. The Darkness was like a ceiling only a few rods away. Once more did a fire-beam shoot upward; I only hoped that the bandit leader would be too preoccupied to notice me.

I drew up to the lip of the ditch; there crouched Shekkar beneath an overhang, the bodies of several Shadow creatures nearby, looking semisubstantial again in death.

I prepared to hurl the pot at him, but he spotted me and fired the red beam. My horse was stricken, collapsing with a death-scream; I fell into the ditch, losing my grip on the pot. I barely avoided being crushed by the pitiful beast, but that didn't worry me. The pot!

It bowled along the rocky earth like a ball in a yard sport. The bandit leader saw it and kicked it aside.

My head throbbed as if struck with a bludgeon. I sensed—an opening, as of a door or window, like I had in the temple when my dinner appeared from nowhere. I looked up, and now I could peer down the very throat of the Shadow-maelstrom.

Shekkar had advanced with his fire-gun, perhaps to finish me, but now he stared upward, too. Of a sudden the wind changed direction, with such violence that he was knocked down.

The wind! By the dust it carried I could mark its movement. It came from every direction into this ditch—then up!

Shekkar cried out. I watched him rise from the ground like a leaf caught by a dust-devil. He flew ever upward, struggling and screaming, into the throat of the maelstrom. Then the world-turned-nightmare faded from my sight.

X

I spluttered and waved my arms, the sting of smelling salts sharp in my nose.

"Milady?"

The lupine form crouching over me was a welcome sight. I reached up and tousled the fur of his neck as I might a child's hair. The blue sky beyond Wolfhead was a vision even more welcome.

"The Darkness is gone," I observed.

"As are the outlanders and the bandits," said Belita.

"And I am still here," said Wolfhead. "That you did this still amazes me. I am indebted to you both."

"No more than we are to you, Wolfhead," I denied.

The Gray One's ears perked. "Wolfhead?"

I flushed. "I'm sorry. I had to give some sort of name to you. And Wolfhead had—popped up in the conversation."

The man-wolf grinned. "It is not undescriptive. But I do have a name, my lady, unused a thousand years. I am Amarrok."

"Then let me say at last that my name is Wylona," I returned. "And this is Belita, my dear friend and adviser."

"Yes," said the Gray One. "Your woman of Power. We introduced ourselves while you were out."

I rode upon Belita's horse, while she and the Gray One led it and discussed the days of the Old Ones. I was content to watch the landscape.

Bodies were still scattered about, of men, horses, dogs, and also of the Shadow creatures. The latter melted like cheese in the sunlight. I saw the prison-tent and the abandoned juggernaut, yet this land seemed like a different world compared to its own self of just a few hours before.

From far off came a timid wolf howl. We stopped, and Amarrok answered. Three furry shapes limped toward us from the rocky hills—the only survivors of the Gray One's pack.

"My brothers," Amarrok sighed. "I have used them for my own purposes as much as any Dark Old One."

The wolves greeted him in a friendly fashion nonetheless, and he dropped to all fours for a minute, speaking in a language of growls and yips.

"They have received Akria's call from the south," he explained, rising again onto two feet. "Evidently her mission was a success. Your male survivors did reach a place of safety."

Amarrok stared down at the ground for a moment before

speaking again. "I fear, dear Wylona, that I must take my leave as soon as Akria comes."

"Why?"

"To tell you the truth, lady, I had not expected to live out the day. And however much I'd like, I can hardly return with you to the Dales."

He did have a point. I couldn't imagine the Gray One and the court ladies sitting down to sup at the same table.

"But your wise woman has given me a spark of hope."

I raised an eyebrow as I turned to Belita. She explained.

"It is rumored that there lies a land to the north of the Waste, called Arvon, where Old Ones live in peace, protected by illusions from modern men. It is only a legend, even amongst wise women, but Amarrok has heard of it."

"The territory to the north was known as Arvon in my day," the Gray One said. "That the name has survived, even in legend, gives me hope that this rumor is true. The search will, at least, give me something to do."

We traveled on at a walking pace. When we crested the hills surrounding the shallow valley, a score of furry forms appeared out of the rocky terrain. The three wolves with us hobbled out to greet them, and then Amarrok spoke to them in his lupine language. When he rose again to face us, I knew this tokened a farewell. I dismounted slowly and took Amarrok's paws in my hands.

"L-Lady—Wylona—" the Gray One stuttered. "I must away."

"Will we ever see you again?"

"Perhaps. There is only the Waste between Arvon and Ellsdale, and it is not quite so terrible a barrier as it once was."

I hugged the furry man-wolf and kissed him on the muzzle. Belita embraced him as well, then he and his renewed pack bounded away into the Waste.

The women's campfire drew us like a beacon. We quashed their many questions until we organized them for traveling, and even then we were uncommunicative.

It was a long and tasking trek from Dragonsback to Ronansdale, but we survived. At the very border of the Dale

we were met by a party of men, amongst whom rode Captain
Kegan. It seemed that Kegan and the others had brought Lord
Ghislain of Ronanskeep word of the metal Alizon monsters,
and the old warrior had implored that men be sent in rescue for
the women of Ellsdale. I was glad to see the guard captain safe,
but I could barely suppress my laughter as he told me of the
terrible wolf pack that hounded his men for days.

I met with Lord Ghislain and offered whatever help my tattered band of followers might give. A lesser ruler would have
thought us no better than another group of refugees come to
leech off his generosity, but not the master of Ronanskeep. We
were welcomed into his halls like favored members of his court,
and we settled in gratefully, swearing to toil like the lowest
menials while we imposed.

Of what took place thereafter, better tale-tellers than I have
already written. The supply lines of the juggernauts had been
severed by the coming of the Darkness; the northern Dale
forces had only to keep them from reopening. As they did in
the south, the metal monsters ground to a halt, and they sit
there still, rusted trophies of war, on the border of Ronansdale
and Ellsdale.

The reclamation of our fair land has been a long and tedious
process, but a new keep rises from the ruins of the old, and
above it banners flutter, with the seal of Ellskeep proudly dis-
played.

In the days to come, though, perhaps Ellsdale and
Ronansdale will join as a single land. Ghislain of Ronanskeep
has visited me several times now; he is a brave and handsome
man, but more importantly, he is unafraid of the new or
strange, and he does not find it odd that I've decreed the hunting of wolves for sport to be a punishable offense. Sometimes
he even rides with me to the edge of the Waste, and we two
listen to wolf howls in the night, as though expecting a lupine
voice to call out a human greeting.

Afterword

This story grew out of my interest in wolves, werewolves, and things like them. Many years ago, I came across the use of the term "wolfhead" or "wolfshead" as a synonym for an outlaw. I don't remember where, but I suspect it was in an Andre Norton story. I stored this information away, and as I read the Witch World novels, I was disheartened to find that the most lupine of this world's intelligent creatures—the Gray Ones—were solidly in the camp of Shadow. But, I reasoned, perhaps it was not always so . . .

When the opportunity presented itself to write a Witch World story, I wrote a few paragraphs about a lone rider in a lonely land encountering a somewhat irritated but by no means evil Gray One. Then the double-edged possibility of the word "wolfhead" came to mind, so I thought of a band of human "wolfheads" opposing a creature that could use the name literally. From these fragments an eighty-page story developed that I had to chop to half its size to meet the word limit of the book. Ouch!

I was never good at endings, however; I wonder how Amarrok would fare in Arvon, how well Belita is doing in her craft, and even if Wylona's father Torak is really dead. Someday I may have to write further about them, whether there are more Witch World anthologies or not.

—Michael D. Winkle

WERE-FLIGHT

by

Lisa Woodworth

I

Khemrys

Many times have I heard how my mother rode into the small abbey at Rhystead with a babe at her back, and a dying warrior across her saddlebow. They tell me that he bore the scars of many battles and that there were many fresh grievous wounds. But of this my mother never spoke. Also, Dame Rimia, who had helped her care for him, talked of his appearance and garb, saying it was unlike that of men she had seen. Some of the Dames thought he was from the south, of which we know very little. On that day, a part of my mother died. The remaining years granted her were spent as though she were always listening for a call that never came.

She was Lady Tirath, daughter of a house fallen to the invaders we call the Hounds of Alizon. When their strange machines of war destroyed her family's holding, she escaped turning north to join some kin. Once, as though speaking to herself, she told of how she met my father, Herwyd, in the fens. She was sick nearly unto death from a fever, and he had cared for her as tenderly as he would his own blood. That year they exchanged vows and rode the far Dales, seeking news of her kin and of the fighting brothers from which he had become separated. In time, I was born, and shortly thereafter had come the battle from which they fled to Rhystead. This was the closest I ever came to hearing of my father. She never mentioned this part of her life again.

Most of the Dames were beyond middle years, and they made much of me, undertaking my upbringing with great zeal, fussing over mother and me. She would smile faintly and read to me many of our old tales, which was quite a relief to one as inundated with stories of the Cup and Flame as I. I remember that she always smelled of roses.

At times I walked with Dame Rimia, the stillmistress, and learned the uses of herbs and their lore. Others I spent with one or another of the Dames, learning to figure accounts, to embroider and to mend, to read, to cook and too ofttimes to pray. Our little abbey had so few visitors and was so far from any keep or village I wondered how it had ever come to be.

So fiercely had my mother ridden into the abbey's life, and so quietly she faded out of it. When I had been there eleven summers, she left this life. She had been too ill to rise from her cot, and the community and I had despaired of any change. One day, however, she rose at dawn and dressed herself as though awaiting a bridal. She bedecked both herself and our rooms with flowers, and from deep in the recesses of a chest brought out fine jewels—jewels she had never worn in all our lives at the abbey. They were most unusual in design, being made of amber and deep golden moonstones, shaped like fantastic beasts. I was entranced. Why was she wearing them now?

After breaking fast, I returned with her to our rooms. For the first time in my life, she looked at me with her full attention, as though she were truly seeing me. With one careworn hand, she smoothed back an unruly lock of my dark hair where it fell over the peak at my forehead. The gesture seemed so natural and familiar. I hoped she was at last on the mend, and that things would be different between us now. I sat on a small stool near her feet, and she settled as though waiting. Perchance she had heard of visitors arriving, although I had seen no sign of any messenger.

At last the silence was broken. "Khemrys, I will not be here tonight. All that I have will be found in the chest under the eastern window."

I was familiar with it, and I looked up expectantly. Was our kin coming at last?

The ruddy fire crackled and popped as Tirath spoke again. "I have not been much of a mother to you, and I cannot remedy that. Mayhap you will think kindly of me now and then. You are growing much like your father in looks, and I think that the day will come when you may want to leave the abbey and seek his people. All that we can leave you, daughter, is in the scroll you will find near the bottom of the chest."

She paused, and I waited in dismay. Was she leaving me to seek for herself? Why did she speak as if she were not coming back?

As if in answer to my unspoken question, she sighed and went on.

"I wish that I could tell you more, but it is not permitted me. I *can* tell you that your father and I loved you very much indeed. I remember well his joy the night that you were born. I had been afraid that he would be disappointed that you were not a son to bear the sword. He laughed aloud and praised the Goddess for you. I saw him digging through his gear pack, and when he came back to the fireside, he was bearing these jewels I now wear. A few scant months later he was taken from me— from us, I should say. I hope you will find the happiness that once I knew."

This was the longest speech I had ever had of her, and also the last. She rose and walked nearer the window. Afraid suddenly, I moved closer to her. She looked at me and seemed to be about to speak again, then her gaze rose above my shoulder. Her eyes widened in gladness and recognition. "Herwyd!" Her voice pealed like a bell. "I've been waiting!" Turning, I hoped to find a visitor, but there was no one to be seen. All at once I felt odd and chilled, and looking back to where my mother stood, I saw her crumple to the floor with a sigh. Her face was younger and more beautiful than ever I had seen it, and it wore a look of joyous greeting. I called for Dame Rimia, but by the time she could reach us, Mother was beyond her help, leaving me conscious of a loss of something wonderful. I feel certain that she had some foreknowledge, and that my father did come to her.

For the next three years at Rhystead I became more of a favorite than ever. There were no other girls, and the ladies were all growing older. I did not wish to pledge myself to Cup and Flame, and so I stayed as a sort of boarder. My life was a pleasant one in this quiet backwater, and I rather enjoyed being petted and spoiled.

Mother's chest had held the familiar articles of clothing and linens, but at the bottom I found a badly nicked and dented sword. It was polished to a silvery gleam and wrapped in a cloak that had been much rent and most carefully mended. I knew at once these must be things belonging to my father.

The sword had a most curiously wrought hilt and quillions, being a leopard's head with jeweled green eyes for the pommel and two incurling tails for the latter, most life-like. Even the cunning eyes seemed almost to wink at me.

However, the rune scroll was rather a disappointment, as it was no more than that collection of the bardic tales from which she had read to me as a child. Nowadays I fancied myself quite a woman grown, too old for stories of moss wives, shape-changers, dragons, and the like. I kept it close though and showed no one, not even Dame Rimia, of whom I was exceedingly fond.

Near the end of the Year of the Sphinx, the abbess, who was very old, passed to Flame. We all rather expected that Dame Rimia would take her place, but word came one day from the outside that we were being sent a new abbess. I was disappointed that my old friend had not been selected, but I was excited, too, over the thought of a new face and stories of outside life. Little did I think that my world would change so drastically.

The new abbess was Rosera, and it was rumored that she was the daughter of a very wealthy and powerful family in the south. I wondered if perhaps she knew of my mother's kin, or mayhap of my father's. I had accepted the consensus that he was likely from the south as well. We here in the far north had very little idea of what peoples from other places were like. There was an air of gentle urgency as we cleaned and hung the walls with banners bearing the bright emblems of Cup and Flame. These last Dame Katreen had spent many hours on, and the appliqué work was beautifully done. We cut fresh reeds to dry for the floors, and each of us vied with the others producing some dainty thing to please our new abbess.

Dame Seralda came forth one day with a tiny but exquisite carpet that she had brought with her to Rhystead over seventy years ago. It was a prized possession, although admittedly it had seen better days. We placed it next to the Mother Abbess's bed as a crowning touch.

Late one eve, a messenger came bearing tidings of Rosera's arrival on the morrow. Each of us thought of a number of things that must be done before morn, and our abbey fairly buzzed with activity. I had planned an early expedition to gather sweet-smelling herbs to strew underfoot, so I retired rather earlier than was my wont.

Shortly before dawn, I dressed and went forth, hoping to be back long before breakfast. The Dames did not think our new-comer could possibly arrive before second devotions were done, so I felt quite safe. There was a heavy dew, and I was soon wet through both my kirtle and my underskirt. I worked as quickly as I could, and also I found some lovely dog-roses to brighten the rooms. I saw by the sun that it was now more than two hours past First Flame, and gathering up my skirts, I ran back with my baskets to Rhystead.

Once home, I set my herbs inside the outer door to the still-room, and I had just taken off my muddy shoes when there came the sound of many horses. The abbey emptied, as all were anxious to meet Rosera, and in the excitement I completely forgot what a sight I made in my filthy working garb. As the party came through the large double gates, I was amazed to see at least three times the number of persons we were led to expect.

Besides the usual outriders and escort, there were two or three dozen ladies, most of whom were dressed in the dull colors of the Dames. Some also wore the garments of servants, but there were three among them who were most brilliantly arrayed. These were young girls of noble kin who were being fostered among us until such a time as their families could arrange suitable marriages for them. All were mounted on most splendid horses, the like of which I had never seen.

As they drew rein in the courtyard, various of the Dames went forward to catch the bridles of these fine steeds, I among them. Dame Rimia, as highest ranking, carried the guesting cup. As I approached the horses, they began to shy and to sweat nervously. I thought perhaps they knew I was unaccustomed to such as they. Steeling myself, I grasped the bridle of the young rider closest to me. Her palfrey began to neigh shrilly with eyes starting and ears laid back. It was all the girl could do to keep her seat.

Attention was most suddenly focused directly on me, and all at once I became aware of my state of dress. Frightened and embarrassed, I tried to edge away, but my path was blocked by a stately woman wearing the emblem of the Sacred Cup.

A voice rang out, "Who *is* this wretched urchin and where does she belong?"

"I am Khemrys, an orphan fostered with the Dames," I answered meekly. I hated to incur displeasure right at the start.

A reassuring arm was laid about my shoulders as Dame Rimia's voice broke the disapproving silence. "It was the wish of her mother that Khemrys be fostered here until such time as she is old enough to have a marriage made or to take upon herself the vows of Cup and Flame."

"Who are you who speaks for her?" queried Abbess Rosera.

"I am Stillmistress Rimia. Your Reverence," came the soft reply. I could see the lady immediately recognized the name and was marking dear Rimia as an upstart and would-be abbess. Since no house-name had been mentioned for me, I was probably to be labeled as well.

"See that you keep her away from the horses. One can tell that such as she is unfit to deal with fine blood-stock. And for Flame's sake, can you not clean her up a bit?" I could see already that I was not to enjoy my former state under the rule of this new abbess.

The girls to be fostered at Rhystead along with myself were new to Rosera as well. Alois was a typical Dales beauty, with her hair bright as corn and sea-blue eyes. She came from a coastal family that had doubled its holdings after the defeat of those same Hounds of Alizon who had cost my mother's kin their lives.

Serilla was the second, with hair of a less bright hue and dark eyes that I thought held a rather sly gleam. That first night at sup, she managed to "accidentally" spill her broth across the front breadth of my best dress. I believed it no accident and resolved to watch her most closely.

The third was Lysande, who said very little to anyone. She was dressed as finely as the rest, but to my eye less ostentatiously. Seeing my dismay over the mess made on my only really good gown, she leaned across and whispered that she had another that she would be most glad to give me, as it was in a color not particularly to her liking. I barely had time to murmur hasty thanks before one of the new Dames was shushing us.

After dinner, she caught up with me. "I do not wish you to think that I would try to foist upon you an unbecoming gown, but the fact is, I have never thought it suited well my coloring. If you would come with me, I will show it to you, and you may decide if it will do." I thanked her and followed along to her chamber.

The gown was lovely. It was a deep rust, cut in a fashion I had never seen before. It had a wider and deeper neck than those I had previously worn, and it was fitted closer to the body as well. The over-gown was a rich brown, and both neck and sleeve were bordered with gems and embroidery. I had never viewed anything half so fine. For a moment I feared Lysande was only teasing me and had some other thing in mind as a gift, but she seemed to sense this, and she assured me that she had many others equally as nice and many more that were grander still.

Showing me these, I had to agree. I believe that Lysande had more clothing than the Dames and I combined. And the shoes and belts! Each dress was complete with its own accessories.

Lysande was nearly as dark of hair as myself, being a very

deep brown. Her eyes a deeper blue showed against skin as fair
as mine was brown.

I had never thought much of my own black hair. While my
own green eyes with their tiny golden flecks brought to mind a
cat's, I never had that perfection of coloring as the new girls
showed. This matter was a thing to trouble me.

Our talk was broken by the bells rung for lights out, and I
hurried to my room. Only arriving there, I found my belongings
being spilled into the hall in an untidy heap. It appeared that by
the new order, I was to move to a different room, nearer the
herbarium. This had always been used as a drying room for
certain herbs. It made only a cramped bedchamber. Sighing, I
attempted to tidy my belongings as best I could.

We continued to discover that there were to be a great many
changes for the abbey. The first afternoon, Dame Seralda's precious carpet was found on the rubbish heap, where it had been
flung after the Mother Abbess's own new carpet had been
spread. With a cry, one of the older Dames gathered it up and
shook it off. We told Seralda a polite fiction, and she seemed to
believe it.

The next large change was in the way that the home farm
itself was to be run. New plowing horses were purchased, while
the old ox that had formerly done such labor was slaughtered.
The fowlyard was completely changed to house fine new hens.
For the first time, we had swine to keep as well. Our sheep
were pronounced to have too coarse wool, and were sold to
make way for another breed. And the small vegetable garden
was plowed up to nearly five times its former size. Even new
barns were raised.

The Dames of Rhystead assumed that the new Abbess had a
long purse. But soon it became apparent that this was not the
case. We heard rumors that Rosera had been sending missives
begging monies to both the new keeps and the villages springing up in the area. Also, from time to time small personal items
would be found missing—these presumably being sold for
whatever they would bring. The second time this occurred, I
took the sword, jewelry, and other things my mother had left to
me and fashioned a case for them from oiled skins. I am
ashamed to say that I stole these from the stores room, but I

could see at the time no other alternative. This I buried a little way outside the gates in a grove where Lysande and I were wont to retreat in our meager leisure time.

Her Reverence was a great organizer. She had a chore for every waking moment and made no resting allowance for even the stock. Lysande, Alois, and Serilla were exempt from these, as was herself, but none of the others were, and most particularly not me. As the older Dames who had been in residence at the time of her arrival in due time passed to Flame, Rosera replaced them with ones who had been under her rule at Ulmstead. Thus, it seemed as time went on that I had fewer and fewer friends.

Serilla took great delight in reporting every slightest mistake or happening to Her Reverence, being one of a disposition to thrive on others' misfortunes. Alois was not as cruel, but rather stupid, as if a trait had been sacrificed to make that pink and gold outer perfection. Lysande was kept away from me by dint of service in the sewing room, for she could fashion the most intricate broideries and was much in demand for such by ladies of the neighboring keeps.

After the war's end, when the invaders had been pushed back to the sea, there were many empty keeps, also many men with an eye to becoming powers in their own rights. The south was broken and its rich lands needed much reclamation, but here at Rhysdale there was much land that had never been worked by men. Also, Mother Rosera was making Rhystead over in the image of those great abbeys of the south, and we were in a fair way to becoming a power to be reckoned with in the north.

Our lady was never satisfied with our efforts, however. She complained constantly that things were not at all what they had been in Ulmstead or Norstead, and many of the Dames could be found after twilight devotions in Dame Rimia's chamber. Rimia never did aught than let the discontent have an ear in which to speak. She was a gentle soul and spent much of her time trying to soothe the ruffled feathers.

One morning, though, when Dame Katreen went to rouse her for dawn contemplation, Rimia did not answer her tap. Entering her room, she found that this good woman had passed to

Flame sometime during the night. As Rimia was in apparently good health the previous evening, I secretly feared that Rosera had found some way to make an end of her. But there was no proof of such.

My sixteenth name-day passed unnoticed by any save Lysande, who had fashioned in secret a lovely kirtle of amber shade. This I found on my cot when I went to change before our twilight devotions. I had been feeling miserable, for Her Reverence was bringing a good deal of pressure to bear on me. She wanted me to swear to Cup and Flame or else leave Rhystead altogether. I was now old enough to marry if I would, but no kin had stepped forward to make a marriage. Life permanently under Rosera was unthinkable, and my lot would likely be as hard if I married one of the village boys. Also, I had no liking for such a joining with one whom my heart had not chosen.

However, at sight of the amber gown, my spirits lifted, and I decided to wear it for the remainder of the evening. I knew it must be Lysande's work, for who else could ply a needle with such skill? And who else would do as much for me?

I was nearly late for service, so I slipped in the back and seated myself out of sight in one of the alcoves kept for visitors. Midway through devotions, I became aware of voices from the seats to my far right. Annoyed, I tried to shut them out, but they persisted. When I heard my name spoken, I unabashedly strained to listen.

"Rosera thinks she is bastard get." That was Serilla. "All that is really known is that her mother rode in with some nearly dead man. For all we can guess, the woman may have picked up some wounded man-at-arms to lend credence to the story she had gotten up. And who can know whether she was nobly born herself? From what I have heard, the Dames merely took the woman's own word for that. And did you see the garb she was decked out in tonight?"

My face burned hotly in the blanketing dimness. How I wished it were possible to make her pay dearly for those words! I heard Alois voice in turn her opinion that my name was most likely stolen, and I could bear it no longer. Rising silently, I edged back to the rear door and slipped out.

Anger moved me until I was in the open. Twilight here soothed my raw soul. Even knowing that I would pay later for having left services, I felt no guilt at seeking the twilight. *As well hang for a sheep as a lamb,* I thought.

The moon was nearing full that night. As I slipped through the grass, I could see each blade. The leaves' rustle and the insects' sounds nearly deafened me. My legs felt heavy as well, and I wondered if I had begun to ail as I hurried to my beloved grove.

Once there, I sought my favorite seat. The air, so mild earlier, felt chill to me. Perhaps it had not been wise to come away like this. I must have dozed, for I suddenly felt stifled by the weight of that same dress that had been too light such a scant while before. I pulled it off awkwardly.

All at once, the world about me shifted, and when it tilted back again it was not in the same place it had been before. I struggled to rise, but my legs would not serve me. Then I caught sight of my hand, and hand it was no longer.

A pard's paw was there in its place! I tried to scream with fright, but my voice came out as a yowl. Not knowing what I was doing, I ran, feeling a cat's lean muscles ripple beneath my skin, a pard's long, loping strides.

I do not know where I went that night nor what I did, save that I awoke naked an shivering with chill shortly before daybreak. I did not want to think about it. I dressed hurriedly and crept in through the small door leading to the herbarium. Lying in my bed, I tried to recall all that I had ever heard of shapechangers, and I felt I must be cursed. So I resolved to stay indoors the following nights, thinking that if the full moon's rays did not fall upon me I would somehow be safe.

However, this was not to be. For two following nights when I retired to my room after twilight prayers, I assumed pard form. So changed I would leap out the narrow window into the courtyard, from there to the outer world. Each night I returned before dawn, as it was much simpler to reenter armed with a cat's senses and stealth. As the change came quicker and easier, I enjoyed the freedom it gave me.

On the fourth night, I made the excuse of needing to harvest moon-flowers to allow me to legitimately leave the abbey pre-

cincts and stay out until sunrise. Moon-flowers can be picked
only beneath a full moon. Once this one waned, there would be
no other freedom for another month. Mother Rosera was for
once in complete agreement with me, as she liked a tea made
from these blossoms before sleeping, claiming it soothed her
nerves. I knew I could gather quite a few before shape-shifting,
and I had in mind to try a little experiment of my own. I
thought to consciously will myself back into woman-form, and I
wanted to make sure that there could be no witnesses.

I nearly had my basket full when I became aware that I was
not alone. I sensed the change-time and hurried off into the
grove fairly flying toward a bright patch containing the moon-
flowers needed to make my harvest complete. They were there
but also stones set out in a pattern vaguely and irritatingly familiar. I felt somehow that I should know it, but those voices
sounding closer drove such thoughts from my mind. Serilla and
Alois, who was never far behind her, were ahead of me.

"I think she ran this way," Serilla said. "Doubtless she is
meeting a man. The last two nights when I checked her room,
the bed was empty. That is why Her Reverence gave me permission to follow her tonight."

So! It was no wonder the abbess had been so agreeable earlier! More than ever I must keep control tonight. Now I shivered, thinking how narrowly I must have escaped detection.

"I cannot understand why any man would want to lie with
her—she is as thin as Dame Camelda's washboard, and not
nearly so attractive." Alois's faintly whining voice made answer.

Moon rays shone directly overhead. Those stones about were
returning an answering bluish green glow. I crouched lower
than ever among the flowers. To my horror, I could feel the
excitement that heralded the beginning of my transformation.

Trembling with fear of being discovered, I fought for control.
A wild rhythm sang through my blood, and the very stones'
light pulsed to match the beat of my heart. I sensed somehow
that those could help if I only knew the key.

At any time now I would make the Change. Trembling with
the effort, I felt I had done no work harder in all my life than
hold control.

Just then, Serilla spied me hiding among the plants and pulled me to my feet with cries of triumph. Where was the man I had come to meet? All protests were in vain. I shook off their hold and paid little mind to such accusation. It was far more important to keep Khemrys-shape.

Serilla's voice was tight with anger. "What more could be expected from slut's get?" as she slapped me across the face.

I felt her rings tear my cheek and lip. White-hot rage rushed through me in waves. I lost my hard-held control. Before their horrified gaze, I changed. The beast-madness in me wanted to rip Serilla's throat out, so end her taunting forever. I snarled. Only fearing if I gave into my rage I might be forever trapped in pard-form, I struggled against beast anger.

Alois lifted a rock crumbled from one of the standing stones. She flung it to catch me behind the ear. I was dazed for a moment.

Serilla caught up my discarded gown as they fled. All the Dark fears might be at their heels. My long pard legs carried me to the hills and safety. There could be no going back after this night.

The sky began to lighten once I was high above the village. I lay down to await my transformation back to Khemrys-shape. Only that expected Change did not come. As the day dragged on, I went a little mad at the realization that I was trapped in pard-flesh. For several days I wandered hungry and thirsty, before I gave in to the beast nature. Catching a small reptile I gulped it down. The animal must remain uppermost for my survival.

Nightly I fought to will myself woman, nightly I failed. The place of the Old Ones must have held a power to thus imprison me.

About many of the ancient places of another race there is a feeling of either good or ill. The stones I had come upon that night had not threatened, so I could not understand why I was unable to assume my true form. Perhaps the Old Ones do not like us to tamper with their secrets.

Several months passed and I was drawn to Rhystead, the only home I knew. Most importantly I wanted to see if returning to the stones would at last bring about the Change.

During the day I skulked on the outskirts of the village, wanting no sharp-nosed hound to sniff me out. Near dusk, I crept beneath the open windows on my way through the streets, listening to the talk of those within.

My lips stretched back in the semblance of a smile as I heard the tale of my shift into many forms, finally settling on the guise I now wore. Though I hissed when they spoke of Serilla's bravery in the face of my savage attack. It was accepted that I had been warded off by sight of an amulet of Gunnora, or one of the talismans the Dames had blessed, though none agreed as to which. Most folk were of the opinion I had gone to join the Dark Ones, though a few suggested I had crept off to die of wounds. All had seen Lysande's beautiful gown with the telltale hairs on the inside—that had been ceremoniously burnt in the Cleansing Flame by none other than Abbess Rosera herself. I was saddened by this, thinking of the long hours spent in its making. Why punish the garment for the sins of the wearer?

At last the darkness was complete. I made haste to the standing stones. As the moon was waxing near to full, I hoped for success. I felt unhappy knowing there would be no means of contacting Lysande even in my true form. Had she turned against me also?

So it was with great surprise that I discovered her seated on one of the fallen stones, apparently awaiting me. I drew back, fearing a trap, but scented no one else. As though she were aware of my presence, she rose and called me by name.

Hesitantly, I came forward. She shrank back a step, then she moved toward me, calling in a low voice: "Khemrys?"

I rolled onto my back in the grass and summoned forth a rather rusty purr. My action brought her to gingerly stroke my fur.

Lysande spoke. "Khemrys, there be powers and powers, as all know. I felt a call tonight to come here, and I could not escape that. Only I did not expect to find you still a beast, and so brought clothing, which will be of little use. But also, I brought food, which perchance will."

I rubbed my head hard against her hand, as a kitten will in a playful mood. She looked at me with surprise.

"Can it be you understand? If so, rub your head against my

hand once more." Could it be that Lysande, all, thought me no more than a beast now?

I did as she asked, rubbing against her cheek also for good measure. Lysande smiled.

"Sister, you must leave this place at once. Go into the Waste and hide. For I have heard talk of a man sent to track you. They mean him to slay you, if you are taken, as one possessed of the Dark Old Ones. I will find means of sending word to you if it is ever safe for you to return."

I growled. How could I ever evade such a hunt?

Lysande guided me to where she had concealed the food. Bits of fowl and bread I devoured with great relish, and I wished that I could take away with me the hard journeycake she had so thoughtfully provided. It was thick with dried meats and fruits, to sustain life for quite some time. After this hour I must be vigilant always. Would there never be rest for me? I had not regained my Khemrys-self!

II

Harlyn

The late afternoon sun slanting through my visor near-blinded me. I had no relish for another night's wilderness camp. Summer had crept by at a snail's pace while I was eager to see home once more.

Some distance ahead stood a fine keep nestled in the rolling hills of Rhysdale. Surely its lord would welcome a weary traveler. Thinking longingly of a soft bed and food not half charred, I urged Keldar on. Perchance visions of a stall and rich grains to fill his belly drew him as well.

We had ridden far these last years, Keldar and I. From the Waste south even unto Trevamper, site of the Great Fair of the Dales, we had journeyed for days at a time without seeing another human face. I had a great curiosity to visit other places

and peoples. For a space I sold my sword to one lord or another, fighting men being much in demand in these troubled
times.

At the gates, receiving the customary challenge, I raised my
shield for the warden to see the device emblazoned there. "I
am called Harlyn, and I wish lodging for the night. I serve no
house, and I swear to bring no ill to those within."

This seemed to satisfy him, and he bade me enter. I removed
my helm, tucking it beneath one mail-clad arm as we advanced
into the shelter of the bailey. Men came to bring me the guesting cup, and I gratefully drank the bracing mixture of hot wine
and spices before I dismounted, leading my horse to the stables. The grooms stood willing to see to him. However, knowing the stallion would suffer no other's touch, I dismissed them,
saying that I would attend to all that was needful.

Here the great hall was impressive. The tables had been already set up. Upon these, torches burned with a clear and
steady light. Those making ready the meal were cheerful and
well clothed. About all was an air of peace and plenty.

A plump, motherly woman showed me guest quarters and
offered me the use of a bath. This last appealed to me, as I
feared I greatly needed one.

Leisurely, I soaked away the grime of long travel. Hard soap
was an unexpected luxury, while hot water eased my knotted
muscles and soothed the places where the byrnie had rubbed.
Hearing the bell sound for the evening meal, I made haste to
dry and dress myself. I was curious to meet the lord of this well-
ordered place.

Before the High Seat, I offered greeting. "For the welcome
of the gates, my thanks. For the feasting on the board, my pleasure and good wishes. To the lord of this roof, fair fortune."
This time I sincerely meant the oft-used words.

A tall man rose cup in hand. "To the farer on far roads the
welcome of this house, and may fortune favor your wandering."

At the close of the meal the master of the house gestured for
me to join him. He pulled up a stool like his own, saying, "We
have not had speech other than formal, Lord Harlyn. I would
not wish you to think me an ungracious host."

I assured him that he was anything but that. Noting that all called him Malgwyn familiarly, but with an air of respect, I thought this man was above petty titles, and the liking within me grew.

At length the talk turned to things of general interest. I listened to news of local doings with but half an ear. However, when mention was made of a shape-changer, my attention was caught and held. A few months past, a maiden from the abbey had become a Were and attacked two girls one evening. They only just managed to fend off her attack and drive the beast away.

Interested, I pressed for further details. Few such were forthcoming. The name given of the unfortunate maid was Khemrys. Prior to the incident, there were no known manifestations, and from most accounts she was of good, though mysterious, blood. No other sightings had been confirmed. All thought her dead or else fled afar.

Several newcomers joined our group, the first a tiny woman with close-cropped hair the shade of an autumn leaf. She carried a battered lute as tenderly as one would a babe. Her companion moved with a dancer's tread, though he was of a size I would not care to quarrel with. His expression was shielded by a drooping mustache and a clipped beard. I noted that he marked all possible exits by quick glances and sat protectively close to the lady.

Cries of greeting were raised, and at once she was begged for a song. All sound died save for the hiss of the fire as she began. Old favorites were called for, and others came to widen the circle. The singer had a pleasant, rather husky voice, with a gift for freshening the old and familiar.

Then the woman sang tunes of her own devising. The final dealt with the matter of the shape-shifter spoken of earlier. It was a haunting melody, and surprised all by being sympathetic to the plight of the girl.

She was still singing as I left that merry company for the peace of a bed.

I awoke reluctant to leave this keep. This puzzled me, as such a scant time before I had been so anxious to ride north. In the armory, I put a finer edge to my sword and pounded out the battle-dents in my shield. My dart-gun I reworked, spending several hours refletching darts and fashioning new ones. During the late afternoon I practiced my skill with the men-at-arms in the bailey.

All this time, the tale of the young shape-shifter lay in my thought. Unable to shake that, I found to my surprise the resolution to hunt her down had grown in me.

My announcement of this was made at the evening meal. Some of that wished to join me. But I wished this to be a solitary quest, and some time passed before all were convinced.

At length I sought my chamber. My stripped shield leaned in the corner, awaiting a fresh coat of paint. I stooped to right it, while doing so I caught sight of my face on its polished surface.

I was startled at the haunted eyes. Herein I had the look of a man under geas!

A soft tap at the door broke through my thoughts.

The minstrel of yestereve stood there when it was opened. Tonight she wore soft dove-gray, with milky moonstones on brow and breast. Her circlet was in the shape of the Horned Moon. This was a woman of Power!

I stepped aside to grant her entry. "What seek you here, wise one?"

"You, I know for what you are, but I carry no quarrel within these walls," the answer came. "The need has been laid upon me to come hither. What you would do is needful. Though your kind have little dealing with The Lady, this pattern is of her weaving. Your hunt will be long, and the way difficult, but you will find the one you seek. This I have Seen. Prepare yourself, for the trail will be laid soon. No more has been revealed to me, save this, you ride with her blessing, and mine."

Her hand made a graceful gesture in a pattern that hung in the air with a glow of blues and greens.

When I looked away from it, thinking to ask more, the room was empty. All was as if she had never been. It was long e'er sleep came to me that eve.

Word spread quickly of my quest. When I rode forth three days hence, the few I met along the track to the village bade me good fortune in the hunt. Keldar picked up a stone as I passed through the marketplace. I dismounted and set about prising it free.

The feeling of an unseen watcher grew in me. Whirling, I marked a pair of eyes. Glowing emerald in the near darkness, yet with points of golden flame in their depths, the eyes of a pard regarded me.

For an instant we stood thus, gazes locked, till the beast with a cry turned and fled. It was the matter of moments for my task to be completed. So I rode hot on the trail of the great cat.

III

Khemrys

Replete at last from my first good meal in some time, I stretched my length, claws needling into the soft ground. A full belly made me lazy. I rested my heavy head in Lysande's lap and straightaway began to doze. Her hand caressing me grew slower and slower, and at length her head drooped to rest upon my flank. The moon alone guarded our slumber.

I was roused by a persistent shake that would not go away. Raising a paw with claws extended to slap away the annoyance, I suddenly realized where I was and came full awake. The stars overhead were dimming as the sky began to lighten, and I must make good my escape.

Lysande knelt and kissed my forehead. We parted thus, not knowing if we were to see each other again. I blinked a bit as tears rose in my eyes. I wondered if true beasts ever cried.

When hastening through the village, along a street still empty in the dawning, I heard hoofbeats close at hand. Frantically, I looked for a place to hide, finding it beneath a cart.

From my refuge, I studied the stranger. Some instinct in me warned that this was the hunter sent to bring me down. His helm was looped over the saddlebow. I wanted to study this one, the better to escape his grasp.

What I found there, in other circumstances, would have pleased me. He was well favored, with hair as dark as my own and a finely chiseled face, the firm set of which told me this man owned no master. Fine lines graven about his eyes spoke of a man used to all weathers. The ones at the corners of his mouth argued good humor.

I forced myself to face the unpleasant truth I would have to kill this man, or die myself. As if I had shouted this, he spun, his eyes seeking my hiding place.

We stared so at each other for the beat of a heart. Then I made a great leap past hunter and horse. Breathlessly I fled to sanctuary in the hills, and from there I reached the Waste.

The Waste is a place of dread to lawful folk of High Hallack. A twisted, barren place, it is inhabited by outlaws and creatures more at home in a nightmare. Though the thought chilled me, this must be my hiding place.

Also, there were to be found there by report many places of the Old Ones. Perchance one of these would help me to become Khemrys once more.

My pads were worn and bloodied by the relentless pace. I raced up hills and down, seeking to shake the hunter from my trail. At times it seemed that I had succeeded, and I would have time to catch some unwary creature to satisfy my ravening hunger. After, I would drop, exhausted, to sleep until the pounding of hooves heralded the coming of my pursuer.

At length I reached the place where the Dales joined the Waste. Fall had fled, and Year's Turning, so the land was locked deep in the grasp of the Snow-Bird. Harsh winds slashed at me. Ice balls collected in the tufts between my pads, and I must needs stop to bite them free. Sighting some shelter in the form of outcrop some yards ahead, I hurried on.

The half-blocked wind blew less chill here. Perhaps the storm had erased my trail, and I had eluded him at last.

I was lean indeed, the bones rising sharply beneath my skin. My coat might have faded to the color of parched earth. However, the muscles that served me were still supple, hardened by the long pursuit.

My mind was sharp and clear. I had learned much from the beast. The constant struggle to maintain that part of me that was Khemrys had eased a little. I might tap the resources of the pard for my flight, but the strategies I used were my own.

My musing was interrupted by the sharp scent of a burrower among the stones now sheltering me. Scooping out the soil and smaller rocks protecting it took only moments. Soon the tasty meat filled the cavern of my belly.

A little while later I dug out a den of sorts. Fitting myself into it, I slept.

I awoke to the dazzle of sun on snow. This harsh land was softened by the blanket covering it. Skeleton fingers of the twisted trees pointed skyward, the only sinister note. I romped kittenlike through the drifts. No windborne scent of hunter spoiled my frolic.

Tracking a hare, I dispatched it before it was aware of me. Two days now I had had food and shelter. Regaining my den, I drifted into slumber once more.

This unexpected luck held throughout Snow-Bird, even into the Month of the Frost Sprite. My flanks filled out, and my coat lost its sere look. Roaming the hills, I chanced upon another of those places left by those who knew the land of old.

This place of the Old Ones differed from the one I had stumbled upon at Rhysdale, being in better repair. Only a few of the pillars had tumbled. Beneath one of these I found a hollow for a hiding place. There was a floor in shape like a five-pointed star, a low, circular wall enclosing the whole. All were made of the blue-green stone I now associated with magicks and mysteries. Though here was one feeling of peace and security.

My moon waiting came to an end as the waxing was full within a fortnight. At the back of my neck fur bristled with anticipation. A crushed herb smell was around as I approached the temple-place—for I was sure that such it was.

I strode across the floor, halting where the arms of the Great Star joined. Moon beams woke the sleeping pillars, thus they, too, gave forth radiance.

Being raised in the abbey, I was unsure how to proceed. Cup and Flame are apart from the Mysteries, and our poor library had contained few scrolls dealing with such. I closed my eyes, searched memory for what I had read.

The tale-scroll of my mother had dealt with this! Feverishly, I tried to recall the words one used in addressing those Powers that Be. Alas, that was miles away. I could not consult it directly, but I could almost hear my mother's voice reading aloud the parts.

I *could* hear it aloud! Her voice rose in formal chant, and another, deeper voice echoed her words. They shaped names that fit no tongue of High Hallack, beseeching those who dwelt here to aid me. I felt power flow into me as a man fills a drinking horn. All that they had been, they now gladly gave, to aid me in what I now must do.

Stretching my tawny length to its fullest, I stood with head up. From my throat came a low croon, my petition to those who listened. In my mind I formed a picture of myself, of Khemrys. This would be! I put all newly strengthened will into that wordless cry.

To feel that rippling of flesh and sinew that heralded the Change! I watched my claws shrink, widen; my paws spread, each toe lengthen to a finger; the fur withdraw so sun-browned skin greeted my gaze. I was woman once more!

My hands I pressed to my face, my body, before I dropped to my knees to give thanks to she who had granted this. Though snow lay about this land, I did not shiver or feel its bite, even unclad as I was. Her hand kept me safe and warm throughout that bitter eve.

Morning came, and I examined myself once more, still unable to believe that my quest had ended. A tangle of clothing lay beside me, and lifting it I found a sturdy outfit like unto those that hunters wear. Being of leather, with breeches in place of skirts, I would have a freedom of movement not customarily granted to women. There were thick boots as well, with linings of soft fleece. I pulled them on, the scent of faded roses clung to their folds.

Thinking of the likeness to hunter's garb brought to mind he who tracked me. I wondered whether he had called off his search. Realizing for the first time my vulnerability as Khemrys, I shivered, and prayed he had.

Berries and herbs grew about the temple of the Old Ones in plenty. The winter blast never reached this place where I gathered fruit long out of season in the Dales. To my harvest I added certain herbs of Power and healing, and an armful of stunted heads of grain. These last I patiently ground between two stones until I achieved a coarse flour. Mixing this with water, I formed the mealy cakes that give sustenance to the traveler, liberally spicing them with the dried berries.

More herbs I placed in the sewn-in pouches of my tunic against future need. Gratefully I thought of Dame Rimia and her patient wisdom in pointing out the name and uses of each. How glad I was now that I had listened.

At moon's waning, I had a most frightening dream. I seemed to *see* the hunter, as though from a great height. He and his mount picked their way carefully across the muddy plain. Both looked thin, and their heads drooped against the lashing wind. This land had not been as good to them as me.

I realized of a sudden that I *knew* this ground they were now upon. It was but a few hours' ride from my refuge! All I saw was so real that I woke in a cold sweat.

This dream was surely a warning. I entered that star-guarded place, saying, "For this shelter, the feasting provided, my gratitude." I could not use the address one gave to a human host, but I hoped the watchers here would read my heart.

I stooped to drink at a tiny spring bubbling up behind the temple. Its waters were sweet and chill. There was no means to carry any water with me, and I knew not when I would find another such.

I left on foot, hoping that human tracks would not arouse any suspicion in my pursuer. The melting snow took the pard marks, such as he would search for. Would that my luck held!

IV

Harlyn

I sniffed the pard's sharp musk on the breeze. She was running hard before me into the hills of Rhysdale, I close upon her heels. Now and again I lost sight of her in the dense brush

above the town, but the trail was clear to read. The beast made
no effort at first to conceal her passage. Later, she grew much
more wary.

She had a speed born of fear and utter desperation. I had the
geas, that compelling command that will let one do naught else,
to guide me.

Through summer's end, past the time of harvest and leaf-fall
did we run, Keldar, the pard, and I. I fear none of us had much
rest or food until Year's Turning. The Harpy was past, and the
Year of the Orc at hand when I marked Keldar favoring his
near-side foreleg. I had not yet saddled him for the day's chase,
and I moved closer to check it. The tendon was much inflamed,
and as I watched, the swelling grew greater. I took out certain
herbs and dug roots to make a poultice. There would be no
chase for us for some time to come.

The forage was better here than farther on, so I constructed
a rude shelter. I did not want to permanently disfigure the
area.

Turning from my task to Keldar, I removed the now-cold
poultice. The leg was not so hot and puffed as it had been. I
applied another at once.

I never left my friend hobbled at night. This had amazed
some. Most fighting horses of the Dales are hobbled or taught
to ground-tie when the reins are released. But Keldar was far
more intelligent than those. He never wandered far in night's
grazing and was ready as I for the road each morning. Woe be
unto any who attempted to steal or harm him! He was amply
able to deal such.

Hares were plentiful in this place. I snared several, roasting
one and preparing the others in strips to dry. The night was
still, and no stars shone. A prickling at my neck told me bad
weather was rising.

Later snow began to fall. Softly at first, then feather masses
swirled in a cloud so thick I could scarce make my way to the
shelter I had contrived. My saddle and gear were inside and I
flung great armfuls of dead, dry leaves in after them. These
would provide me with more protection than my single blanket.
I made fast the saddle blanket about Keldar to give him what
aid I could. The snow continued falling. I suspected we would
be trapped here for some time.

Morning came, gray and chill, and still the snow continued. I floundered seeking the buried ruin of last night's fire to rescue the strips of now-frozen meat.

Snow fell throughout the day, obliterating the landscape and utterly covering my makeshift home. At midafternoon I pulled aside the covering of the doorway and crawled out into the dim light to see how my comrade fared.

Keldar had found sanctuary beneath the overhanging branches of a great evergreen. Heavily laden limbs drooped near the earth under the massive blanket of snow they bore. The horse was glad to see me, whickering gently as I stepped inside.

"Ho, friend! Would we were both in Jurby port, eh?" My hooved companion snorted an appropriate sounding response.

He was near invisible in the twilight beneath the branches— for gray-black dappled coat was patterned like shadows on a forest floor.

We ventured forth together, he to forage for what grazing could be found, I to try to locate wood for fire. I spied tracks of a hare in the area where I had had such success previously, and I constructed another snare to lay near its burrow. After gathering masses of deadfall, I checked Keldar's foreleg, finding it much improved.

Days and nights passed much the same for near a fortnight. The trail of the pard would be impossible to pick up, and I despaired of ever hunting her down. What happened to one when a geas was left unfulfilled? I did not like to think of that.

My food supply dwindled, although occasionally I was able to supplement it with a hare from my snares. The journeycakes Lord Malgwyn had furnished were only a memory. I wondered if we two could survive until the weather broke.

At last a day came when the sun showed rather fitfully through the clouds. Thereafter began the slow process of freeze and melt that is so hazardous for travelers. Each night the loud *pop!* of trees exploding from their expanded sap broke the quiet like the crack of the herdsman's whip. To find a trail now would be impossible.

I chafed as each day that passed lessened the likelihood

of my ever picking up that trail. Keldar was eager to be gone
as well. His leg was completely healed, making me thankful
again that I had him instead of one of the less sturdy Dales
horses.

Late one eve near moonrise, I sat musing near the fire,
watching the twisting flames make patterns against the dark.
Seeing them thus brought to mind my mother's face, bending
her will to See what lay ahead in the scrying bowl. Like a sword
thrust that struck. I could See my quarry thus using the fire!
How could I have forgotten my earliest training? Too many
years of concealing differences among Dalesmen had led me to
overlook such a simple solution. Also, I could have alleviated
so many discomforts of the past month with other teachings of
my youth.

I made myself comfortable and began consciously to relax
each separate muscle. Clearing my mind of all but thoughts of
her whom I sought, I looked into the fire. Deeper, deeper into
the writhing colors I eyed. The flames began to recede as another scene took their place.

It was night, as now, with a full moon overhead. I felt a sense
of failure until I realized I was looking at a place other than that
where I now dwelt. It was a temple of—no, I shall not call her
name. It shone with a radiance not of this world, and at its
center—the pard!

Dimly I heard chanting, words and names, though not from
the cat. I saw no others, but an overwhelming sense of Power
made the small hairs at the back of my neck stand upright. The
creature's head was now flung aloft as it uttered a low, crooning
petition. Bathed in moonglow, I watched her begin the familiar
transformation to human semblance.

Now I was near enough to touch her from my point of vision
as her features reshaped into those of a girl just entering wom-
anhood. Her dark hair swept to her hips like a waterfall, concealing most of her slim body. Her triangular face with its wide-
set eyes turned this way and that, in rapturous delight at her
metamorphosis. She looked fit and lean. The storm just past
had not marked her as it had me.

I tore my eyes away from the girl to mark the place. Certain
landmarks led me to believe it but a few days' ride from my

shelter. The picture then began to fade, and the last sight I had
was of Khemrys, (for it could be none other), arms raised high
in thanksgiving. Then all was gone save the flickering of my
now-dying fire.

As I drifted into sleep that night, her face still called me with
a haunting pull strong as that of the geas laid upon me.

At dawn we headed north out of the valley, riding hard toward the place of my vision.

My supplies were near nonexistent, save a few strips of the
meat I had managed to dry. So it was with great relief I came
upon one of the cache-sites of a Waste-dweller.

These were dangerous to the uninitiated, as supplies are
scarce and precious, so that the owners often set traps for would-
be thieves. But I was in desperate straits and wary of the risk.

A rock heaved ahead in one place broke through a covering of lattice concealed by dirt and pebbles. Revealed below
was a deep pit lined with row upon row of sharp spikes, tips
coated with a green substance that I guessed as a deadly
poison.

Once the trap was sprung, it was an easy task to remove what
stores I required: some meal, dried fruits, and the seeds that
would sprout into greens. I replaced the cairn as I found it.
Even one beyond the law I did not want to rob, thus I left the
greater portion for my unwitting host.

For near a week I followed the trail laid by the flame
that night. Keldar and I picked our way carefully, as the
ground was still sodden and nigh impassable. However, the
fair weather held, and I had great hopes of cornering my
quarry at last.

However when I reached the Star Temple, the girl was gone,
and only the broken stems of herbs and a few distorted
footprints bore mute witness to her sojourn. I had not truly
expected to have the hunt end so easily, and I was, in an odd
way, proud of the skill of my prey.

We camped there that night, for there was a sweet-flowing
stream and good grazing nearby. I mounted the low steps
to the star-form pavement to voice a wordless plea to those
who once dealt here for aid in the ending of this quest. More

and more was I filled with rightness, a sense of a pattern
nearing completion. Only the fulfillment of the geas would
free me, and I began to find within myself the reason for its
being.

Stooping to fill my flask with the clear water, I noticed a dark
glint among the plants nestled 'round the spring. I knelt to better see and found a few brown hairs tangled in the woody
stems. Gently I freed them and put them in my belt pouch.
Mayhap they would be a lucky talisman.

The tracks leading out showed that the girl, for she wore that
guise now, was heading north, farther into the heart of the
Waste. It would have been wiser for her to remain in pard-form
in this most dangerous country.

Not only those fleeing the law sheltered here. Creatures
of Shadow and things of an earlier, grimmer age slunk about
as well. The deaths such granted were not the clean ones
of hunter's dart or arrow, but something more horrible, while
death to the body did not necessarily follow. I hoped the
girl would chance upon none such monster before I caught up
with her.

V

Khemrys

The thick mud sucked at my boots with every step. At times I
lost my footing in the mess and fell sprawling. In no time I bore
the look of a moss wife out of legend. Why not? I thought.
Were not Weres legends, also?

Now I longed for a pard's speed to cross the mire. But I
feared to make the transition and perhaps be once more locked
within the beast.

*   *   *

Thankfully I stumbled upon a shallow pool ringed by twisted trees. The water led me to make camp here. Cold as it was, I must have a clean body and clothing.

Brush gave me a fire. So far I had marked no signs of inhabitants in this desolate land. Only the ruins bore silent testimony of man's hand upon this region.

Taking advantage of the warm afternoon sun, I stripped and stepped into the chilly water. I swirled water over the oiled surface of my leather. Stretching them across a flat rock to dry, I returned to my own scrubbing.

I was glad to shape-change once I left the water. The air was growing quite brisk, as I took pard-form. Checking the damp leathers and finding them not yet wearable, in fur I settled in.

At sunrise, I became Khemrys once more, tending things only hands could do. The fire rebuilt, the leathers redonned, I heated one of the rough cakes on a stone to make it more palatable. As I sat crunching the coarse near-tasteless stuff, I thought wistfully of baking day at Rhystead, the tiny cookies rich with eggs and seeds, the mouth-watering smell of the hot bread fresh from the great ovens.

I was so lost in such a gluttonous dream I did not see the three burly forms slipping silently through the trees. As closer they edged, I finished the last of my crumbly stuff and stood, wiping my hands on the seat of my breeches. Even though those had been drying for nearly a full day, their dampness clung, chill and unpleasant to my skin.

A loud crack of a nearby twig revealed the lurkers. There was no time to flee for they were upon me, foul hands riffling through my pouch and clothing. Dumping my precious herbs to the ground, one lout crushed them to dust beneath his heel.

The tallest one spoke. "It were kind o' ye, gurrl, tae build us that beacon fire. So as to make the findin' of ye easy. Belikes t'come here lookin' for a man. No fine-livin' high lady comes to the Waste without she has a good cause."

I stared at him with wordless hate. The second held my arms firmly pinned at an unnatural angle to my body. I dared not struggle, as the slightest movement caused me excruciating pain. This one seemed gratified at an involuntary cry and twisted my arms a little harder. I bit my lip.

When the third one ran his eyes and hands insultingly over my body, I stiffened, trying to think of a means of escape.

The first ripped open my jerkin laces and commented on the smallness of my breasts. As he and the stocky, toadlike one roughly pulled my tunic over my head, I began steeling myself, willing the swiftest transformation I had yet attempted.

The clothing beneath the rudely questing hands changed to the sleek golden hide of the cat, the hands so painfully held to the sharp-clawed paws of a terror from the hills. My long form twisted in their grasp. Now the hunted became the hunter.

My would-be captors paled. The tall, hulking one drew a wicked-looking sword. I backed, snarling, ears laid flat to my head. The grasp at the nape of my neck still held by the third was a fatal mistake—for him. I writhed, thanking the power that be for the loose folds of skin there. Four deep gashes in his face and neck matched more on his pale chest. He gasped, clutching the burning, blood-welling stripes and freeing me in the process.

"Ye murdersome beast! Die, you!" the man with the blade snarled. I dodged neatly, knocking down the bulky one who made a warding-off sign at me as I ran past him. I managed a snap at the swordsman in retreat, then I turned tail and fled for my very life, leaving the no-longer-pleasant grove behind me.

I ran until I dropped from exhaustion. How could I have been so foolish as to light that fire? It was luck of a sort that nothing worse had been drawn to me by the beckoning flame. I must consider my actions hereafter, for every man's hand would be against me.

As I lay panting, the distant thunder of hoofbeats sounded. Lifting my head and squinting, I could perceive the outline of a rider some distance away. The silhouette was vaguely familiar, and confirmation came on the wind. The hunter had returned. Leaping to my feet, I leaped ahead, disregarding the aching protest of every joint and muscle.

VI

Harlyn

The girl was clever. Although she had been in no little hurry, great care had been taken to make her track near invisible. Patiently searching each time it faded out, I was able to find a tiny branch awry, a crushed leaf, a bit of ash from a buried fireside. I was sure that these had been left by my quarry.

In spite of the tedious nature of the search, we were able to cover more than twice the ground of a single girl on foot. Soon, with any luck, I would have her in sight.

Near dark I came upon the stiffening body of a man. The scavengers had not yet begun their work, and I saw that he bore the signature mark of the pard. His face and chest had been raked to the bone by scimitar claws, one nicking the great vein of the throat. The tracks leading away told the tale of two others making a hasty exit.

The pard's prints were there as well, and I remounted, turning Keldar's head to follow. We must be fairly close now. Since I was certain the dead man and his companions had richly deserved their fates—I spared no further thought for them.

By starlight I raced. Recklessly across uncertain terrain and luckily without mishap I gave Keldar his head. Near false dawn I saw the prints had lost their evenness, as if their owner reeled with exhaustion. She could not be far ahead of me now.

I slowed my steed lest I betray my calling too soon. The rising sun revealed a small outcropping of rock in the near distance. Toward that the pull of the geas led me. The land where I now rode was familiar to me. Many times I had come this way hunting with my father and brothers. We were but a few leagues' distance from my childhood home, and the warring pull of home and kin-ties vied strongly with the compulsion of cornering my prey at last.

A tawny flash from the rock ahead gave me knowledge that

my presence had been marked. She fled unsteadily, as though
her legs could no longer quite support her weight. Heading toward a deep crevasse, she sought to conceal herself and mayhap
lose me once again in the process.

But this time, her luck failed her. For I knew the sides there
rose smoothly vertical, and the entrance was the only exit. No
escape for Khemrys this time.

Arriving at the narrow entrance, I dismounted, leaving my
helm hanging from the saddlebow. Keldar snorted suspiciously,
as though he were unsure whether I was quite aware about my
action. I ruffled the thick mane where it hung over his canny
eyes, and, turning toward the crevasse, made to confront this
Were-girl.

VII

Khemrys

Stumbling, I leaped across the outcropping and spied a deep
fissure in the rock ahead. I knew I could squeeze myself in
easily, and from there either hide from his piercing gaze or else
render myself invulnerable to sword thrust or dart blast, for no
sunlight broke that gloom. There would surely be some means
of egress, would there not? I tried hard to reason, but my mind
was foggy with fatigue, and I knew it would be fate that would
decide in the end.

Slipping through the opening, I made my way toward the
back. Overhead, the walls were as smooth as the sides of a
polished horn cup. I wished I had not been born with the
Were-curse, for it had been my bane from start to finish, and
though I would much miss the luxury of cat senses, I would
most gladly forswear all to be able to live without the constant
pursuit.

There was no exit other than the way I had come, and the
jingling of harness and mail made certain my hiding place had

been discovered. I was trapped. With bone-chilling certainty I knew that this was the final confrontation that I so dreaded. I would have no chance unless I was able to slay this man. Now I feared that it would be I who was slain.

Dimness within became utter dark as the man's body cut off what feeble light reached hither. I backed until the wall was hard against my hindquarters ready to spring, but what I saw made me stop. The outline of a strong hand held a dart-gun pointed straight at me!

I froze, squeezing tight my eyes against death. A click of metal on stone made me open them again. The man had thrown his gun away! He drew closer, and I could see even in the minute light that he was smiling. Did he think to kill me with naught but bare hands?

Puzzled, I saw those hands spread wide, as though to show me he meant no harm. There was not a single sound as we stood thus, regarding each other. Then his smile widened, and his body seemed to lose its familiar outline like a heat-softened candle. The body crouched, assumed a lean length with smoke-gray fur sprouting like spring grass. Fascinated, I watched a tail form and lengthen, his strong nose and lean chin stretch forward into a cat's muzzle. I had never seen a transformation from the observer's point of view. How gracefully everything seemed to flow and change!

Then I shook my head as if to clear it. What was I thinking of at a time like this! This was no hunter sent to slay me, but another of the breed of my father and myself! I was not alone anymore.

Cautiously he approached me, as though not sure what sort of reception I would grant. He was larger than I and even more graceful from mottled head to smoky tail-tip. Nose to nose we stood until I flung decorum to the four winds and began to purr and roll. We tumbled about thus until we tired, and picking our way through the narrow opening, we lay at last in the sun-warmed grass at the very feet of the great horse. He did not seem to note anything unusual about our appearance, and I wondered, for it had always been my experience that all mounts feared me greatly.

As though he could read my very thoughts, the snowcat became man once more. "Keldar's kind are of a breed our kin raise themselves, and they accept us for what we are. I am Harlyn, Wererider of the Gray Towers, and a merry chase you've led me, pretty lady."

His speaking voice was a rich baritone with an underlying rumble not unlike the purr of a great cat. Feeling suddenly shy, I too shifted back to Khemrys's shape, and I could not meet his eyes. Seeing my embarrassment and confusion, he tenderly gathered me close. I had reached safe haven at last.

Afterword

As long as I can remember, stories about shape-changers have numbered among my favorites. When I first read The Year of the Unicorn *I was enchanted, although I was disappointed to find that there were no female Wereriders.*

After many discussions with Andre, I discovered that there could be, although not necessarily in the direct line of descent. I kicked around a variety of ideas until a poem by a writer featured elsewhere in these collections set the final note in my mental chord. I'd like to thank her, the many friends who nagged/encouraged me (you know who you are), but most of all Andre, who has so graciously allowed us to play in her marvelous world.

—Lisa Woodworth

THE SWORD-SELLER

by

Patricia C. Wrede

The tiny sword-seller's booth was almost hidden behind a row of tinker's stalls and jewelry stands; Auridan very nearly passed by without seeing it at all. When he did notice it, he paused. Then he shouldered his way toward it with a smile. He needed a sword, and half the fun of a fair was hunting bargains in the smaller booths.

The booth's proprietor, an old man in a dark blue robe, looked up as Auridan ducked under the awning. Auridan braced himself for the usual exhortations, but the man regarded him with a silent, unblinking stare. Auridan gave a mental shrug and bent over the counter. He was surprised at the disorder he found; knives, daggers, and swords of all lengths were jumbled as randomly as a child's game of catch-straws. Some had sheaths, some did not; some were polished and sharpened, others were black with age. A cursory glance was enough to tell Auridan that nothing here was likely to be worth haggling over. He shrugged again, and turned to go. As he did, a glint of color caught his eye.

Auridan stopped. A blue stone winked at him through a gap in the crisscrossed pile of weapons. Auridan moved two swords and four daggers and uncovered an ancient short-sword without a sheath. The blue stone was one of a pair set in the hilt, amid carving so clogged with grime that it was impossible to determine what the decoration represented. The blade of the sword was black with age, and thicker and wider than those Auridan was used to. Almost in spite of himself, Auridan lifted the sword, testing the heft. The hilt fit his hand as if it had been made to measure, and the balance of the blade was perfect.

"That sword is not for sale," a harsh voice rasped.

Auridan started and looked across the counter into the unfathomable eyes of the sword-seller. "If it is already spoken for, you should not display it with the rest of your wares," Auridan said in mild annoyance. He twisted the blade from side to side, studying it with regret. It would be a deal of work to clean and sharpen, but something about the weapon called to him . . . He shook himself, and held the sword out to the sword-seller.

The old man made no move to take it from him. "I did not say the sword was spoken for," he said.

"No, I suppose you didn't," Auridan replied with a smile. "But what else am I to think when you refuse to sell it?"

"Think as you will," the man said, "so long as you do not think to buy that sword."

"As you will," Auridan said. Again he held out the sword. The old man sat watching him with the same unblinking stare.

"Very well, then." Auridan set the sword down gently atop the welter of other weapons in front of the old man. His fingers uncurled reluctantly from the hilt, and as he stepped away from the counter he was surprised to find that his breathing had quickened. "Good day, and fortune follow you," he said, and turned away.

"Wait."

Auridan looked back, but kept one hand poised to lift the fringe of the awning. "What is it?"

"The sword is not for sale. It is given. Today, it is given to you. Take it."

Auridan stared. Was the old man mad? Even an old and battered sword was worth a good deal, and this weapon was well made. The sword-seller looked as though he could make good use of whatever coin it would bring. "Why would you give me the sword?"

"That is my affair," the old man said. "The sword is yours. Take it."

Auridan heard finality in the sword-seller's voice, and the man's eyes were bright and knowing. They did not look like the eyes of a madman. Auridan reached for the hilt of the sword, then hesitated. Whatever the reason for this strange offer, he could not take such advantage of an old man. His hand went to the pouch at his belt and removed half of the scanty coins remaining. He held them out to the sword-seller. "Here. It's not the worth of such a weapon, by any means, but—"

"The sword is a gift!" the old man snapped. "Did I not say it?"

"I'll take it as a purchase, or not at all," Auridan said. Briefly, he wondered if he had not run as mad as the old sword-seller. Forcing a merchant to take coin at a fair! Whoever heard of such backward bargaining?

The old man snorted. "Take the sword and go."

Auridan shrugged. He tossed the coins onto the counter, where they made tiny noises as they clinked against the jumbled weapons and fell into the spaces between them. Only then did he put his hand to the hilt of the ancient sword.

"For your courtesy, I give thanks," Auridan said, and picked up the weapon.

He thought he saw a flash of worry in the sword-seller's eyes. Then the man said, "You are a blank shield. I am sometimes asked to recommend such men to those who seek to hire them. If someone asks, where shall I send him?"

Auridan blinked in surprise, but said courteously that he could probably be found in the serving tent after sunset. He thanked the man and left, wondering why he had bothered. He doubted that anyone would seek to hire a mercenary by such roundabout methods. Still, he thought the suggestion had been well meant. He put the matter out of his mind and began looking for a leather-maker's booth where he could buy a sheath for the sword.

For the next several hours, Auridan strolled among the booths and tents, enjoying the warm sunshine and watching the

eager, noisy crowds. The annual Fyndale fair had been resumed
shortly after the end of the long war with the Hounds of Alizon, and it had grown every year since. Ten merchants' flags
had flown above the booths at that first fair; now, four years
later, there were thirty or more, and the tents and carts and
tables of the lesser tradesmen sprawled in a disorderly semicir-
cle around the gray stone pillar where men swore to keep the
peace of the fair.

Auridan remembered that first fair well. Unlike so many of
his erstwhile comrades in the war against Alizon, he'd been
restless and disinclined to settle down. By a lucky chance, he'd
met one of the lords from the south who'd been dispossessed
during the war. Auridan had taken service with him, and they
had spent several years fighting in the southern part of High
Hallack. Eventually, the lord and his men had prevailed, but
the substance of his keep had been wasted in the struggle, and
Auridan was not of a mind to squat there waiting for the man to
rebuild his fortune. He had taken the lord's blessing, and the
few coins that could be spared, and come back to Fyndale in
search of another patron.

He studied the crowd as he walked along, and for the first
time began to doubt the wisdom of the decision he had made
with such blithe confidence. Most of the fairgoers looked pros-
perous and contented—good signs for the merchants, perhaps,
but not so promising for a blank shield mercenary looking for
someone in need of a guard or a soldier.

Well, if nothing else, he could hire on with a merchant returning home from the fair, Auridan thought philosophically.
Merchants were notoriously nervous about bandits, particularly
when there were profits to protect, and from the look of things,
this fair would be profitable for nearly all of them. Feeling
somewhat more cheerful, Auridan headed toward the serving
tent, to purchase a cup of wine and consider what to do next.

Two drinks later, he had still not thought of anything. He
was just beginning his third when a light, musical voice said,
"Fair fortune to you, traveler. Are you the blank shield the
sword-seller told me of?"

Auridan looked up, and his reply died on his lips. The
woman who stood beside him had the kind of beauty song-

smiths broke their strings over. Her thick, butter-colored braids
coiled into a high knot above a classic oval face. Her skin was
fair and flawless, her eyes a serene hazel. She was tall and
slender, and her cloak and robe were of fine wool, heavily embroidered. She could be no more than twenty, but her bearing
proclaimed a confidence beyond her years.

She must be daughter to one of the Dales lords, Auridan
thought dazedly; then his bemused wits began working again
and he rose to his feet and raised his hand palm-out in greeting.
"Fair fortune to you, lady. I am Auridan; how may I serve
you?"

The woman's lips compressed very slightly; then she sighed
and motioned for Auridan to seat himself once more. She took
the place beside him and said, "I wish to hire a man to guide
and guard me on a journey. I have been told that you are a man
of honor, and would suit my purposes."

"I have done such work before," Auridan admitted. "What
direction do you travel, and with how large a party?"

The woman bit her lip and looked down; suddenly she
seemed much younger, barely out of girlhood. Then she raised
her chin and said defiantly, "I wish to go north, to Abbey Norstead. And the party will consist of we two only; I will take no
others with me." She added solemnly, "It is why I particularly
wish to hire an honorable man."

Auridan swallowed a chuckle, but shook his head. "I fear
you have not considered, lady," he said gently, even as he wondered why such a girl as this would wish to enter the abbey.
"The effects of the war linger; travel is still not safe. I cannot
believe your kinsmen would allow—"

"The last of my kin by blood is at Abbey Norstead," the girl
broke in pointedly.

"Then you'd do far better to stay in Fyndale for a week or so,
until the fair ends, and hire passage in a merchant's train. I'm
sure that at least one or two will head toward Norsdale."

"I've no mind to wait so long," she retorted. "Nor do I wish
to move at a snail's pace, stopping at every village and hamlet
in hopes of another sale."

"I see you've journeyed with merchants before," Auridan
said, amused.

"Two travelers alone may well be safer than a larger group," she persisted. "For two can hide, or slip away silently in darkness, where more cannot."

"A single guard may also be easily taken by two or three outlaws, who would never think to attack a stronger party," Auridan pointed out. "And with such a one as you to tempt—"

"I am not helpless!" she interrupted angrily. "I know the use of a sword, though I am better with a bow."

Without thinking, Auridan raised a skeptical eyebrow. The girl saw, and her eyes flashed. "You think that because I am beautiful I have no thoughts in my head save silks and jewelry, and no skill in my hands but embroidery!" she said scornfully. "Faugh! I'm sick to death of men who see nothing but my face!"

Before Auridan could answer, a man's voice cut across the hum of talk surrounding them. "Cyndal! There you are at last!" The girl stiffened, and Auridan looked around for the source of the cry.

He found the speaker quickly—a tall, brown-haired man of perhaps thirty years, dressed in a tunic of fine crimson wool. He was making his way quickly through the crowd, his eyes fixed on the girl beside Auridan. "Hervan," the girl muttered, and she spoke as if the name were a curse. "He would!"

The brown-haired man reached the table. He ignored Auridan and said in a chiding tone, "My dear Cyndal! What do you here, and in such company? My lady has been frantic since she found you missing!"

"I don't believe you, Hervan," the girl replied, unmoved. "Chathalla knew I was going out, and I've barely been gone an hour. She wouldn't fuss over such a thing."

"Chathalla's nerves are particularly fragile just now," the brown-haired man said defensively.

"Your concern for your lady wife does you credit," Cyndal said in a dry tone.

"I could wish you had had as much consideration. What she will say when she knows where I found you . . ." He glanced disapprovingly around the serving tent, and his eyes came to rest on Auridan.

"Don't tell her," Cyndal suggested.

"Don't be ridiculous, Cyndal. You shouldn't be wandering around the fair alone; you know that. Come on, I'll take you back to the tent."

"I haven't finished my discussion with Auridan," Cyndal said.

"Cyndal, be reasonable!"

Hervan's tone was patronizing, and Auridan felt a wave of dislike for the young Dales lord. He decided to intervene. "But she is," Auridan put in pleasantly. "Being reasonable, I mean."

Hervan stared at him in blank astonishment, and Auridan gestured at the cup of wine he had been drinking. Fortunately, it was still three-quarters full, and he had set it down between Cyndal and himself, so that it was impossible to tell to which of them the cup belonged. "My lady has not yet finished her wine. Surely you do not think it would be reasonable for her to leave it behind?"

"Indeed." Hervan looked from Auridan to Cyndal, and the question in his expression was clear. Cyndal's lips tightened, but she presented Auridan as graciously as if they were at the court of one of the High Lords of the Dales instead of in a serving tent at a fair. She did not, Auridan noticed, mention what she had been discussing with him.

Hervan's expression cleared before Cyndal was half finished with her explanation. "A blank shield? How fortunate! I am in need of a Master of Arms; come to me tomorrow and we'll talk of it."

"Why, thank you, my lord," Auridan said, forcing his lips into a smile. "Tomorrow evening, perhaps? I would not wish to interfere with your fairing."

"I will look for you then," Hervan promised. "Now, Cyndal—"

"But Lady Cyndal still has not finished her wine," Auridan cut in smoothly. "Surely it won't matter if she stays here a little longer. I will be happy to escort her back if you wish to return and reassure your lady wife."

Hervan hesitated visibly, but he could not refuse without giving the impression that he did not trust Auridan. That would make Hervan look foolish, since he had just offered to take Auridan into his service. Hervan bowed graciously, showered Auridan with insincere thanks, and left at last.

Auridan turned to Cyndal. She was looking at him with an expression of mingled resignation and scorn, and he wondered whether she thought he had believed Hervan's playacting. "I think that now I understand exactly why you wish to go to Norstead," Auridan said before she could speak. "But I thought you said that you had no kin outside the abbey. Lord Hervan does not act like a stranger."

Cyndal's eyes widened; then, suddenly, she smiled. Auridan swallowed hard. Cyndal had been lovely before, but the glowing expression of relief and gratitude increased her beauty tenfold.

"Hervan was my uncle's stepson," Cyndal said, and Auridan gave himself a mental shake. He *had* asked, after all. "When my uncle saw that he was unlikely to have children of his own, he made Hervan his heir. Hervan has been lord in Syledale since my uncle died two years ago."

"And it took you two years to decide that you'd rather enter an abbey than live in his household?" Auridan said skeptically.

She laughed, but her expression sobered quickly. "No, it's only in the last few months that he's been acting that way, since he's known Chathalla will bear him an heir after Midwinter. I decided on the way to Fyndale that it would be easier on everyone if I went away for a while. My mother's sister at Abbey Norstead is the only blood relation I possess, so it's reasonable for me to go there."

Auridan stiffened as wild speculations chased each other through his mind. If the impending birth of an heir had triggered Hervan's subtle persecution of his cousin-by-marriage, Hervan's actions might well be rooted in something deeper than mere distaste for Cyndal's presence. And whatever the cause, it was certainly not a safe situation for a mercenary to become involved in. He opened his mouth to tell Cyndal as much, and found himself saying, "Have you told Lord Hervan of this plan of yours?"

"Not yet," Cyndal admitted. "I thought I would have a better chance of persuading him if Chathalla and I had all the arrangements made before I spoke to him of it."

"I see." Auridan was more confused than ever. "And she agreed to your traveling with a single man-at-arms?"

"I didn't mention that," Cyndal said. "She'd worry. I'll just tell her, and Hervan, that you've agreed to be my guide and head the men who'll accompany me. They won't think to ask how many men there will be."

"Why the need for all this subterfuge? Why don't you just take the five or six men you need with you?"

"Because Hervan wouldn't provide them, and I can't afford to hire that many!" Cyndal snapped. "And if you aren't going to help me, I don't see why I should answer any more of your questions."

"In that case, I shall escort you back to your cousin," Auridan said, rising. "I strongly recommend, however, that you explain matters to Lord Hervan before you approach me or anyone else on this subject again."

"That can be no concern of yours, since you do not wish to take me to Norstead," Cyndal said coldly as she rose to follow him.

Auridan scowled at her. "By the Nine Words of Min, lady, do you not realize how much trouble you would make for any man like me who accepted your offer unknowingly? Blood-kin or no, Lord Hervan stands as your protector! Were I to agree to take you to Norstead without his permission, I'd have to go on into the Waste and earn my bread by scavenging, for no lord would hire me afterward."

"Oh." Cyndal's voice was thoughtful, and she was silent for a long time. They had nearly reached the visitors' tents when she said, "I'm sorry; I hadn't thought of it that way. But if Hervan agrees, will you guide me?"

"Certainly," Auridan replied, then wondered whether the wine had not been stronger than he had thought. He gave a mental shrug. Time enough to worry once the girl got Lord Hervan's agreement to her plans; from what Auridan had seen, it did not look probable.

Cyndal did not appear to share Auridan's doubts. "Thank you," she said with a smile that took his breath away. "You are coming to speak with Hervan tomorrow, are you not? I'll talk to him before then."

Auridan nodded absently, and she directed him toward one of the tents on the outer perimeter of the camp. They finished their walk in silence, except for the obligatory courtesies exchanged when he returned her officially to her step-cousin's care. Then Auridan hurried away to his own campsite, feeling unreasonably relieved and irrationally anxious at the same time.

To give himself something to think about besides Cyndal, Auridan spent the evening worrying at the hilt of his new sword with polishing cream, strong soap, and a pile of old rags. He worked slowly to keep from accidentally dislodging the stones in the hilt. Even so, by the time he was ready to sleep he had removed most of the ancient grime from the carving that decorated the hilt. In the flickering firelight, all he could tell was that the two stones were the eyes of some wild-haired creature. Reluctantly, Auridan sheathed the sword, telling himself he could examine it more closely in the morning.

When he awoke, his first action was to reach for the short-sword. He was surprised to see how different the carving looked in daylight. The blue stones were indeed eyes, but what he had taken for hair was a crest of intricately carved feathers that stood out around the head of a serpentlike creature. The serpent's body twisted around the hilt of the sword, forming a series of ridges that made the sword less likely to slide in the hand. Auridan studied it, wondering from what tale the swordsmith had taken such a creature. A snake with feathers was strange enough to be a relic of the Old Ones . . .

Auridan shivered, then shook his head and smiled. The Dales were full of strange things left behind by the Old Ones, but one did not find them for sale at out-of-the-way booths in Fyndale. For while the leavings of the Old Ones might be dangerous indeed, there was always someone eager to take the risk in hopes of the power he might gain. Any merchant daring enough to traffic in such items would be charging enormous sums for them, not giving them away to mercenaries. Auridan pushed the remnants of his uneasiness to the back of his mind, and went off to get himself some breakfast.

When he finished eating, Auridan took the sword to a busy tinker's stall and had the blade cleaned and sharpened. It cost more than he had expected, but it was worth it to have a good sword at his belt again. He spent the day wandering through the fair, but as soon as the sun disappeared behind the mountains he headed for Lord Hervan's campsite.

The guard who greeted Auridan did not seem surprised by his request to speak with Lord Hervan, and he was immediately ushered into one of the tents. He found Hervan, Cyndal, and a quiet, gentle-faced woman seated on small folding stools inside. Hervan rose, frowning, as Auridan entered.

"This is my wife, the Lady Chathalla," Hervan said, gesturing at the unfamiliar woman beside Cyndal. He paused, studying Auridan, then said abruptly, "My cousin claims she wishes to hire you to take her to Norstead."

"She mentioned the possibility," Auridan said cautiously. He saw Cyndal shift, and Chathalla put a restraining hand on her arm, and he wondered what he had walked into this time.

"Indeed." Hervan's voice was barely a fraction friendlier. "And you approve of this proposal?"

Auridan raised an eyebrow. "Approve? My lord, I am a mercenary. I approve when I am paid."

Hervan gave a bark of laughter. "Very good. Sit down, then, and we'll talk."

As Auridan turned, looking for a fourth stool, he heard a short, hissing intake of breath. He straightened hurriedly. Hervan was staring at the carved hilt of Auridan's short-sword, and his expression was curiously blank. "My lord?" Auridan said cautiously.

Hervan ran his tongue over his lips. "The decoration of your swordhilt is . . . quite unusual."

"Really? I had thought it some whim of the smith who made it," Auridan said. "Have you seen similar work before, Lord Hervan?"

"Possibly." Hervan's tone was carefully casual, but his lips were stiff with tension. His eyes darted up to Auridan's face, then as quickly away. "Enough. What is your price for escorting my cousin to Norstead?"

Auridan blinked, somewhat bewildered by this abrupt change in attitude, then named a sum he knew to be reasonable. Hervan nodded, but he did not look as if he was devoting much of his attention to Auridan's words. Instead, Hervan was watching Cyndal, and after a moment he said almost pleadingly, "You're sure you want to take this trip, Cyndal? You won't change your mind?"

"Yes, I'm sure, and no, I won't change my mind," Cyndal said.

Hervan glanced at Auridan again and said heavily, "Very well. You wanted to leave tomorrow morning, didn't you? I'll see that everything is ready."

"You mean, you'll let me go without any more arguing?" Cyndal said, amazement and disbelief warring in her voice.

"I've no choice!" Hervan swung around to face her. He sounded desperate, and angry, and somehow frightened. "Cyndal . . ."

"What's wrong, Hervan?" Cyndal asked almost gently.

Hervan hesitated, and his wife leaned forward and said quietly, "Yes, please tell us."

Hervan jerked as if he had been stung, and his expression hardened. "Nothing. Nothing whatever." He looked at Auridan and said, "I'll have your payment ready in the morning."

Auridan nodded, and the bargain was swiftly concluded. He bowed his thanks and left, puzzling over the implications of the little scene. Hervan had all the earmarks of a badly frightened man, but why would the design of Auridan's swordhilt have frightened him? Auridan kicked at a rock in frustration. Hervan was lord of a Dale, however small; there was nothing Auridan could do to make him explain.

Briefly, Auridan considered leaving the sword behind, but he needed a weapon and he could not afford to buy another. Nor could he refuse to escort Cyndal, however uneasy her stepcousin's attitude made him. Even if he had not given his word to both Hervan and Cyndal, Auridan could not afford to pass up such a commission. His purse was nearly flat, and it would be at least a week before he could expect any income from an alternate position, supposing he could find one quickly. Auridan grinned suddenly. It was pleasant to have honor and necessity in agreement, for once, about his future course of action.

They left early the following morning, before the fairgoers emerged from their tents to crowd the space around the booths. Lord Hervan had provided a pretty chestnut mare for Cyndal that Auridan thought would be more than a match for his own gray. Hervan had also arranged saddlebags full of supplies for both Cyndal and Auridan, and he had a purse with Auridan's fee ready and waiting. He even suggested a route—the old track near the top of the ridges. Auridan thanked him without mentioning that he had been intending to take the high trail anyway. At this time of year, any outlaws would be watching the main road for unwary merchants; the high trail would be far safer for so small a party. Hervan's farewells to his step-cousin were perhaps a little stiff, but Auridan had to admit that in everything else the man had done as much or more than he had promised.

Cyndal was in a sober mood after taking leave of her cousin, and for the early part of the morning she rode in silence. But the warmth of the day and the cheerful calling of the birds proved too much for her to resist, and by the time they stopped for a midday meal she was laughing and talking with Auridan as though he had stood guard over her cradle.

Auridan was surprised at how comfortable he was with her. His previous experience with noblewomen had not led him to expect anything remotely resembling this casual camaraderie. Before he thought, he said as much, and Cyndal grinned.

"You've probably only seen proper noblewomen, like Lady Chathalla," she said without rancor. "Penniless females like me aren't usually allowed out in public."

"*Do* the Dales hold any other women 'like you'?" Auridan asked, studying her with exaggerated admiration.

"Hundreds," Cyndal said, and her smile faded. "I'm one of the lucky ones. If Chathalla weren't so nice, I'd have been stuck in the kitchens or the back gardens with fewer prospects than a serving wench. I've seen it happen; Uppsdale isn't very far away, and I remember how Lady Annet treated Ysmay. And Ysmay had dowry enough to marry, in the end; I don't even have that."

"Surely your uncle—" Auridan stopped short as he realized that, camaraderie or not, this was not the sort of question a blank shield ought to ask of a noblewoman.

"My uncle didn't think of settling anything on me for a dowry," Cyndal said. "He was more concerned with making sure no one would be able to object to Hervan as heir. And it was lucky he did; things were rather difficult for a while after he died. If he hadn't made such a point of Hervan's being his heir, blood-kin or not, I'm not sure what would have happened to any of us."

Auridan nodded sympathetically and changed the subject. He had seen enough in recent years to be able to guess more than he wanted to know about what Cyndal was not saying. The thought of this beautiful girl helplessly caught up in one of the sometimes bloody struggles over a Dales rulership made him wince. Then he smiled at himself. Beautiful Cyndal might be, but helpless? Little as he knew her, he knew she was not that.

Despite his enjoyment of Cyndal's company, Auridan grew increasingly uneasy as the day wore on. In the late afternoon, clouds began sweeping in from the west, turning the day gray and adding to his irritability. Finally Cyndal noticed his nervousness and demanded to be told what was wrong.

"I won't be treated like a porcelain ornament," she said. "And I can be dreadfully stubborn. So you might as well explain what's bothering you, and save us both the trouble."

"If I knew what it was, I'd tell you," Auridan replied. "It's just a feeling, that's all."

They rode until just before dark. A cold drizzle began to fall as they struggled to set up camp in the gloom, and they heard the rumbling of thunder among the nearby mountains. Auridan rigged an inadequate shelter for Cyndal from seven leafy branches and a blanket, then was exasperated when she insisted on joining him in hunting firewood.

The storm hit with a crash while they were heading back toward their camp with the second load. Rain slashed through the branches of the trees above them, soaking their cloaks in minutes and half blinding them. Auridan shouted to Cyndal to keep close; in the dark and the rain it would be all too easy to become separated and lose the way. He thought he heard Cyndal shout agreement, but a few moments later, a brilliant flash of lightning showed her forging through the trees ahead and to his right.

The thunderclap that followed drowned out Auridan's call.

Cursing, he blundered toward where he thought she was. He ran into a tree and lost several of the branches he was carrying. As he struggled to get a better grip on those that remained, he heard Cyndal scream.

Auridan dropped the firewood and leaped forward. The scream had come from just ahead of him; he ought to be able to find her easily enough. He heard Cyndal scream again, and another flash of lightning lit the woods.

By its light, Auridan saw Cyndal plunging wildly into the trees. Just behind her, its head a man-height above the ground, was a creature with a long, sinuous body like a giant snake covered with feathers. Auridan grabbed for his sword as the light faded, and forced his feet to move faster. The image of the enormous snake hung before his eyes, as though the lightning had etched the scene into their surface. Then he realized that the snake was glowing. It moved forward without hurry, following Cyndal.

Auridan stumbled after it, determined to reach the snake before it could harm Cyndal. The chase seemed to last for hours, the darkness punctuated by occasional flashes of lightning. Auridan was grateful for the storm; the brief flares of light were the only way he had of being sure the snake had not yet reached its prey.

Suddenly the snake disappeared, like a puff of smoke scattered by the wind. Almost at the same moment, Auridan heard Cyndal give another scream. Desperately he threw himself forward. He had an instant's confused impression of plunging through something like a thin curtain into dryness and warmth and flickering torchlight, and then he collided with Cyndal.

They teetered together in a tangle of dripping hair and soggy cloaks. Auridan recovered first and instinctively raised his sword. Then what he was seeing finally penetrated, and he stared in astonishment.

He was standing just inside a curtain of blackness that blocked the mouth of a huge cave. Torches burned in iron sconces hanging from the walls of the cave. Directly across from Auridan stood the statue of a plumed snake rearing up twice the height of a man, its mouth open in a silent hiss. Before the statue was a low table, and in front of it stood three men. The first was an old man robed in green. Next to him stood the sword-seller in an identical robe of dark blue. Then Auridan stiffened in shock. The third man was Lord Hervan.

"Your champion has arrived at last, Sympas," said the first man. He laughed unpleasantly, and his eyes never left Auridan. "Not a very prepossessing sight, is he?"

"Appearances are not everything, Kessas," the sword-seller replied calmly.

Kessas snorted. "It took you long enough to get him here."

Auridan stared at the two men in bewilderment. Beside him, Cyndal raised her head to study their surroundings. Auridan felt her shudder against him as her eyes fell on the statue; then she went rigid with shock. *"Hervan?"*

Hervan looked at her with a miserable expression. "I'm sorry, Cyndal! I didn't *know!*"

"Didn't know what?" Cyndal demanded. She sounded more like herself, and Auridan grinned.

"I didn't know what Kessas would ask! I . . . made a bargain, I thought it was the right thing, the only way to be *sure* . . ."

"What are you talking about, Hervan?" Cyndal said sharply.

"This," Hervan said. He looked away from her. "Your being here."

"What your step-cousin is trying to tell you is that either you or he will die tonight," said Kessas. Auridan made an involuntary gesture with his sword, and the old man gave him an unpleasant smile. "Precisely," he said.

"Hervan, *why?*" Cyndal said urgently.

Hervan raised his head. "Syledale. You know what it was like, after your uncle died! I wanted—I wanted to be sure nothing like that would ever happen again. There had to be an heir no one could question, but Chathalla hadn't shown the slightest sign, not once in over three years. So I bargained. I didn't know!"

"Enough," said Sympas sternly. "You made your agreement, and you must abide by it. By your own will, you are Kessas's champion."

"And I suppose you intend me to be yours," Auridan said.

"I chose you for that purpose, yes."

"What happens if I refuse?"

"If there is no contest, the color of the serpent remains as it is, which is the green of Kessas," the sword-seller replied. "Since he is dominant, his will would prevail and the girl would be sacrificed."

Cyndal made a small noise and reached for the dagger at her belt. Auridan's eyes narrowed. "And if I agree?"

"The outcome of the contest determines the color of the serpent," Sympas said. "If Lord Hervan wins, Kessas remains dominant and the girl dies. But if you are the victor, the color of the serpent will change to blue, and you and the girl will go free."

"You leave me no choice," Auridan said.

"Then stop this chattering and let the contest begin," Kessas snarled.

Auridan raised his left hand and unfastened the clasp of his cloak. He let the soggy mass slide to the floor and stepped forward. Reluctantly, Hervan drew his sword and came to meet him. Auridan saw that Hervan's blade was a twin to his own, and his lips twisted. Not an identical twin, he thought; he would be willing to wager that the stones in the hilt of Hervan's sword were green, not blue.

Warily, Auridan circled his opponent. He had no idea how good a swordsman Hervan was, and still less what difference the two strange swords might make in the fight. Hervan was equally unwilling to close with him, but finally he could wait no longer. He stepped forward and swung.

Green and blue sparks flew as the weapons touched, and Auridan felt his sword arm tingle. He forced himself to concentrate on fighting. Hervan was an excellent swordsman; Auridan could not afford to let himself be distracted. He parried a vicious thrust, and more sparks flew. They grew thicker and brighter with each blow, until the very air seemed to shine with green and blue light.

Finally, Hervan broke through Auridan's guard. Auridan twisted aside, but not quite in time. The point of Hervan's sword grazed his left shoulder. Auridan felt a painful jolt in his left arm from shoulder to fingertips. He ignored the pain, for Hervan's desperate attack had left an opening. With all his strength, Auridan brought his sword down across Hervan's, just

above the guard. The force of the blow tore the weapon from
Hervan's hand. Before he could recover it, Auridan's blade was
at his throat.

Hervan stood motionless, staring at Auridan with wide eyes.
Auridan hesitated, and heard the sword-seller's voice say, "You
have won; now make an end."

Auridan shook his head. He stepped back, kicking Hervan's
sword well out of reach, and lowered his own weapon. "If I
have won, that is the end," he said. "There is no need for killing."

"You must!" Kessas's voice was frantic. "The power will not
be bound unless the victory is sealed in blood!"

"I won't kill him," Auridan said stubbornly.

"Fool!" Kessas cried. "Kill him or we'll all die! Look there!"

Auridan looked up. The serpent statue was glowing. Blue
and green light rippled up and down the carved plumes, the
shimmering colors shifting crazily from one feather to another,
and cracks were appearing in the stone. Kessas's face was a
mask of terror. Then, with a loud grinding noise, a large chunk
fell out of the nose of the statue. Another followed. "Run!"
shouted the sword-seller.

Auridan ran. He heard Kessas shrieking curses behind him,
but he did not look back. He saw the black barrier at the mouth
of the cave vanish as Cyndal darted through it. An instant later,
Auridan followed her, with Sympas right behind him. Auridan
turned and pulled Hervan out just as the roof of the cave collapsed with a roar.

For a moment, they stood in the darkness outside, panting
with exertion and coughing in the cloud of dust spewing from
the mouth of the cave. The rain had subsided into a cold drizzle
once more, which added to their discomfort. Sympas seemed
the least affected; he stood staring almost wistfully back toward
the cave. At last he looked up.

"The power of the serpent, for good or for ill, is broken, and
I am free at last," he said to Auridan. "For that, my thanks."

"Thanks are well enough," Cyndal said with irritation, "but I
want an explanation. What has all this been about?"

The sword-seller smiled. "A fair question, though perhaps
not fairly phrased. The feathered serpent that you saw in the

cave was a . . . source of Power. In itself, it was neither of the Light nor of the Dark, but could serve either as its servants willed it.

"My brother and I were bound to the serpent long ago. We were intended to hold the serpent's Power for the Light, but over the years Kessas delved too deeply into the things of the Dark, and it swallowed him. Then he began searching for a way to bind the Power of the statue to himself alone.

"He found it in you." The sword-seller looked at Cyndal. "Your mother bore a trace of the old blood, and she passed it on to you. That and your beauty made you the perfect sacrifice, whose blood would bind the Power to Kessas. So Kessas made his bargain with your cousin: a son and heir in exchange for you."

"He didn't tell me what he was going to do!" Hervan said. "I wouldn't have agreed if I'd known."

"You did not ask," Sympas said sternly. Hervan looked down, and Sympas continued, "I learned of Kessas's actions too late to stop what he had set in motion. My only hope was to counter what he had done by choosing a champion of my own." His eyes met Auridan's, and he smiled. "I chose better than I knew."

"That was why you tried to give me the sword!" Auridan said.

"Yes. I was concerned when you insisted on paying, for it meant I had no hold on you to draw you here. So I sent you to Cyndal, hoping that you would become involved in her plans. In the end, it was as well that you were free to choose, for you could not otherwise have destroyed the serpent."

"I didn't—"

"The laws that governed the Power of the statue were very rigid. Blood sacrifice would bind its Power to Kessas; a contest to the death would bind its Power to the victor. You won the fight, but refused to kill your opponent. Neither Kessas nor I had won, and the conflicting Powers tore the statue apart. Had you taken the sword as I meant you to, I think you would not have been able to keep to your resolve."

Auridan looked at Hervan. The Dales lord looked cold and miserable and worried. Auridan still didn't like him much, but he was glad he had not been forced to kill the man.

"What about Chathalla?" Hervan asked urgently. "Will she be all right, now that . . ." He waved at the pile of rubble where the mouth of the cave had been.

"Your lady will suffer no hurt by this," Sympas assured him.

"You are luckier than you deserve, Hervan," Cyndal said.

"I know," Hervan said without looking at her.

"Then do not seek again to bend old Powers to your wishes," Sympas told him.

"I won't," Hervan assured him. Then he looked at Cyndal and said tentatively, "Will you still be going on to Norstead?"

"I think it would be best," Cyndal said gently. "If Auridan is still willing to guide me. But I will return before Chathalla has her child."

"Thank you," Hervan said.

The sword-seller looked at Auridan. "If you have no other questions for me, I must go."

"What about this?" Auridan said, holding out the short-sword.

"Keep it," Sympas said, and smiled. "You have paid for it twice over, once in coin and once in service."

"I'm not sure I want a sword that gives off blue sparks in a fight," Auridan said.

"The sword drew its Power from the statue; with the statue gone, you have no need to worry," Sympas assured him.

Auridan did not see how Sympas could be so positive, but he did not like to offend the man. He nodded and sheathed the sword, reminding himself mentally to clean it as soon as he was somewhere dry.

"Farewell, and again, my thanks." Sympas turned and started walking up the mountain.

"Wait! Where are you going?" Cyndal said.

The sword-seller looked back and smiled. "Home," he said, and this time when he walked away no one stopped him.

Afterword

*Writing "The Sword-Seller" was, in many ways, going back
to my roots as both reader and writer. I don't remember when
I read my first Witch World book; it's almost as if they came
with the bookshelves my parents gave me for my birthday
when I was nine or ten. I do remember that I was "too
young" when I first read one—half the time, I didn't understand what was going on. I didn't care; I loved them anyway.
It wasn't long before I was old enough to understand them,
and I loved them even more. Images from the books have
haunted me for years—Kaththen wrapping a scarf around and
around her changed face, Crytha hurling the Shadow Sword
like a spear, a line of cloaked women on horseback riding
slowly away from Norstead Abbey. The books have unques-
tionably influenced my work from the very beginning, and it
has been a pleasure and a privilege to contribute to this volume.*

—Patricia C. Wrede

Biographical Notes

M. E. Allen

Mary Elizabeth Allen was born in Darbyshire, England, and grew up in New Jersey. This gave her such an appreciation of different world views that she took to fantasy and science fiction like a duck to water. She now lives in New York City where she works as an editor for a hardcover publisher and writes anything that catches her fancy. Her latest oddity, a time-travel regency romance titled *Current Confusion,* was published under the pseudonym Kitty Grey.

Jayge Carr

Jayge Carr started writing on a dare. One evening, angry at what she was reading (not an Andre Norton novel), she tossed the book across the room and snarled, "I could write a better book than *that*." Her other half, working at his desk, looked up and said, "Why don't you?" "Because I'm not a writer," she replied, with great logic. At which he said, with greater logic,

"How do you know until you try?" The trying has produced several books, including the upcoming *Knight of a Thousand Eyes* (sorry, *not* fantasy, hard SF) coming out from Bantam next year, and dozens of short stories.

Juanita Coulson

When Juanita Coulson was eight years old, her mother gave her a typewriter. That led to rapid addiction to storytelling via the printed word. A first professional submission, at age eleven, received a kindly rejection from Scribners. Riding Marion Zimmer Bradley's coattails, however, with a coauthored SF short story in 1963 met with better success. Since then, Coulson has published works of science fiction (currently the *Children of the Stars* series), fantasy (*The Web of Wizardry*), historical romance, gothic suspense, and nonfiction. When not writing, she performs (and occasionally composes) SF and fantasy songs, reads a wide range of fiction and nonfiction, gardens, and crochets. The rest of the time she and her husband, Robert "Buck" Coulson, also a writer, try to keep their ten-room farmhouse—with its three libraries—in some semblance of order; that's often a losing battle, but an enjoyable one.

A. C. Crispin

Ann Crispin is the author of the bestselling Star Trek novels *Yesterday's Son* and *Time for Yesterday*. In addition, she coauthored *Gryphon's Eyrie* with Andre Norton. She is currently writing and editing a science fiction series, *StarBridge*, about a school for young people of different species located on an asteroid light-years away. She lives in Maryland with her husband, son, three cats, two horses, and an overworked dinosaur of a CPM computer on which she processes many words indeed.

Esther M. Friesner

Esther M. Friesner is the author of thirteen fantasy novels, the most recent being *Hooray for Hellywood,* which concludes the *Here Be Demons* trilogy, and *The Water King's Laughter,* which is the fourth volume in the *Chronicles of the Twelve Kingdoms* series. She holds a B.A. in Spanish and Drama from Vassar and an M.A. and Ph.D. in Spanish from Yale, where she taught for a number of years. She enlivens home life in suburban Connecticut through participation in the local Society for Creative Anachronism. She is also a W.I.T. (Wench in Training) with the fifth Connecticut Regiment, a colonial recreation group.

Sharon Green

Sharon Green states that she has been reading fantasy and science fiction from the age of twelve and writing even before then. Having heard a speech of Robert Heinlein's that included the advice, "Don't talk about it, do it!" she has been doing it ever since. To date she has seventeen novels and five short stories in print.

P. M. Griffin

P. M. Griffin has been writing since her early childhood. She is the author of the *Star Commandos* series as well as a number of short stories, which have appeared in *Magic in Ithkar 3, Catfantastic,* and *Tales of the Witch World* Volume 1, and elsewhere.

She lives in Brooklyn, New York, with her cat, Cougar, and works as a computer support person by day, reserving the evenings and nights (plus weekends, holidays, and every other "spare" moment!) for writing.

Caralyn Inks

Caralyn Inks attended the 1984 Clarion West Writers Workshop and survived the 1989 San Francisco earthquake. In between living through aftershocks of various magnitudes, she writes, designs toys, and rides herd on sixteen-year-old twins, two cats, two rabbits, a rat, and a dog.

Patricia Shaw Mathews reports:

"I have read science fiction since I was ten; my favorite Witch World novel is *Year of the Unicorn* and my favorite Norton book is *Star Ranger*. My first published story was, 'There is Always an Alternative,' a Darkover story; I have also published three other Darkover stories, an Ithkar story, and a fantasy tale in my own world; and the joke about the income tax for off-worlders, the '1040-ET.' I live in New Mexico and sometimes go to the Santa Fe Opera. I work as a self-employed contract accountant, which is to say, a high-class temp without benefits."

Patricia A. McKillip

Patricia McKillip is the author of various young adult novels, among them *The Forgotten Beasts of Eld* and her first science fiction endeavor, *Moon Flash*. Other works include *The Riddle-Master of Hed* trilogy, an adult science fiction, *Fool's Run*, and, most recently, *The Changeling Sea*. She was born in Salem, Oregon, lived in the San Francisco Bay Area for a quarter of a century, and has been living, for the past two years, in upstate New York.

Ann Miller and Karen E. Rigley

Ann Miller of Texas and Karen Rigley of Utah set up collaboration before they met in person. Since their first novel, *Comanche Moon*, they have worked as a team in the field of the short story as well, and the duo's articles on writing and collaboration are in constant demand. Their sf/fantasy stories include "Supercat," in *Catfantastic*, and "Stones of Sharnon," Ann's story in *Tales of the Witch World* Volume 2, which inspired them to write "Godron's Daughter."

Marta Randall

Marta Randall's first science fiction story was published in 1972; since then she has written six novels and numerous shorter works. Her most recent novel is *The Sword of Winter;*

her young adult biography of John F. Kennedy was published by Chelsea House in 1987. She has edited the *New Dimensions* original anthology series, and served two years as President of the Science Fiction Writers of America, and she teaches science fiction and fantasy writing workshops through the University of California Extension at Berkeley. She and her husband, Chris Conley, live in Oakland, California; she is the mother of Richard and Caitlin, and surrogate parent to a houseful of cats and one house-sized dog.

K. L. Roberts

Kenneth Roberts is a writer and illustrator who lives in Florida. He has worked in a great variety of jobs on his way to being a writer, including clerking, doing computer analysis, and other classically struggling-writer vocations. He is currently working on a portfolio of illustrations based on David Lindsay's *Voyage to Arcturus,* and on a writing project with an anthropological basis, concerning the future of civilization in the next century.

Mary H. Schaub reports:

"After a distinctly wheezy, asthmatic childhood, I did manage to negotiate a college education (although I had to drop my chemistry major early on due to allergic reactions, and finish in math education). Between corporate bookkeeping, I found one-on-one private tutoring more rewarding than substitute teaching. Since 1970, however, family health problems have largely confined me at home. In 1973, I sold my first story on the second try; after that, a blizzard of rejections sleeted amid sporadic sales until Miss Norton included a story of mine in one of her Ithkar anthologies. Since then, I have been dabbling in the Witch World, completing (to my considerable surprise) my first novel set there during the Turning's vast upheaval (Tor will publish it as part of the forthcoming *Witch World Chronicles*). My book allowed me to explore the wonderfully musty corners of Lormt's fabled archives. It was a relief to wander there mentally, since any bodily blunder among dusty parchments would speedily result in my eviction for disturbing the scholars' peace with my sneezing."

Carol Severance

Carol Severance is a Hawaii-based writer with a background in art and journalism. She has published stories in anthologies and magazines and is a novelist and prize-winning playwright. She shares her Hilo home with a surfer, an anthropologist, and an undetermined number of geckos.

Elisabeth Waters

Originally inspired to write by the works of, among others, Andre Norton and Madeleine L'Engle, she has been writing for ten years and lives in California with a well-known author, and a dog that's part wolf. *Changing Fate,* her first novel, won the first Gryphon Award and has been bought for publication by DAW Books.

Michael D. Winkle

Michael D. Winkle was born in Tulsa, Oklahoma, and has lived in the same general area ever since. He received a B.A. in English from Oklahoma State University in 1984. He has had several short stories, novelettes, and serialized novels published in various fan publications. His first professional sale, a short Cthulhu Mythos tale entitled "Typo," was to the now-defunct *Fantasy Book.* "Wolfhead" marks his second professional appearance. He has written two novels, which are in search of a publisher, and has a third in progress.

Lisa Woodworth

Active in the Society for Creative Anachronism and Oklahoma fandom, her years of reading led to an attempt to share in that magic. "Were-Flight" marks her first professional appearance.

She is currently working on the "Furkindred" shared-world

project published by Miscellanea Press and trying to stave off chaos in Oklahoma, where she lives with her husband, three children, and assorted pets.

Patricia C. Wrede reports:

"I started writing in seventh grade and have been doing it off and on ever since. I received my A.B. from Carleton College in Minnesota, where I majored in Biology, and I started work on my first novel just after I graduated. Since then, I've published seven and a half books (*Sorcery and Cecelia,* the half book, was a collaboration with Caroline Stevermer) and a number of short stories. My most recent novel, *Snow White and Rose Red,* is part of Tor's Fairy Tales line. My interests include chocolate, desultory gardening, other people's cats, and my husband, who knows that the way to my heart is to give me another set of bookshelves."

THE BEST IN FANTASY

☐ 53954-0 SPIRAL OF FIRE by Deborah Turner Harris $3.95
    53955-9 Canada $4.95

☐ 53401-8 NEMESIS by Louise Cooper (U.S. only) $3.95

☐ 53382-8 SHADOW GAMES by Glen Cook $3.95
    53381-X Canada $4.95

☐ 53815-5 CASTING FORTUNE by John M. Ford $3.95
    53826-1 Canada $4.95

☐ 53351-8 HART'S HOPE by Orson Scott Card $3.95
    53352-6 Canada $4.95

☐ 53397-6 MIRAGE by Louise Cooper (U.S. only) $3.95

☐ 53671-1 THE DOOR INTO FIRE by Diane Duane $2.95
    53672-X Canada $3.50

☐ 54902-3 A GATHERING OF GARGOYLES by Meredith Ann Pierce $2.95
    54903-1 Canada $3.50

☐ 55614-3 JINIAN STAR-EYE by Sheri S. Tepper $2.95
    55615-1 Canada $3.75

Buy them at your local bookstore or use this handy coupon:
Clip and mail this page with your order.

Publishers Book and Audio Mailing Service
P.O. Box 120159, Staten Island, NY 10312-0004

Please send me the book(s) I have checked above. I am enclosing $_____
(please add $1.25 for the first book, and $.25 for each additional book to
cover postage and handling. Send check or money order only—no COD's.)

Name _____

Address _____

City _____State/Zip _____

Please allow six weeks for delivery. Prices subject to change without notice.

ANDRE NORTON

BESTSELLING BOOKS FROM TOR